POWER

MW01221980

"Whose temple is this?" Elysia asked.

"Athena's," Damon answered.

Moving up the three stone steps, Elysia ran her hand over the flat marble. "Still smooth."

"This temple does have a dark history, though. You've heard of Medusa, right?"

"The gorgon?"

He nodded. "She was once a priestess in this temple. Gorgeous, they say, and totally devoted to Athena. But Poseidon had a thing for her. And he followed her here. When he found her alone, he took her, right here on this altar."

Elysia's gaze dropped to the marble beneath her hand. "Right here?"

"Right there. When Athena found out what Medusa had done, she turned her beautiful hair into snakes and her lower body—that which had tempted Poseidon so—into a snake."

"I remember this story. But the way I heard it, Poseidon raped Medusa."

"Why would Athena punish her for that? Rape isn't the female's fault. Medusa was a victim. No, Athena turned Medusa into a gorgon because there's power in sex, especially when it's performed in a sacred place. And she punished Medusa because when Medusa claimed that power here, in the virgin goddess's own temple, Medusa broke free of Athena's hold."

Elysia looked back down at the altar, and as color rose in her cheeks, Damon knew exactly what she was imagining. The same hot and wicked thing he was imagining. "Power, huh?"

"Incredible power."

She bit her lip. "Does Athena know we're here?"

"Doesn't have a clue. She only monitors this island during the survival phase of recruitment."

Elysia hesitated for only a second, then walked her hands down the edge of the altar, shifted to her side when she reached the end, and moved between it and Damon. "In that case…" The instant her hands made contact with the hard wall of his chest, electricity fanned out beneath her touch, making his muscles quiver and ache for more. "I might be up for a little power grab."

TITLES BY
ELISABETH NAUGHTON

Deadly Secrets Series
(Romantic Suspense)
REPRESSED
GONE

Eternal Guardians Series
(Paranormal Romance)
MARKED
ENTWINED
TEMPTED
ENRAPTURED
ENSLAVED
BOUND
TWISTED
RAVAGED
AWAKENED
UNCHAINED

Aegis Series
(Romantic Suspense)
EXTREME MEASURES
LETHAL CONSEQUENCES
FATAL PURSUIT
SINFUL SECONDS
FIRST EXPOSURE
ACAPULCO HEAT
*(in the Bodyguards in Bed
Anthology)*

Stolen Series
(Romantic Suspense)
STOLEN FURY
STOLEN HEAT
STOLEN SEDUCTION
STOLEN CHANCES

Against All Odds Series
(Contemporary Romance)
WAIT FOR ME
HOLD ON TO ME
MELT FOR ME

Firebrand Series
(Paranormal Romance)
BOUND TO SEDUCTION
SLAVE TO PASSION
POSSESSED BY DESIRE

Rising Storm Series
Season 1, Episode 3:
CROSSROADS
Season 2, Episode 7:
BLINDING RAIN

Anthologies
BODYGUARDS IN BED

AWAKENED

ETERNAL GUARDIANS

ELISABETH NAUGHTON

Copyright © 2016 Elisabeth Naughton
All rights reserved.

ISBN-13: 978-1537189741
ISBN-10: 1537189743

Cover art and design by Patricia Schmitt/Pickyme
Editing by Linda Ingmanson

This book is a work of fiction. References to real people, events,
establishments, organizations, or locations are intended only to provide a
sense of authenticity, and are used fictitiously. All other characters, and all
incidents and dialogue, are drawn from the author's imagination and are
not to be construed as real.

No part of this book may be reproduced, scanned or distributed in any
printed or electronic form without permission. Please do not participate in
encouraging piracy of copyrighted materials in violation with the author's
rights. Purchase only authorized editions.

"Be still my heart; thou hast known worse than this."

—Homer

CHAPTER ONE

"Twenty-five years is nothing but a blink of an eye to the gods. And peace is as fleeting as the wind. It will end. It will end soon."

How many times had Elysia's mother said those words to her? How many times had Elysia ignored the threat because she thought those who wanted to hurt her would come from Olympus and not from within her own realm?

She rushed out of the Argolean castle through the tunnel she often used to slip away unnoticed, and ran into the forest unable to breathe, unable to think, unable to focus on anything but reaching her favorite spot. The one that overlooked the bay and always calmed her.

Binding... Nereus...

She stopped on the bluff far above the ocean, leaned forward, and rested her hands on her knees as she sucked back air. Tears burned her eyes. Tears she wouldn't let fall. Her parents were arranging a binding between her and the Council leader's son, Nereus. She didn't want to be bound to anyone. Especially not to anyone associated with the Council, the governing body that advised her mother the queen, though more often than not they worked to undermine her mother at every turn. Elysia's parents were convinced the binding would ease tensions between the two political factions in their country, but Elysia didn't care about politics. She didn't care about Nereus. Yes, they'd gone to school together, but they'd never run in the same circles. She barely knew him.

She pressed the palms of her hands against her eyes. She didn't want a binding of any kind. *And my mother knows that.* She didn't need a male to complete her. She had no desire to provide heirs for the throne. In fact, she couldn't wait until her parents produced a male heir so she could forget about all this ruling crap they were preparing her for.

But what really hurt…what burned deep in the center of her soul was the fact that her mother was going back on her word. All her life, the queen had told Elysia that if she chose to be bound someday, the choice of whom she spent her life with was up to her. Elysia's grandfather, King Leonidas, had forced Elysia's mother into not one, but two political marriages for his benefit. Thankfully, circumstances had kept Elysia's mother from completing those bindings, and eventually she'd been bound to Elysia's father. Argolea was supposed to be a different—better—place than it had been for her mother. History was not supposed to repeat itself. Not now. Not over twenty-five years later.

"Lys? Are you okay?"

Talisa's voice echoed somewhere close, but Elysia couldn't make herself turn to see where her cousin stood. The bitter bite of betrayal was all she knew. That and a searing urge to run.

"Elysia?"

Maximus. That was her other cousin, Max. The three of them were supposed to go hiking together this afternoon on Max's one day off from training with the Argonauts. Dammit, she should have known they'd find her here, in her favorite spot.

"What's wrong?" Max asked.

Everything. Everything was wrong. And she couldn't stay even a second longer to tell them.

"I…I have to get away." Away from this castle, away from her parents, away from everyone trying to control her. Dropping her hands, she turned slowly and stepped back toward the bluff.

Confusion darkened Talisa's violet eyes. Wisps of black hair that had slipped free of her ponytail flitted around her worried features. At her side, Max—as blond and buff and big as his father, the Argonaut Zander—reached out for her. "Lys, wait."

Elysia closed her eyes before either of them could touch her and pictured the field outside the witches' tent city at the base of the Aegis Mountains. The witches manned the moving portals that were banned by the Council. *Banned per Nereus's father's orders.* The Council was always trying to control the Argolean people. Putting restrictions on them without the monarchy's approval and banning the portals so its citizens couldn't cross into the human realm without permission. Nereus and his father would try to control Elysia like that if she agreed to this binding. They'd take away her freedom. They'd turn her into someone she didn't want to be. But she wouldn't let them. Because she belonged to no male.

"Elysia," Max said. "Dammit, just wait."

His words disappeared in the wind as she flashed across the distance with the telekinetic power all Argoleans possessed in this realm. Air whipped over her cheeks, brushing her hair back from her face. She breathed it in, letting go of her anxiety and stress.

Her feet connected with solid ground. She opened her eyes and looked across the meadow toward the tall oak trees on the far side. In the distance, the colorful flags of the witches' tents waved in the breeze. Her heart leapt with excitement. Freedom was within her grasp.

Eight females emerged from the trees before she could take two steps toward that freedom. Eight females who clearly weren't witches.

They were each dressed in tight black pants, sleeveless leather tops, and kickass stiletto boots. Each one sporting long, flowing hair in a variety of colors, their Barbie doll faces and curvaceous bodies clearly designed to seduce. And each held a bow and arrow aimed directly at Elysia's heart.

Sirens. Zeus's band of deadly female warriors. Elysia drew to an abrupt stop. Occasionally, Sirens passed through their realm when they needed to speak to the queen about matters relating to the gods, but they always came through the guarded portal in the capital city of Tiyrns. And Elysia had heard nothing in the castle the last few days that gave her any indication Sirens were expected today.

"This is a surprise," Elysia said, trying like hell to keep her voice steady. "Are you lost?"

The brunette in the center stepped forward, her arrow never once wavering from its target. "No, but you are, Princess."

The way the Siren sneered the word "princess" put Elysia on instant alert. They clearly knew who she was. "I… Whatever you're here for, I'm sure I can help you."

A slow smile spread across the brunette's perfect face. "I'm sure you can. Seeing as how you are why we are here."

Oh shit… "I don't—"

"Understand?" The brunette lifted her brow. Several Sirens rushed up to Elysia's side and grasped her arms. "You will soon. Thank you for saving us a trip into the capital. Much less messy this way."

"Wait." Panic rose in Elysia's chest, and she pulled back on the Sirens' hold. "Let go of me. You can't just—"

"Oh, but we can." The leader lowered her weapon as the others pulled Elysia to a stop in front of her. "By immortal decree, Zeus has the power to choose any female from any realm to serve with his Sirens. And you, Princess, have just been chosen. Say good-bye to everything you know and love."

That panic went stratospheric. Elysia had wanted to escape Argolea and everyone trying to control her in this realm, but not like this. Service with the Sirens could last millennia. And with them, she'd be more of a prisoner than she was here. "No. I can't—"

"Bring her." The brunette turned, and to the other Sirens, she said, "There is much to do, and Athena is anxious to see if this one can make the cut."

"Mm…" Aphrodite swung her long legs over the side of the enormous bed and stretched her arms above her head. "That was wonderful." Curly auburn hair the color of autumn leaves spilled down the pale skin of her naked spine as she turned and cast a coy look over her shoulder. "You get better and better, Damianos."

The two naked nymphs who'd joined them scurried off the bed and rushed out of the room. Aphrodite pushed to her feet, all long lines and perfect curves, and crossed to the chaise.

The nymphs could disappear after the fact, the lucky females, but Damon could not. Rolling to his side, he propped his elbow on the mattress and rested his head on his hand as he watched Aphrodite slide a white silk robe onto her pale arms and tried not to be resentful of that fact. "Good thing, since my purpose is only to serve."

Aphrodite smirked. "And you do it so well, *erastis*."

Lover. He hated the way that word sounded.

The goddess moved back to the edge of the mattress and sat, then reached out and twirled a lock of Damon's hair around her finger. "Speaking of serving, a new class of Sirens is set to arrive."

She pushed out her full, plump lips in a sexy little pout. "Athena is going to try to steal you from me again."

Damon looked up at the goddess of love and desire and tried to feign disappointment, though inside, excitement leapt at the possibility of a break. Aphrodite's temple wasn't a bad place to spend your days—wide soaring rooms, tall stately pillars, marble everything, fountains and baths that promised both pleasure and relaxation, and the sweet scent of heliotrope wafting on the air, awakening the senses. But lately he couldn't help thinking there had to be more to life than this. More than meaningless pleasure. More than casual sex. More than catering to Aphrodite, a goddess who cared only about herself.

"A new class, huh?" He rolled back into the mountain of pillows and laced his fingers behind his head, remembering that Athena and Aphrodite didn't always get along. Jealousy was forever an issue between them—between any of the ruling Olympians— and he'd learned long ago not to show interest in any immortal other than the one currently in his line of sight.

"You don't want to go, do you?" Aphrodite slid her finger down his throat and across the dusting of hair on his bare chest. "I could tell Athena you're too valuable, which you are."

This was where he needed to be careful. He couldn't show too much enthusiasm, or Aphrodite would never let him leave. "Of course not. Training new Sirens is as enjoyable for me as spending time with your husband is for you."

Aphrodite's lips curled. Everyone knew she couldn't stand her husband, Hephaestus. Her gaze hovered on Damon's face. "That boring?"

She was beautiful, even Damon couldn't deny that. Meadow-green eyes, flawless skin, high cheekbones, and lips made only for seduction. But though physically he was still attracted to her, more and more lately, he was finding it difficult to be aroused in her company. Sex with Aphrodite was as empty as his life these days. There had to be more. A reason he was here. A future that held some kind of purpose. Something other than…immortal perfection.

He drew his hand from behind his head and brushed the back of his fingers against the smooth curve of her jawline. "Infinitely boring. When I'm with the Sirens, I count the days until I return to your temple."

Which was a flat-out lie. Working with Athena's Sirens, training them in combat, strategy, warfare—even seduction—was a thousand times more fun than being stuck in Aphrodite's claustrophobic pleasure palace.

Aphrodite sighed and smoothed her hand over his chest again, dropping her gaze to where she touched him. "I suppose I could consider letting you go. So long as I know you're pining away for me. Absence, they say, does make the heart grow fonder."

Damon had never found that to be true, but he refrained from saying so. He wasn't about to do anything to jeopardize this chance to escape, however short his respite might be. "It does. Very much so."

She leaned down and kissed him, sliding her tongue along his at the first touch and tasting him deeply. He didn't pull away, didn't say no, knew it was pointless to do so. Instead, he slid his fingers into the curly mass of auburn hair framing her face and kissed her back. Her mouth turned greedy against his, and she wriggled out of the robe she'd just pulled on, then pushed the sheet from his hips.

Yeah, there has to be more than this, he thought as she climbed over him. More than aphrodisiacs to keep him hard, more than meaningless sex, more than immortals using him for their pleasure. There had to be a hell of a lot more. Somewhere.

He just hoped he found it before he went mad.

CHAPTER TWO

Max flashed to the meadow outside the witches' tent city. A burst of light behind him illuminated the grass. The light returned to the hazy normal of mid morning as the portal closed and Talisa stepped up at his side.

"How do you know this is where she went?" Talisa asked.

"Because I've seen that look in her eyes before. You've seen it too."

"The running look." Talisa's jaw clenched. "*Skata*. If she crossed into the human realm, we're going to have a hard time finding her."

Max agreed, and that was his biggest fear. Elysia occasionally crossed into the human realm when she needed to get away from the craziness of royal life, but he couldn't really blame her for that. Life in the castle was nuts on a good day, which was the major reason Max spent as little time there as possible. People were always hovering, watching what you were doing, waiting on you like an invalid. As heir to the throne, Elysia had to live up to an impossibly high standard, one that would drive him batshit crazy if he had to live it on a daily basis.

No, he couldn't blame her for running, but she knew not to cross into the human realm alone. Hades's daemons still patrolled that realm. Argoleans—especially any linked to the monarchy or the Argonauts—were not safe there. The fact she'd flashed so impulsively didn't just set him on edge, it set off every protective instinct he had as an Argonaut.

Or—since he wasn't a full-fledged Argonaut yet—as a *guardian-in-training*.

Resentment bubbled inside him. He was thirty-five fucking years old now; he'd trained long enough, but the Argonauts still treated him like a freakin' kid. And he didn't see that changing anytime soon.

Pushing down the bitterness as best he could, he headed toward the tent city. "Come on. Maybe she hasn't crossed yet and we can catch her before she gets herself into trouble."

Behind him, Talisa huffed, her black boots crunching over twigs and rocks. "Dream on. I heard my parents talking last night. My father thinks the only way they're going to head off a coup is through a political binding."

Max stopped and looked toward his cousin. Talisa's father was the leader of the Argonauts, and he was bound to the queen's half sister, just as Max's father, Zander, was bound to the queen's other half sister. The three female cousins—Elysia, Talisa, and Max's younger sister, Zakara—had all been born within a few months of each other, but where Elysia and Zakara were somewhat soft and naïve, Talisa was not. At just under six feet, with jet-black hair pulled back into a messy tail and porcelain skin she wished people didn't notice, Talisa was as tough as anyone Max had ever met.

"They're going to marry her off? To whom?"

Talisa's violet eyes held Max's. Eyes that were so captivating, people often forgot she was a weapon just waiting to be fine-tuned. Like him. "Nereus."

"*Skata.*" Nereus was the absolute worst match for Elysia. The *ándras* had picked on her back when they were kids, and Max had needed to step in to scare the living crap out of the asshat on more than one occasion. He seriously doubted Nereus had changed his ways in fifteen years.

He headed back up the hill, a new frustration burning through him. "No wonder she fucking ran."

Talisa's long legs ate up the space to catch up. "Maybe we're wrong. Maybe she just had an argument with her parents. It could be nothing."

"Not if our luck holds," Max muttered.

They reached the outskirts of the tent city, but the second they stepped onto the dirt road, Max knew something was wrong.

Nothing moved in the village. No witches milled through the streets. The laughing children who normally played around the tents were nowhere to be seen. In fact, no sound echoed from the city save for the colorful flags high above, flapping in the morning breeze.

Max reached back for the parazonium—the ancient Greek sword all Argonauts carried—in the sheath concealed at his back. At his side, Talisa quietly pulled twin daggers from their holders on her lower spine. Slowly, they moved into the village and drew to a stop the moment they rounded the first corner.

A witch wearing a long pink skirt and dark jacket lay sprawled at the entrance to a tent, an arrow sticking out of her chest. Talisa knelt to feel for a pulse. A grim expression crossed her face as she looked up at Max and shook her head.

The hair on Max's nape stood straight. He stepped past the dead witch and moved to another body, this one in the middle of the road, and felt for a pulse. Nothing. Picking up his pace, he rounded another corner and gasped at the scene laid out before him.

Bodies littered the ground, some sprawled in the middle of the street, others halfway out of tents as if they'd been fleeing. All with arrows protruding from them.

"Holy gods," Talisa whispered as she came up behind him. "What happened here?"

"I don't know." A blinding red rage colored Max's vision. A rage he'd inherited from his forefather Achilles but which he could usually control. Moving toward the closest body, he pulled an arrow from the witch's back and stared at the weapon.

"What army in our realm uses arrows?" Talisa muttered.

The rage inside grew hotter. "They weren't from our realm. They—"

A cough echoed from a nearby tent. Talisa whipped in that direction and darted for the tent flap.

"Godsdammit. Talisa. Wait." Fear rushed in, overtaking the rage as Max dropped the arrow and followed. They could still be in that tent. Talisa could be walking into a trap. Talisa didn't listen, though, and disappeared into the tent before he could stop her. Gripping the blade tightly, Max readied himself for a battle, but when he stepped inside, fear gave way to relief.

A female lay sprawled on the ground near the far tent wall. Blood seeped from a wound in her abdomen. An arrow lay broken on the ground at her side. She twisted to look toward them, her face as pale as snow. "It's you. I thought…"

"Shh." Talisa moved quickly to the witch's side. "Try not to move." She sheathed her daggers, then pressed her hand against the witch's wound. "What happened here?"

"The young. Delia took...the young." The witch's face scrunched in pain. Bright purple hair hung limply around her face. "Need to...make sure they're okay."

Delia was the leader of the coven. Max breathed slightly easier knowing she'd managed to get the young out in time.

"We'll find them," Talisa said. "Don't worry. Can you tell us who did this?"

The witch exhaled a long breath and closed her eyes. "They...came through the portal. We didn't...expect them."

Max tugged off his jacket and handed it to Talisa, who pressed it against the witch's wound. Kneeling on the witch's other side, he laid a hand over the witch's brow. Her skin was cool and clammy. "Sirens?"

Talisa's wide-eyed gaze darted to his.

"Y-yes," the witch breathed.

"What the hell are Sirens doing in Argolea?" Talisa whispered.

Max didn't know, but whatever their reason, it clearly wasn't good. "We have to warn the Argonauts. They could be halfway to Tiyrns by now."

He pushed up, but the witch grasped his arm, stopping him. Her cold fingers closed over the ancient Greek text that ran down his forearms and entwined his fingers. "They're not...going to Tiyrns. They...left."

Max focused on the witch's jet-black eyes. "What do you mean, left?"

"They went"—the witch cringed—"back through the portal. With her."

A warning tingle rushed down Max's spine.

"Her who?" Talisa asked. "Who did they take with them?"

"The...princess. They took...the princess."

The rage came storming back, coloring everything red. Max jerked to his feet, but before he reached the tent door, Talisa was in front of him, her hand pressed against his chest, her violet eyes as hard and focused as he'd ever seen them. The same ancient Greek markings that branded his forearms stained hers as well. "You're not going after them."

"Like hell I'm not."

"These are Sirens, Max. *Sirens*. Zeus's lethal warriors."

"I don't care."

"Well, I do. You'll not last ten minutes with a pack of Sirens, no matter how tough you think you are. Use your brain, dammit. We need more than you and me for this."

A muscle in his jaw ticked as he stared down at her. She was right. As always, she used logic before reflex, a trait he'd yet to perfect. "We'll get the Argonauts. Then we'll go after them and kill every single Siren."

Talisa dropped her hand, but her expression said she wasn't sure even that would be enough. "Fine, but we're taking the witch with us. We can leave her at the castle for your mother."

"No," the witch croaked.

They both looked back her. The witch stared at them with clouded dark eyes. Talisa moved back to her side and pressed her hand over the jacket against the witch's wound again. "It's okay. Max's mother is a healer. The best in the land. She'll help you."

The witch shook her head and gripped Talisa's hand. "No. The Argonauts…can't…they won't…win. I overheard them. He's chosen…her…for the Siren Order."

Max's eyes grew wide. Zeus had marked Elysia? For the Siren Order?

Fear wrapped around his chest and squeezed like a boa constrictor. Elysia would never last. While she had the strength and fortitude to one day rule their land, she wasn't a warrior. She was more like her mother than her father. She didn't know the first thing about fighting or warfare or strategy. If someone didn't do something fast, the Sirens would destroy her.

His gaze darted to Talisa, and a new sense of urgency rippled through his veins. "We have to get her back."

Talisa looked up at him. "I—"

"You can't, Guardian." The witch drew a shuddering breath. "It's too late. They've already taken her to the island of…Pandora."

Elysia came awake with a start. Sunlight blinded her. She blinked until her vision cleared and squinted up at palm trees swaying gently in the breeze.

Her mind spun, but she couldn't grasp a memory or even an explanation. Pushing up on her hands, she felt something soft and grainy against her palms. One look confirmed she was sitting in sand.

Her gaze drifted to the right, where waves lapped gently against a beach. Stumbling to her feet, she turned and took in her surroundings. The beach was bordered by thick brush and a jungle of trees. In the distance, cliffs rose from the sand. Beyond, tall mountains reached toward the sky.

Her spine tingled. She had no memory of this place. Nothing looked familiar. Panic built in her chest, made it hard to breathe. Glancing down at her hands, she realized she was wearing a short, khaki cotton skirt and a matching halter top. No shoes. Nothing else. Just flimsy fabric that blew softly in the breeze.

Think, Elysia.

Elysia! That was her name. She knew that much for sure. But everything else was lost—how she'd come to be here, what had happened to her, even what she was supposed to do next.

She glanced up and down the beach. No other people. No footprints. No signs of life. Lifting her forearm, she noticed her skin was pink but not tanned or sunburnt. She hadn't been out in the sun long, which meant...what? That she'd been left here? By whom? And when?

She looked around for some kind of shipwreck but couldn't see one. An eagle cawed high above. Blocking the sun with her hand, she squinted toward the sky. The bird held something in his talons. Something that looked like...

He let go of the object. A box floated down to her with the help of a small red-and-white parachute.

She stepped back as it drew close. The box landed in the sand feet away. The object was as long as her foot and as wide as her hand. Dropping to her knees, Elysia lifted the box and studied it from all sides. It was made of wood—oak, it seemed to her. And stamped on two sides was the Greek letter for Sigma, cut with an arrow.

Sigma...arrows...oak and eagles...

The eagle and oak tree were symbols of Zeus, the king of the gods. And the Sigma insignia cut by an arrow was that of Zeus's elite Siren warriors.

A shiver of foreboding rushed down Elysia's spine. She wasn't sure how she knew all that—especially when she didn't know anything other than her name—but something told her she was right.

Licking her lips, she eased back on her heels and flipped the latch on the box. Inside sat a scroll of parchment paper that looked to be ancient. She drew it out and unrolled the paper.

Welcome to Pandora, Siren Recruit—

Your trial begins now. In order to join the incoming Siren class, you will be put to the test. Only the strongest and sharpest recruits will succeed, so be mindful of everything you do from here forward.

Our order was formed thousands of years ago by seven original Sirens, each of whom completed seven labors to prove their worthiness. Below you will find the first of seven similar labors. Once a labor is completed, a new box will be delivered to you. Upon fulfillment of all seven labors, you will join the Siren class at Siren Headquarters on Olympus. Should you fail at any of your labors, you will remain on Pandora until such time as you succeed, or the island's inhabitants find you.

There is no way off this island save completion of the labors, so do not waste time looking for an escape. You have been chosen by Zeus for this task, recruit. Prove your worth.

—Athena

Elysia read the letter three times. Athena? The goddess of war? The head of the Sirens? Holy *skata*. A new, more intense shiver rushed down Elysia's spine. She'd been chosen for the Sirens. She didn't know the first thing about being a warrior. Sure, her father was an Argonaut, but that didn't mean she—

Her gaze skipped over the beach once more. Yes. Her father was an Argonaut. A great warrior. She searched her mind for anything else…a memory, an image, something about him…but came up blank. She couldn't picture him. Didn't know his name. It was like trying to see through thick fog. She knew the thoughts and memories were close, but for some reason, she couldn't reach out and grasp them.

She read the scroll one more time and noticed a note at the bottom.

Labor One: Build a shelter that can be defended from predators.

Elysia's gaze lifted to the trees, and her stomach tightened with fear. What kind of predators lived on this island? If Zeus and Athena sent Siren recruits here as a test, something in the back of her mind warned the predators had to be far worse than lions and tigers and bears.

The brush behind her rustled, and she jerked in that direction. Her heart rate shot up. Pushing to her feet, she gripped the scroll and watched with wide eyes. Maybe finding some kind of shelter, away from whatever lurked out there, wasn't a terrible idea.

She glanced toward the canopy again. From above, she'd have a better view of anything coming toward her. Since she and Talisa and Max had built numerous tree forts when they were younger, she knew how to climb. She—

Whoa. Who were Talisa and Max?

Again she tried to make connections between the names suddenly popping into her mind and any kind of logical memory, but nothing made sense. Why couldn't she remember?

The brush rustled again, jerking her out of her thoughts. Moving quickly down the beach away from whatever was lurking, she circled the cove until she was at least a hundred yards away. In the trees, she spotted vines she could tie together to create rope. One look at the sun told her it was early afternoon. She had plenty of time before dusk.

She worked through the heat of the day, swiping away the sweat with her forearm as she braided vines together to create multiple ropes. By the time she was finished, she was hot, sticky, and thirsty. Climbing the closest tree until she was about fifteen feet above the ground, she tied the rope around the trunk and a thick branch, then dropped back to the beach and repeated the process in another tree, stretching the vines until she'd made a hammock well out of reach of any predators. It wasn't the best "shelter," but it was strong enough to hold her weight, and this high, she had a good view of the beach, the bluff to her left, and anything moving through the thick brush below.

Just as she finished tying the last rope, an eagle cawed above. A low whistle sounded, and another item floated toward her, falling in the hammock she'd just created. Carefully, she climbed out onto the hammock and grasped the box.

The same Siren symbol was stamped into the wood. Elysia flipped the lid open and pulled out another scroll. This time there was no letter. Just the following words:

You have completed Labor One. Well done, recruit.
Labor Two: Find and transport fresh water.

"Yeah, no shit, I need water," she muttered, dropping the scroll and box in her lap. Her mouth was dry as paper, and her energy was seriously lagging. She could survive weeks without food, but without water, she'd be dead in three days. She glanced toward the sky again. The sun was already dropping toward the ocean, which meant she only had an hour or so before it set.

She did not want to be caught in the jungle at night. She still didn't know what was out there, but she had a strong hunch it wasn't good. Water was a must, though.

Scowling, Elysia climbed out of the tree, stopped with her feet in the sand, and perched her hands on her hips as she scanned the area. Finding water was only half her problem. Transporting it—as the scroll said—was another issue altogether.

Her gaze dropped to the box still in her hand. It was made of wood, but she doubted it was waterproof. Though some plants in the jungle stored water...

Turning away from the beach, she brushed vines and palms out of her way and moved toward the inside of the island. Bamboo held water. This was a tropical island. There had to be bamboo somewhere close.

The temperature grew higher the farther she walked, and perspiration slicked her skin, making the flimsy cotton outfit cling to her body. The ground angled steadily uphill. Glancing left and right, she studied every bush and tree for something she could use to transport water, but nothing looked useable. Just when she was sure this was a lost cause, she spotted a tall plant with a thick stalk and small leaves.

Bamboo. Relief swept through her. But as she stared at the trunks, a frown pulled at her lips. How was she supposed to cut the damn thing? Bamboo was strong as shit. A dagger or axe or sword would come in handy right about now.

Or a parazonium like the Argonauts carry.

Yeah, that would be a total help. But…whoa…how did she know what the Argonauts used for weaponry?

As much as she wanted to rack her brain for the answer, she didn't have time. Her gaze dropped to her feet. Pushing the brush away with her toes, she spotted an old section of bamboo, three feet long and as wide as her arm. It was hollow inside and open on both ends. Biting her lip, she scanned the jungle floor and noticed a banana tree.

Her stomach grumbled. Banana trees meant food. They also held water. And they were a helluva lot softer than bamboo.

She still didn't know how she knew any of this, but it seemed to make sense, so she went with it. Maybe she was a biologist or a botanist or something. That would explain her knowledge base.

And what the hell is a botanist?

She rolled her eyes, then glanced at the ground again and found a smaller piece of bamboo as long as her hand and as wide as her thumb. She moved to the banana tree, located a rock, and used it to hammer the smaller section of bamboo into the trunk, creating a tap.

Several seconds passed, and nothing happened. Frowning, she turned toward the bamboo. That was probably her best bet, but how was she going to cut it? A trickle of liquid sounded at her back. Whipping around, she stared at the banana tree and grinned. Water flowed from the tap in the trunk as if a faucet had been turned on.

A smile spread across her face. Grasping the trunk, she lowered her mouth below the tap and drew a mouthful of liquid, then grimaced.

The water was definitely fresh, but it tasted like bananas. Not her first choice, but better than nothing. And water from a plant meant she wouldn't have to worry about boiling to decontaminate as she would if she'd found a stream or spring.

Swiping her wet hands on her skirt, she reached for the bamboo piece she'd found, wrapped several large banana leaves around one end, and tied them in place with more vines she wove together. After setting the makeshift bamboo bucket under the tap, she found a spot on the ground, sat back, and waited for the water to fill.

Not bad for a princess. She rested her forearms on her updrawn knees and smiled. Not bad at all.

Holy *skata*. Her grin faded. Princess? Where the heck had that come from? Princess of what?

Again she searched her memory, but the fog just seemed to grow thicker. What in Hades was happening to her? Why could she remember random bits but not the whole picture?

Brush rustled somewhere to her right. Her heart raced all over again, and she stumbled to her feet. Another eagle cawed above the thick canopy, but she didn't look up. Her focus was locked solidly on that brush—and whatever the hell was lurking inside.

A third box floated through the tree limbs and vines and landed at her feet. Elysia's gaze remained on the brush, which had grown still. Was she letting her imagination get away from her? The letter had warned of predators, but she'd yet to see anything—or anyone—else on this island.

Long seconds passed, but whatever had caused the brush to rustle was clearly gone. Elysia's gaze dropped to the box at her feet. Cautiously, she reached for it, opened the lid, and read the note inside.

> *Impressive work, recruit.*
> *You have completed the first two labors.*
> *Now you must venture away from your safe haven.*

"News flash," Elysia muttered. "I've already done that." She kept reading.

> *Labor Three: Seven spears are located on the island.*
> *Find and bring one back to your shelter.*

"You have got to be kidding me." A freakin' spear would have helped her hack down some bamboo. That should have been the second labor. But besides that, the light was already starting to fade. She didn't have time to go on some stupid treasure hunt. There was no way she was getting lost in the jungle at night.

She checked her tap. Water trickled out of the plant but, thankfully, showed no signs of stopping. She needed to give it at least another fifteen minutes so she'd have enough water for the night.

Her gaze skipped over the jungle again. It wouldn't be dark in fifteen minutes. Instead of sitting here twiddling her thumbs, she might as well look around this area for that stupid spear.

Decision made, she closed her hand around a long, thin piece of bamboo. She swung it through the air, figuring a cane was as good a weapon as anything—just in case. Mentally noting where her bamboo tree was located, she headed east and counted footsteps so she knew how to get back. On the sixteenth step, her foot sank into a mud bog.

"*Skata.*" She wrenched her leg up. But before she could pull her foot free, the ground dropped away, dragging her down a river of mud with a scream that rang in her ears.

CHAPTER THREE

Max flashed to the courtyard of the Argolean castle with the witch cradled in his arms. A split second later, Talisa appeared at his side.

Castle guards took notice of them and rushed over. "What happened?" one asked.

Max handed the witch off to the guards. "She's injured. Get her to my mother." To Talisa, he said, "Come on, we need to find the queen."

They moved into the castle, their boots clicking across the great Alpha seal set into the marble floor of the massive entry. Pillars rose all around them. A grand staircase swept up and to the right.

"What time is it?" Talisa skipped stairs to keep up with him. "At this hour, the queen's probably with my father, getting her daily report on the Argonauts' missions."

The queen always met with the leader of the Argonauts at the end of the day, unless he was out in the field. Since Max's dad, Zander, along with the Argonauts Orpheus and Aristokles were on patrol today in the human realm, Max figured Talisa was probably right. At the second-floor landing, he headed for Theron's office.

Voices echoed from the open door as they approached.

"No, it didn't go well at all," the queen said. "I'm sure she hates us right now."

"Hates is too tame a word," the Argonaut Demetrius, Elysia's father, said from somewhere in the room.

"Are you saying you want to change your mind?" Theron asked.

"I don't know how we can," Isadora answered. "You said that spy our guards caught in the tunnels was definitely wearing the insignia of the Council."

Max and Talisa both slowed.

"He was," Theron answered. "And he's still not talking. But we all know the Council does not like the changes you've instigated since becoming queen. They don't like the way you've elevated females in this realm and given them a voice. They don't like that you've welcomed the witches into society, and they definitely don't like the fact you opened our borders to the Misos."

Max glanced toward Talisa. The Misos were the population of half-breeds—a half-Argolean, half-human race—who'd come to Argolea as refugees when their colony was destroyed by daemons in the human realm.

"Twenty-five years later," Theron went on, "and they're still grumbling about that. These are old-school *ándres* and old-school politicians, my queen. Unless you do something to show them that tradition still exists here, they're going to move against us all and revert this realm back to what it was when your father ruled. I don't see another option, at this point. A political marriage aligning the monarchy with the Council is the best option you've got to prevent a major coup."

Talisa tensed at Max's side, and silence echoed from the room. Max knew just what his cousin thought of arranged bindings. For a female, it was a prison sentence. But at the moment, it was nothing compared to what was happening to Elysia.

He moved into the room without knocking.

Theron glanced over with a scowl. "Maximus, whatever you need can—"

The second he spotted Talisa, the Argonaut leader's expression softened. He was a big guy—easily six feet five and two hundred fifty pounds of pure muscle—but as he pushed out of the chair behind his desk, a warm smile broke across his face, making him look less like a warrior and more like a father.

That expression darkened when he glanced between his daughter and Max, though, clearly reading Talisa's worry. "What's going on, you two? What's happened?"

Talisa stepped toward her father. "*Patéras*—"

"Elysia is gone." Max looked toward the queen, standing near the windows with her slim arms crossed over her chest.

"What do you mean by gone?" Seated on the couch to Max's left, pushed to his feet and pinned Max with a hard look.

He was bigger than Theron, closer to seven feet, with dark hair and eyes that hinted of danger and secrets. For as long as Max could remember, Demetrius had been the most intimidating of the Argonauts, and now was no exception.

"We had plans to go hiking today," Talisa said at her father's side before Max could find the words. "All three of us. But when we met up with Elysia, it was apparent she was upset. She flashed before we could stop her. Max and I tracked her to the witches' tent city. We're pretty sure she was planning to cross into the human realm."

"*Skata.*" Demetrius's jaw hardened, and he flicked a look at his mate. "I told you hate was too tame a word."

The queen stepped forward, pale blonde hair falling to her shoulders in a wave, looking absolutely tiny next to her massive mate. "You said planning. Did you catch her in time?"

"No," Max answered. "She was already gone when we arrived."

"*Skata.*" Demetrius said again, running his hand through his dark hair. "She knows she's not supposed to cross without a guard." He moved toward the door, flicking one look at Theron. "We need to get to her before she finds trouble."

Theron rounded the desk. "I'll send word for Titus and Phin to join us."

"You won't find her," Max said after them.

Both males stopped and looked back.

"He's right." Talisa moved up at Max's side. "She never made it to the human realm."

Demetrius stepped toward her, eyes narrowed and very focused. "What are you saying?"

Talisa looked toward Max, and as their eyes locked, he read the worry and apprehension in her violet gaze. She didn't want to say it. He didn't blame her. He didn't want to say it either, but someone had to.

Max set his jaw. "She's on Pandora."

Demetrius stared at him a long moment before his eyes grew wide with both fear and shock and darted toward his mate.

"Pandora?" Theron moved back into the room. "How? No one knows how to get to that island. Even the queen and

Demetrius, who were trapped there, don't know how to reach it again."

"Sirens know," Talisa said.

For a heartbeat, no one moved, no one spoke. But Max felt the fear swirling through the room with the force of a tornado. And in that moment, he knew he'd failed again. If he'd been faster—if he'd been smarter—he could have stopped Elysia in time and kept her safe. But he hadn't. And now his only hope was that someone stronger could save her before it was too late.

"Sirens came into Argolea through the moving portal," he finally said. "They slaughtered the witches, and they took Elysia. Took her because Zeus marked her for the Siren Order."

This was by far the stupidest thing Damon had ever agreed to do.

The cut in his thigh was already starting to knit together thanks to his fast-healing genes. If the Siren recruit didn't find him soon, he wouldn't need to be rescued. Then she'd fail her next labor and would end up stuck here for good.

"Come on, chickadee," he muttered as he leaned back against the rock wall. "The light's starting to go."

The monsters on this island came out at dusk. If you weren't somewhere safe by sunset, all bets were off. While Damon didn't particularly care what happened to some recruit who probably wouldn't make it through the full seven years of training—very few actually did—*he* didn't want to get trapped on this island for all eternity with her. Being shipwrecked with the immortal world's deadliest monsters wasn't Damon's idea of a vacation. Not by a long shot. No matter what Athena thought of this girl.

A rustling sounded to his right. Slowly, Damon pushed to his feet. Gripping the tree limb he'd picked up, just in case, he held still and hoped whatever beast had just awoken couldn't smell him and went on its horrifying way.

A sword would be nice. Or one of the Sirens' trusty bow and arrows. Leave it to Athena to stick him here with nothing to defend himself. Then again, she'd done this to him dozens of times over the years, and he'd agreed to it. Why should this be any different?

The thick brush rustled again. Damon's heart picked up speed. He gripped the club tighter, hoping it was his recruit making all that noise. He was tougher than any seasoned Siren, but with no weapon, even he didn't stand much of a chance against a monster that breathed fire or struck out with claws like machetes.

Silence settled over the jungle. Sweat beaded on Damon's bare chest as he held his breath and waited. Several tense seconds passed, and he exhaled when he realized there was nothing there. Then the brush burst open, and a manticore, a beast with the body of a lion and the head of a human, sporting glowing red eyes and three rows of razor-sharp teeth, roared and charged.

"Fuck. Me." Damon didn't bother to fight. He darted into the trees to his right and sprinted for the beach.

The Siren recruit had built a shelter in the trees—a smart choice considering most of the monsters on this island couldn't climb. At this point, Damon didn't care if he ruined her little test or even that he had to save himself. He wasn't about to be some beast's lunch because of her.

His foot hooked a root he didn't see, and he tumbled forward. The club flew from his fingers. At his back, the manticore roared louder. Damon landed with a grunt against the ground, but before he could jerk upright, his momentum took him over again, and in a daze, he realized he was rolling down a steep hillside, tumbling faster with every crack against the forest floor.

Pain echoed from his back, his shoulder, his injured leg. Somewhere above, the manticore roared, but all he could see was the jungle spinning around him. His body finally came to a bone-jarring halt. With a groan, he tried to push up on his hands, but pain exploded all across the back of his skull, stopping his momentum.

He sucked in a deep breath. Warm liquid gushed from the cut on his leg, telling him he'd ripped open the wound. His vision grew spotty. He was losing blood fast. The monster would smell that. More would likely come. He wasn't making it to that tree fort. He had to find a place to hide and wait. Somewhere he could regroup and give his body time to heal.

Somehow, he managed to drag himself forward, but his head was so light, he had trouble focusing. And before he was able to pull himself into the brush, the edges of his vision darkened.

Shit.

Oh yeah. This was definitely the dumbest thing he'd ever agreed to do. Because as much as he hated Aphrodite's pleasure palace, at least there he'd been in one piece. And alive.

In a matter of minutes, he'd be neither.

Elysia stilled in the trees where she'd been hiding since she'd heard the roar above on the hillside.

That groan didn't sound like a monster, though. It sounded like a man.

Another roar echoed, shooting her heart rate into the stratosphere. She dropped the paper she'd fished out of the latest box to fall from the sky—the one that had arrived just after she'd located one of those illustrious spears in a pile of rocks at the bottom of the hill she'd tumbled down—and wrapped her fingers around the hilt of the weapon. *Kill an animal and prepare your first meal.* That was her fourth labor. Until she'd heard the roar, she hadn't truly believed there were any animals on this island. Now she knew differently. But from the sound of that roar, she'd be smart to avoid that particular animal. Or thing. Or monster.

She stepped to her left, intent on heading back to the shelter she'd built in the trees, but as she moved out from behind the tree, she spotted the body.

It was male, sprawled facedown on the ground, unmoving. Eyeing the hillside where she'd heard that roar, she cautiously nudged the man's shoulder with her foot.

He didn't move. Heart pounding, she knelt and searched for a pulse against his wrist.

He was alive, just out cold. Judging from the blood against the rocks near his right leg, though, badly wounded.

Common sense told Elysia to leave him. He looked to outweigh her by at least a hundred pounds. Even if he could walk, injured the way he was, he'd just slow her down. And right now, the only thing she cared about was getting back to safety. But her conscience kept her from walking away. What had her mother always said? *Power does not come from strength of arm, but in a ruler's ability to show compassion to those in need.*

She frowned, because—again—she could remember words and information, just not the person saying them.

Looking back at the man, she bit her lip. *Skata*, she couldn't leave him. At least not until she got him somewhere safe.

She circled him, knelt at his side, and ripped off one bottom leg of his pants. After tying it quickly around his upper thigh to slow the bleeding, she scanned the small valley they'd both tumbled into. A sheer rock wall rose to the right, at least eighty feet in the air. The hillside climbed to the left. Behind her, the valley narrowed as it curved down and away.

She looked back at the rock wall. The light was starting to wane, and from her position, it was hard to see, but a shadow to the right could be the opening to a cave.

All kinds of monsters might be living in that cave. Apprehension kept her from moving forward. Another roar echoed from the ridge above, sending a shiver down her spine.

Monsters or not, whatever lived in that cave had to be better than what was waiting out here to eat them.

Hooking the spear in the tie at her waist, she leaned down, slid her arms under the man's shoulders, and pulled him with her as she stepped back toward the shelter.

Her muscles ached. Pain shot up her back while sweat beaded every inch of her skin. Clenching her jaw, she pulled harder, dragging his body along the ground, trying to make as little sound as possible. Long minutes passed. When she finally reached the mouth of the cave, she laid him on the ground, drew a deep breath, then pulled out her spear—just in case—and stepped cautiously into the space.

No signs of life. No bones or weird smells. Slowly, she moved deeper into the cave.

The ground was mostly sand, the walls smooth stone. The cave ran back about fifteen feet and stopped. Breathing easier, she leaned her spear against the wall, returned to the man, and dragged him inside. When she was six feet in, her bare foot slipped. She grunted as her weight went out from under her and she hit the sand on her butt. The man landed on top of her legs, pinning her to the ground. Her grunt turned to a moan of frustration and flat-out annoyance.

She was hot, sweaty, and ready to be done with this guy— whoever he was. All she wanted to do was get back to the beach and her hammock high above the ground. Using every last bit of strength she had, she managed to roll him off her, swiped at the sweat from her forehead, and knelt in the sand beside him.

"Whoa."

Shaggy light brown hair framed a weathered face that was both masculine and striking. His nose was straight, his cheekbones strong. A thin layer of scruff covered a square jaw and chin, making him more ruggedly sexy than handsome. Bruises marred the skin near his right temple, but they didn't detract from his mesmerizing looks, and the thin scar that ran across his upper lip only made her wonder what had happened to him in the past.

Her gaze drifted down his thick neck to strong, toned, bare shoulders. An intricate rose tattoo covered his right biceps and shoulder. The rose was the symbol of love, of beauty, purity, and passion. Roses were usually associated with females, especially those who worshipped the goddess Aphrodite.

She frowned, unsure how she knew that, and let her gaze drift lower, over his pecs, down his strong, carved abs to a tapered waist, and finally the dark pants covering his narrow hips and strong legs.

Her throat grew dry as she visualized what was under those pants. Forcing her gaze to his legs, she shook her head. The man was unconscious, and she was ogling him like a piece of meat. Yeah, that wasn't creepy or anything.

Still…he was seriously hot.

Her gaze slid back up to his stunning face, and out of nowhere, déjà vu hit her square in the chest. She'd seen him before, she was sure of it. Not in person, but in a picture or a book.

Although that didn't make a whole lot of sense. How would she know any man on this island? If he was here, it meant he was somehow linked to the Sirens—and through them to the gods. Her people made it a point to stay as far from the gods as possible.

"Twenty-five years is nothing but a blink of an eye to the gods. And peace is as fleeting as the wind. It will end. It will end soon."

Her mother had said those words to her. She remembered hearing them as clearly as she'd heard that monster roar. But she didn't know why they'd been said. Or when. Or even where. She couldn't remember the context or what her mother had looked like saying them, but she knew they were real. Just as she knew her mother had said them sometime recently.

A dim roar echoed from outside, shaking Elysia from her scattered thoughts. She looked toward the cave opening. The monster sounded as if it were still up on the hillside, but she didn't want to take any chances. Pushing to her feet, she grasped the spear and headed for the mouth of the cave. If she had any hope of making it safely to morning, she needed to find firewood and enough brush to camouflage her location.

Hers? *Theirs...*

She stopped outside the cave and frowned. Common sense told her to forget about the mystery hottie inside and hoof it back to her shelter high in the trees. Sirens attacked, they didn't rescue.

But something in the center of her chest wouldn't let her walk away. She didn't know if it was duty or honor or sympathy or weakness, but she couldn't leave him. He was as much a victim in all this as she was. Which meant...

She was fucked. When the monsters came to eat them in the middle of the night, she'd have no one to blame but herself.

"Yeah," she muttered, marching into the trees. "You're perfect Siren material, Elysia. Way to go."

CHAPTER FOUR

"There are three phases to Siren training."

Demetrius watched as Skyla leaned against Theron's desk, crossed her arms over her chest, and looked out at the group assembled in the Argonaut leader's office. As Athena's right-hand Siren for over three hundred years, Skyla had firsthand knowledge of the Siren training schedule, but hearing the details didn't tame the darkness swirling inside Demetrius. And sitting here chatting about what was happening on Olympus wasn't doing shit to save his daughter.

"The first," Skyla went on, "is a series of tests designed to push a recruit to the limit to see if they're worthy of the Order. The second deals with basic training in a variety of areas—warfare, strategy, marksmanship, physical endurance, etcetera. The third focuses on sharpening and honing the skills learned earlier."

"How long does each phase last?" Isadora asked from where she stood near the windows.

Demetrius heard the strain in his mate's voice. She was as worried about their daughter as he was. He glanced at her delicate jaw clenched with worry, and the tense line of her shoulders. But where she, as queen of their realm, had to stress not only about what was happening with Elysia but about the repercussions of any kind of rescue attempt on Argolea, all Demetrius could do was focus on the ways he was going to make Zeus and Athena pay for fucking with his family.

"The first phase is an undetermined length of time." Skyla tucked a lock of long blonde hair behind her ear as she glanced the queen's way with green eyes tinged with sadness. "Basically, it lasts however long it takes the recruit to pass the given tests. Phase two covers the first three and a half years of training, while phase three covers the last three and a half years. Upon completion of the full seven years, each recruit is then tested in each area until their skills match Athena's expectations."

"Her expectations differ from one recruit to the next," Daphne cut in from where she stood next to her mate near the wall. "The tests in the first phase are not static. They change from one recruit to the next. There is no fairness in the world of the Sirens."

While Daphne had never been inducted as a Siren, she'd been chosen by Zeus to become one. She'd completed the full seven years of training and had passed every test except marksmanship. In lieu of another exam, Zeus had asked her to carry out a mission for him—to find and destroy the rogue Argonaut Aristokles. But instead of destroying Ari, she'd fallen in love with the guardian. And it was because of her that Ari, who'd once been thought dead by his kin, had returned to Argolea and to the Argonauts.

Ari wrapped an arm around Daphne's shoulder and drew the nymph protectively to his side.

"That is true. She does. And"—Skyla looked back at the queen—"even if a recruit completes the first test, that's not a guarantee she'll be passed on to the second level of training."

"What do you mean?" Demetrius asked, his concern growing by the second.

Skyla drew in a breath. "The first level is all about survival. A recruit—in this case, Elysia—is dropped into a harsh and dangerous environment and given the opportunity to showcase her survival skills."

"Pandora." Demetrius's jaw hardened. The witch had told Max the Sirens had taken his daughter to Pandora. He knew all too well about the dangers on that godsforsaken island. Both he and Isadora had been trapped on Pandora long ago and had barely survived. The island was inhabited by all the worst creatures in Ancient Greece—hydras, keres, harpies, manticores...and those were only the ones Demetrius and Isadora had encountered. There were hundreds more lurking in the shadows, just waiting to attack his unsuspecting daughter.

"Yes." Skyla met Demetrius's gaze. "Pandora has been the Siren testing island of choice for years. According to Athena, it's the best possible place to separate the girls from the Sirens."

Isadora's eyes slid closed, and even though that darkness inside screamed to be released, Demetrius moved behind his mate and massaged her slim shoulders, hoping to alleviate at least a little of her stress.

"Each recruit is given seven labors," Skyla went on, looking over the group. "Seven tests of their worthiness. After they complete a labor, they're given a new one. Points are tallied by Athena. The recruits who complete the tasks the fastest receive more points. The top seventy-five percent of the finishers are moved on to stage two of training. The bottom twenty-five percent are not."

"So there's a chance she could be returned," Theron said from the couch where he sat next to his mate, Casey. "If she doesn't complete the tasks fast enough."

"No." Skyla sighed. "No, there's no chance she'll be sent back."

"I don't understand." Isadora shifted beneath Demetrius's hands. "If she can't complete the labors in time, what happens to her?"

Skyla glanced toward her mate, the Argonaut Orpheus, perched on the edge of the desk at her side. With a frown, he reached for her hand. Skyla's fingers curled around his. But she still didn't answer.

"The bottom twenty-five percent are ejected from training," Daphne said when Skyla couldn't. "If they can't cut it in training, Zeus doesn't think they're worthy of this world. They're executed."

Every muscle in Demetrius's body went tight and rigid. In front of him, Isadora gasped and turned to press her forehead against his chest.

"That won't happen to Elysia." Orpheus's gray eyes sharpened. "Elysia's half-Argonaut. She's been running with Max and Talisa in the forests of this realm as long as I can remember. That girl might not be a warrior, but she's a survivor. She knows how to take care of herself. She'll make it through the seven labors."

Isadora looked up, and when Demetrius met her gaze, he saw the resolution in her eyes. And the hope.

He gave a little nod even though he didn't feel any hope himself. Isadora closed her eyes briefly, then turned to look back at the group.

Inside Demetrius, that darkness bubbled right to the surface. If anything happened to his daughter, Zeus and the Sirens wouldn't know what hit them. He'd make them pay for this with his dying breath.

"Orpheus is right." Skyla nodded. "Elysia will make it off Pandora. I did." She nodded toward the nymph at Ari's side. "Daphne did. I have every confidence she'll get through this and make it to Olympus."

"So tell us about the second phase of training," Casey said from the couch. "She'll be on Olympus for that, correct? That's what we're all interested in. We can get to Olympus. We can't get to Pandora."

"Yes, the second phase takes place on Olympus. But if you're thinking we can mount some kind of rescue, that's not going to be easy."

"During the first few years," Daphne said, "the recruits are always with a trainer. Always. They're never left alone. They're not even allowed to run training missions in the human realm until the third phase, which, I'm sorry to say, won't happen for Elysia for at least three and a half years. Even if you could come up with a rescue plan, you'll never get to Elysia unnoticed. Someone is always watching. And even if you *could* get there unseen, and assuming she *could* get away from her trainers for a few moments to meet you, there's no way to get her a message to tell her what you have planned. Not to mention she wouldn't remember who you are even if you could warn her."

"What do you mean she wouldn't remember us?" Callia, the queen's other half sister and the Argonaut Zander's mate, wrinkled her brow.

"That's the part I haven't gotten to." Skyla shifted uncomfortably against Theron's desk. "All recruits' memories are blocked until they make it through phases one and two of training. After that, when they're in phase three and Zeus and Athena are convinced they're dedicated to the Order, those memories are slowly returned."

"Dear gods." Isadora leaned back into Demetrius as if the world had just rocked out from under her. "She won't remember any of us."

Demetrius closed his hands around her upper arms, holding her tightly so she didn't fall. But really he was using her to hold himself up, because the more he stood here listening to Skyla, the more he realized their chance of getting Elysia back anytime soon was slipping away.

"Our best chance for any kind of rescue is when she's in the human realm," Orpheus said beside Skyla. "Until then, I don't see how we can even get to her."

"That's over three years away," Zander said in disbelief, perched on the armrest of the couch next to Callia.

Three years…

Demetrius squeezed Isadora's arms. Yes, their daughter was strong, but he wasn't sure she could last three years. Elysia knew how to take care of herself, but she had a gentle heart. She wasn't a warrior like the Argonauts. In a combat situation, Elysia's first instinct wouldn't be to kill but to protect.

Demetrius's gaze drifted toward Theron's daughter, leaning against the far wall, her marked forearms crossed over her chest, her jaw clenched, her muscles tensed and ready for a fight. Animosity swirled in the darkness inside. Talisa was the warrior, not Elysia. Talisa was the female Zeus should have chosen, and even she knew it. But Zeus never did what was expected, and Demetrius knew far too well that the reason the god had picked Elysia was to fuck with the monarchy. Zeus hated Isadora more than any other because she had the one thing he wanted most in the world: the Orb of Krónos. The four-chambered disk created by the Titan Prometheus that housed the classic elements—earth, air, water, and fire—and had the power to release the Titans from Tartarus.

That was Zeus's ultimate goal. To take back the Orb so he could control all the worlds, not just the heavens. Only Isadora stood in his way. She possessed the Orb, and as soon as the Argonauts found the water element, she was going to destroy it so no one—mortal or immortal—could release the Titans and start the war to end all wars in the definitive quest for power.

"What about Nick?" Theron asked.

Demetrius looked toward the leader of the Argonauts. Nick was Demetrius's half brother, the leader of the Misos race—half human, half Argoleans—who lived within their realm. But by a twist of fate, Nick was also a god.

Hope leapt inside Demetrius. In the chaos since Elysia's abduction, he'd overlooked their biggest weapon. A god who was nearly as powerful as Zeus himself.

"Nick might be a help to us in three years," Orpheus said, "but the minute he steps foot on Olympus, all the gods will know. They have a twisted god sense like an alarm. I guarantee if Zeus even sniffs Nick anywhere close, the king of the gods will lock Elysia down so tight, we'll never find her. No, our best bet for any kind of rescue is to wait until she's in the human realm."

That hope fizzled and died.

"I know three years sounds like a long time," Skyla said. "But it will pass quickly. And it's but a blip in Elysia's lifespan."

Skyla was right. Three years was nothing for Elysia. Argoleans, being descendants of the original seven Greek heroes, were blessed with long lives—at least five hundred years. Argonauts, and those of the royal family, lived longer. Closer to eight hundred years. But Demetrius still wanted his daughter back now...not *three years from now*.

"She will be repeatedly tested over the next three years," Skyla went on. "But she'll make it. I agree with Orpheus. I think we focus on a plan to bring her home when she's in phase three and is running training missions in the human realm. It's the safest choice all around."

Murmurs echoed across the room as each Argonaut spoke softly with those around them. Demetrius looked down at his mate, who turned sad and worried eyes up at him. He saw the logic, understood it, but all he could think about was Elysia trapped on Pandora, fighting for her life.

"What about seduction?" Max asked loudly from the back of the room.

Demetrius's head came up, and a whisper of foreboding rushed down his spine. Voices in the room quieted.

"You didn't mention that as one of the training segments," Max said as all eyes turned his way. "But we all know that's part of the whole Siren gig, isn't it? Forced sexual training to turn an innocent female into a hardened seductress? If we wait three years to go after her, Elysia won't be the female she is now. Not even close."

Demetrius's lungs squeezed so tight, it felt as if the hands of the Fates were crushing them into dust. He'd forgotten about the seduction piece. He'd been so afraid for Elysia's safety, he hadn't stopped to think about just what kind of training she'd be subjected to.

"Seduction is only one facet of the training," Daphne said uneasily. "And she could get lucky. My trainer was…gentle."

Demetrius's gaze shot toward Skyla. The former Siren let go of Orpheus's hand and crossed her arms over her chest again. But this time, her focus dropped to the floor, and her trainer, Demetrius deciphered, hadn't been so nice.

The darkness swirled faster inside.

Isadora stiffened beneath Demetrius's hands. "Maybe you'd better tell us what's involved in this…seduction training."

Skyla's worried eyes met the queen's. "Are you sure you want to know?"

Isadora swallowed hard. "Yes."

Skyla glanced at Demetrius. And when he saw the apology in her green irises, he curled his fingers in the sleeves of Isadora's blouse and only just held back from flashing straight to Olympus to kick some immortal ass.

"It's intensive." Skyla sighed. "And Max's guess was right. It will change Elysia. In ways none of you can imagine."

Damon couldn't stop staring.

Peeking between shuttered eyelids, he watched as the Siren recruit pulled a skewer from the fire and touched the sizzling meat on the end of the stick. She winced and jerked her hand back, then blew on her fingers to ease the burn.

He should already be back on Olympus. His wounds were healing. Even though things hadn't gone as planned, he'd done what he'd been sent here to do—to play the victim so the recruit could rescue him.

Color him shocked. In all his years playing this part for Athena's recruits, he'd only ever *acted* as a victim. After being chased by that manticore, tumbling down the hillside, and passing out at the bottom of the ravine, though, he'd seriously been one. Lucky for him, the recruit hadn't just been in the area, she'd gotten him to the safety of this cave, torn off part of her skirt, and fastened a bandage to his wounds. Then she'd gone back out into the wild, found herbs known for their healing properties, come back, built a fire, and cooked up a brew that she'd applied to his wounds to aid his recovery. And as if all *that* wasn't heroic enough, she'd gone back out into the dark where all those monsters lurked, found and killed a rabbit, brought it back here, and cooked it so they had something to eat.

Who the heck was this chick? He'd never come across a recruit so levelheaded and selfless. Nowhere in labor five was the recruit expected to heal or feed him. She just had to rescue him. So why in Hades was she bothering to take care of him? Didn't she know she'd already done what Athena wanted her to do? Every other recruit he'd ever encountered cared only about completing the seven labors and getting off this hellhole of an island.

Knowing he couldn't just come out and ask that—especially when he was still pretending to be injured—he feigned sleep as he watched her blow on the skewer of meat and carefully pull a piece off the stick, pop it into her mouth, and slowly chew.

Damn, but he could see why Zeus had marked her for the Sirens. The female was gorgeous—long silky hair the color of melted chocolate, mesmerizing coffee-colored eyes, high cheekbones, and a regal nose. She was slim—more athletic than curvy—and her breasts were small and firm in the miniscule halter top the Sirens had dressed her in before dropping her here, but he liked that about her. She wasn't altered like the Sirens. Not yet, at least. If she made it to the third phase of Siren training, though, she would be.

Zeus took pleasure in remaking each of his Sirens into the most seductive form he could imagine—small waist, big tits, long legs, firm ass—a form of magical plastic surgery that took a recruit from competent warrior to deadly seductress. And he did it for a reason. Because Sirens—by definition—were the very creatures males—mortal or immortal—could not deny. They used their sexuality as a weapon, and when they had a male exactly where they wanted him, then they were at their most deadly.

Damon hated the thought of Zeus tampering with this female. She was already perfect. Why the fuck did Zeus feel the need to mess with natural beauty?

Heat rolled through his belly and slid lower. And as he watched her, Damon recognized the stirrings of an arousal he hadn't felt in years. Sure, he was male. His body responded to a female's touch whether he wanted it to or not. But this was different. This was an arousal that came from within. From interest. From lust.

She set the stick on the rocks around the small fire she'd built, wiped her hands on her even shorter skirt thanks to her bandaging techniques, and crawled across the sandy floor of the cave toward him.

Muscles flexed in her thighs, and Damon's own muscles tightened as she drew close. The scent of honeysuckle surrounded him, and the heat in his groin intensified, thickening his cock and leaving him hard and hot and achy in a way he hadn't been in years.

Her soft fingers landed against his thigh. Carefully, she untied the bandage and looked down. Tucking a lock of hair behind her ear, she tipped her head and muttered, "Hm. That's strange."

Damon seriously hoped she wasn't staring at his hard-on. Knew if she hadn't noticed it yet, she would in a second. He continued to hold as still as possible.

The pads of her fingers pressed all around the wound. A twinge shot through his skin, but it faded quickly beneath the warmth of her touch. The wound had already healed; he could feel it. There was probably nothing left but a thin red line.

"You, Elysia," she said as she lifted her fingers from his skin, "can now add healer to your list of attributes."

He almost burst out laughing at the way she was talking to herself, but bit his tongue to keep from giving himself away. Disappointment and relief swirled through him at the loss of her touch. But it was quickly overridden by the realization that she'd said her name.

Siren recruits weren't supposed to remember their names. They weren't supposed to remember anything about their old lives.

"So why aren't you awake yet, Mr.—" She gasped and, seconds later, whispered, "Oh my."

And right then, Damon knew she'd spotted his hard-on.

So much for feigning sleep.

He held his breath and waited for her to call him out, but she didn't. Long, silent seconds passed. Finally, she muttered, "Screw Siren training. Looks like I can already add seductress to that list."

The sexy little smile that curved her lips sent the blood rushing right back into Damon's cock, and even though he knew he was supposed to be hightailing it back to Olympus right this second, he didn't want to. He wanted to stay right here in this cave and figure out what it was about this recruit that fascinated him so.

Because there was something special about her. Something he couldn't quite put his finger on. And before he left her, he wanted—no, he *needed*—to know just what that was.

The sound of shuffling dragged Elysia out of a delicious dream. She'd been playing in the surf when a sexy sea god had risen up from the warm, waist-deep waters, drawn her into his strong arms, and consumed her with a hot and heavy kiss.

She blinked several times, pushed up on her hands, and stilled. The shuffling sound that had awoken her wasn't the wind or the waves. It was the brush that she'd piled in front of the cave's opening last night being pushed aside.

"Sorry." The man she'd rescued from that manticore ducked under the overhang and stepped into the cave. "I didn't mean to wake you."

Slowly, she sat up and focused on the torn black pants that rode low on lean hips, exposing the carved V of his hipbones that drew her gaze down. To what he kept hidden underneath those pants. To what she'd watched come to life last night when she'd touched his leg.

She swallowed hard and forced her gaze up, over cut abs and pecs, to strong sexy shoulders, and finally that stunning face. His features were the same chiseled angles and lines she'd studied last night, except this morning his eyes were open. And in the sunlight shining in through the cave's opening she could see the color. Deep brown rimmed in a halo of gold. Spellbinding eyes. Hypnotic. Captivating.

He laid a piece of bark on the sand in front of her, and set a bunch of bananas on top. "Not as impressive as whatever you cooked last night, but it should suffice for breakfast."

Elysia's mouth went dry, not because he was awake and feeding her. Because he was the spitting image of the sea god she'd just been fantasizing about.

She tucked a lock of hair behind her ear, her stomach churning with both nerves and uncertainty. "Um, thanks."

"Damon."

She glanced up to his face. His really gorgeous face. "Excuse me?"

"My name's Damon."

"Oh. Um, I'm Elysia."

"I know." He sat in the sand across from her and rested his forearms on his updrawn knees. "I remembered hearing you say your name last night. I was kind of in and out a bit then, I'm afraid."

Her fingers stilled in the process of peeling a banana. *Crap*, he'd heard her talking to herself. Yeah, that made her look totally tough.

"Thank you for saving my life," he said in that same sexy voice she'd heard in her dream.

Heat rushed to her cheeks. How the heck had she dreamt about his voice? He hadn't spoken last night. She'd never heard his voice before.

She quickly pulled the banana open, broke off a piece, and popped it in her mouth. "Oh," she said around a mouthful. "You're welcome."

He watched her eat, making her feel even more self-conscious. And halfway through her meal, she realized she was eating something shaped suspiciously like—

Ooookay. Not going there. She set down the rest of her banana and swiped her hands on her skirt.

"I'm not a god."

Her hands stilled, and that heat swept down her neck. Had he somehow sensed her dream?

"I'm sure that's what you're wondering," he said quickly. "I mean, because of what's on this island and all. But I'm not. I'm mortal. Like you."

She wasn't sure what she was. At the moment, she was having trouble just remembering her name.

"And I'm not a Siren recruit," he went on. "Obviously."

From the corner of her eye, she watched the edge of his lips curl in a sexy smirk. One that pulled on the scar near his upper lip and made his entrancing eyes absolutely sparkle.

The heat shifted to her breasts and trickled down her belly to pool between her thighs. And the memory of that dream—of the sea god's mouth covering hers—made her legs tremble.

"So I'm sure you're wondering what I'm doing here," he continued.

She was. But she couldn't quite find her voice to ask. Her throat was too thick, her mind too clouded to stumble over words.

"I was a plant. By Athena. Part of your fifth labor."

"Fifth?" Her brow wrinkled. "But I haven't received my fifth labor yet."

"You completed four and five out of order. But trust me, you finished the fifth one already."

She had no idea what he was talking about. "Athena sent you?"

He nodded. "I work with the recruits. I'm one of the trainers. In this phase, we're used to weed out those who will move on from those who aren't strong enough."

"So my fifth labor was…"

"To rescue someone from danger."

"Oh. Well. It's a good thing I stumbled across you, because I was pretty sure I was alone on this island."

"Not alone." He winked at her. "Not even close."

The simple act ignited a low burn in her belly. One she liked. Too much. Especially considering where she was.

She swiped her hands across her skirt again, averting her gaze. "So you're one of the trainers I'll be working with on Olympus? If I make it that far?"

"Possibly. There are many trainers."

"Are they all mortal, like you?"

"Most are. The gods employ many mortals on Olympus to aid in their endeavors."

Elysia chanced a look at him in the dim light. He wasn't human. She wasn't sure how she knew that, she just did. He had some kind of otherworldly blood in him, she just didn't know what kind.

Her gaze strayed to the rose tattoo on his right shoulder and biceps. His skin was tan and unmarked save for that rose, his muscles ripped and distracting, but her gaze kept flicking back to that tattoo. "The rose is a symbol of Aphrodite, is it not?"

"It is." His gaze narrowed. "How do you know that?"

Elysia's mind spun. How did she know? She'd learned it somewhere, she just couldn't pull the memory into focus. "I'm not sure." When her gaze met his, she realized he was studying her speculatively. "Was I not supposed to say that?"

He was silent for several seconds, staring at her with such intensity she was sure she'd said something wrong. Nerves tightened her belly.

"I'm surprised, to be honest. All Siren recruits' memories are wiped clean. The memories are eventually returned, usually in the third phase of training, but that's not for many years. You said your name last night, which also surprised me. Most recruits don't know their name. What else do you know or remember?"

Elysia looked around the dimly lit cave. "Just bits and pieces really. Nothing concrete. I remember being in some kind of classroom, learning about the Olympians."

"Do you remember where you grew up?"

She tried to put the pieces together, but all she saw were fragmented scenes—being in a school, running through a forest, chasing a blond-headed boy and a dark-haired girl, glimpsing a city of white marble and stone from the hillside and feeling a rush of...contentment.

Was the city of white her home? She couldn't put a name to the city. Couldn't even put a name to the boy or girl she saw in those visions.

After several moments, she shook her head. "No. I have no idea."

The intensity left his gaze, and he seemed to breathe easier. "I guess whoever wiped your memories didn't do a very good job. I'm sure that will be addressed if you make it through the seventh labor."

Elysia's stomach tightened. She didn't want to lose what few memories she had. "Maybe I—"

A shrill whistle echoed from beyond the cave opening, and Damon turned that way. "Speaking of..." He pushed to his feet and moved for the opening. "That sounds like your next box."

Elysia wasn't sure she was ready for another box. She just wanted to go on sitting in this cave with the sexy man she'd rescued, wondering who he was and fantasizing about that dream.

When he stepped out into the sunlight, a whisper of worry rushed through her. Did that mean he was leaving? He'd said he was only here to aid her in the fifth labor. Was he heading back to Olympus?

She quickly pushed to her feet and followed. Sunlight blinded her as she stepped into the warm morning. Blinking several times, she searched for him, then relaxed when she spotted him ten feet away, lifting a small box from the ground.

Muscles flexed in his strong back and shoulders as he rose to his full height and dusted off the box. And her stomach did a weird flip when he turned her way, smiled that sexy half grin, and handed her the box.

"I think this is for you."

Hesitantly, she reached out. Their fingers brushed against the smooth wood. And the moment they did, sparks of heat and electricity ricocheted into her fingertips, up her arm and down to her chest, bringing everything else to a standstill.

"Aren't you going to open it?" he asked in that deep, familiar voice.

Her gaze narrowed. She knew him from somewhere. They'd met before. A long time ago. She was sure of it. She just didn't know where.

"*Oraios?*"

Beautiful. He'd called her beautiful. Something in her chest went all warm and liquid at the simple word, and her stomach did that weird flop thing again as he stared at her.

No, she definitely didn't want him to leave. She wanted to know more about him. Wanted…something she was pretty sure she wasn't supposed to want as a Siren recruit.

She wanted him.

Heat rushed up her cheeks, and she pulled her hand from his, looking down at the box. What was this thing she was feeling? Yearning, craving…lust? Sirens were highly sexualized warriors— Elysia knew that—but she wasn't supposed to feel lust so early in her training… Was she?

She cleared her throat and focused on the box. She wasn't sure what she was supposed to be feeling, but she knew if she wanted off this island, she had to get through these labors. Her fingers shook as she worked the latch, and embarrassment rushed through her when she realized he had to see it.

Great. Now he knew she was interested.

She freed the latch and pulled the scroll from the box. Then frowned.

"What does it say?" he asked.

"It says I have to find something called an aegis. It's hidden somewhere on the island."

"The aegis is a shield, sometimes bearing the head of a gorgon."

"Do you know where?"

"No."

Her gaze dropped to his firm mouth, and she watched as his top teeth sank into his bottom lip. A burst of heat rushed through her, imagining those teeth nipping at her own lip. But it faded quickly when she realized he was probably leaving at any moment.

Why wouldn't he? His job here was done. Disappointment washed through her all over again.

"I might have an idea where to look," he said.

Hope lifted her gaze back to his eyes—his mesmerizing, hypnotic eyes—and that heat came rushing back. "Does that mean you'll help me find it?"

He grasped the spear leaning near the door of the cave, took her elbow with his other hand, and steered her into the jungle. "That depends on whether or not you want me to stay."

Ribbons of electricity arced from her elbow into her chest and down to her groin, warming her in a way she'd never felt before. Electrifying her in a way that made her feel alive.

"I want you to stay," she said quickly.

He smiled down at her as if he liked that. "Then for now, *oraios*, regardless of the consequences, I'll stay."

CHAPTER FIVE

Damon walked behind Elysia as they trekked through the jungle, mesmerized by the sway of her hips in the short skirt and the flex of muscle in her thighs and ass. He really needed to pull his head out and stop drooling over her. She was a recruit. Assuming she made it through the labors, odds he'd be assigned to her during her training were slim. The attrition rate for recruits was high. The likelihood she'd be booted before she made it to seduction training was even higher.

All kinds of sultry, erotic images filled his mind as he thought of training Elysia in the art of seduction—her naked in Aphrodite's pleasure pools, tied blindfolded to his bed, writhing as he drove her to the brink with his hands and tongue and body.

Tearing his gaze from her delectable ass, he swiped the perspiration from his forehead and told himself she was just a recruit. *Just a recruit.* So she was hot. They were all hot. So she'd rescued him. She was supposed to rescue him. And so she remembered things she wasn't supposed to remember. That didn't make her special. It just meant whoever had wiped her memories had done a shitty job.

If she isn't that special, then why in Hades haven't you left yet?

"Good fucking question," he muttered.

Elysia glanced over her shoulder. "Did you say something?"

"No. Don't mind me."

"Huh."

Fabulous. Now she was trying to piece together what he'd said. He swiped at his forehead again and looked down at the path to keep from staring at delectable backside. He shouldn't be here.

They'd been wandering around this damn jungle for a good four hours, and he had no idea where that stupid aegis was located. He wasn't helping her. She didn't need him. The smart thing would be to forget this mini-obsession and head back to Olympus before Athena cued into the fact he'd gone AWOL.

His chest smacked into something hard, and a soft grunt sounded at his front. Too late he realized Elysia had stopped and that he'd run right into her.

"Damn it." He reached for her shoulders so she didn't fall facedown and pulled her back against him. "Sorry."

"Shh." Her hand gripped his at her shoulder.

Heat rushed from her back into his chest and stomach and thighs, and with just that little contact, he grew hard and achy, exactly as he'd done last night.

Holy hell, he wanted this female. Wanted her in a way he hadn't wanted another in he couldn't remember how long.

"Do you hear that?" she whispered.

He couldn't hear anything but his pounding heart and raging libido. But her words forced him to focus on the jungle around them. When brush rustled somewhere to their right, he realized they weren't alone.

Adrenaline spiked, kicking him into action. Grasping her hand, he pulled her off the path, his eyes scanning the vines and trees around them for anywhere they could hide.

A hillside rose to their left. He pulled Elysia with him as he moved around the base, looking for a copse of trees or a boulder where they wouldn't be seen or—

He spotted what looked to be another cave. Moving quickly, he pulled Elysia in with him, only to realize it curved to the right six feet and stopped.

"What are we—"

"Shh." He pushed her as far back into the darkness as he could, until her back was pressed up against the rocks and he closed in at her front. "The monsters on this island are only supposed to come out at night, but I wouldn't put it past Zeus—or Athena—to change the rules."

The gods were always doing shit like that. Twisting the order of things to fit their needs. He hated that about them. Hated their selfishness and how he was stuck in the middle of their stupid world.

"You're still in the sunlight." Elysia's fingertips curled into his shoulders, and she pulled him into the warmth and softness of her body. "Get closer so they can't see you."

His adrenaline spiked all over, this time not from fear but from awareness. The silky skin of her thigh brushed his leg, but she didn't stop. Just continued to pull him in tighter. He lifted his hands to brace himself against the rocks so she wouldn't feel threatened, but the hard tips of her breasts grazed his chest, distracting him from his surroundings. And when she pulled him in again, his awakening erection pressed against her warm, soft belly, making all thoughts but her fade into the background.

Holy Hera. She had to feel that. It was highly inappropriate, not only because they were currently being stalked by monsters but because this wasn't a seduction session. He wasn't supposed to be turned on by her. He wasn't even supposed to be with her.

She didn't move, just held him tightly against her. He knew he needed to pull back, to put space between them, to do something, but he was too afraid to move and alert her to his raging erection.

Slowly, he released the rocks above his head, let his hands drop to her shoulders. Her skin was smooth and silky, the muscles firm and strong. His gaze drifted down to her face, but this far back in the corner, darkness made it hard to see her expression. He could tell she was looking up at him, though. Knew from the warmth of her breath against his neck that she was watching him. Sensed by the way her quick breaths lifted her chest to rub against his that she was as aroused by him as he was by her.

She shifted closer, and her breasts pressed harder against him, sending the already pounding pulse in his ears into overdrive. His hands drifted down her shoulders, along her slim torso to rest on her hips. And when she sighed and moved even closer still, whatever reservations he'd had before seemed nonexistent.

He lowered his head, eager to find her mouth in the dark, but she stiffened against him, and sucked in a breath that was more shock than arousal. He stilled. Listened. And realized what she'd heard.

A voice. Feminine. Just one, though.

"Did you hear that?" Elysia whispered.

"It's another recruit," he whispered back.

She lifted her head, and even though it was still too dark to see her eyes, he knew questions swirled in her dark eyes.

"There are several recruits on this island," he went on, even though all he wanted to do was kiss her. "All searching for the same things."

"The aegis? Is there more than one?"

"I don't know."

Her fingers slid from his shoulders to his chest, and she gently pressed him back a half step. "Then we have to get back to searching."

He knew she was right, but he wasn't ready to let her go.

Reluctantly, he stepped back. The voice had faded, which meant the other recruit must have moved on. Before he could back out of the cave, Elysia said. "Wait. Do you feel that?"

The only thing he felt was her heat still swirling around him like a vortex in the small space, but he stilled and tried to focus so he could figure out what she meant. Cool air drifted over his calves.

"This cave goes farther back," she said with excitement. "We should check it out. Just in case."

"Let me look." Damon crouched. She was right. The cave opened to a crawl space big enough for a person. What he'd thought was sunlight from the opening was actually light coming from deeper in the cave. "There's some kind of illumination."

Elysia knelt beside him, her arm brushing his in the process, sending shards of heat all through his torso. She shifted in front of him on her hands and knees and moved into the crawl space. "Come on."

He hesitated for only a split second, watching the sway of her sweet ass as she wiggled through the tight space. If another recruit found the aegis before she did, all his little fantasies about her were going to poof right out of his grasp. If he wanted to go back to what they'd just been about to do, he needed to stop fucking around and get busy.

A scraping sound echoed ahead. Damon crawled after Elysia, grunting as his shoulders and back hit the top of the tunnel and his knees scraped along the rocky floor. Just when he was sure this passageway was nothing more than a hoax, Elysia gasped.

He pushed to his feet when the tunnel opened to a large room. Light shone down from a hole in the ceiling, illuminating a pedestal made of stone. He let his eyes adjust, then sucked in a breath when he saw what had made her gasp.

A metal shield that looked to be millennia old sat on the pedestal. As he drew close, Damon caught sight of the silhouette of a mermaid imprinted into the metal.

"Wow." Elysia stopped in front of the shield. "I thought you said it was a gorgon head."

"I've never seen an aegis from the Sirens." Truth was, he'd never stuck around long enough to care what items a recruit had to find after rescuing him.

Elysia grazed the shield with her fingertips. A burst of light filled the room, highlighting the walls, the floor, the tunnel they'd just crawled through. She pulled her hand back, and the light slowly dimmed until it was nothing but a bright spot at the base of her neck. A turquoise amulet appeared at her throat, anchored by a chain around her neck. An amulet surrounded by swirls of silver that oddly resembled marine life.

Wide-eyed, Elysia reached up to touch the amulet. "It's cool, like water."

Damon ran his own fingers along the edge of the jewel. "That makes sense. The ancient Sirens were thought to be mermaids. Seductive females enchanting sailors who ventured near."

"I've read Homer."

Surprise lifted his gaze from the amulet to her face, highlighted by the glow of the stone. And again he was struck by the fact she remembered more than she should. "You have?"

"Long ago, when I was in school."

"In the same school where you learned about the gods?"

"The same place."

Memories flickered in her eyes, ones he couldn't read. But he could tell that whatever she was seeing was more than a fragment. And that meant she wasn't simply a memory swipe gone wrong. She was different from the other recruits. Somehow, she was more than any other female who'd been marked for the Sirens. And for reasons he couldn't explain, he *had* to know more about her. He had to know everything.

"Damon?"

"Yeah?"

"Are you all right?"

He wasn't sure. All he knew was that she was closer than she'd been moments before. Had she stepped in or had he? He glanced down only to realize his hand had moved from the amulet at her throat to lie over the beat of her heart—and her left breast.

Realizing what he'd done, he dropped his hand and moved back. Holy Hades, this female was doing a number on him. Arousing him in ways no female had, making his thoughts scatter and swirl. What the hell was happening to him?

"The, uh, amulet is a sign," he managed. "It means you're in the top seventy-five percent of recruits. You only have one labor left. Congratulations."

A wide smile spread across her gorgeous face, one that told him she'd liked where his hand had been. And just that fast, confusion fled and the need to touch her and know her and possess her came rushing back.

"That's good." She stepped closer. So close her seductive heat surrounded him. "Very good. So long as you stay to help me with the last labor, that is."

Oh man. Her eyes were vast dark pools. And he was falling under their spell. Just as those sailors had fallen for the ancient Sirens' hypnotic voices.

Her hand landed against his bare chest, igniting a fire in his blood. He lifted his to close around her long, slender fingers. Whoever she was, whatever she was, he no longer cared. All that mattered was having her.

He lowered his mouth to hers, and the instant her lips brushed his, desire flared hot and urgent through every cell in his body. He gripped her hand tighter against his chest, slid his tongue along the seam of her lips, then groaned when she opened and let him in.

Heat. Life. Home. The words swirled in his head while her tongue stroked gently along his. This was familiar. This was new. This was all-consuming in a way nothing and no one had ever been before.

She broke the kiss and stepped back long before he was ready to let her go. Cool air whooshed over his lips and bare chest. Before he could pull her back, she turned away. "Oh my gods, it's the seventh labor."

In a daze, he realized she'd moved toward the pedestal. A small wooden box sat near the aegis, as if it had floated through the skylight above.

Which, considering who was sending them, was no surprise. They'd set it up to happen just that very way.

Did that mean Athena knew he was here? She had to. She knew everything the recruits did on this damn island. He was going to be in some serious shit when he got back to Olympus.

His gaze drifted to Elysia. As he watched her open the box and read the scroll inside, arousal flared in his belly and spread into his groin. He'd deal with Athena's consequences later. All he cared about right now was the female in front of him.

Elysia's face fell. Worry immediately clamped a hand around his chest, distracting him from his thoughts. He moved toward her. "What's wrong?"

She turned to face him with wide, sickened eyes. "It's the last labor." She held out the scroll. "I have to kill another soul."

*K*ill *another soul...*

The words echoed in Elysia's mind as she sat by the fire on the beach that night. Darkness pressed in all around them, and every once in a while, the sound of branches crashing sounded from the jungle, but Elysia didn't even turn to look. The thuds were far off, and as Damon had told her, the monsters on this island didn't like flames. They were safe so long as the fire didn't go out.

"You've barely eaten," Damon said across the fire, where he stoked the hot coals with a thick branch.

Elysia looked at the fish he'd caught and cooked after they'd returned to the beach, sitting on a piece of bark he'd used as a plate beside her. "I'm not hungry."

"You have to eat."

Kill another soul...

Her stomach rolled. Eating was the last thing she needed to do. Pushing to her feet, she paced ten feet into the darkness, then turned and paced back. No, what she needed to do was find a way off this island. She couldn't kill someone. What did the Sirens think she was? A monster? She couldn't do that. She'd gladly bind herself to anyone her parents paired her up with over this.

Her feet stilled, and her brow lowered. Bind herself? What in Hades did that mean?

"I hope this isn't your way of telling me I should worry."

Elysia looked over at Damon across the fire. A sexy half smirk toyed with the edge of his lips, distracting her from her thoughts. "What?"

He lifted his brows, cueing her into his meaning.

She frowned. "I'm not going to kill you, if that's what you're thinking."

"Just making sure." He patted the log beneath him. "Why don't you come sit down?"

Confusion clouded her thoughts. "Why are you still here?"

"I'm not sure—"

"You said you were only here so I could complete the fifth labor. If that's true, then why haven't you left?"

"I thought you wanted me to stay."

She did. But she wasn't entirely sure why. Yes, she was attracted to him, yes he was hot, but there were a hundred things she needed to focus on other than hot and attractive. And he'd even admitted there would be repercussions to his staying, so why the heck was he still here? Especially now when she couldn't even string a thought together without flipping out?

"*Oraios.*" He rose and crossed to her. "Come here." Gently, he took her hand and led her around the fire. When they reached the log, he said, "Sit."

Elysia lowered to the log, her mind flipping between memories she couldn't bring into focus, to thoughts of him, to the seventh labor she didn't want to think about.

His hands landed on her shoulders and began kneading the tight muscles. "You're tense."

Of course she was tense. The Sirens wanted her to *kill* someone. Someone who'd never done a single thing to her.

"I know you're conflicted," he said long minutes later. "If it helps at all, most of these recruits will not make it off this island."

"So, what, my killing them is a way to put them out of their misery?"

"I didn't say that. I—"

"Could you do it? Kill someone you don't know? Someone you've never even met?"

"I have," he said quietly.

"You have?" Surprise rippled through Elysia, and she looked up at him. "When? Who?"

Damon's gaze met hers, and his hands paused their massaging. Something dark passed over his eyes. Something mysterious. "I'm not sure."

"How can you—"

"I don't remember it. But I know I've killed. Many times."

He was talking in riddles. She didn't know what he was saying. And considering how scattered her mind was at the moment, she was almost too afraid to ask.

Sighing, he let go and sat on the log beside her. Leaning forward, he rested his forearms on his knees and clasped his hands. Firelight flickered over his rugged skin and the rose tattoo that seemed to dance over his shoulder and biceps. "I was in some kind of accident in the human realm. The Sirens found me and brought me to Olympus. The gods nursed me back to health. When I awoke, I had no memory of my previous life."

Elysia studied his features. A thin layer of stubble had formed on his jaw, making him look darker and sexier than any male had the right to look. "How long ago was this?"

"Twenty-five years ago."

"And you can't remember a single thing?"

He shook his head. "Everything was blank when I awoke. The only thing familiar was the blade. That's how I know I've killed. My fighting skills are reflexive. I know I was some kind of warrior in the past, I just don't know where or for whom."

"And the gods didn't tell you?"

"They didn't know either. But they saved my life. That's why I serve them."

"And you never had any desire to return to the human realm? To find out who you used to be?"

He shook his head again.

"What if people are looking for you, though? Your family?"

"I don't think I have a family."

"But if you can't remember—"

He turned to her. "I'd feel them, Elysia. If they were there, I'd know. I've never felt any connection to anyone or any place. No loss. Until I met you, that is."

Something warmed in her belly. "What do you mean?"

He sighed again and looked back at the flames. "I don't really know what I mean. You asked me why I've stayed when I should already be back on Olympus. I guess the answer is because I feel some kind of connection to you that I've not felt with anyone else."

"Because I can remember things I'm not supposed to remember and you wish you could do the sa—"

"That's not why I've stayed." He looked at her again. Only this time his eyes were so focused and intense, heat rushed straight to her core. "Maybe at first that's why I didn't leave, but there's something else. Something more. Some connection I can't define. And I know it's selfish of me, but I don't want to leave until I figure out just what it is."

Her heart picked up speed until it was a whir in her ears, and as their eyes held, she felt the connection he spoke of too. It was more than sexual. It was more than a similarity in their blank memories. It was familiarity. A kinship. As if they'd known each other before, as if they'd crossed paths in a past life, as if their souls were predestined to meet by the Fates spinning the threads of life.

His gaze dropped to her fingers, and he reached for her hand. Warmth encircled her palm as his fingers slid along hers, rough where she was soft, strong where she was weak. "I know you don't want to complete the seventh labor. I know it's asking you to do something you're not comfortable doing. But I keep coming back to this feeling that I was sent here for a reason, that our meeting was not a random coincidence. Until I figure out why I feel that way, I can't leave. If Athena should discover that I've stayed, though… If she pulls me back to Olympus before I figure that out…"

Understanding dawned. "Then we'll never see each other again."

"Yes." His gaze lifted to hers, fathomless chocolate eyes rimmed in gold focused solely on her as if she were the only thing he could see. "If you don't complete the seventh labor and make it to Olympus, we'll never know the truth."

He was right. He could be whisked back to Olympus at any moment, and if that happened, neither of them would ever learn what was so compelling about the other. But was her desire to discover who and what he was to her strong enough to override her ethics? Did it justify killing someone? Especially another recruit?

"I don't think I'm ready to let you go," he whispered, leaning toward her. "At least not yet."

Her heart pounded hard against her ribs. She wasn't ready to let him go yet either, but she didn't know what to do. And the more time she spent with him, the less sure she was about everything, everyone, including herself.

Her breath caught as his soft, masculine lips brushed hers, and all thoughts but him, this, them slipped from her grasp.

"Help me," a voice said weakly.

Damon pulled back. "Did you hear that?" Pushing to his feet, he stared past the fire toward the darkness.

"Hear what?" Elysia turned to look.

"Help me," the voice called again.

"There's someone out there."

Slowly, Elysia rose. "It could be another recruit."

Damon grasped her hand. "Or it could be someone looking for me."

Sweat beaded on Elysia's spine as Damon pulled her away from the log. He grasped the spear from the sand and held it out for her. She shook her head. "You take it."

A worried expression passed over his features, but he didn't argue, instead moved around the fire and drew her with him.

The firelight faded the farther they moved down the beach. Only a sliver of moonlight illuminated the white sand and waves lapping gently against the shore.

"Help me, please," the voice said again, this time closer.

Elysia's fingers tightened around Damon's. "It's female."

"Yeah. Stay close. It could be a trap."

Those nerves kicked up in Elysia's belly. Of course it could be a trap. Athena was recruiting more than one female for the Sirens, which meant there were probably multiple amulets on this island. If another recruit had already found one, Damon and Elysia could be the prey instead of the hunters.

Fear lanced through her. Not just for herself, but for Damon as well. She slowed her steps and pulled on Damon's hand. "Maybe we should go back."

"Oh, thank the gods," a voice said somewhere close.

Elysia squinted in the darkness and felt her heart drop when she realized it was too late to turn around. A blonde Siren recruit, wearing the same ridiculous getup as Elysia, sat in the sand only feet away, leaning against the base of a palm. No amulet hung from her neck.

"I didn't think anyone would come," the female said. "Please help me."

Elysia's gaze fell to the recruit's calf, covered in blood.

"What happened?" Damon asked.

"A harpy." The recruit braced her hands against the sand and shifted with a grimace. "It came out of nowhere. I injured it, but before I could get away, it grabbed my leg. I thought I was going to die."

Damon handed Elysia the spear, then lowered to his knees to check the recruit's wound.

The recruit jerked back before he could touch her, and wide, fear-filled eyes stared into his face. "No, don't. It's still out there. Harpies can track blood. You have to kill it before it comes after me."

Damon glanced up at Elysia, and she read the question in his eyes. She would never have an easier chance to finish the seventh labor than she had right now.

Sickness rolled through Elysia's belly, and she quickly shook her head.

Damon sighed, leaned back, and ripped his remaining pant leg at the knee. Pushing to his feet, he handed the black scrap of fabric to Elysia and took the spear from her hand. "Use this. I'll go see if the harpy's still close."

Elysia grasped his arm. "But—"

"I'll be fine. I know how to take care of myself."

He did. She knew that. He was a warrior, not a nobody like her. But she didn't want him stalking off when he was upset with her. She knew he wanted her to go to Olympus with him, and she knew this was her best shot to do that. But couldn't he see that by doing what Athena wanted—by killing an innocent—Elysia would be altering that person he'd just claimed he felt so connected to? "Damon."

His eyes met hers, but when she looked into their chocolate depths, she realized they weren't filled with anger or frustration. They brimmed with sadness.

"I get it," he said softly. Then, closing his hand over hers against his arm, he squeezed. "See what you can do to help her. I'll be right back."

Relief and confusion warred inside Elysia as she watched him disappear into the jungle. What was this crazy connection between them? Why did she feel so drawn to him when she barely knew him? The sound of brush rustling slowly faded until all she could hear was the whoosh of waves rolling against the shore.

The recruit grimaced. "Who is he?"

Elysia's chest pinched as she knelt and slid the cloth under the recruit's calf. "I'm not sure."

"What's he doing here?"

"I'm not sure about that either."

"Seems like you're not sure about much."

Elysia frowned because, at the moment, she wasn't sure about anything. *Especially* Damon.

The recruit moved her hand against the sand, near her thigh. And from the corner of her vision, Elysia spotted the silver chain wrapped several times around the recruit's palm. A silver chain that was oddly similar to the silver chain around Elysia's neck.

Slowly, Elysia's gaze lifted to the recruit's. Only this time the recruit's eyes weren't frightened or pained. They were cold. Cold and hard and dangerous.

"I'm sure about something." The recruit pulled a dagger from behind her back. "I'm sure you're my ticket to Olympus."

CHAPTER SIX

The detached look in the recruit's eye told Elysia the female had killed before. But the excitement she saw lurking behind that look told her the recruit had enjoyed it.

The recruit swung out with the dagger. Elysia jerked back and fell onto her butt in the sand. The recruit growled and lurched forward. Elysia tensed and reached for the recruit's wrists. Her fingers wrapped around the slim bones, wrestling to stop the blade from reaching her. Pushing against the recruit with all her strength, Elysia shoved the female back. The recruit growled again and threw her weight to the side, sending them rolling across the beach.

Sand flew up into Elysia's eyes and nose and mouth. She sputtered, grunted, but didn't let go. The recruit snarled and jerked her left hand back, then nailed Elysia in the temple with something hard and sharp.

The amulet wrapped around her palm.

Elysia's head snapped back, but she still didn't let go. Grunting, she shoved her knee into the recruit's ribs. The recruit groaned and shifted, but managed to yank her left arm free and grip the blade with both hands.

Elysia fell on her back onto the sand, grappled for the hilt of the blade. The recruit braced her knees on both sides of Elysia and angled the tip of the blade over Elysia's heart.

"Too bad you're gonna die," the recruit growled. "I could have found a use for a scrapper like you on my team. Cleaning my boots."

Elysia's muscles screamed. Pain shot through every inch of her body. Sweat dripped from her forehead as she fought to keep the blade from piercing her flesh. But she was losing. The tip shifted closer. Tears pricked Elysia's eyes with the knowledge she wasn't strong enough to win this fight.

"*Emmoni!*"

The recruit lifted her head at the sound of Damon's voice and looked toward the trees. Elysia shoved hard with every ounce of strength, thrusting the recruit's arm—and the blade—away from her.

The recruit gasped and tensed. Wide-eyed, she looked down at the blade piercing her own chest.

Blood spurted. She fell forward onto Elysia. Footsteps sounded, followed by Damon's voice, yelling, "*Emmoni!*"

Oh gods. *Oh gods...* Elysia grunted and shoved the recruit off her. Shaking, she shifted to her knees in the sand and sucked back air.

Damon skidded to a stop in the sand and gripped her shoulders. "Are you okay? *Emmoni,* talk to me."

That word... He kept saying that word. She didn't know what it meant. "I..." Her breath came fast and shallow. She couldn't find the words. "I'm...okay."

He pulled her in tight to his chest. "Thank goodness."

Elysia wasn't ready to thank any god. Her gaze strayed to the recruit past Damon, lying bloody and unmoving on the sand. The dagger stuck straight from her chest. Disbelief and sickness rolled through Elysia all over again. "Oh my gods... Is she...?"

Damon let go of Elysia and turned. Kneeling near the recruit, he felt her neck for a pulse.

When he lifted his hand and stood, Elysia knew the answer. Bile rose in her throat. She doubled over, resting her hands on her knees as she gagged. "I'm going to be sick."

Damon gripped her shoulders and turned her away from the body. "Listen to me. You defended yourself. You didn't do anything wrong. You did what you had to do to survive."

"But she—"

"She set you up. The harpy was already dead, Elysia. She separated us on purpose so she could go after you. She thought you'd be the easier mark."

The sickness slowly receded. Her gaze strayed back to the lifeless recruit.

She'd killed another person. It didn't matter that she'd done it in self-defense. She'd taken a life, and nothing could change that.

"Hey," Damon said softer, lifting her chin with his finger. "Look at me. You did the right thing. I'm just sorry I wasn't here to do it for you."

Elysia's eyes closed, and the fight slid right out of her.

Damon caught her before she fell and pulled her into his chest. "It's okay. You're okay. I've got you."

She wasn't sure how anything could be okay now, but she let him hold her, let him be the strength she didn't possess. Long minutes passed. When the shakes slowly subsided, she sniffled. "I'm sorry I'm not tough. If my cousin Talisa were here, she wouldn't be shaking like a leaf. She'd be cleaning her weapon and moving on."

His hand stopped its gentle friction against her spine. "She wouldn't?"

A memory flashed behind Elysia's eyes. Of Talisa's jet-black hair blowing in the wind, her smiling violet eyes, and her wide grin as she released the string of her bow and the arrow hit the tree trunk dead center.

"No, she wouldn't." Surprise rippled through Elysia. She remembered her cousin. Easing back, she looked up at Damon. "Talisa is a warrior. Like you. Not at all like me."

"I've got news for you, *oraios*." Damon's sweet brown eyes softened, and he rubbed his thumb against something wet on her cheek. "You are a warrior. You proved it these last few days. Very few recruits make it this far." His fingers drifted to the amulet around her neck. "And only a handful do so as fast as you."

"But I had your help."

His lips curled. "You didn't need my help. And I'm pretty sure I didn't do anything but slow you down."

Their eyes held, and heat gathered in her belly. The same heat she always felt whenever he was close. "So what happens now?"

"I don't know." His fingers slid up her throat to cradle her jaw. "I don't really care. All I really care about right now is this."

His lips covered hers, and she opened at the first touch, drawing him into her mouth and soul and heart. Her eyes drifted closed, her body warmed. It was crazy. It was fast. It made absolutely no sense. But she didn't care either. All she wanted was more.

His tongue brushed hers in long, languid strokes. She wrapped her arms around his waist and trailed her fingertips up his back. His strong, muscular body pressed against her from thigh to chest, and everywhere they touched, heat ignited, sending arcs of electricity straight to her sex.

Light flashed, a blinding white she saw even behind closed eyelids. Damon called her name. But she couldn't respond. Because, suddenly, she was floating, flying, tumbling.

Her feet hit something solid. Darkness descended. In a daze, she realized her body was no longer warm but cool. She blinked several times and opened her eyes, only to discover she was no longer on a beach but in a field. Golden wheat surrounded her, and ahead, a monstrous mountain rose toward the blue-green sky.

She gasped, turned quickly, and stared wide-eyed at soaring marble temples in the distance.

"Breathtaking, isn't it?" a voice said to her left.

Elysia jerked that way. The voice wasn't Damon's. It wasn't even male. It was female. Coming from a voluptuous raven-haired beauty dressed in skintight black leggings, a low-cut black tank, kick-ass knee-high boots, holding a sleek and deadly bow and arrow.

"Welcome to Olympus, recruit. I'm Khloe, your advisor through the next phase of training." The Siren nodded toward a smaller, not nearly as ornate building far across the field. "That's Siren Headquarters, your home for the next three years." She motioned for Elysia to follow. "If you thought Pandora was tough, just wait till you see what Athena has in store for you next."

Holy Hades, she was on Olympus.

Elysia glanced toward the shimmering temples again, then realized Khloe was still walking. Hustling to catch up, she fell into step behind the Siren. "Um, there was a male on Pandora. A trainer. Is he back already?"

Khloe glanced over her shoulder with narrowed blue eyes. "A male?"

"Damon. Do you know him? Is he back?"

Khloe stopped. "Damianos was on Pandora? With you?"

Elysia nodded, but a shiver of foreboding rushed down her spine. This Siren clearly knew him.

Khloe's gaze swept over Elysia, from the top of her head to the tips of her toes. Disbelief shone clearly in her eyes when they returned to Elysia's face. "You were quite taken with Damianos?"

That shiver kicked up to a full-blown tremble, and something in the back of Elysia's mind warned not to give too much away. "Um…"

A condescending grin curled Khloe's plump, perfect lips. "All the recruits are. A specimen like that? How could you not be? Word of advice, recruit? Forget about that male. He's only here on loan, until Aphrodite calls him back."

"Aphrodite?"

"He didn't tell you?" She rolled her eyes. "Of course he didn't. It's no fun for him if the unsuspecting recruit knows the truth. He's Aphrodite's favorite love slave. I didn't realize Athena had sent him to tempt the recruits on Pandora, but I guess it makes sense. I mean, why not whore him out sooner? Soon enough he'll be prostituting himself for the sake of the Sirens." She grinned. "Or Athena will be putting him to good use."

Shock and disbelief rushed through Elysia, and her mouth dropped open. Khloe didn't seem to notice. The Siren turned toward the compound and kept walking as if the world hadn't just rocked right off its axis.

"Don't worry, recruit," Khloe called. "You're not the first to fall for his slick charm and wicked animal magnetism." The Siren chuckled. "I guarantee you'll not be the last."

"You know the rules, Damianos." The goddess Athena and head of the Siren order paced around behind Damon in her palatial office at Siren Headquarters. "Rules keep this compound running like a well-oiled machine. Without rules, we have no order. And without order, we have no *Order*."

Damon clenched his jaw. Personally, he had no use for the Sirens. Most thought of the deadly females as an otherworldly police force, crossing in and out of the human realm to maintain law and order among the mythic races. But Damon had been on Olympus long enough to know the truth. More often than not, the Sirens carried out Zeus's dirty work when Zeus didn't want to do it himself. And though usually Damon could overlook that for an excuse to escape Aphrodite's pleasure palace, today it was all he could do to keep from telling Athena just what he thought of her *Order*.

"Remaining on Pandora after you fulfilled your duty was a violation of the rules, Damianos," Athena went on, circling to his right. "If you cannot follow the rules, then you won't be allowed inside the compound again."

Whoa. Back up. Damon shifted in his seat. She was kicking him out of the compound? For good? If that happened, it'd be years before he'd be able to see Elysia again. Assuming, that is, that she made it through the second phase of Siren training. And no way in Hades did he want to think of her *making it through that training* without him.

"I realize I violated a rule." *Careful. Be humble here.* "But I was injured. By a manticore. I wasn't able to return to Olympus on schedule."

Athena's gaze narrowed. She was the epitome of a Siren. Flawless face, curly locks that hung to the small of her back, a compact, curvaceous body, big tits, small waist, and legs that seemed to stretch for miles. But she was also a lethal warrior, and Damon knew her looks were meant to deceive. The same way all Sirens were trained to deceive.

"I should have returned as soon as I was able," he said when Athena only continued to stare at him with knowing, speculative eyes. "That's on me. I know that. It won't happen again."

She held his gaze so long, sweat formed on Damon's brow. She was going to ask him why he'd stayed, and when she did, what would he tell her? That he'd become obsessed with one of her recruits? She'd never allow that. She'd kick him out right now if she knew that. She'd undoubtedly seen what had happened between him and Elysia on Pandora. The Sirens monitored the whole island. He had to make her think he'd just been using the female, the way he was used by Aphrodite every damn day.

"Look." He shifted in his seat and frowned as if this conversation were beneath him. "Call it a moment of weakness due to an injury. I'm male and mortal and flawed. And I spend most of my days with Aphrodite. What can I say? The recruit was attractive, so I stayed. But I didn't get lucky as I wanted, so no harm, no foul. Right?"

Athena's gaze sharpened. "It is not your job to seduce recruits in the survival phase of training."

Be humble... "I know that."

"You will not attempt so again."

He breathed easier. The goddess was falling for it. "I won't."

"The recruit has developed feelings for you."

Something in Damon's chest tightened, but he forced himself not to react.

"I've no doubt the damage you caused will be undone by her seduction trainer, but it is still unacceptable."

It wouldn't be undone if Damon had a say in it. "So we're good here?"

"Not quite." Athena stood in front of her desk and looked down at Damon as if he were a bug she wanted to squash with the heel of her boot. "There is still the matter of your insubordination."

"But I thought—"

She leaned back against the shiny steel surface and crossed her arms under her ample chest. "I'm fully aware that your time in Aphrodite's palace is...how shall I put this? Lackluster? Just as I'm aware you enjoy your time away. You've proven yourself a useful instructor not just in seduction but in warfare, combat, and strategy. The Sirens would hate to lose your expertise. If you are going to remain part of this compound, however, you must be reprimanded for your failure to follow rules."

"What kind of reprimand?" he asked warily.

Athena considered for a moment, then said. "A month. In the pit."

Holy shit. A month in the isolation pit. Insanity by boredom. "And at the end of the month?"

"You will be reinstated to your current position as trainer."

Which meant he would still be assigned to a recruit for seduction.

"Of course, it's your choice," Athena said dryly. "If you'd rather return to Aphrodite's palace and leave the Sirens behind for good, you may do so now."

That wasn't even an option. "I'll take the punishment."

"Good." Athena rounded her desk. "Your month begins at sunset. Report here in an hour. In the meantime, go tell Aphrodite you won't be at her beck and call for quite some time."

Damon rose. He didn't want to see Aphrodite. He wanted to find Elysia and tell her why he'd be absent the next few weeks. But he had something more important to do first. "Don't you think the news would be better coming from you?"

Athena glanced up from the file she'd already started reading. "No. You're Aphrodite's property. You made this mess. You're the one who must deal with the consequences."

"What in Hades do you think you're doing?"

Athena turned at the sound of Zeus's aggravated voice and frowned. She knew she was his favorite daughter, hence he'd given her the task of managing his Sirens, but sometimes she wished he'd just take a hike and leave her alone to do her job. The king of the gods was always second-guessing every one of her decisions.

"What you asked me to do." She looked back at the Siren report on conflicts currently happening in the human realm. "What does it look like?"

Zeus stepped out from behind the bookshelf where he'd been lurking during her discussion with Damon and glared down at her. She was tall for a goddess—just over seven feet—but the king of the gods towered over everyone. "It looks to me like you're delaying our progress. A month? A month is forever."

Athena rolled her eyes and closed the folder. "A month is nothing, and you know it."

"But—"

"Our plan is working." She met her father's dark gaze. "Their attachment has already been solidified. Trust me. Absence will only make their hearts grow fonder."

Zeus frowned. "I've never found that to be true."

No, of course not, because you don't have a heart.

There was a reason Athena chose combat over pleasures of the flesh. A reason she was still known as the virgin goddess of warfare. Because she'd watched her father confuse lust for love one too many times. And because she'd witnessed the fallout of that lust and how his licentious appetites had altered the course of mortal and immortal history. If the god could think with his head instead of his dick, he would have had every ounce of power long ago.

"Look," she said, working for patience as she always did when dealing with the king of the gods. "A month will ensure we are able to begin training the Argolean princess in all manner of combat before he returns. When his time in the pit is finished, she'll be moving into her first phase of seduction training."

Zeus's dark eyes narrowed. "And won't that look convenient? When he is assigned as her trainer?"

"He's not been assigned as her trainer."

"Then how—"

Holy Hades, the god had no faith. She lifted the mirror from her desk and held it out for him to see. "We didn't have to assign him as her trainer. He's doing that himself."

Fog swirled in the mirror and slowly cleared, revealing an image of the Hall of Sirens, deep in the lower levels of Siren Headquarters. Tall columns rose to the ceiling, and rows and rows of wooden file folders filled the massive space. Damon appeared in the entrance and quickly rushed down the stone steps. He searched the rows until he found Elysia's drawer, pulled it open, and located her assignment sheet. The image in the mirror zoomed in on the page listing her assigned trainers in each phase. Zeus watched with wide eyes as Damon erased another's name and wrote his own under SEDUCTION TRAINER.

Zeus met Athena's gaze. "How did you know he would do that?"

"I had faith in the information you provided me when your witch messed with his brain."

Understanding filled his eyes. "That she is his soul mate."

Athena nodded. "Now that he's encountered her, he will always find a way to be with her. He can't help it. It's biological at this point."

Zeus laid the mirror on Athena's desk, and a slow smile curled one side of his mouth. Athena knew her father didn't enjoy his wife's meddling in his affairs, but Hera's soul mate curse was turning out to be a boon for all of them. "To his detriment."

"Yes," Athena said, relaxing because the god was finally getting it. "Have faith, dear father. Time is nothing in the grand scheme. You've waited twenty-five years for revenge against the Argonauts and their queen."

Hunger filled Zeus's dark eyes, and Athena knew he was imagining a future where he controlled more than just Olympus. He was picturing one where he controlled everything.

"Soon, Father." Athena stepped close. "Soon the world will know what it means to quake with true fear, and when it does, no one will be able to stop us."

CHAPTER SEVEN

There was hell, and then there was *heeeeeellllllll.*

Zagreus was stuck in the latter.

"No," Clotho, the youngest of the three old biddies he was currently stuck serving said as Zagreus moved around the kitchen table refilling coffee cups. "Lachesis is the measurer of the thread, and she says when it's time."

Atropos harrumphed. "He's cheated death one too many times. If you ask me, it would solve all kinds of problems if we cut the boy loose here and now. I could do it easily. Smother him with his blanket in the night. He's already down in that pit. No one would know for days. It could look like an accident."

Clotho leaned forward with wide blue eyes, her diaphanous robe shimmering with the movement. "Oh, for crying out loud. Can't you even come up with something more original? You've always been smother-happy. For someone whose only responsibility is to cut the thread of life, the least you could do is put a little thought into his death."

"Now, girls," Lachesis said, holding up her hands to calm her sisters. "We already discussed this and agreed that death is off the table. There's still much for him to do."

"See?" Clotho glared at Atropos. "You just put your abhorred shears away. No one likes you anyway."

Atropos crossed her arms over her chest with a huff. "Stupid mortal lover."

Clotho gasped, then glared again. "Pathetic death monger."

Zagreus bit the inside of his cheek so he wouldn't be tempted to add his own sharp-tongued comment to the grumbling, wrinkled biddies and refilled the next cup.

Oh yeah, this was total hell. His father had fucked him royally on this one. Instead of sending Zagreus to the Underworld as punishment for betraying him, Hades had sentenced Zagreus to this. To the Kingdom of Moira, the realm of the Three Fates, the diaphanously robed incarnations of destiny who determined all life and death in the cosmos and who always managed to meddle in the gods' fucking affairs. His included.

Zagreus scowled as he shoved the coffeepot back on the burner and brought the cream and sugar to the table. Hades was probably getting a good laugh out of this. Imagining his son in servitude to the three old hags, cutting the Fates' gnarled toenails and cleaning the wax from their ears—all jobs Zagreus had been forced to do over the last twenty-five years, even when he'd been on the verge of vomiting.

But that wasn't the worst part. No, the worst part about this hell was that he couldn't escape. The Kingdom of the Moira was worse than any maximum security penitentiary. Hades had handed Zagreus over to the Fates with no stipulation on his sentence. And since the Fates determined all destiny, even that of the gods, Zagreus had no choice but to suck it up and keep picking out earwax.

"No one's dying," Lachesis said louder. "What we need to decide is at what point to intercede."

Atropos rolled her eyes. "Always with the interceding. If they can't figure it out themselves, I say they get what they deserve."

"No shit," Zagreus muttered as he moved around the table. On this, he agreed with the white-haired Grim Reaper. Couldn't those dumbfucks see they were being moved around like chess pieces? Zeus and Athena were orchestrating the entire fucking situation.

Clotho looked up sharply. "What was that, Ziggy?"

The sound of that bloody nickname made Zagreus see red, but he bit down hard to keep from backhanding the old hag and muttered, "I said 'oh, chips.' I was getting chips for your afternoon snack. I almost forgot."

He moved quickly back to the kitchen before any of them could stop him.

"Low sodium for me!" Clotho called. "You know I have to watch my salt intake!"

"Low sodium, my ass," Zagreus muttered as he opened and slammed cabinets in the kitchen. Clotho ate anything and everything she wanted. She was just trying to make his life a living hell by requesting random shit...*and she's succeeding.*

"I don't believe it's time to intercede," Lachesis went on from the other room. "There are too many variables still up in the air. Much will depend on her reaction to seeing him when he emerges from the pit."

"*She* is the problem," Atropos said. "If the wonder-spinner over there hadn't put *that* soul into the princess's body, none of this would be an issue."

"They're soul mates," Clotho said in a sing-songy voice. "Even your cynical old heart can't deny true love."

"Oh holy hell," Atropos responded. "They barely know each other. It's not even close to true love. And considering what Zeus has planned for the male, I've a feeling it will never get that far."

Zagreus leaned back and peeked through the doorway toward the table where the three wrinkled Fates sat. Just what was Zeus planning? Zagreus hadn't been subject to the Fates' torment twenty-five years ago when the male Damon had first been brought to Olympus. Hades had decided to torture Zagreus for a while in the Underworld before realizing Zagreus was immune to his cruelty. It wasn't until six months later that Hades had tossed his son here and Zagreus had been forced to listen to the Fates' monotonous conversations.

Usually, those conversations were boring as hell, and Zagreus tuned them out. He always perked up when their discussions involved the gods, though. This time, from what little he'd been able to glean, he was sure Zeus was scheming for something. Though what that something was, Zagreus didn't know. Considering Zeus was involving the princess of Argolea in his plan, though, Zagreus had a feeling it had to be something big.

"We shall see," Lachesis said, lifting her mug and taking a sip. With a frown, she glanced back toward the kitchen.

Zagreus ducked behind the doorjamb just before she spotted him.

"Ziggy! This coffee is cold." Then more quietly, Lachesis said, "After twenty-five years, don't you think that male would finally get it right?"

"I'm telling you," Atropos muttered, "Ziggy's a few nuggets short of a Happy Meal, if you know what I mean. I could easily put him out of his misery, as well."

"Oh hush, you," Clotho whispered. "We already decided against that too. I like our Ziggy."

For one swift second, Zagreus pictured himself picking up the hot coffeepot and hurling it toward the Fates. Then common sense kicked in, and he realized if he did that, he'd never get out of this realm. And that was his only goal. To find a way to escape. Fuck true love and destiny and whatever the hell Zeus had planned. All Zagreus cared about was freedom.

That and all the vile, malicious ways he was going to make his father pay for sending him to this hellhole when he finally got free.

"Let's go, Highness," a female voice rang out from ahead. "You're sucking up the tail end."

Elysia clawed her way out of the bog, grappling at reeds and grass and anything she could hold on to for leverage, and pulled. Gasping in a breath, she dragged herself up onto the grass, then fumbled her way to her feet.

"Better put some muscle into it," the Siren yelled louder, "or you're gonna be last *again*."

Elysia gulped in another breath, eyed the other recruits running away from her, and pushed her legs forward. Every muscle in her body ached, and mud slid down her face to mess with her vision, but she was determined not to be last. Last on the training course meant she was the last to eat, and that meant she had to sit on the floor like a dog because all the chairs would already be taken. Last meant she had to stick around the mess hall for cleanup duty. And last meant she'd be working her fingers to the bone until midnight and would miss out on the sleep she desperately needed before she had to get up and do it all again.

She'd been on Olympus for only a month, but she'd already learned a very valuable lesson: whatever you'd done to complete the seven labors on Pandora didn't count. You either excelled on the Siren training field now, or you failed and were cast out of Olympus.

She wasn't entirely sure what that meant. No one had answered her question when she'd asked where Zeus sent the recruits who didn't make the cut. And part of her was afraid to know the truth. Because just knowing no one would talk about it meant wherever those females went couldn't be good.

An image of white towers shimmering in the late-afternoon sunlight flickered behind her eyes, and a sense of longing filled her chest. Over the last month, the images had sharpened. She saw faces now. Heard voices. Knew the memories were of her home and family far away, but she still didn't know where. Common sense told her not to let anyone know. Damon had made it more than clear that recruits weren't supposed to remember their pasts. She wasn't sure why she could, but none of the other recruits had any recollection of their lives prior to being dropped on Pandora. If she ever hoped to see her family again, she needed to stay quiet about what she knew. And remembered. And, more importantly, felt.

Her mind shifted from home to Damon, but instead of longing, a bitter anger filled her chest. One that gave her the energy she needed to keep going.

She rounded the last corner on the track and spotted the giant oak a hundred yards away that marked the end of the course. The other recruits were only twenty yards ahead, caked mud covering their shorts and tanks and every bit of bare skin. She clenched her jaw and pushed her legs harder, using all the rage and humiliation she felt for the male and how he'd tricked her. Her arms pumped faster, her steps grew longer...

She drew up alongside a nymph from some island off Greece. The recruit glanced her way with wide eyes. Muddy tangles of hair slapped Elysia in the face, but she forced herself to run faster. The nymph grunted and lurched ahead. Grinding her teeth, Elysia quickened her steps, leaned forward...

And watched in disbelief as the nymph swept past her to cross the finish line a tenth of a second before her.

Elysia tripped and stumbled to her knees in the dirt. Laughter rang out around her—from the other recruits, from the three Sirens running this training segment, from everyone *but* Elysia.

"Last again, Highness." Khloe rested her hands on her hips and shook her head. "That's not an improvement."

"Considering she's related to an Argonaut," the Siren Allegra said, "you'd think she'd be an asset, not a liability."

"A life of luxury has obviously done nothing but make her soft." The third Siren—Maia—looked down at Elysia with an air of disgust "Don't worry. We'll break her of it before long."

"Head back to the compound to shower before dinner," Maia told the rest of the group. With one more disgusted look in Elysia's direction, she signaled the other two Sirens and moved into the trees.

The recruits spoke in hushed whispers as they followed the Sirens and disappeared from view. With her hands braced on the ground in front of her, Elysia dropped her head and drew in a deep breath that did little to settle her still-racing heart.

She was fooling herself. She was never going to cut it as a Siren. She couldn't even make it through a simple obstacle course without wanting to fall over and die.

"Come on." The nymph who'd just beat Elysia across the finish line tucked a hand under Elysia's arm and tugged her to her feet. "You'll feel better once you've had a shower and hot food."

Skeptical, Elysia looked up at the blonde, whose hair and face and body were as coated in mud as her own. "Why are you being nice to me?"

"Because something tells me you could use a friend." The nymph let go of Elysia and grinned. "Sorry I didn't let you win. I have this ultracompetitive nature that kicks into gear sometimes. I'm not always good at controlling it."

Elysia didn't need a friend, she needed a miracle. And she wasn't ready to trust anyone on Olympus just yet, especially another recruit. She stepped around the nymph. "I don't want anyone to *let* me win. I can do this on my own."

The nymph skipped to catch up to her. "I know you can. You're already faster than you were just a few days ago. In no time, you'll be blowing past all of us."

Elysia huffed as she picked her way around vines and tree limbs and moved up the hillside.

"I'm Sera, by the way. Well, Seraphine, but that's a mouthful, and not in a good way. You're related to an Argonaut?"

That's right. She was. A kickass Argonaut who could grind these Sirens into dust. Not only that, Khloe had called her "Highness." Which meant…

Holy *skata*. That meant she was the daughter of Argolean royalty.

Elysia's thoughts spun out of control as the realization set in. If she was royalty, there was no way her parents would have given her up to the Sirens willingly. And if that were true, it meant someone could be searching for a way to rescue her from Olympus right this very minute.

"Elysia?"

Elysia blinked several times only to realize the muddy nymph was staring at her. "What?"

"I asked what an Argonaut is."

Crap. Their minds were supposed to be wiped. She needed to pretend she was as clueless as the girl at her side. "I don't know. An astronaut, maybe?"

Elysia began walking and told herself not to get excited just yet. *Could be searching for her* was the catch. And even if someone *was* looking for her, the chances they could make it into Olympus were slim to none.

"That would be cool," Sera said. "Astronauts are people who read the stars in the human realm and give out fortunes, right?"

Lordy… Did the Sirens realize they were creating idiots by wiping every recruit's memory?

Elysia bit her tongue as she swiped at a prickly vine so she didn't add another cut to her already scraped legs and stepped out of the trees onto the training field at the edge of the Siren property. Past the white buildings of the compound, the sparkling temples of Olympus could be seen in the fading afternoon light, as majestic and ornate as the Siren compound was drab and plain.

"I'd love to know my fortune." Sera stopped at Elysia's side. "Wouldn't you? I mean, it'd be cool to know if we're going to pass and become Sirens, wouldn't it?"

The nymph talked a mile a minute, which wasn't exactly a thrill to Elysia, especially when she was so tired she could barely stand up straight. But at least it kept her mind off the fact every muscle in her body ached. And off the fact all she really wanted to do was search every one of those temples for Aphrodite's palace so she could tell Damon to go to hell for the way he'd tricked her.

"Wouldn't it be wild if you ran into your Argonaut relative in the human realm when you were on a mission for the Sirens? Maybe your relative could read all their fortunes."

Sera's babbling drifted to the back of Elysia's mind as a memory hit. One of her father tucking her into bed at night when she'd been young. Singing her a lullaby, then leaning down to kiss her cheek. "*Sweet dreams,* agkelos. *Because of you, I am blessed.*"

Agkelos. Angel. He'd always called her that. A sharp pain lanced her heart. One that stole her breath and made her miss that sparkling city more than a snowflake misses cold air.

Would she ever see him again? Would she see anyone she loved again?

"I'm starving." Sera stepped past Elysia and headed for the Siren compound. "Let's go get some food."

Elysia drew in a deep breath and let it out. Slowly, the ache in her chest dimmed, but as she began to walk, it was still there. And something inside her said it would be there until she finally found her way home.

"Since I lost on the field—again," she said to Sera, hoping to take her thoughts off a father she wished she could forget, "there won't be much left by the time I get to eat."

"Don't worry." Sera winked back at her. "I'll load up my plate and save you some of the good stuff."

Elysia narrowed her eyes on the blonde's ponytail, covered in mud and swinging as she moved. What did Sera want from her? She'd already beaten Elysia. It was clear Elysia was the worst of the recruits at this point. What could the nymph possibly get from hanging out with her besides ridicule?

Sera glanced over her dirty shoulder and smiled. "I can't stand most of the food anyway. I think in my previous life, I must have been a chef or something. Ooh, wouldn't that be cool? If cooking was part of the training? I'd love to get my hands on a mixer and whip up some cakes and pastries." She giggled and looked ahead. "Correction. Maybe I was a sugar addict in my earlier life."

Elysia's suspicion slowly faded, and in a whir of understanding she realized exactly what Sera would get from hanging out with her. Friendship. The girl was as much an outcast as Elysia.

Damn that Damon. Because of him, she was suspicious of everyone around her. It was time she forgot about the male for good and got on with what she needed to do next.

Which was training to become the best Siren she could be. Because the hard truth was that it didn't matter if anyone was looking for her. They weren't going to find her. She wasn't going to let herself be cast out, which meant she didn't have a choice. She had to make this work.

They rounded the corner of the mess hall, and in the setting sunlight, a male stepped out of the headquarter building across the courtyard and moved onto the wide porch. Elysia immediately tensed, then relaxed when she realized it wasn't Damon.

Don't think about Damon! "Who is that?"

Sera turned to look. "One of the trainers."

A tingle rushed down Elysia's back. The male was tall—close to seven feet—broad shouldered, with legs the size of tree trunks. She'd sort of hoped Damon had been lying about male trainers in the compound. Until today, she'd yet to see one. "Have you worked with him? I've only worked with the Sirens so far."

"Me too. I don't think the male trainers come on until later."

Great. Elysia said a silent prayer Damon was comfortably back with his slutty goddess by then. "How do you know he's a trainer?"

"Because I heard some of the other girls talking about him. I think his name is Erebus."

They watched as Erebus crossed the training field, his massive legs eating up the space as if it were nothing. He was the personification of darkness—jet-black hair, dark eyes, mocha skin—and being as big as he was, he commanded attention.

Sera stepped close and lowered her voice. "Word is he's a minor god from the Underworld who Hades lost to Zeus in a bet. Zeus supposedly loans him to the Sirens now and then to help with training. Can you imagine having *him* assigned to you for seduction training? Gods only know what kind of kink he's into." Sera fanned her face. "I'm getting hot just thinking about it."

Elysia dragged her gaze from the stunning male and looked at her new friend's dirt-streaked face. "Seduction training? What's that?"

Sera's pretty blue eyes widened. "Don't tell me no one's told you about seduction training."

A whisper of apprehension rushed down Elysia's spine. "No, they haven't. What is it?"

"Only the most pleasurable, challenging, exciting part of Siren training." Sera looped her arm through Elysia's and pulled her toward the mess hall. "It's when they assign a male to a new recruit, and he teaches her how to seduce and pleasure."

Elysia's stomach pitched. "You don't mean—"

"Yep." Sera grinned. "Sex. In any and every way possible. It's part of the whole lure-a-male-in training we have to go through. Sirens aren't just lethal warriors, they're irresistible male magnets. In order to be inducted into the Order, a Siren has to know how to pleasure and be pleasured so she can carry out her mission at any time. I've heard some recruits are so wrecked by their seduction training, they can't move for days. I also heard some trainers continue their lessons for *years*. Gods"—she sighed, a wistful look on her face—"can you imagine? Being pleasured by a sex god like Erebus *for years*?"

Elysia's mind snapped right back to Damon even though she didn't want it to. To the sight of his toned chest and abs. To the feel of his body pressed against hers. To the way he'd tasted when he'd kissed her. Only this time, those memories melded with images of his naked body moving over hers, skin slapping, sweat dripping, and their mingling voices groaning in the dark.

Her skin grew hot; her heart rate shot up. She swiped at the perspiration suddenly beading her neck and looked down at her wet fingers.

She wasn't interested in Damon anymore, dammit. She wasn't interested in any male. So why was she sweating just thinking about Damon teaching her all those wicked things Sera had mentioned?

"Hey, you okay?" Sera glanced sideways as they reached the door to the mess hall. "You look a little pale. Don't worry. Your chances of being assigned to Erebus are slim. I'm sure you'll get someone else. We don't get to choose, after all."

"We don't?"

"Nope. It's up to the gods."

Skata. That was exactly what she was afraid of. Not that she'd be assigned to Damon, but that he'd be assigned to seduce someone else.

CHAPTER EIGHT

"I don't know." Seated on the arm of the couch in the living room of the house she shared with Orpheus on the outskirts of Tiyrns, Skyla crossed her arms over her chest and bit her lip. "I can tell you how to get in and out of the Siren Headquarters, but you have to cross into Olympus to do that. And that won't be easy. Not to mention you'll be spotted as soon as you reach the gates."

Max leaned forward in his chair, desperate for the former Siren's help. "Orpheus still has his invisibility cloak, doesn't he?"

Skyla frowned. "That thing hasn't been used in over twenty-five years. There's no guarantee it'll even work."

"But Orpheus is part witch," Talisa said in the seat beside Max. As soon as Max had told Talisa his plan, the female had jumped to help. If no one else was going after Elysia, they would. "He can charm it. It doesn't have to work forever. Just long enough to get one of us into Olympus."

"I don't know." Skyla's brow wrinkled. "You'd have to get Orpheus to agree to that, and he's firmly in the queen's camp on this."

Panic rose in Max's chest. This had to work. A month had already gone by, and they still didn't have a plan. Wasn't anyone else worried about Elysia? "Yes, but—"

"In the queen's camp about what?" Orpheus asked, striding into the room. He crossed to Skyla, leaned down, and kissed her cheek. "Hey, my beautiful Siren." Then, nodding toward Max and Talisa, he said, "What are these two yahoos doing here?"

Skyla sighed. "Trying to convince me to help them break into Olympus and rescue Elysia."

Max stiffened as Orpheus turned gray eyes their way. Beside him, Talisa drew in a breath.

"Don't tell me we're back to this," Orpheus muttered.

"*Patéras.*" Four-year-old voices sounded from the other room, and seconds later, Orpheus and Skyla's twins, Melita and Kyros, rushed into the room and threw themselves at Orpheus's legs.

Orpheus chuckled and swooped the girl with the bouncing blonde curls into his arms and kissed her plump cheek. "There's my daemon girl. Did you drive your mother batshit crazy today?"

"Orpheus…" Skyla sighed and massaged her forehead.

Orpheus grinned. At his feet, Kyros lifted his arms in the air and chanted, "Hold you! Hold you!"

"Hold *me*," Orpheus corrected.

"No, hold *you*!" Kyros yelled.

Rolling his eyes, Orpheus looked down at his mate. Skyla only shook her head and crossed her arms. "You wanted them."

Orpheus hefted the boy up until he had one child in each arm, and when the two were busy chattering away with each other in some weird twin language Max would never understand, Orpheus pinned Max with a hard look. "No one's going to Olympus."

"Just hear us out." Max rose. "It's a simple plan. We use your cloak, sneak into Olympus, find Elysia, wait until the cover of darkness, then sneak her out. My father said you used to use the invisibility cloak all the time to gain access to Olympus unseen and that no one was ever the wiser."

"Yeah," Orpheus answered, "when I was young and stupid. And you're forgetting a very important fact here. No one was waiting for me those times. Zeus knows we're desperate to get Elysia back." He looked at Melita. "Don't you dare stick that finger you just licked in my ear." Then to Max, "He'll be expecting a rescue of some kind. You go, and you'll be walking into a trap, which is exactly why the queen shot this idea down when you brought it up weeks ago."

Max's jaw clenched. "You don't under—"

"There's also the small issue of protection should you even complete a successful rescue." Orpheus handed Melita to his mate as she rose and reached for the girl. "We can't protect her here."

"Zeus and Athena can't cross into Argolea," Max countered. "They're Olympians. This realm is off-limits to the Olympian gods."

"No, but their Sirens can." Orpheus moved to the couch, set Kyros on the cushion, pulled a sucker from his jacket pocket and handed it to the boy. Kyros squealed in glee, then his little face scrunched up in all seriousness as he worked to pull the wrapper off.

"Me too! Me too!" Melita chimed.

Orpheus moved back toward Skyla and handed the girl perched on her mother's hip a lollipop.

"Seriously?" Skyla scowled at her mate. "They won't eat dinner now."

Orpheus grinned. "Dinner's overrated. Besides, candy makes them like me best."

Skyla rolled her eyes and set her daughter on the chair where she'd been sitting.

Orpheus's smile faded as he tucked his hands into his pockets and refocused on Max. "Look, I get what you're trying to do, but it won't work. Sirens can pass through our borders at will. Even if we man the portal to make sure they don't enter Tiyrns unnoticed, there's nothing stopping them from crossing through the moving portals. We can't police those. We've tried. Pulling the princess from the Sirens at this point would be considered an act of war to Zeus, and I won't be a party to something that will cause a repeat of what the Sirens did to the witches."

Orpheus's mother had been a witch, and he had a strong connection to Delia's settlement. Luckily, most of the coven had escaped in time, and those who'd been killed hadn't been civilians but part of their defense team. But that didn't make it right, and Orpheus had been livid when he'd seen the carnage Athena's Sirens had caused. The memory of it still made Max see red.

"He has a point," Talisa said softly.

Max understood Orpheus's point, but he glared his cousin's way. She was supposed to be on his side with this.

"I know you kids are worried about Elysia," Orpheus said, gentling his voice. "I get that. But immortal law states Zeus can choose any female he wants for his Sirens. I hate it as much as you both do, but he chose Elysia, and there's nothing we can do to change that. The queen and her sisters have pooled their gifts to look into the present, and they've seen that Elysia made it through the tests on Pandora and that she's already started the next phase of training. That's a good sign." He glanced at his mate, then back at Max and Talisa while the twins happily sucked on their candy, oblivious to the turmoil in their world. "She'll be on Olympus for at least the next three years. She's safe there. The best we can do is continue monitoring her progress and search for a solution that won't result in all-out war. I know your instinct is to jump, Max, but as a future Argonaut, you have to start thinking about the bigger picture. You can't just focus on your personal wants."

That was rich coming from a guy who'd spent hundreds of years saying fuck you to the world and doing only what he wanted.

"You're talking years," Max said, fighting the rage that wanted to consume him. Didn't they care? Didn't they realize what it was like to be plucked from one life and thrown into another? What it was like to be forced to fight and kill for something you didn't believe in?

He knew. He knew all too well. He could still feel the cold. Could still hear the screams. Sometimes, late at night, he could even feel his blade sinking deep into flesh as he watched the last bit of life bleed out of his victim.

Max didn't want that for Elysia. He'd do anything to save her from the nightmares that still haunted him. It didn't matter who the Sirens ordered her to kill. Once she let the darkness take her, it would never let go.

"Yeah, I am talking about years." Orpheus's gray eyes narrowed. "Years where Elysia is safe and no one else is killed because we acted rashly."

Frustration, anger, disbelief coiled through Max, and he turned away, fighting the urge to shove his fist through the wall. He didn't need a lecture from someone who'd only developed a conscience because of a female. Orpheus hadn't bothered to clean up his treacherous ways until he'd fallen in love with Skyla.

"We're just worried about Elysia," Talisa said. "She's not me or Max. Fighting, combat, and warfare do not come naturally to her. Her survival skills were strong enough to get her through the tests on Pandora, but she's not a warrior. And when it comes to being a Siren and killing… She won't be able to do that. Not unless they break her."

"She's Demetrius's daughter," Orpheus said. "She might not be a warrior, but she's strong. She can get through the training."

"Maybe." Talisa's voice softened. "But even the training will change her."

"The girl is right." Something in Skyla's tone made Max turn. The former Siren looked toward her mate with haunted eyes.

"What do you mean?" Orpheus's expression grew worried as his focus zeroed in on his mate.

"Elysia won't be the same." Something dark passed over Skyla's eyes. Something that gave Max hope. "The Siren training *will* change her. Seduction, combat, the war strategy they drill into the recruits' heads... I know I told the queen she'd be okay, but, Orpheus, Athena and Zeus wipe the recruits' memories so they won't question what they're being taught. It's reprogramming. By the time Elysia remembers who we all are, it'll be too late. They'll already have their killer."

"But you made it through okay."

Skyla shook her head. "I made it *back* because of you, and it took hundreds of years. Most Sirens are not that lucky. And even I'm not the same person I used to be before. You know that."

Max held his breath as he looked between the two. Orpheus and Skyla's love story didn't span years, it spanned centuries. They'd known each other when Skyla had first joined the order and Orpheus had been a reckless youth with no regard for rules. It had taken death, reincarnation, and more than a little forgiveness to bring them back together. It had also taken a love that knew no bounds.

Orpheus's expression grew grim as his gaze held Skyla's, and in the silence, Max's heart beat faster.

Skyla reached for her mate's hand. "I know it's wrong, but I wish...I wish someone would have come after me all those years ago. I wish I'd never been a Siren."

Pain and regret swamped Orpheus's features as his fingers closed tightly around his mate's. "I'm an Argonaut now," he said softly. "The queen's already decided. I can't be involved."

"You wouldn't have to be," Max said quickly. "If anyone finds out, I'll say I stole the invisibility cloak."

Orpheus scowled Max's way like that was the stupidest thing he'd ever heard.

"He stole the Orb of Krónos from the castle once," Talisa pointed out. "That wouldn't be a stretch."

"I was a kid then." Max sent his cousin a sideways glance at the mention of the magical disk that had the power to release the

Titans from Tartarus. "And thanks so much for reminding everyone about that incident."

"I'm just saying." Talisa rolled her eyes. "Some people wouldn't be surprised to hear you stole something else."

"This is insanity." Orpheus let go of Skyla's hand and rubbed his forehead. "Forget about the fact you'd be putting your life on the line and could quite possibly get caught by any number of gods. Assuming you can find Elysia and get her out of Olympus, you can't even bring her back here." He dropped his hand. "If the Sirens found out she was in this realm, all hell would break loose. You'd have to go on the run in the human realm, and even then they'd hunt you like dogs. They'd never stop. "

"We could take her to the half-breed colony." Talisa looked up at Max, then at Orpheus. "There's still therillium in the caverns beneath the colony. Once it's glowing, the ore has the ability to cloak our location. We could stay hidden indefinitely. The colonists did so for years."

Orpheus frowned. "And look how well that turned out. The colony's in ruins today."

"Because someone didn't keep the ore lit," Max said. "We're smarter than that."

"Insanity." Orpheus looked toward the ceiling and shook his head.

Skyla reached for her mate's arm. "They can do this, Orpheus. They could save her. It's not a terrible plan. In fact, I think it could work."

Worry lines creased Orpheus's brow as his gaze met Skyla's. "You really think it's a good idea?"

"I do. Let them do for her what you couldn't do for me."

Orpheus closed his hand over Skyla's against his arm, sighed, and looked between Max and Talisa. "You're both willing to risk your futures for this?"

"Yes," they answered simultaneously.

"And the Argonauts?" Orpheus zeroed in on Max. "Because if you do this, you'll never serve with the guardians. It doesn't matter how relieved Demetrius or Isadora are that Elysia is safe. You'd be disobeying a direct order from the queen. I might not always agree with everything Theron does as head of the Argonauts, but if he didn't go after you for that, he'd be breaking the law. With the political climate the way it is now in Argolea, the Council would demand you be punished for insubordination. And I'm not talking about just kicking you out of the Argonauts. I'm talking about a sentence of death."

Max knew full well what it meant to break the laws of the Argonauts. His father had been preparing him to join the guardians both mentally and physically since he was ten years old. Tradition was sacred in their land. But he also knew some things were more important than laws and traditions.

Max stood a little taller. "I'm fully prepared to face the consequences. If they can catch us."

"And that's a big if," Talisa added.

Orpheus shook his head. "Stupid young fools. The whole world will be after you."

Skyla let go of Orpheus's hand, sidled up against him, and wrapped her arm around his waist. "If memory serves, the whole world was after you not all that long ago, daemon, and you managed to prove everyone wrong."

Orpheus draped his arm over her shoulder and looked down at her. "I got lucky."

"No, you just had someone who believed in you. Elysia needs someone to believe in her just as much. This is the right thing to do, Orpheus, and you know it."

Orpheus's grim expression said he wasn't convinced, but when he looked back at Max, his eyes hardened. "I can't guarantee the invisibility cloak will work more than a few hours. The thing's ancient."

Hope surged through Max's veins. "A few hours are all we need."

"No, you need a fucking lobotomy. And if you rat me out for helping you, I will kick your ass from here to Olympus myself. We clear?"

Max smiled for the first time in weeks. "We're clear."

Talisa exhaled a long breath. "Thank you. Thank you both."

"Don't thank either of us yet." Orpheus glanced back at his mate. "Though you, Siren, can show me all kinds of thanks for going along with this asinine plan as soon as they're gone."

"Asimime plan!" Melita giggled and popped the lollipop back in her mouth.

"Ass-a-time!" Kyros laughed as he rolled onto his back on the couch, kicked his chubby little legs in the air, and waved his candy. "I want ass-a-time too!"

"That's a good idea," Orpheus leaned close and nipped at Skyla's ear. "I could use some ass time myself."

"Down, daemon." Skyla smiled and pushed him away. "There are young in the room."

"They're four. They have no idea what we're talking about."

"No, but the other young do."

"Oh yeah. I forgot about them." Orpheus chuckled and kissed Skyla's cheek.

Max frowned at Talisa, whose gaze darted anywhere but at Orpheus and Skyla. That familiar resentment burned inside him. The "adults" were treating him like a kid again. Someday soon he'd make everyone see he was as much a warrior as the rest of the Argonauts. Someday soon they'd all realize just what he was capable of.

"Now that we have that settled…" The former Siren turned toward Max and Talisa, her expression growing serious once more. "Let's talk about what you'll find when you get to Olympus."

After a month in the pit—which was exactly as it sounded, a hole in the ground beneath one of the buildings on the Siren compound—Damon was eager to rejoin the Sirens as an instructor. And way more than ready to see Elysia again.

He'd thought about her nonstop in the pit, and even though something in the back of his head warned this growing obsession for her could be trouble, he'd decided to ignore it. He'd spent the last twenty-five years on Olympus feeling no excitement, no emotion, nothing but disinterest. Something about Elysia brought him to life in a way nothing and no one had before. Something he needed to know more about.

He showered and changed in his room in the instructor wing, checked in with Athena to figure out where they were in the training cycle, then headed down to the mess hall for some food. After filling his plate, he took his tray to a table near the wide windows that overlooked the training field where recruits swung blades and shot arrows during their daily skills sessions.

Damon scanned the recruits until he found Elysia, and his pulse ticked up at just the sight of her. She stood on the far side of the field, a bow in her hand, aiming an arrow at a target set on a stump. Kastor, a mortal Damon had worked with in the past, walked around her, lifting her elbow, repositioning her grip on the bow, giving her tips on when to release the arrow.

Heat rushed through Damon's body, condensed in his groin, and sent electrical spirals all through his limbs. She was dressed in the standard Siren fare—tight black tank, slim-fitting dark pants, and knee-high boots—but even from this distance, he could see that she'd changed. Muscles that hadn't been there a month ago were now obvious in her arms and legs. And her skin, though still paler than most, was darker from hours outside in the sun.

Kastor stepped around her, brushing his body against hers in the process. Jealousy whipped through Damon as he watched. He wanted to be the one touching her like that, lifting her arm, helping her hold the bow. His only consolation was that he—not Kastor— *would be* the one pressed up against her later tonight, teaching her all about the pleasures of seduction, hearing her scream his name and beg for more.

"Holy Hades." Erebus set his tray on the table beside Damon and pulled out a chair. "I thought the last class was bad. Is it just me or are these recruits getting weaker by the year?"

Damon glanced up at the god. Kastor wasn't a threat. As soon as Elysia saw Damon again, they'd pick up right where they left off. His blood warmed just thinking about the night ahead, and the jealousy slipped away. "It's probably just you. You're getting older and less patient with every class."

"Probably true." Erebus frowned. "Good to see you, man. I heard you were in the pit. That had to be fun."

Most people steered clear of Erebus because of his size and his perpetual darkness. Most, but not Damon. He liked the god. Enjoyed being around Erebus's perennial bad mood because it was a complete one-eighty from Aphrodite's light and airy pleasure palace.

Damon huffed and reached for his water. "More fun than hanging with Athena."

"I'll give you that."

As Erebus was in charge of all the instructors, he worked closely with Athena to keep the training schedule running smoothly. The goddess might be a mighty warrior herself, but she had zero personality and rarely cracked a smile. In that respect she was a lot like Erebus.

Erebus pointed toward the windows with his fork. "And I guarantee it was more fun than being stuck out in the field with those yahoos."

"Are they really that bad?"

"Let me put it this way." Erebus leaned one elbow on the table. "Do you remember Ambrosia?"

Ambrosia had been a nymph Zeus had pegged for the Sirens. The poor female had been hot enough for the order, but she hadn't known the hilt of a sword from the blade, and she'd been so clumsy, she'd spent most of her time in the infirmary. When Athena had realized the nymph was more of a danger to herself and the other recruits than the monsters on Pandora, the goddess had finally pulled Ambrosia out of the Siren class and sent her to serve Aphrodite as a maid. Damon still saw the girl in Aphrodite's pleasure palace from time to time and felt sorry for her, but the nymph didn't seem to mind her station in life. In fact, she rather enjoyed cleaning up after the goddess and her toys. "Yeah, I remember her."

"She was Heracles compared to what's out on that field now."

Damon barked out a laugh. "You're so full of shit."

"I'm not." Erebus cut into his meal. "After a month, we should already be moving on to strategy, but most of these chicks can't even shoot an arrow yet. I mean, look at that one there." He pointed toward the far side where Elysia lined up another shot. "Hot, right?"

"Totally hot." Arcs of electricity spiraled straight into Damon's groin again as he watched the muscles in Elysia's arm flex and she pulled the string back and released. The arrow skewed to the right, missing the target by ten feet.

"Kickass body, gorgeous face," Erebus went on. "One conversation with her and you can tell she comes from some kind of nobility. And according to her chart, she sailed through the seven labors on Pandora in record time. But the female can't shoot an arrow to save her life, and she's even worse with a blade. I mean, where does Zeus find these broads? 1-800-soft-r-we?"

A bead of worry slid down Damon's spine. "You said they were all bad."

"They are." Erebus swallowed a bite. "But she's at the back of the class for sure. Her reflexes are atrocious, and she's slower than snail bait."

Damon's worry morphed to a quick pulse of panic. The Sirens kept tallies on all the recruits and compared them at checkpoints during the training. If Elysia was still at the bottom of the list by the next checkpoint, she'd be removed from the Sirens. And removal from the Sirens didn't mean she'd be reallocated to a new position on Olympus like Ambrosia—that had been a special case. Removal from the Sirens usually meant death.

"She's got heart," Erebus said, scooping up another bite. "I'll give her that. She was a little ball of fury when she arrived here from Pandora. Whatever happened there sure lit a fire inside her."

Damon's arousal cooled, and he frowned. He could only imagine what had ignited that fire. No doubt one of the Sirens had mentioned his name and told Elysia just who he was. That, coupled with the fact he hadn't been around to explain his side, had to have left her spitting mad. Good thing he was scheduled to see her tonight so he could make a little of that up to her.

"I sure hope she's better at seduction than she is combat." Erebus shook his head. "Might be the only thing that can save her at this point."

She would be. Damon would make sure of that.

A tingle ran through him at the thought of what tonight would bring, but as he continued to watch Elysia shoot that bow, it slowly dissipated. He'd have to find a way to tutor her in marksmanship as well as seduction. Those weren't the kind of late night hookups he'd fantasized about in the pit, but they were just as important if he wanted to keep her around.

And he would keep her around. Because he wasn't about to let her get kicked out of the Sirens. Whatever it took, he'd make sure she stayed right here on Olympus. With him.

CHAPTER NINE

Every muscle in Elysia's body ached.

Around her in the Siren barracks, lockers slammed, voices murmured, and running water echoed from the showers. Kicking her dirty boots under her bed, Elysia reached for the towel from her locker and swiped at the mud on her face. All she wanted was a hot shower, a belly of food, and a full night of sleep, in that order. Considering fifty other recruits all wanted the same things, her odds of getting any quickly weren't looking good.

"You weren't last today, Highness."

Elysia stiffened when she spotted the two recruits standing at the end of her bed, each covered in as much mud and dust as she and holding their own towels. The one who'd spoken was an Amazon—tall, athletic, and deadly with a bow, and she used the word "Highness" like a sharp weapon. The other was a wood nymph—petite, fair, and fast as a cheetah. Both had been kicking Elysia's ass in the training competitions all week. Neither had bothered to learn Elysia's name, preferring instead to call her Highness, in reference to a conversation they'd overheard between the trainers about why Elysia was so "soft."

"She got lucky," the nymph said with a hint of disdain in her voice. "It won't last."

The Amazon chuckled, and both females turned, speaking in hushed voices as they headed for the showers.

On the bed beside Elysia's, where she was pulling off her dirty socks, Sera shook her head. "Don't even think about it. They're not worth the effort."

Elysia clenched her jaw as she reached for the shampoo and soap sitting on her shelf. "They're right, though. I did get lucky. If Damaris hadn't slipped and fallen in the mud, she would have beat me on the obstacle course today."

"Maybe." Sera shoved her dirty socks in a bin beside her bed. "Maybe not. You were catching her. You're getting faster. Those bimbos know it too, or they wouldn't bother taunting you,"—she winked—"Highness."

Elysia frowned. "Don't you start with that too."

"Why not? You could be royalty, you know. Why else would the trainers be whispering about it?"

Elysia rolled her eyes and slammed her locker. She *was* royalty. She just didn't want anyone to catch on that she knew who she was. Which meant acting all put out when people teased her. "Yeah, right. Maybe I'm really the Queen of England."

Sera's brow wrinkled. "What's England?"

Skata. Someone had wiped Sera's mind a little too vigorously. Elysia reached for Sera's arm and pulled her up from the bed. "A cold, wet place. Come on. We need to hit the showers before all the hot water's gone."

They rounded the corner toward the bathrooms just as Athena stepped into the barracks with a Siren on each side. Voices quieted. The water shut off. Several recruits rushed out of the showers, dripping wet and wrapped in towels.

"Gather round," Athena said. "I have an announcement."

Elysia and Sera glanced at each other, and whispers drifted over the group as Athena's gaze skipped from one face to another.

Tonight," Athena said, "the evening meal will not be served in the mess hall. This marks the beginning of the next phase of your training. Upon showering and preparing yourselves, you're to gather in the grand foyer where you will be blindfolded and assigned a seduction trainer. Your first lesson begins tonight. He will instruct you on what to do. If you please your trainer, you will be rewarded with dinner."

Gasps and excited whispers echoed through the room, but Elysia's stomach flipped as she stared at the gorgeous goddess and pictured Damon.

Athena glanced over the group, her dark hair falling in soft curls past her shoulders. "Are there any questions?"

One recruit at the back of the group, a wood nymph who was almost—but not quite—as bad at Siren training as Elysia, held up her hand. "What about, um"—the nymph's face grew pink—"protection?"

"Before you each began your first phase of training," Athena answered, "you were charmed in such a way that your body is now resistant to all disease and your fertility was suppressed. The spell lasts seven years, until such time as you finish your training. If you pass your final exams and are inducted into the Order, a new spell will keep you protected throughout your time with the Sirens."

"Well, at least we don't have to worry about getting pregnant," Sera muttered at Elysia's side.

Elysia shushed her, but her stomach rolled.

Sex. Athena was suggesting they have sex. No, not suggesting, ordering.

"Are there any other questions?" Athena asked. When no one responded, she nodded at the two Sirens at her side and said, "Good." The two Sirens stepped out of the room and returned, each carrying several boxes. "The Sirens are placing your specified attire for the evening on the end of your bunks. They are different for each of you. Remember that your seduction trainer has chosen your ensemble to fit his plans. He will know if you choose to alter it, so be forewarned."

When the Sirens finished handing out boxes, they returned to Athena's side.

"Enjoy your evenings, ladies, but remember this is not for fun. Seduction training is an integral part of our curriculum, and you will learn to pleasure, to be pleasured, and to seduce if you are to join our ranks. Fail at this, and you fail at everything." Without another word, Athena turned and left the room with the Sirens on her heels.

Voices kicked up as soon as they left—excited whispers, giddy laughter, shrieks of anticipation. But Elysia couldn't share in the exhilaration, because all she felt was a rush of sickness.

"Wow." Sera turned toward Elysia with wide eyes and a huge grin. "I guess that throws a wrench into our evening plans."

Elysia's gaze locked on the silver box sitting on the end of her bed, the one that hadn't been there only moments before. Moving back toward her bunk, she lowered herself to the mattress.

"Hey." Sera followed. "You okay?"

"Not really."

Sera sat on her own bunk. "What's wrong?"

Elysia glanced around. The others were all in the bathroom, already doing their hair and makeup. No one could hear their conversation, but she softened her voice to a whisper just in case. "I, ah, kinda already made out with one of the trainers."

Sera's eyes grew wide, and she grinned. "Holy shit, you little minx, you! When did you find the time?"

"It wasn't here. It was on Pandora. He was the one I had to rescue."

"Wow. So...what? After rescuing him, you just jumped his bones? Way to go."

Elysia rolled her eyes. "Can you focus for one minute? It wasn't like that. He stuck around and helped me with the next few labors. And, I don't know, we talked, and one thing led to another and...and then we kissed."

Sera considered for a moment. "If he stuck around when he was supposed to leave, that's not exactly a bad thing. It means he was interested. Clearly, seduction is where you're going to earn back your points."

"Now I sound like a slut."

Sera laughed. "That too is not a bad thing. You are training to be a Siren after all."

Sighing, Elysia looked down at her hands.

"Okay, spill," Sera said. "Something more than just kissing this dude is eating at you and has been since you arrived on Olympus."

"I don't know. I just..." Elysia lifted her hands and dropped them. "I didn't know who he was when I kissed him. It wasn't as if I was trying to seduce him. I liked him. A lot. Then I got here and discovered he's one of Aphrodite's boy toys and that she pimps him out to the Sirens for seduction training."

"Ouch. Yeah, that news would totally blow. I get it. No wonder you've been in such a funk. But, think about it logically. The odds you'll get him as your trainer are really slim. I mean, there are fifty of us. If he stuck around with you on Pandora when he shouldn't have, Athena's probably assigned him to someone else already."

"Yeah." Elysia twisted her hands in her lap. "Probably."

Sera stared at her a long moment. "Which is just what you're really afraid of, isn't it?"

"Stupid, huh?" Elysia's heart pinched as she looked at her friend. "He belongs to Aphrodite. I'm pissed he didn't tell me who he was, and I don't even want him as my trainer."

"But you don't want him to train anyone else either," Sera finished.

"Yeah," Elysia whispered. "Exactly."

"That"—Sera moved to sit next to Elysia and wrapped an arm around Elysia's shoulder—"totally sucks."

Elysia huffed a sound that was a half laugh, half groan. "Thanks for the news flash."

"Well, look on the bright side. Maybe your seduction trainer will be so hot, he'll make you forget all about what's-his-name."

"Yeah, maybe," Elysia agreed.

But as her gaze drifted to the box on the end of her bed, she knew odds were a whole lot better she was going to spend the next few months fantasizing her trainer was Damon. And cursing the recruit whose nights would now be spent pleasing him.

Damon stood in the shadows of the main hall and watched from afar as the recruits spilled into the room, more than fifty females from all different backgrounds. Tall pillars rose all around the room, and iron chandeliers lit with a thousand lights illuminated their wide eyes and expectant faces.

Less than half of the recruits would make the cut by the end of their seven years of training. Some would be shipped off to various parts of the globe to serve Zeus and the gods in other ways—as handmaidens, as pleasure slaves, even some as breeding stock—but the rest would be terminated.

Most probably didn't realize that fact. Zeus liked to keep those details secret. It was a shitty deal all around for those that didn't make it, but Damon had learned long ago that after the recruits left the Siren compound, there was little he could do for them. Except Elysia. He was determined she'd make it. She had to. Because losing her was no longer an option.

His gaze skipped over each female as she entered. Excitement lit their eyes as they caught sight of the trainers assembled on the periphery. The recruits were each dressed in an outfit of their trainer's choosing—some in skirts that showed off their legs, some in skintight pants, all wearing heels and heavy makeup and with enough cleavage to drown a man. As Zeus had handpicked each recruit, they were all beautiful, but those eventually inducted into the Order would be altered in the image he preferred. Zeus claimed his Sirens were altered to draw the attention of any male they crossed, but Damon knew the truth. Zeus didn't appreciate individuality. He wanted his minions to fit his mold. And he changed them to prove he was in ultimate control over every aspect of their lives, even their looks.

What good was being king of the gods if you couldn't lord it over each and every one of your subjects?

Disdain rippled through Damon. A familiar disdain after twenty-plus years on Olympus. Thankfully, his interactions with Zeus were few and far between. He shifted his weight against the wall and crossed his arms over his chest, searching for Elysia.

He searched faces but still couldn't find her. Where the hell was she? She couldn't have been kicked out of the class already. He'd know.

Hushed whispers carried on the air. Footsteps sounded as the room filled. Around him, trainers murmured throaty approvals. But Damon barely spared them a glance. He continued scanning faces, searching for Elysia. The last of the recruits stepped into the room, and the wide double doors on the far side closed.

Panic spiked in his chest, and he pushed away from the wall.

Footsteps sounded to his left as Athena climbed three stone steps and stood on the raised platform to address the group. "Quiet down," she said in her throaty, sex-kitten voice. "We're about to begin."

Damon barely cared about Athena's little announcements. He moved toward the group and scanned each face again. She had to be here. She couldn't miss this.

Voices quieted as all eyes turned toward Athena, who tonight was dressed in a low-cut, sleeveless red blouse and black leggings capped with four-inch silver heels. With long, delicate fingers, she reached for a scroll from the Siren standing next to her. "Tonight you move into the second phase of your training. Seduction is as elemental to a Siren as is her ability to kill."

And this growing need inside Damon was as elemental as anything he'd ever felt. He stepped closer to the crowd, searching faces, sure he had to have missed Elysia with her hair and makeup done.

"Forget everything you know about seduction," Athena went on as Damon continued scanning. "Your assigned trainer will rewrite your history with both seduction and pleasu—"

The double doors on the far side of the room burst open, and Elysia stumbled into the room.

Heads turned. Eyes shifted her way. On the platform, Athena frowned and muttered, "There is always one in every group." Then louder, "Recruit, take your place."

From the corner of his eye, Damon saw the look Athena sent Naila, her right-hand Siren. Naila nodded and looked back toward the double doors Elysia tried to close with as little sound as possible.

They were making a note of her disruption, docking her points for being late. Damon would have to find a way to help her regain those points before the next checkpoint.

His focus zeroed in on her, and the stress faded as warmth gathered low in his belly. Her hair fell in soft, dark waves to the middle of her back, and her eyes were made up just enough so they sparkled. His gaze drifted down, over the simple blue blouse he'd picked out for her, the slim-fitting black pants and sensible flats, then lifted back to the long string of pearls around her neck that fell to her cleavage. He'd debated what to send her for tonight, and finally decided something that put her at ease would be best. He wanted her to trust him. Trussing her up in some revealing ensemble—though he definitely planned to do that later—wouldn't be his smartest first move.

Sirens passed through the crowd of recruits, and as one stepped in front of Elysia, Damon realized Athena had stopped talking. The Siren held up the blindfold, and Elysia's gaze flicked Damon's way. For a split second, their eyes held across the distance, making every muscle in Damon's body tighten with excitement and anticipation.

He couldn't read her from this distance. Was she happy to see him? Angry? Excited? He'd never know, because the Siren covered her eyes with the blindfold before he could tell and moved behind her to tie the sash.

His pulse sped up, but instead of breathing easier, all he could think about was what he was going to say to her when they were finally alone.

Athena's voice echoed through the room once more as she called off each recruit's name. One by one they were brought forward, handed off to their assigned trainer, and led out of the room. Damon's pulse beat hard and fast as he waited. When Sera's name was called, Erebus sent Damon a predatory wink and moved across the wood floor toward the unsuspecting nymph.

"Elysia," Athena said when there was only one recruit left. Lowering the scroll in her hands, Athena moved slowly down the three stone steps toward the female. "You were late."

"Y-yes, my lady." Elysia managed a pathetic bow and turned toward the sound of the goddess's voice. "I'm sorry. I didn't...I won't let it happen again, my lady."

Damon's jaw tightened as he watched. Athena was purposely intimidating the poor girl, all because she got her shits and giggles the same way her father did—from scaring others.

"See to it that it does not. In the meantime, you are at the bottom of the list in the standings. The first elimination is coming up in a matter of weeks. That means you need to step things up or you'll be on your way out. Do I make myself clear?"

Damon bit down harder. *Stay where you are, dickhead. Don't make things worse for her.*

"Yes, my lady."

Athena's eyes narrowed on Elysia in an assessing, almost rapacious way. There was something sinister in Athena's gaze, an undertone of disgust that made the hairs on Damon's nape stand straight.

Had Elysia offended the goddess? Did Athena know something about Elysia's past the girl didn't? The goddess could hold a grudge like nobody's business. If Athena had already pegged Elysia to fail, making sure Elysia passed was going to be a tougher job than Damon had anticipated.

Silence lingered. Finally Athena turned to leave. But as she did, her gaze found Damon's, and even though he tried to stay still, every muscle went tense and rigid.

This was where it got tricky. When he'd altered Elysia's chart, he'd purposely placed her at the bottom of tonight's list. The other recruits were already paired up. If Athena balked here and wanted to make a switch, she'd have to call them all back. That would waste time and could cause problems. He was banking on the fact she'd let it slide.

Athena's gaze narrowed to hard, sharp points, a warning reflecting deeply in her bitter eyes. Damon held his breath and waited, knowing he was playing a game of roulette he couldn't win, hoping and praying this one gamble would pay off. Several heartbeats of heavy silence elapsed before Athena turned out of the room without another word, her heels clicking like cannon fire against the hardwood as she left.

Damon exhaled. Told himself he'd dodged a major bullet. Reminded himself to be careful around Athena from here on out. Elysia clearly wasn't the only one on the goddess's shit list.

Breathing easier, Damon returned his attention to Elysia. Instead of moving toward her, though, he simply watched. Watched the way her breasts rose and fell under the blue blouse with her shallow breaths, watched as she licked her lips and shifted her weight, watched the adorable way she twisted her fingers still behind her back as she waited.

He wanted those hands running over his body. Wanted her warm breath fanning his cheek. Wanted those succulent lips pressed against his as they'd been on Pandora. But first he wanted her to want the same things.

He cleared his throat, and she immediately stiffened. She was nervous. More nervous than he'd expected for someone who'd had no problem kissing a total stranger in the jungle. He took that as a good sign.

His footsteps sounded across the floor. As he drew close, the familiar scent of honeysuckle surrounded him. His skin tingled. Electricity arced through his body. Even before his fingers grazed hers, he knew she felt it too. Knew from the way she trembled and held her breath. Knew from the heat suddenly swirling around him like a vortex.

He didn't speak. Simply slid his palm along hers and wrapped his thick fingers around her much daintier ones. Pulling her toward the double doors on the far side of the room, he led her out and down a long hall lit with pale sconces, and finally into one of the many private training rooms in this wing of the compound.

This was not where he wanted to spend his first night with her, but considering what he had planned, this was the safest place for both of them.

He closed the door after her. Left her standing in the middle of the room as he lit candles around the periphery. Elysia's breaths grew shallow and fast. Grasping her at the shoulders, he turned her toward him, then slowly pushed her back. Her muscles tensed in obvious fear. When the backs of her legs hit the front of the chair, she relaxed.

Her hands landed on the armrests of the high-backed Queen Anne, and she lowered herself to the soft cushion. Leaning close so she could feel the heat of his body and the brush of his skin, Damon fingered the long strand of pearls from the edge of her throat down to the V of her cleavage.

Elysia went completely still. Drawing in a whiff of her delectable scent, Damon let his fingertips hover on the bottom pearl, right at the apex of her cleavage, and watched as her succulent breasts rose and fell.

Gods, she had the best breasts, small and firm and high, and at the moment not nearly as exposed as they'd been on Pandora. He wanted to feel them in his palms. Wanted to hold them and squeeze them and lick them until she was quivering. But he held back. Because what he had planned needed to come first. And because when he did those things, he wanted her writhing and begging for more.

Reluctantly, he lifted the necklace from her skin and drew it over her head. She shivered as if he'd removed an article of her clothing, which only made his pulse beat faster and his pants grow even tighter. Moving around behind the chair, he reached for her right hand and gently pulled it back, then did the same to her left. She tensed as he used the pearls to tie her wrists together behind the chair, but didn't voice a protest.

"Relax, *oraios*," he said softly as he pushed to his feet and walked around the chair. "Nothing bad is going to happen to you."

He pulled the blindfold free. Elysia's dark eyes widened, and in a rush, he saw exactly what he'd missed in the ballroom when she'd looked at him across the distance. He saw shock, disbelief, and rage. But mostly, he saw betrayal.

"You," she muttered.

She was pissed. He had that coming. "Yes, it's me. I know you think—"

"You don't know a thing about me. You never did." Disgust rushed across her features as her gaze swept over him like a broom brushing aside nothing but dirt. "All you know is being a yes-boy for the Sirens and man whore for some slutty goddess."

CHAPTER TEN

Damon stiffened at Elysia's sharp words. She tried not to let his reaction faze her, but something inside shrank with mortification.

She wasn't this girl. The angry jilted lover. She didn't want to be that girl. Didn't want to feel a thing for him. But she did. Her chest pinched so hard at the sight of him, pain spiraled through every cell.

Skata. She wasn't about to be enchanted by this gorgeous male any more than she'd been on Pandora, but one look at his thick legs, cut muscles, and trim physique and she was a quivering mess. He was dressed in loose black drawstring pants and a lightweight, short-sleeved, button-down shirt that showcased the rippling muscles in his arms and exposed just a hint of the rose tattoo on his shoulder and biceps. And when her gaze lifted to the shadow on his square jaw, his tanned and weathered skin, and his chocolate irises rimmed with gold, her resistance wavered.

Don't do it. Don't fall under his spell. Because that's all it was. A spell. The same kind of spell Aphrodite clearly uses to turn hot males like him into manipulative man whores.

She stiffened her spine.

"I see a month with the Sirens has exercised your tongue well," Damon said.

"My tongue gets plenty of exercise, thank you very much."

A wry smile spread across Damon's lips, making him look that much sexier, and Elysia's cheeks heated when she realized just where his thoughts were heading.

"Not like that," she snapped. Then, when she realized this was her chance to make him squirm a little, she added, "Actually...just like that. There's this really hot ebony god who's been helping me—well, flirting with me, really—in the field. He's—"

"Tall guy? Scar near his left eyebrow?"

Suspicion drew Elysia's brows together. Damon didn't seem the least bit jealous. Panic sent her pulse up. "Yes. But he's—"

"A minor god." Damon crossed his thick arms over his chest, the movement pulling on his shirt. "His name's Erebus. And I guarantee he wasn't flirting. Unless your name was Sera. I noticed him eyeing her a month ago. He's been assigned as her seduction trainer."

Elysia's eyes widened. "*He's* Sera's trainer?"

"Jealous?"

No, Elysia wasn't jealous. She was a little afraid for her friend. Erebus was huge. Before she could say so, though, Damon's words hit her.

She tugged at the pearls tied around her wrists, which—as he'd planned—kept her completely immobile against the chair. "You were here a month ago? I'd have seen you if that were the case. What did you do, run back to Aphrodite's temple for a little fun?"

He moved to her left and disappeared behind her chair. "Actually, Athena had a job for me."

Elysia huffed. "Another recruit to manipulate?"

"Something like that," he muttered.

Heat burned her cheeks when she remembered the way she'd fallen for his ruse. The injured, innocent male. She nearly huffed again. There was no such thing as an innocent male.

"I've spoken to a few of your field trainers." Damon moved around her right side. "And it seems you're in a precarious position." He stopped in front of her again. "You need me, Elysia. You need high marks in seduction if you're to make it through the first elimination round, and I'm your seduction trainer."

Her temper spiked. He was the last person she wanted to learn seduction techniques from, now or ever. "How did I get stuck with you? I want someone else."

"There is no one else. Everyone's been paired up, *oraios*."

"Don't call me that. We both know you use that on every female you seduce.

He stepped closer. "Perhaps you'd prefer I call you *thisavrós*."
My treasure.

Elysia stiffened.

"Or *chará*."

My joy.

The breath caught in her lungs.

Resting his hands on the arms of her chair, he eased forward until he was a breath from her lips. "Or better yet, *emmoní.*"

My obsession. He'd called her that on the beach. Just after she'd killed that recruit. When he'd come rushing up to help her.

Skata, don't remember that beach. Don't remember your time with him on Pandora. Don't remember anything about the slimy male.

"Yes, I like that." Warm breath with a hint of mint washed over her face and ran down her neck, bringing every nerve ending to life. "*Emmoní,*" he said again in that deep, sexy, titillating voice. "My obsession. That's what I'm going to call you. Because that's what you've become. A drug I can't stop craving."

Elysia's mouth grew dry, and behind her back, her fingers trembled. He was manipulating her. The same way he'd manipulated her on Pandora. She knew that. But her heart beat hard against her ribs just the same, and her skin tingled in anticipation of his touch.

"You lie," she whispered.

His gaze held hers. Intense. Unwavering. Smoldering. His lips so close, she could almost taste him. And his hot breath cascading over her flesh only made her breaths faster and shallower and her heart race beneath her ribs.

She wanted to kiss him. Wanted to hit him. Wanted... She didn't know what she wanted. She couldn't seem to think when he was close, and when he looked at her—really looked at her as he was doing now—the same connection she'd felt on Pandora flared hot inside her. A host of emotions rippled through his gorgeous eyes as they held hers, ones she felt all the way in her toes, ones she sensed he felt as strongly as her.

He blinked, and the connection was broken. Cool air swept over her as he straightened. And though she knew she should be relieved, disappointment washed over her like a tidal wave.

He walked around behind her chair and pulled the string of pearls from her hands. The strand broke, scattering pearls over the floor. "We're done here."

Surprise rippled through Elysia. She pulled her hands together and rubbed her wrists as she twisted in the chair. "What do you mean, done? We haven't done anything yet."

"Return to your barracks."

Panic tightened her chest. He was dismissing her? Just like that? Sure, she didn't really want to stay and be seduced by him, but if she went back now, everyone would know she'd failed seduction just as she'd failed every other task assigned to her in this place. "But—"

His gaze met hers once more, only this time it wasn't smoldering. It was hard and cold and very guarded. "You're dismissed."

Elysia slowly pushed to her feet as he moved toward the candles and blew them out one by one. A new sense of dread trickled through her.

He was right. She couldn't fail seduction. She did need him. "Damon—"

"I said you're dismissed, recruit." He didn't turn toward her, but in the dim light, she watched his jaw clench down hard. "Don't make me say it again."

Dazed, Elysia stepped out into the dimly lit hallway, completely unsure what had just happened. All she knew for sure was that Damon was her trainer, and that sometime between the moment he'd untied her blindfold to now, she'd upset him.

She ran back over their conversation. Knew there had to be a moment when something had flipped. She was the one who had every right to be upset, not him. Then she remembered the way he'd stared into her eyes as if searching for the truth, and her breath caught.

She hadn't been able to hide her disgust. Hadn't even tried. And now he knew just what she really thought of him. But instead of reacting indifferently, as she'd expected someone like him to be, he'd seemed...hurt.

Her pulse beat hard. She pressed a shaky hand against the wall. Tried to make sense of what was happening. Couldn't, because he had no reason to be hurt, unless...

Her throat grew thick, and the axis her world was perched upon tipped and swayed.

Unless the connection they'd shared on Pandora truly had been real.

* * *

"Elbow up." Damon brushed by the redheaded recruit and nudged her elbow higher. "Draw the string back closer to your ear."

The recruit did as he said and released. The arrow sailed toward the target, striking the outer circle with a thwack.

"Better."

The recruit—he couldn't remember her name—lowered the bow and looked up with a flirty smile. "It's easy when you have the best instructor."

Damon's gaze skipped over her. She was dressed in familiar, tight Siren garb, and she was hotter than hot—hourglass figure, firm tits, with high cheekbones, a slim nose sprinkled with freckles, and full, pouty lips that drew attention straight to her mouth. But even with her fuck-me looks and come-get-me caresses every time he stepped close, he wasn't interested. The only female he was interested in was a temperamental brunette. The same one who'd made it more than clear last night she'd rather slit her wrists than be anywhere alone with him ever again.

His gaze skipped across the training field toward the far side where Elysia held a wooden sword and was currently getting her ass kicked by another recruit. Her dark hair was piled on the top of her head in a messy bun. Sexy, damp tendrils tickled her cheeks and the back of her neck. She swung out with the sword and completely missed her target. The other recruit—an Amazon Damon had already discovered had nothing but attitude—shoved her foot against Elysia's lower back and pushed. Elysia fell to her knees in the dirt with a grunt.

Damon cringed. Erebus was right. She was awful. After a month, she should be much further along in combat, marksmanship, and archery.

Frowning, he looked away from her, still unable to stop thinking about last night. Could he really blame her for her reaction? She was right. He was a yes-boy for the Sirens. A slut for Aphrodite. He fucked Aphrodite whenever she called him. He fucked her slaves whenever she ordered him to do so. Then he went along with the sadistic goddess when she pimped him out to the Sirens so he could fuck their recruits. He was the epitome of a man whore, and they all knew it.

Disgust rolled through him, a familiar disgust he tried not to analyze too deeply. So Elysia didn't want him. He was no worse off now than he'd been before he'd met her. He'd always enjoyed his break from Aphrodite with the Sirens. Seduction training with the recruits wasn't forced sex as it was in Aphrodite's temple. Hell, he didn't even have to fuck the recruits if he didn't want to. He just had to teach them to be seductive. And if he wanted to fuck them and have a good time… Well then, that was up to him, wasn't it?

His gaze skipped back to Elysia, and he watched as she pushed to her feet, dusted off her hands, and lifted her practice sword once more. The Amazon waited until Elysia swung out, then hooked her leg around Elysia's and dropped Elysia right to the ground.

"*Fuck me.*" She was so getting cut at the first elimination, it wasn't even funny.

The redhead he'd been working with brushed her voluptuous breasts against his arm, drawing his attention her way. "What was that? An offer?" She trailed long, slender fingers down his arm and batted insanely long eyelashes up at him. "I'm game. If we slip away now, no one will notice."

Kadmos was her seduction trainer. Damon remembered seeing the male lead her out of the great hall last night. Kadmos helped Poseidon manage the oceans when he wasn't with the Sirens, a much more interesting assignment than Damon's lot with Aphrodite. And while the mortal was large and built and alpha enough and could probably get any sea nymph he wanted, Damon had a feeling he didn't need to do a lot of training with this recruit. She oozed sex appeal and was already trying to practice what she'd learned last night on Damon.

Still not interested.

He reached for the recruit's hand and pulled it away from his arm. "Let's stay focused on archery."

The recruit pushed out her lips in a sexy little pout and slid her fingers along his arm again. "Why say no when saying yes feels so right?"

Damn, she was good. "Pick up your bow, recruit, and try again."

The recruit dropped her hand with a huff, but Damon barely noticed. His attention was already back on Elysia, pushing herself up from the dirt and dusting off her pants. Mud streaked her clothing, her face, and her arms, and sweat made her clothing cling to her soft skin. But to him, she'd never been more beautiful.

No, she might not be interested in him any longer, but he still needed to make sure she survived the first elimination.

Luckily, since they were forced to spend their evenings together for the next few weeks anyway, there was one thing he could do to make sure that happened.

He just knew it would be pure torture for him.

Emerging from the showers that night, Elysia found Sera standing in front of the full-length mirror hanging on the door of her locker as she clasped a chain around her neck.

"Oh, hey," Sera said as Elysia drew close. "I was just about to go looking for you. You better hurry up. You're gonna be late."

Elysia's gaze skipped over Sera's revealing outfit—strapless top, short skirt, bare legs that seemed to stretch for miles in the four-inch heels—and a whisper of jealousy raced along her nerve endings. Sera's hair was a mass of messy waves around her pretty face, and her lips sparkled with some kind of pink lip gloss Elysia knew would drive Erebus absolutely wild.

Elysia tucked the towel tighter around her damp skin and dropped down onto her bunk. "I've got plenty of time."

That wasn't a lie. She'd looked in the box Damon had sent over before she'd taken her shower. Instead of the revealing outfits and high heels all the other recruits received from their trainers, he'd sent her yoga pants, tennis shoes, and a plain white, short-sleeved T-shirt.

There was absolutely nothing sexy about the getup. And considering the way he'd kicked her out of that private room last night, she had a feeling nothing sexy was going to happen tonight or ever.

Rejection pulled at the corners of her mouth and left a hole the size of a crater in the middle of her belly. He didn't want her. So what? She didn't really want him. She'd already told herself that. And she didn't care if she'd hurt him with her reaction last night or not. He'd hurt her by lying about who he was.

So why in Hades was she bothered by the clothes in that damn box?

"We didn't get a chance to chat much last night," Sera said as she checked her makeup in the mirror. "You were already asleep when I got in."

Actually, Elysia had been feigning sleep because she hadn't wanted to discuss her disaster of a night. Or hear about how awesome Sera's had been.

Pushing to her feet, Elysia pulled underwear and socks from her locker. "Yeah. I was beat."

"If you'd been awake, I'd have told you what I heard. Erebus, my seduction trainer, is friends with the guy who was camped out with you on Pandora."

"That's not a surprise since they're both trainers here."

"Right." Sera ran her fingers through her hair, still studying her reflection. "Turns out he got into some deep shit for staying with you. That's why he hasn't been around. Word is Athena gave him the choice between going back to Aphrodite's temple or spending a month in the pit. He chose the pit."

Elysia's hands paused in the process of pulling on her T-shirt. The recruits had all been warned about the pit when they'd first arrived at the compound. If any tried to leave the premises, if any decided not to follow orders they'd be thrown in the pit for an unspecified length of time. It was isolation, filth, extreme cold, and insanity by darkness all rolled into one, and Elysia had heard horror stories of past recruits who'd lost their minds after only a week in that hellhole.

Elysia's pulse sped up. "Wait. You're telling me he chose the pit over Aphrodite's pleasure palace?"

"Uh-huh." Sera looked Elysia's way. "Sounds like you did a number on that guy. I guess you're better at seduction than you thought. Hey, who'd you get paired up with last night? You never told me."

Slowly, Elysia lowered to her bunk again, the socks in her hand, her thoughts skipping right back to last night and Damon's reaction when she'd accused him of being—she cringed nothing but a man whore.

"Lys?" Sera asked.

Elysia blinked and looked up. "Yeah?"

"I asked who you were paired up with."

Damon. She'd been paired up with Damon, which made zero sense. If Athena had been pissed enough to toss him in the pit for what he'd done on Pandora with her, there was no way she'd have let him anywhere near Elysia again. Unless...

"Oh my gods." Elysia pushed to her feet when she remembered her strange confrontation with Athena last night after all the other recruits had been paired off with their trainers. At the time, blindfolded and unable to read what was going on around her, Elysia had thought the eerie silence was a result of the way she'd stumbled in late. But now Elysia knew it was because Damon had been the only trainer left in the room. And that Athena had cued in to something Elysia was just now realizing.

Damon had somehow changed the assignments so he'd be paired up with her. That was the only explanation that made sense. Their being seduction partners wasn't a random coincidence at all. It was his doing because—she remembered the hurt in his eyes last night—because he really did care for her. And that meant the connection they'd forged on Pandora was truly real.

Elation filled her chest, but it quickly deflated when she remembered the things she'd said to him in that room.

A need to set things right pushed Elysia into action. She tugged on her yoga pants, shoved her feet into the tennis shoes Damon had sent over, and rushed for the door. "I have to go."

"But…" Sera turned to look after her. "You haven't even dried your hair!"

Elysia didn't care how she looked. Damon had seen her at her worst on Pandora and hadn't cared. He'd just wanted to be with her.

"My obsession. That's what I'm going to call you. Because that's what you've become. A drug I can't stop craving."

Her heart raced as she tore out of the barracks, crossed the courtyard in the dark, and rushed toward the Hall of Seduction, anxious to see him again. He hadn't lied, not about what he'd felt. He'd been telling the truth. Just as he'd been telling the truth on Pandora when he'd said, *"I keep coming back to this feeling that I was sent here for a reason, that our meeting was not a random coincidence."*

Maybe it was reckless. Maybe she was setting herself up for heartbreak, but she didn't care. She felt the same way. She'd remembered a lot about her life over the last few weeks, and she knew she'd never had an attachment like this to another male, and that she'd never wanted one. But she wanted Damon now. Needed him. Not because she was on the verge of failing as a Siren, but because he made her feel things she hadn't felt before. And because she didn't want to end up bitter and jaded like the females instructing her. She wanted to live. Wanted to love. Wanted to experience everything she could before it was taken away from her.

Her sneakers skidded to a stop outside the private room Damon had taken her to last night. Drawing a breath that did little to settle her pulse, she lifted her hand to knock, then changed her mind. Grasping the door handle, she turned and pushed the heavy wood door open with her hip and stepped into the room. "Damon?"

No candlelight met her eyes. The room was completely dark. A shiver of fear rushed down her spine.

"You're late."

His voice was deep, low, somewhere to her left. Exhaling with relief, she turned toward the sound, desperate to tell him everything she'd just realized. "I know. I—"

He stepped around her out into the light of the hall. "Follow me."

Confused, Elysia looked after him, already striding down the corridor away from her. Letting go of the door, she hustled to catch up. "We're not staying here tonight?"

"No."

He didn't slow his pace, didn't touch her, didn't even look at her, and as Elysia lengthened her stride to stay with him, she realized he wasn't dressed as he'd been last night either. Instead of lightweight clothing that was easy to remove, he wore the same fitted black fighting pants he'd worn in the training field earlier today, a black T-shirt, and a black hoodie that accentuated the width of his shoulders.

Reaching the end of the hall, he pushed the heavy doors open and stepped out into the cool night air.

Moonlight lit the path. Tall trees rose high above, their leaves rustling in the evening breeze. He didn't slow his steps as he moved down a series of stone steps that led into the forests beyond the compound. Shivering, Elysia followed, wishing she'd thought to bring a jacket, wishing he'd stop so she could talk to him, praying he'd look at her just once so she could apologize and tell him she wasn't the bitch he thought her to be. "Damon, where are we going?"

He didn't answer. Worry skittered along her nerves, but she fought it back. Was this part of her seduction training? Olympus was the playland of the gods. Was he taking her to a secluded waterfall? A hidden cottage? Excitement erupted in the center of her chest and flowed like lava into her belly, warming every cell along the way. Was he taking her to a place that had special meaning for him?

They reached a clearing. Moonlight shone down from above, illuminating the short grasses and flowers along the ground. The forest closed around them in a circle. Damon crossed to the middle of the clearing, tugged off his hoodie, and tossed it on the ground.

Elysia stopped at the edge of the clearing and listened for the rumble of a waterfall, searched the tree line for some kind of cottage, or tent or structure where this seduction lesson was supposed to happen. All she saw was a field and Damon standing in the moonlight, facing away from her.

"Catch."

She looked up to see a wooden object sailing toward her. Reflexively, she winced but caught the training sword just as it reached her.

"What is this for?" she asked, staring down at the sword.

"For training. Which you sorely need."

Her gaze lifted across the moonlit meadow. In his hand, Damon held another wooden sword.

Two things clicked in Elysia's brain at once. One, he hadn't brought her out here for any kind of seduction training. And two, he didn't have any intention of teaching her about seduction at all…probably ever again.

"You're sucking up the tail end of the class," Damon said. "If you've got any intention of moving on, you need to get a lot better fast."

Elysia glanced back at the sword in her hand. "So this is…"

"The only thing that's going to save your ass."

Disappointment swept through Elysia. A disappointment she had no one to blame but herself. "And the seduction training—"

"Is a waste of time."

Her gaze met his. Moonlight highlighted the thick muscles in his arms and neck, his hard jaw, his focused eyes. But there was absolutely no friendliness in his features. The male before her now was but a shadow of the one she'd met on Pandora. "Then how will I pass that portion of the training?"

"I write your evaluation. I'll give you high marks."

"Just like that? Without any work?"

"We both know that's all it would be. Work. So let's save ourselves the time and energy and move on to something we know you can improve on."

Rejection burned through her. Rejection and a swift shot of pain because she realized she'd hurt him way more than she'd thought. He'd told her he had no memory of his life before Olympus. He knew nothing more than being a servant to the gods and had no choice about his station on Olympus. And she'd faulted him for that. Faulted him and accused him of being a whore.

Her mouth grew dry. "If you don't want to be my seduction trainer, then why are you doing this?"

"Because we're required to spend our evenings together for the next few weeks. And because you need the extra help."

Even after all the pain she'd caused him, he still wanted to help her. A tiny ray of hope wriggled its way through the rejection. An apology wasn't going to work here. He'd never believe her, and he'd probably think she had ulterior motives if she tried. The only way to make it up to him was to re-form the connection they'd forged on Pandora. Which meant taking things slow, as they'd done there.

"Lift your sword," he said. "You need to learn how to defend yourself the correct way."

She didn't want to lift her sword. She wanted to throw her arms around his neck and kiss him. But she couldn't. Not yet at least.

Drawing a breath, Elysia held out her sword and stepped forward. And told herself she could do this. She had to. Because she didn't believe their meeting was a random coincidence anymore. Somehow, she had to make him remember that he didn't believe it was a coincidence either.

CHAPTER ELEVEN

Damon was sweaty, hot, and more than a little sexually frustrated.

Five nights spent tutoring Elysia in archery, sword fighting, and marksmanship techniques without touching her had left him horny as hell. Especially when she showed up for their sessions in skintight spandex, a crop tank that revealed the sexy strip of skin across her belly, or when she'd pause to take a breath, then smile at him all sultry and absolutely adorable in the moonlight.

He shoved his muddy boots in the bottom of his locker, pulled out the fresh pair, and sat on the bench in the locker room. Around him, trainers prepared for their evenings with the recruits, showering, changing, shaving…laughing and razzing each other about whose recruit was the fastest learner. Most of the trainers resided in the compound during the training segments, but their dormitory was on the far end of the compound and not easily accessible after a full day on the field. Damon frowned as he looked around. At least these lucky pricks got to get it on with their females after a day like this. Damon had to go right back to cut and thrust, fancy footwork, and the best place to slice a person to make them bleed out quietly.

Erebus caught Damon's eye from across the room, and Damon quickly rose, pulled on his black T-shirt, and shoved his feet into his boots. Yesterday, he'd gotten stuck listening to Erebus drone on about what a natural Sera was at seduction. If Damon had to hear what she could do with her mouth one more time, he was going to explode. And not in any way he wanted to explode.

Running a hand through his damp hair, he headed for the door, thankful to escape before someone caught him. At his back, he heard his name called, but didn't slow his steps. Though why he was rushing toward even more sexual frustration, he didn't know.

He reached the clearing long before Elysia. Sitting on a log near the entrance to the meadow, he munched on a handful of nuts and mentally ran through the hand-to-hand combat moves he needed to show her tonight. It would mean touching her, which he wasn't sure he was ready to do just yet, but the elimination checkpoint was coming up in a matter of days. If he didn't show her some basic moves now, she'd pass everything else, fail combat, and still be cut.

She was doing better. Not great, but better. If she kept working as hard as she'd been working the last few days, she might skate through the checkpoint unscathed. She'd never be the best warrior in the group, but she had skills. She just needed to hone them if she wanted to someday be a Siren.

Did she want to be a Siren? The thought echoed in his mind. He wasn't sure. Hadn't ever asked her. He only knew that he couldn't let the alternative happen. More than anything, he just wanted to get to a point where he didn't have to worry about her. Where he wouldn't have to spend his nights out here in the moonlight alone with her. Where he didn't have to agonize over touching—or not touching—her every damn second of every stupid day.

Skata, he wanted to touch her more than he wanted food.

Frowning down at the almonds in his hand, he pitched them into the trees, then looked back in the direction he'd come. Where in Hades was she? She was almost forty minutes late.

He pushed to his feet, ready to go looking for her, when twigs cracking drew him to a stop. Seconds later, he spotted a silhouette moving toward him.

His body heated at just the sight of her, irritating him even more. "You're late again." Swiping his hands against his thighs, he fought back the arousal. "The moon will be setting soon."

"I'm not late," Elysia said in a soft, sexy voice. "You were early."

"How do you know how early I wa—"

She moved into the light, and all words died on his lips.

Gone were the spandex and tank. In their place, she wore a soft yellow sundress with loose, ruffled shoulders, a nipped-in waist, and a hem that hit just at her knees. Pale yellow flats covered her feet, her hair was pinned up in a messy knot, and silver drops fell from her ears, catching the rays of moonlight shining through the trees.

The arousal came rushing back, hot and fierce. "What…? Where…?" He held out his hand. "You can't train in *that*."

She clasped her hands behind her back and smiled. A warm, gorgeous smile that lit up her entire face. "What? This?" She looked down at the dress, then back at him. "I didn't have time to change."

His eyes narrowed. "You weren't wearing that on the training field earlier today."

"Oh, you noticed." Her smile widened. "I'll take that as a good sign."

She stepped past him, leaves and twigs cracking under her dainty shoes as she moved, and as she swept by, the scent of honeysuckle surrounded him, reminding him of the sultry hours he'd spent with her on Pandora.

"I'm not really up for another lesson in combat," she said over her shoulder, meandering through the trees, away from the meadow. "I think I'd rather go for a walk instead."

Damon looked after her, stunned and…shit, hard. "And I think if you're not serious about training, then maybe it's time you went back to your barracks."

She flicked him a flirty look over her shoulder but only kept walking away. Away from him. Away from the Siren compound. Away from anyone who might see what she was up to.

Her hand landed on the trunk of a tree, and she hummed a tune he couldn't quite make out as she weaved through the birch and maple in the grove. The sleeves of her dress fluttered as she moved, dragging at his attention, and when she turned at the giant oak, then disappeared from view, his heart leapt into his throat.

His feet were heavy against the ground, his heart a whir in his chest. A walk? She wanted to go for a walk *now?* He didn't buy it. A voice in the back of his head told him not to follow. The woman had already wrecked him enough for one lifetime. He didn't need to trail after her like a freakin' puppy dog. Again.

Skata. Forget being sexually frustrated. Now he was simply fucking frustrated.

And still horny as hell, dammit.

Muttering curses, he trailed after her, hoping she hadn't already gotten herself lost. That was all he needed. To spend the next five hours out here in the dark, trying to find her before one of the Sirens realized she was missing.

Moving around a boulder, he finally spotted her ahead, a blur of yellow in the pale light. A frown pulled at his mouth, a mixture of relief and more frustration. Quickening his steps, he moved out of the shadows and into the moonlight. Then drew to a stop when he spotted her standing at the edge of a small pool, one foot out of her flats, her toes testing the water.

"It's warm." A smile split her lips. The same sexy grin she'd sent him on Pandora that had done crazy things to his blood.

"We need to go back. This is too far off the property."

"There's plenty of time for that. I think we should get in."

His gaze shot to the water and the steam rising from the surface. Images of her naked and reclining in the hot liquid filled his mind and heated his blood all over again, forcing him back one shaky step. "We don't have time for that."

When she didn't answer, he turned away and motioned with his arm. "Come on. Since you're not dressed for a lesson, I'll walk you back."

One soft yellow flat landed on the path in front of him. He stilled, and his pulse ticked up. Slowly, he turned, then nearly swallowed his tongue. Because Elysia was already tugging the yellow sundress up her sweet and tempting body.

"No, thanks." Slim legs made to wrap around a male came into view, followed by pale pink panties covering her tempting sex and the curve at her hips, a flat belly and luscious breasts resting in the cups of a pale pink bra. She pulled the dress over her head, tossed it on the rocks, and grinned with pure seduction as she reached back for the clasp of her bra. "I think I'd like to take a swim instead."

His mouth grew dry as he watched her flick the clasp free and catch the cups of her bra before they slid free of her breasts. And the blood rushing straight to his cock made him as hard as the rocks beneath her feet.

"You should join me, Damon." She let go of the bra. It fell at her feet, revealing her gorgeous, perfect breasts and pink-tipped nipples. Her fingers found the lace at her hips and stilled. "If you're not scared, that is."

* * *

Elysia knew she was being bad. But for once, it felt so good to be bad, she didn't care what anyone thought.

She slid her fingertips beneath the waistband of her silky panties. Damon's eyes darkened, but he didn't move closer. Didn't reach for her. Just continued to stare at her naked flesh as if he couldn't look away. And even though that wasn't exactly the reaction she'd hoped for, she took it as a good sign. She'd been flirting with him all week during their "lessons," and she'd gotten absolutely nowhere. It was as if the male was suddenly immune to her charms. This was her last-ditch effort to break through his barriers, and if the bulge in his pants was any indication, that effort was slowly starting to have an effect.

She pushed the silk down her legs, stepped out of the undergarment, and kicked it toward her dress. His gaze zeroed in on the thatch of curls at the apex of her thighs, and her nipples pebbled, sending shards of heat straight into her sex as he continued to stare. But he still didn't move. Didn't speak. Didn't reach for her. And she knew if she had any hope of getting through to him, she had to get him naked too. Right now.

She turned away, giving him a nice view of her ass, and picked her way over the rocks. Stepping into the hot springs, she sighed as heat surrounded her calves, her thighs, her hips and waist. "Gods, this is amazing." She turned to face him and lowered herself into the water, groaning at the way her muscles immediately relaxed. "You should really get in." Her gaze dropped to the bulge—even bigger, now—in his pants. "If you can move, that is."

"You're playing a dangerous game, *oraios*."

Beautiful. Not *my obsession* as he'd called her before she'd fucked everything up, but it was a start. One she could work with.

She fanned her hands through the water and grinned. "I don't know what you mean."

"You know exactly what I mean. Come on. Get out."

"Nope." She leaned back against the rocks, resting her head on a smooth stone, and closed her eyes. "I'm staying. You can go back if you want, though I'm sure Athena will pepper you with all kinds of questions about what happened to me when I turn up missing."

"You'd do that just to get me in trouble, wouldn't you?"

Doubt whipped through her, and she opened her eyes. Did he really believe that? Gods, she *had* wounded him. Horribly. He'd told her on Pandora that she was the first person he'd ever felt connected to. She was probably the only person he'd ever opened up to about his blank memories.

She sat upright, not even caring that her nipples were on the edge of the water or that she wasn't posing sexily for him. All she wanted was to take back all the awful things she'd said and thought about him over the last month. All she needed was for him to know she hadn't meant them. "Damon—"

"Fine." He reached behind his head with one arm to tug his shirt up. "You can have your fun for now. But I'm not staying all night, so soak your fill. Then you're getting out and going back."

A tingle rushed straight through Elysia as carved abs, perfect pecs, cut shoulders, and muscular biceps came into view. Not to mention his gorgeous face and the hint of stubble that made him look that much more dark and dangerous. No male should be this beautiful. It wasn't fair. And he wasn't even a god. She was sure if the gods knew he was this hot, they'd punish him. Which, strangely, made his assignment with Aphrodite all the more understandable.

Not wanting to think about Aphrodite, she pursed her lips and relaxed against the rocks again as he bent and tugged off his boots. "Okay, Zeus."

His fingers paused over the snap at his waistband, and he lifted his gaze to hers. "Do *not* call me that."

The look was so adorably irritated, she laughed. "You don't like the king of the gods?"

He pulled the snap free and pushed the dark fabric past his hips. "Can't stand the pompous asshole."

Elysia's mouth went bone dry as she watched his thick, toned thighs, covered in a thin layer of dark hair, come into view. And when he kicked the pants away, straightened, and slid his fingers beneath the elastic waistband of his black boxer briefs, she was pretty sure she drooled.

His fingers pushed the fabric down an inch and stopped just as the carved V of his lower abs caught the moonlight. "You're gonna turn around, right?"

It took several seconds for Elysia to realize he was speaking to her, and she forced her gaze up to his face. "You saw me naked."

"You didn't exactly give me a choice. We both know you're not interested in seeing this."

But she was. She wanted to see everything. Her cheeks heated, and her gaze lifted back to where his fingers held his boxers in place. She wanted to tear the garment free with her fingertips. With her teeth. Wanted to lick and taste everything beneath.

Her heart pounded so hard, she was sure he had to hear it. But she swiveled away from him because she knew if she didn't, he wouldn't get into the water. And she needed him naked and in the water so she could move on with the rest of her plan to prove she wanted to pick up where they'd left off on Pandora.

Water splashed behind her, and her stomach trembled as she imagined all that warm water caressing his rock-hard muscles and tan skin.

"Well?" she asked, figuring it was safe to turn. "Isn't it nice?"

He frowned and sank back against the rocks opposite her, the waterline hitting him mid-chest. "It's okay, I guess."

"You guess." She smiled. "It's awesome. After today's workout, I needed this."

Steam rose around them. He laid his head back on the rocks and closed his eyes. "I saw Minos had you running the obstacle course."

She watched the water lap at his nipples, and her own nipples tightened beneath the surface. "Yeah." She swallowed hard, working to keep her voice from shaking. "I can handle everything but the hill. After we come out of the mud, I lose it on the hill every time."

"That's because you're trying to take the shortest route. It's steeper there. If you go around the rock outcropping, the hillside is more gradual. You'll pick up speed and beat the others to the top."

Elysia hadn't thought of that. No one went that way. She hadn't even known it was an option. "Okay, I'll try that next time. Thanks."

He sighed and relaxed farther in the water, and as she studied his profile tipped upward in the moonlight, something about him struck her again as…familiar.

"I wonder what kind of warrior you were," she said.

He lifted his head, his brows drawn in confusion. "What?"

"Before you came to Olympus. On Pandora, you said the gods told you that you'd once been a warrior. It's pretty obvious from the way you wield a sword. I wonder if you were a knight or a gladiator or maybe a pirate."

He huffed a sound that was part laugh, part annoyance, and leaned his head back once more. "Yeah, right. I was a pirate. Aye, matey."

She smiled because this was what she'd missed the last month. This easy connection they'd shared on Pandora.

"If you were from my realm, you'd have been an Argonaut."

His eyes slowly opened, but when they focused on hers, all humor was gone. "From your realm?"

She nodded. "Argolea."

He pushed upright. "You remember where you're from?"

"Sort of. Certain things have come back. My mother is the queen of Argolea, and my father is an Argonaut. One of the seven descendants of—"

"The seven greatest heroes in all of Ancient Greece. Yeah, I've heard of the Argonauts. I'm not stupid. Zeus and Athena don't think too highly of them."

Elysia shrugged and fanned her hands through the water once more. "Which explains why they took me as soon as I turned twenty-five. You probably don't know how old you are, am I right?"

"No." His gaze followed the sweep of her fingers along the surface, and a sadness she hadn't expected to see crept into his eyes. "I don't."

Inwardly, Elysia cringed. She'd just screwed things up again when they were finally heading in the right direction. Reminding him that he would probably never know where he'd come from or what had happened to his own parents was not the way to get back to where they'd been before.

She pushed away from the rocks and tiptoed across the rocky bottom of the hot springs toward him. "So Sera told me an interesting story."

He tensed as she drew close. "About Erebus?"

"No." She stopped mere inches away, but forced herself not to touch him. "About you."

Unease flickered in his eyes. "What about me?"

"About you and Athena and the pit."

The muscles in his shoulders tightened.

"Why didn't you tell me where you'd been for the last month?"

His gaze skipped over her features. Unsure. Hesitant. Confused. "Because it wouldn't have mattered. You'd already made up your mind about me."

"I had." Her heart skipped a beat because he wasn't moving away. "And I was wrong."

Long seconds passed. He didn't speak. Didn't move. Just looked at her. Really looked at her, as he'd done on Pandora.

She eased closer, until her thighs skimmed his in the water and her fingers found the strong, solid muscles in his arms. "You chose that pit over Aphrodite and her palace. You chose it for me."

His pulse pounded beneath his skin, a rapid thump, thump, thump that fueled the fire inside her. "Elysia—"

"Don't say it doesn't matter." She brushed her body against his beneath the water—his ripped, strong, very aroused body. "Because it does. It's the only thing that matters. And I'm about to show you just how much it matters to me."

When he didn't push her away, she slid her hands up his chest and around his nape, drawing them even closer together. The hard, rigid length of his cock pressed against her belly. But it was his whispered "*Emmoni*," that made her heart lurch and her mouth find his in the moonlight.

Damon couldn't move, could barely breathe. But when Elysia's tongue slid along his lips, coaxing him to open, all rational thought slipped right out of his grasp, and biological instinct took over.

He wrapped his arms around her waist beneath the water and pulled her up against him. Then devoured her the way he'd wanted to devour her since she'd left him on Pandora.

Her mouth turned greedy. Her fingers slid up and into his hair as he kissed her deeper. She stroked her tongue over his in long, languid strokes and rocked her hips against his until he groaned. Closing her arms around his neck, she hoisted herself up in the water and wrapped her legs around his waist so she could press all her slick, sultry heat against the hard length of his cock.

She pulled back from his mouth, her lips swollen and pink in the moonlight, and looked down between them. "You're still wearing your boxers."

Damon sucked in a painful breath. Every bit of energy in his body was gathered where the heat of her sex caressed his aching cock. "Yes," he rasped.

Her gaze lifted to his face. Wispy tendrils had pulled free from her updo and glistened from the steam rising off the pool. Tiny droplets of water caressed her cheek and slid down her jaw and over her neck. And her eyes sparkled with both passion and lust. A lust that only made him harder. "Do I need to teach you the art of seduction, instructor?"

In the midst of probably the most painful moment of his life, Damon laughed. "No."

"Well, you clearly need a refresher. You're supposed to be naked right now. *And in me.*"

His pulse stuttered, because that was all he wanted too. But when she smiled and moved in to kiss him again, all the doubts he'd had this whole last week rushed in, preventing him from making that dream a reality.

Gently, he moved his hands to her hips—her slim, naked, gorgeous hips—and unwound her legs from his body. "*Emmoní*, stop."

Her hands slipped free of his shoulders, and as her feet found the sandy bottom of the pool, she looked up with worried eyes. "What's wrong?"

"You were right about me. I'm all those things you said the other night. I'm Aphrodite's property." His throat felt so thick, he wasn't sure he could speak, but he forced the words past his lips, because he was done keeping secrets. "I've fucked hundreds of females for her, with her. I've taught so many Siren recruits the art of seduction, I can't even rememb—"

Her damp fingertips landed against his lips. "I know, and I don't care."

He gently pulled her hand away and frowned. "You should. I'm not a person. I'm a thing. I don't have a soul. I'm nothing but a pleasure sla—"

"You're more than that." She moved close again, brushing her body along his and sliding her fingers across his jaw in a way that made every inch of his skin tingle. "So much more. You stayed with me on Pandora when you didn't have to. You helped me get through one of the toughest parts of the tests. And then you chose the pit over returning to Aphrodite's temple. A soulless person doesn't do that. A soulless person wouldn't have cared. And then, even after I said all those ugly things, you still didn't turn away. You stayed and you tutored me in combat and marksmanship and archery, all because you didn't want to see me fail."

"You don't know what Zeus does to the recruits who don't make the cut."

"A soulless pleasure slave would not care."

Her eyes went so soft and dreamy, something inside him cracked. "I didn't care. Not about any of the others. Just you. I don't think I could bear it if something happened to you."

When a hint of a smile toyed with her lips, he knew what she was thinking. That he was a total nutcase.

Stepping back, he brushed damp hands over his face and tried to sound semi-sane when he knew he wasn't. "I know it's crazy. I know it doesn't make sense. I've told myself that a hundred times. But something about you...I don't know. It makes me feel alive. In a way I've never been before." He dropped his hands and looked at her in the moonlight. "I like that feeling. I like it a lot. I like you. And I'd rather suffer endless days in that pit if it helped you, than spend an emotionless existence in Aphrodite's debauched palace."

She stepped into him again, wound her arms around his neck once more, and pressed that perfect body of hers against his from chest to knee. "I like that you like that feeling. I like that you like me. And I'm sorry that I said those ugly words. I'm sorry I rushed to judge you. I just..." She sighed and looked down at his mouth. "I just felt such a connection to you on Pandora that it overwhelmed me. And when I got to Olympus and you weren't here, and when that Siren told me who you were—"

"I know." His hands found her waist, and his fingers brushed the soft skin of her lower back. "I don't blame you, *emmoní.*"

"You should." Her eyes held his. Sparkling dark pools that seemed to see all the way into that soul he still wasn't sure he possessed. "Damon, you have every reason to hate me. But if you let me, I'll do whatever it takes to make it up to you."

His heart pinched, and even though he still didn't understand the intense feelings he felt for her so quickly, he knew there was no way he could ever say no to her. "I think you just did."

She smiled again, a warm, rich, genuine smile that lit up her eyes. And as his gaze dropped to her damp lips, that biological instinct came roaring back. Urging him to touch her. To taste her. To make her his so she'd never leave him again.

He kissed her, drawing her into his mouth and heart. Her arms tightened around his neck, and she opened, stroking her tongue along his until the blood pounded in his groin. Changing the angle of the kiss, he slid one hand down her lower spine to clasp her ass and pull her hips tight against him. She gasped into his mouth, then groaned as she wrapped her legs around his hips once more and kissed him harder.

Pleasure arced through his groin, making his cock twitch and pulse. She rocked her steamy sex against him. Kissed him again and again. Sliding his other hand around to her front, he cupped one succulent breast and squeezed, then found her nipple with his thumb and forefinger and pinched.

A tremble rushed through her body, and she pulled her mouth away, dropped her head back, and moaned.

His face fell against her damp chest. He breathed deep as she rocked her sex harder against his painful erection. Desire coursed through every inch of his body, and he knew it would be so easy to free himself from his boxers and slide inside her, but he didn't want that. He wanted her to enjoy. Wanted to feel her passion rise. Wanted to watch as he took her over the edge and into mindless oblivion.

Releasing her breast, he wrapped his other arm around her waist and cupped the other cheek, lifting and lowering her in the water with both hands to increase the friction on her clit. "That's it, *emmoní.*" He pressed his lips against the succulent line of her throat. "Ride me. Use me."

Her moans grew longer. Deeper. Her fingers dug into the flesh at his shoulders. Pain skipped down his spine, melding with the sparks of electricity radiating outward from his groin. He bit down gently on her neck, licked the spot, and suckled.

"Oh gods, Damon."

"Yes, *emmoní.*" He pulled her in tighter, lifted to press against her clit harder. "Let go. Come all over me. I want to feel your release. I want to feel everything. Don't hold back."

Every muscle in her body tensed. She rubbed faster and gasped. And when she cried out, cresting the wave of release, he held her tightly and watched her go over. And nearly came himself.

She collapsed against him, a sweaty mess of damp skin, limp bones, and wet hair. Her face fell against his neck, and he held her close, running his hands up and down her delicate spine as the last waves of the pleasure rippled through her.

"Oh my gods," she breathed. "That was amazing."

He smiled, because if she thought that was amazing, he couldn't wait to show her more. "I'm glad. It was pretty amazing for me as well."

She pushed back and looked down at the water, then up at his face. "You're still hard. You didn't—"

He pressed a kiss against her lips. "I can wait."

"But I don't want you to wait. I want to feel you—"

Chuckling, he pulled her hand away before she could grasp his erection and send him over that edge with just one squeeze. "You will. Trust me. Just not tonight."

"Why not tonight?"

He brushed a damp lock of hair away from her forehead. "Because I'm your seduction trainer, and because I want to do at least one part of this right."

Her eyes softened, and she slid her arms back around his neck. "I think you already seduced me, *ómorfos.*"

He grinned at her use of the word handsome. "I did. But there's still much more to teach you. And we don't have enough time tonight for what I want to do to you next."

A blush rose in her cheeks, and her teeth sank into her bottom lip in such a sexy, innocent way, his cock throbbed all over again. Ah hell. If she kept looking at him like that, he wouldn't be able to resist much longer.

"Um, Damon?"

His gaze lingered on her bottom lip, plump from her teeth. Gods, he wanted to bite that lip. Suck on it. Devour it.

"There's something I need to tell you."

"Yeah?"

"I'm not a virgin."

That got his attention. His gaze lifted to her eyes. "What?"

"I'm sure most of the recruits don't remember whether they are or not, but you need to know…I'm not."

Jealousy raced through him. An irrational jealousy, considering his sexual history. "Who was he?" His brow dropped when he thought about that history. "Or was he a he?" It could have been a her. Or an it.

He cringed. *Please don't say it was an it.*

She laughed and skimmed her fingertips over his shoulder. "Yes, it was a he. What do you think I'm into, satyrs or something?"

He shrugged, more relieved than he wanted to admit. "You could be." And he'd definitely seen kinkier shit in Aphrodite's temple.

"Well, I'm not. It was just a he. I don't remember a lot about him. Just his eyes. He was human. Not a lot of details have come back to me, but I know I used to cross over into the human realm when I wasn't supposed to. Argolea is a very patriarchal society, and as heir to the throne, I had a lot of restrictions placed on me."

"Got it. So, were you like... Did you love this guy?"

"Love?" Her brow wrinkled as if she were trying to remember back. "No, not in love. I think I used him to see what sex was all about."

The shocked way she said it, as if she'd just uncovered a horrible secret, made him laugh. "And did you? Like it, I mean?"

A shy smile pulled at her lips as she looked down at his shoulder. "I'm not sure. That part I don't really remember. I know it was nothing like what we just did here in this water—that I definitely won't forget. That was good." Her sultry gaze lifted. "And hot." She moved closer, rubbing her body against his beneath the water. "And I would very much like to give that and more back to you right now."

His cock thickened all over again. "Stop, or you'll make me come with nothing but your words."

"Can I do that?"

"You have no idea what you do to me."

"I like that. And I definitely want to see that."

He grasped her hands before she could reach his waist. "Not tonight."

Her lips pushed out in a sexy little pout. And as the blood pulsed in his erection, making him painfully hard, he knew the female didn't need an ounce of seduction training. She was the most arousing thing he'd ever met. The kicker was, she had no clue.

He brought her hands to his lips and kissed her knuckles one by one. "I don't want a quickie in the water, and we don't have time for all the things I plan to do to this body. Besides, when I come"—he lifted his head to gaze into her hypnotic eyes—"I want you screaming in pleasure right along with me."

Her eyes darkened with lust, and when he took her mouth, she sighed against him and sank into his kiss. Their tongues tangled, and her arms closed around his shoulders once more in the water, making Damon's heart swell. Not because anything was about to change—he knew his lot in life and that it would never be any different—but because he finally felt alive. And because he had this female to thank for that.

He'd cherish that; cherish *her* for as long as he could. And when her training with the Sirens was over and she finally left him for good—hopefully years from now—then he'd find a way to deal with the remnants of a life whose only purpose was to serve.

Even if it meant living in his memories.

CHAPTER TWELVE

Elysia left Damon outside the doors of the seduction hall with a kiss that, even now as she crossed the compound in the dark, still vibrated through her toes.

Biting her lip, she remembered the way he'd touched her, the words he'd said, all the things he'd made her feel in such a short amount of time. Her chest grew warm and full as she followed the stone path. She'd taken a big risk tonight, and for a moment, when Damon had only stared at her like she'd grown a third eyeball right in the center of her forehead, she'd thought she'd taken that risk for nothing. But now she knew she'd been right. He wanted her just as much as she wanted him. From this moment forward, everything would be different.

A smile curled her lips as she passed out of the light of a decorative light pole and moved into the shadows. She wondered with whom he was scheduled to work in the field tomorrow. Was already planning ways she could catch him between sessions and pull him into a dark corner for a quick kiss. If he hadn't convinced her she needed to go back to her room tonight, she would have—

A hand grasped her arm and yanked her off the path and into the brush. Elysia yelped and tumbled sideways. Before she could scream, another hand clamped over her mouth and pulled her back into a hard, male body.

"Shh," a voice said near her ear. "Don't draw attention. I'm here to help you."

The voice quickly registered, as did the familiar scents of leather and pine. She jerked the hand from her mouth and swiveled around. "Max? What the hell are you doing here? How did you get into Olympus?" She looked back toward the pathway. "If anyone sees you—"

"You remember me?" Max's familiar silver eyes widened. "Skyla said you wouldn't remember anything."

Skyla... *Skyla*... Elysia searched her memory and quickly found the link. "Skyla's a Siren..."

"You do remember." Max's brows drew together. "How is that possible?"

Damon had asked her the exact same thing. "I don't know, but it's not important now." She reached for his arm, her hand closing over the ancient Greek text running down his forearm that marked him as an Argonaut. "You have to leave before someone sees you."

"Not without you." He flipped his hand over, closing it around hers, his wide palm and long fingers familiar against her skin. "I'm taking you home. Come on. Talisa's waiting for us at the gate."

Home... Longing swept through her as he tugged her toward the edge of the path and looked both directions. Longing for a place she only knew in her mind. Yes...she needed to go with him. Home. To Argolea. To her parents. To her old life. To a world where she was no longer a prisoner.

Adrenaline pulsed through her veins as she closed her fingers around his much larger ones and stepped with him. The black cape hanging from his shoulders rustled in the darkness, drawing her gaze.

She'd seen that cape before. Had played with it—with Max—when she was younger. It was an invisibility cape. It belonged to her mother's friend Orpheus. Max must have borrowed the cape to come here and rescue her. And Talisa...

Talisa was also her cousin. Memories rushed through her mind like a movie set on fast-forward. Talisa was the daughter of Elysia's Aunt Casey and Uncle Theron. And Theron was the leader of the Argonauts. He'd been talking with Elysia's parents in the castle the day Elysia had been captured by Zeus's Sirens. Elysia had overheard them discussing—

Binding...

Nereus...

Elysia's eyes grew wide as the memory swept over her. They'd been discussing her arranged binding. Her parents had been preparing to marry her off to someone she didn't want. That was why she'd run, and Zeus's Sirens had intercepted her before she'd been able to cross the portal.

A whirlwind swirled through her chest, twisting her lungs like a tornado twists metal into shreds. She missed her family, missed her home, but she didn't want to go back to that. Couldn't. Because going back to that meant leaving Damon.

"Wait." She pulled back on Max's hand.

Max turned to look down at her, his blond hair catching the lights from the path behind him. "What's wrong?"

Elysia looked up at his strong jawline, his familiar silver eyes, and the compassion in his rugged and handsome features.

More memories rushed in. They weren't just cousins, they were friends. The best of friends. He was eleven years older than her, but he'd never treated her as an imposition, and he'd always watched out for her like a brother. She knew he'd do anything to keep her safe. Just as she knew he would never understand her need to stay on Olympus with Damon.

"I can't go with you."

"What? Why not? You can't stay here."

"There's more I need to do. I was sent here for a reason. I know that reason now."

"Did they freakin' brainwash you? You were sent here because Zeus is a prick. Because he wants revenge against the Argonauts."

"I don't care."

"Well, you need to care, because—"

Voices echoed from the far end of the path, followed by footsteps drawing close.

Panic rushed through Elysia, and she pulled Max back into the brush and held her breath.

Two recruits approached, laughing and chatting about their evenings. They moved right past the brush where she and Max lurked without so much as a sideways glance and disappeared inside the barracks.

When the double doors snapped closed, Elysia turned toward Max and squeezed his hand hard. "You have to go."

"But—"

"I'm fine, Max. Look at me. I'm not hurt, I'm not brainwashed, I'm good. Truly, I am. But I can't leave. I won't. And if you stay here any longer, someone *will* catch you. I won't risk that. Tell the others—tell my parents—that I'm okay. Tell them that I love them and miss them, tell them…"

Her mind caught on another memory. Words her mother had spoken to her not long before she'd come here.

"Twenty-five years is nothing but a blink of the eye to the gods. And peace is as fleeting as the wind. It will end. It will end soon."

She looked up at Max in the shadows. "Tell my parents it's too risky. If I go back with you, there will be no more peace. Zeus will attack Argolea. You yourself said he took me for revenge. If I go back with you now, he'll retaliate. I won't risk that. I'm fine here, Max. I really am."

"But…" His frantic eyes searched her face, and his fingers closed around hers. "We can keep you safe. We have a plan. Just come with me."

She wanted to. She wanted to go home, wanted to see her parents, but she wanted Damon more. And after the words he'd said and the things he'd made her feel tonight, she knew she couldn't leave him now.

"You have to go." Her throat grew tight, her hands shaky as she pushed him back toward the path. "Go, and don't come back. I couldn't live with myself if they caught you."

"But…"

She rose up on her toes, threw her arms around his broad shoulders, and hugged him tight. "I'll find you. When I get through my training and they send me into the human realm, I'll find you. I promise I won't forget you. I won't forget any of you."

Before he could protest again, she tugged the hood of Orpheus's invisibility cloak over his head. He vanished from sight, but she knew he was still there. She just hoped he did as she said and left before what limited magic was left in the cloak ran out. "Now go."

She stepped past him, raced the rest of the way down the path, and skipped the steps to the porch of her barracks. Pulling the door open and moving inside, she told herself she was doing the right thing. She knew she was.

But her heart still squeezed so hard, it felt as if it shrank a size in her chest. Because by staying here with Damon, she'd just given up her one chance to be free.

* * *

Damon couldn't stand still. He hadn't seen Elysia since he'd kissed her good night outside the doors of this building nearly forty-eight hours ago.

Seduction training was only scheduled six nights a week. On the seventh—which had been Sunday—the trainers were given the night off. Since Athena had assigned classroom work to the recruits during the day, and because she'd sent Damon and Erebus to Hephaestus, the god of metalworking, on Monday to pick up a new set of weaponry for the Sirens, Damon hadn't been in the field. Which meant he hadn't even been able to catch a glimpse of Elysia since their magical night in the hot springs.

Athena had purposely sent him on that little errand just to spite him. Hephaestus was Aphrodite's husband, and the god knew full well who Damon was to his wife. Everyone on Olympus knew what Damon did for Aphrodite, and Hephaestus, clearly, had reason to despise him.

Fury burned hot through Damon's gut when he thought back to that encounter. The only reason he wasn't a bloody, bruised mess right this minute was because Erebus had been there to run interference. As Damon paced the length of the private room while he waited for Elysia, he wished like hell he could send Athena on an errand or two. The goddess was still pissed he'd switched up the seduction schedule so he could have Elysia. He'd been stupid to think she'd just let that go. He had to be careful with Elysia from here on out. He didn't want Athena targeting her because of him. And if she planned to make it impossible for Elysia to pass just to get back at him—

The door opened. Damon looked in that direction just as Elysia stepped into the room. Her hair fell in a sleek mass past her shoulders, and she was dressed in another sweet sundress, this one light blue with a heart-shaped neckline that showed off her delectable cleavage. Slim spaghetti straps held the organza fabric in place as it nipped in at her waist, rounded her hips, and dropped to hit mid-thigh, accentuating the long, toned length of her legs.

Desire rolled through his belly, pushing aside all the fury. But it was the shadows in her pretty dark eyes that put him on instant alert.

He reached for her hands. "What's wrong?"

"Nothing. I'm just...just a little homesick today." She drew a deep breath and forced a smile he knew she didn't feel. "Athena kept us on the training field longer than usual. I got here as soon as I could."

Of course Athena had. The goddess enjoyed making him suffer.

Don't think about Athena. Damon brushed a silky tendril away from Elysia's face and forced his focus on this, on them, on the moment he'd been anticipating for two damn days. And after hearing she was homesick, he felt even better about what he had planned. "I missed you."

"Mm." She leaned toward his hand and sighed. "I missed you too. I haven't been able to stop thinking about the other night." Her gaze shifted to the right and the lone candle he'd lit. "Are we—"

"No." Desire came roaring back, a hot and needy fireball that rolled through his blood. Grasping her hand tightly in his, he moved toward the candle and blew it out. "We're not staying here."

"We're not?"

He shook his head as he pulled Elysia with him out into the hall. Tugging the door closed, he held one finger to his lips to tell her to be quiet, then leaned close to her ear, drew in a whiff of her sweet honeysuckle scent, and whispered, "I have something special planned."

Dim light filled the hallway from sconces set every twenty feet along the wall, but it was enough to see the spark of excitement in Elysia's eyes that told him she approved. His pants grew tight. Anticipation curled through his belly as he pulled her down the hall, pushed the far door open, and led her away from the buildings.

Darkness surrounded them as they moved into the trees that bordered the Siren property. He led her through the woods until they reached their meadow. Slowing his steps, he turned toward her, reached for her other hand, and laced their fingers together. "Okay, close your eyes."

"Why?"

"You'll see. Trust me."

She narrowed her eyes in a skeptical way, but the sexy little smirk on her lips told him loud and clear that she did trust him. And that warmed his heart more than anything else.

Her eyes fell closed. Studying her delicate features in the moonlight, he imagined where he was taking her. Excitement curled like fire in his blood.

A pop sounded, and a whir of light illuminated the meadow. Elysia gasped as the portal opened. He squeezed her hands in reassurance as they flashed through time and space.

Solid ground formed beneath their feet. She wobbled, and he reached for her shoulders to make sure she didn't fall. When she opened her eyes and looked past him, she gasped all over again, making him smile.

Her gaze drifted over the crumbling columns and massive ruins behind him, illuminated by the waning moon. "What the…?" She turned to look down the rolling, forested hills to the ocean far off in the distance sparkling like a sea of diamonds in a spray of white light. "Where are we?"

"Pandora."

Fear rushed across her features.

"Don't worry. This is sacred ground. We're safe here. The monsters on this island can't cross into the temple, I promise." He closed his hand over hers once more and pulled her with him toward the broken and chipped marble steps of the ruins. "Come on. I want to show you something."

They moved up the steps and into the temple. Moonlight illuminated the dozens of crumbling columns lining the inside of the temple in two parallel rows. The ceiling was missing in places, and twigs and leaves that had blown in over the years skittered along the cracked and broken floor. Darkness beckoned from the edges of the temple, but Elysia's wide eyes told Damon she wasn't seeing the ruins. She was seeing it as it had once been. Massive, grand, and absolutely spectacular.

"Wow. This is incredible. Whose temple is this?"

"Athena's."

The whites around her mesmerizing dark irises grew even wider.

Damon chuckled and pulled her deeper into the temple with him. "Don't worry. She's not here, nor is anyone else. After Zeus trapped the monsters of the world on Pandora, this temple fell into ruin. It hasn't been used in hundreds of years."

Steps led down into what had once been a large central pool in the middle of the temple. Now only twigs and leaves and broken marble were scattered across the bottom, but as Elysia studied it, Damon knew she was seeing it filled with water, illuminated by carefully positioned holes in the ceiling high above to let in light. To the right and left, chipped benches offered seating. Past the pool, an altar made of marble was perched on a dais, and beyond that, an enormous statue of Athena overlooked everything.

"It's amazing." Elysia let go of his hand and turned in a slow circle. "Can you imagine what it was like in its day?"

Damon glanced around. He didn't see amazing. He saw an ostentatious place where the gods lounged like fat kings and mortals worked their fingers to the bone, rushing around serving the gods like royalty. Exactly as they did on Olympus. "Probably pretty boring. Athena is still known as the virgin goddess. Ironic that she makes her Sirens peddle sex when she's such a prude."

Elysia smiled and stepped toward the altar. Moving up the three stone steps, she ran her hand over the flat marble. "Still smooth."

Damon's stomach tightened, anticipating those delicate fingers sliding along his skin. Soon…

Tucking his hands into his pockets so he wouldn't reach for her yet, he moved up two steps toward the end of the altar. "This temple does have a dark history, though."

"Oh, really?"

"You've heard of Medusa, right?"

"The gorgon?"

He nodded. "She was once a priestess in this temple. Gorgeous, they say, and totally devoted to Athena. But Poseidon had a thing for her. And he followed her here. When he found her alone, he took her, right here on this altar."

Elysia's gaze dropped to the marble beneath her hand. "Right here?"

He nodded again, and a heavy tingle zipped through his groin. "Right there. When Athena found out what Medusa had done, she turned her beautiful hair into snakes and her lower body—that which had tempted Poseidon so—into a snake."

"I remember this story. But the way I heard it, Poseidon raped Medusa."

"Why would Athena punish her for that? Rape isn't the female's fault. Medusa was a victim. No, Athena turned Medusa into a gorgon because there's power in sex, especially when it's performed in a sacred place. And she punished Medusa because when Medusa claimed that power here, in the virgin goddess's own temple, Medusa broke free of Athena's hold."

Elysia looked back down at the altar, and as color rose in her cheeks, Damon knew exactly what she was imagining. The same hot and wicked thing he was imagining. "Power, huh?"

"Incredible power."

She bit her lip. "Does Athena know we're here?"

"Doesn't have a clue. She only monitors this island during the survival phase of recruitment."

Elysia hesitated for only a second, then walked her hands down the edge of the altar, shifted to her side when she reached the end, and moved between it and Damon. "In that case…" The instant her hands made contact with the hard wall of his chest, electricity fanned out beneath her touch, making his muscles quiver and ache for more. "I might be up for a little power grab."

He was still one step lower than her. Leaning to the side, he skimmed his fingers up the back side of her thigh. "You might be, huh?"

"Mm-hm." Her fingers tiptoed to his shoulders, and she eased closer. "What did you have in mind, *ómorfos*?"

Gods, he loved it when she called him that.

"Just this." He tipped his head and leaned around her, brushing his lips softly against the side of her neck. His hand moved higher, tracing the back of her thigh and circling inward until his fingertips skimmed the bottom of her sweet little ass. "And this."

Elysia trembled, wrapped one arm around Damon's neck, and used her other hand on his jaw to tip his mouth toward hers. Their lips met, and her sweet scent surrounded him. And as he pushed her lips open with his tongue and drove into her mouth the way he wanted to drive into her body, all the frustration and waiting of the last two days exploded inside him in a burst of white-hot lust.

He moved up the last step, fisted the back of her skirt, and pulled it higher. Wrapping his other arm around her waist, he hoisted her up onto the altar, and pushed between her legs.

Her hands landed on his shoulders, but instead of pulling him in, she drew back from his mouth. "Athena isn't going to show up here and turn me into a gorgon, is she?"

"We know where to hide on this island. We won't let her." Damon nipped at her swollen bottom lip. "And this isn't about her. It's about you. And me. And this."

He claimed her mouth again and stroked his tongue back along hers, dragging her into a kiss that wasn't only filled with promise, it burst with passion and with trust and with every bit of hope she made him feel.

Tonight was about her. About making her feel special. He might not be able to give her back her family and her home, but he could show her how blessed he was to have found her.

And, maybe, just maybe, by showing her that here in this temple, she could steal a little of Athena's power for herself and find a way to pass that first Siren elimination.

CHAPTER THIRTEEN

Elysia was in heaven. The sweetest and most perfect heaven she could imagine.

She ran her fingers up to Damon's jaw and kissed him gently, softly, groaning against his tongue as it tangled with hers and she drew him into her body and heart and soul.

He moved closer, slid his hands over her shoulders and pushed the straps of her dress to fall around her biceps. Easing away from her mouth, he lowered his lips to her right shoulder and kissed a line of heat all the way to the base of her throat.

Elysia moaned and dropped her head back. Stars twinkled above, but she couldn't focus on any one. His wicked tongue circled the bones at the base of her throat, distracting her from the view. And when he licked his way up the other side of her throat and kissed his way out to her other shoulder, all she could focus on was him.

Electricity arced inside her. Grasping his face in her hands, she pulled his mouth back to hers and kissed him again, wanting to taste him deeply, wanting to feel him everywhere. His hands moved around to her back while he drove her wild with his mouth. He found the zipper of her dress and inched it down. Cool air washed over her spine and was quickly replaced with a wave of heat as his palm brushed the length of her back.

Her stomach tightened. Tingles rushed over her skin as his hands drifted back to the straps against her arms and he pushed the dress down her rib cage, freeing her breasts from the molded cups of her dress.

He drew back from her mouth. Groaned at the sight of her nipples pebbling in the cool night air. A shiver raced down her spine while he looked his fill. He'd seen her naked the other night in the hot springs, but he hadn't stared then as he was doing now. As if he couldn't get enough. As if he was memorizing every curve and plane. As if he was plotting his path to touch and taste and lick and suck.

"Damon." She fisted the center of his black T-shirt in one hand and pulled him toward her. "I want you."

His dark gaze lifted to hers. Hot. Focused. Filled with so much desire, her sex clenched in anticipation.

In one swift move, he reached back, pulled the T-shirt over his head, and tossed it on the ground. "I'm all yours, *emmoní*."

Laughing, she closed a hand around the edge of the rose tattoo on his right biceps and pulled him into her. And when his lips found hers and his tongue immediately drove into her mouth, the laughter turned to a moan of approval.

She wrapped her legs around his waist and rocked against the length of his erection. Dragging his lips from hers, he pressed hot wet kisses against the corner of her mouth, across her jaw and down her throat. He cupped her breast in his hand, squeezed as he worked his lips down her collarbone. Leaning her head back, Elysia clutched his strong arms and moaned. He lifted her breast and lowered his head, taking the tip into his mouth to lick and lave and suckle, and the pleasure was too good to fight. She let go of his arms, braced her hands on the altar behind her and arched her back, giving him more, giving him whatever he wanted, giving him everything.

His erection pushed against the heat between her legs every time he shifted, making her moan, making her body tremble. He circled her nipple, scraped his teeth along the tip until she quivered, palmed the other breast, and did the same.

"Lie back," he whispered.

Elysia lowered herself to the altar. Cool stones pressed against her spine. Damon's hands landed on her hips, and, gently, he scooted her back, his hot breath washing over her breasts, her abdomen, and finally her thighs. Lifting one foot, he tugged off her shoe, did the same to the other, and set her feet on the edge of the altar. And when he had her positioned the way he wanted, he lifted his gaze to hers, smiled a possessively devilish grin, and slowly pushed her skirt up until it pooled around her hips.

His gaze drifted down, and then it was his turn to groan long and deep. "Oh, *emmoni.*"

She shivered at what she knew he was seeing. She'd bypassed panties tonight as well, hoping she wouldn't need them, and now she was glad she had.

His hands landed against her inner thighs, pushing her legs wide. Tingles ran over her skin where he touched, and when his hot breath fanned the sensitive flesh between her legs, she trembled.

"You are the most beautiful thing I've ever seen." He pressed his lips against her hipbone, moved to the apex of her sex. Holding her breath, she watched as he lowered his head and trailed his tongue down her center and back up again.

"Oh, Damon…" Her eyes drifted closed. She dropped her head back and moaned. Pleasure arced outward from her sex as his tongue found her clit and circled. Lifting her hips, she helped him find a rhythm. Groaned when he drew the hard bud into his mouth and suckled. Shuddered each time he released her to trace his tongue down to her opening and back up again.

Yes, this was heaven. The only kind of heaven she wanted. He skimmed one hand up and over the skirt at her waist to cup her breast. The other slid down her inner thigh, across her sex. One thick finger pressed deep inside her as he continued to torment her with his tongue.

Electrical energy gathered in her core. She grasped the silky locks of his hair while she rocked against his mouth. Heat raced down her spine. Tingles radiated outward from her sex. Shifting against the altar, she rose to meet his mouth, lowered, arched her back, trembled because the pleasure was so damn good.

He licked faster, drove deeper with his finger. Drew her clit between his lips and suckled. And when the orgasm hit, it was like a bolt of lightning crashing into her. White light exploded behind her eyelids, causing her to arch her back and scream his name.

Slowly, she became aware of Damon's lips caressing the inside of her thigh, moving up to the sensitive line of her hip, then across her lower abs. And she felt the rain. Soft droplets striking her nose, her breast, her leg, her foot.

Blinking several times, she opened her eyes and lifted her head to look down at him. His hair was damp from the rain, but he didn't seem to mind. A victorious grin curled his wicked lips. "Feel powerful yet, *oraios*?"

Yes, she did. But not powerful enough.

Pushing up on her hands, she grasped him at the shoulders and pulled his mouth back to hers. Rain pelted their cheeks, their noses, ran down to slide over their fused lips. His tongue darted into her mouth, and he groaned. She tasted him mixed with her desire, but it wasn't enough. She wanted more. She needed everything.

She pressed him back, climbed off the altar, grasped him at the shoulders, and turned him so his back was against the cool, hard stones. Her hands swept down to the waistband at his hips, and she popped the button free while she kissed him again. His fingers threaded into her damp hair as he leaned into her, devouring her mouth while she ripped his pants open and shoved her hands inside to grasp his firm, toned ass.

"Elysia," he whispered against her lips. "My Elysia."

She shivered because he wasn't wearing underwear either. Tearing her mouth from his, she shoved his pants all the way to the ground and dropped to her knees. "I need to taste you. Now."

He groaned at the words. His cock sprang up, hard and hot and pulsing. While he kicked off his boot, she clasped her hand around the steely length and drew it toward her lips.

"*Skata*, Elysia." He kicked off the other boot and pushed his pants the rest of the way down his leg. "Let me get these o—" Her mouth closed around the tip. "Oh holy gods."

He fell back against the altar as she took him all the way into her mouth. The head of his cock brushed the back of her throat. Releasing him, she ran the flat of her tongue along the underside of the head, then sucked him deep all over again.

"Fuck, *emmoní*, that feels so damn good." His fingers slid into her hair, and he gripped the back of her head, pushing forward with his hips so his cock breached the opening of her throat. Relaxing her gag reflex, she sucked him deeper, loving the way he moaned and rocked and trembled against her.

Her sex tingled. She dropped one hand between her legs and stroked her aching clit as she drew him deep, released, and did it again. Fire flared hot inside her. He swelled in the back of her throat. She stroked her fingers faster, but it wasn't enough. She wanted more. She *needed* everything.

Releasing him, she pushed to her feet and shimmied out of her dress. "Get up on the altar. I need you now."

"Yes, *emmoní.*" His voice was thick with lust and desire as he kicked his pants the rest of the way off and scrambled onto the hard stone. The rain fell faster. Somewhere above, thunder rumbled like an ominous warning.

Elysia climbed over him, braced her knees on each side of his hips, and leaned forward to kiss him. His mouth immediately opened, his hands slid into her hair, pulling her into him. Shifting her knees back, she found his cock with her hand and stroked him from root to tip until he groaned.

"*Skata,*" he whispered against her lips. "Take me. Use me. Fuck me, *emmoní.* Do everything you want to me. I'm yours. Only yours."

Elysia's heart raced beneath her breast. Eyes locked on his, she leaned back on her heels, positioned his cock between her legs, and drew the tip through her wetness. He shivered beneath her. When the tip ran over her clit, she joined him and groaned.

Power crackled in her veins. Damon's hands landed against her thighs, sending shards of heat all through her limbs. He flexed his hips as she stroked her sex along his cock. Lifted to give her more friction.

"That feels so fucking good," he groaned.

So did he. But it still wasn't enough.

"Watch," she whispered. "I want you to watch as I take you."

His gorgeous gaze drifted down her naked body, the lust in his eyes making her nipples harden and her stomach quiver. Watching him as he watched where their bodies touched, she drew the head of his cock to the opening of her sex and slowly pressed down.

A muscle in his temple pulsed, and his mouth fell open in a silent groan as she slowly took his thick, steely heat inside. She wanted to keep watching him, but the sensation was too delicious, the way he stretched her and filled her so completely too much to resist. Closing her eyes, she gave in to the desire and dropped all the way down, tightening her muscles around his rigid length until they both groaned.

"Oh fuck," he gasped.

Electricity sizzled inside Elysia. Pressing her palms against his pecs, she lifted until the tip slid almost all the way out, then dropped down, taking him deep in one quick thrust.

"Oh *fuuuuck*," he groaned.

The energy gathering inside snapped and popped. Elysia lifted again, lowered once more, squeezed his cock as she rode him. Every rock of her hips dragged the head of his cock along her sensitive walls, making her tremble. Her pulse raced. Perspiration formed along her forehead and spine to mix with the rain falling faster from above. She shifted until he hit that special place. Until every thrust was a repeat stab against her G-spot. Until everything else faded away and all she felt was him, this, them, exactly where they were joined.

Her head fell back, her eyes slid closed. She rode him harder, took him deeper…wanting, needing, craving, begging for something she couldn't name.

"Ah gods," he gasped beneath her as he drove up to meet her. His fingers tightened against her hips, lifting and lowering her in time to his thrusts. "Don't stop."

Thunder crashed above. The rain grew heavier, dragging Elysia's eyes open. She looked down at Damon and the rain pelting their bodies in large, fat droplets that slicked their skin and rolled down Elysia's cheeks. A heady rush of energy mixed with desire and heat rushed through her, making her fuck him with longer, deeper, tighter strokes. He gasped again, but she couldn't stop. She felt drugged with an erotic hunger she couldn't sate. One that took control of her body. Pushed her faster. Overwhelmed her with a power she'd never felt before.

"Elysia…" He groaned her name, thrust up harder to meet her downward strokes. Lightning flashed in a series of white bolts across the dark sky, illuminating the columns of the temple, the altar beneath them, Damon's tensed and gorgeous face dripping with water, and, finally, her wet hands braced against his hard, muscular chest. Pressing down one more time, she squeezed as hard as she could, and when her orgasm hit, it sent a blinding wave of heat and energy and light straight from her core that consumed everything in its path.

Even her.

* * *

Damon blinked up into the rain as Elysia lay limp against his chest. The drops slowed their relentless pounding and faded to nothing more than a light mist. Above, he watched the clouds roll and part until the twinkle of starlight once again filled the night sky above the temple.

Holy Hades. No, holy…fuck. *That* was not at all what he'd expected. *That* had not been normal. Considering whom he served, he'd done just about everything there was to do sexually, but he'd never done *that*. He'd never felt *that*. And the pressure suddenly condensing in his chest—a pressure so intense it stole his breath—wasn't helping him decipher what the hell had just happened. Neither was the strange voice in the back of his head whispering…*she's the one.*

He tried to breathe through it, told himself he was only reacting to what he'd seen. To the image of Elysia naked and riding him in the midst of a storm that seemed to come out of nowhere—lighting flashing behind her, rain pelting their bodies while her hair flew around her face in a wild, angry tangle. But it was the look in her eyes he couldn't forget. The way her dark irises had glazed over. As if she were in a trance. As if she were on fire. As if she were possessed. Only somewhere deep inside, he knew that look wasn't causing the pressure now in his chest. This pressure was from something else. Something bigger. Something he had no frame of reference to explain.

She's the one.

"Wow." Elysia shifted her head against his chest, sending her damp hair skipping over his bare skin. "*Wooooow.*"

The pressure turned to a full-on panic that snaked all through his ribs. He couldn't think. He couldn't breathe. He needed space. Needed to go.

His hands shook as he grasped her arms, rolled her off him, then scooted out from under her and slid off the table. His bare foot hit the edge of a step he'd forgotten was there, and he stumbled. His weight went out from under him, and before he could stop himself, he fell flat on his ass on the hard, cold floor.

"Damon?" Elysia gripped the edge of the altar and looked down at him. "Are you okay?"

He sucked in a deep breath as he met her gaze. And the moment he did, he had another flash of her climaxing in the middle of that rainstorm with the lightning and thunder around her. Of the way her orgasm had triggered his, and the rush of emotion that had sucked him under, chewed him up, and spit him back out.

His head grew light. Tearing his gaze from hers, he stumbled toward his clothes. "I'm…"

Holy fuck, he was *not* okay. He was wrecked. Seriously fucking wrecked. From *sex*.

Which made no freakin' sense, because he did not *get* wrecked from sex. He had more sex than most of the gods, and he never felt a damn thing besides a quick release. His fingers trembled as he pulled on his damp pants and tugged on his soaked shirt, then sat on the steps and fumbled with his boots.

He needed space. Needed to think. Needed—

"Damon?"

—her. He needed *her*.

Blinking several times, he looked up to see Elysia standing next to him in her dress, her hair still wild and tangled, her eyes now drawn and worried.

"Are you okay?" She knelt beside him and placed her palm over his forehead. "You look pale."

She's mine.

"You're not okay." Concern raced across Elysia's features as she rose. "What happened? Did I do something wrong?"

Nothing made sense. But as he pushed to his feet, one thing did.

Her. She made sense in a lifetime of confusion and disappointment and emptiness.

He closed his arms around her and pulled her into his chest, unable to find the words, still unsure what he was feeling. The pressure remained, as did the voice, but knowing he'd upset her added a new layer of anxiety he couldn't ignore.

"You're shaking," she whispered, her hands landing softly against his back. "Tell me what I did wrong."

A shriek sounded above the temple, and they both looked up as a winged creature with the torso and head of a golden-haired woman and the body of a giant bird soared through the opening in the ceiling and headed straight for them.

Damon's eyes widened on the harpy with razor-sheep teeth and claws that could tear a man to shreds, but his feet wouldn't move. Harpies couldn't enter sacred ground. They couldn't come into Athena's temple, even if that temple was in ruins.

"Damon! Get down!"

Elysia threw her weight into Damon and knocked him behind the altar. Damon tumbled to the ground on his back. The harpy screeched and soared back toward the hole in the ceiling. Outside, another shriek echoed. Followed by a third.

"There are more coming. Get *up*." Elysia pulled hard on Damon's arm, forcing him to his feet. Grasping his hand, she tugged her with him toward the corner of the temple, behind three broken columns set in a triangle they could use as a barricade.

Damon's head felt light. His brain fuzzy. He slid to the ground and leaned back against a column. "Harpies...can't enter here."

"Well, they just did." Elysia scanned the temple. "We need a weapon. Damon, where can I find a weapon in this temple?"

Elysia's words echoed around Damon, but he couldn't seem to filter out the background voice. The one that kept repeating... *She's the one. She's yours. She's everything...*

"Damon! Focus!"

Another harpy shrieked. Damon blinked several times, only to realize Elysia was holding him by the shirtfront with both hands. His gaze lifted to her frightened eyes. "W-what?"

"Weapons. This is Athena's temple. She's the goddess of war. Even if this place is ancient, there have to be weapons stored somewhere. Where would they be?"

A third harpy screamed somewhere inside the temple.

Weapons... Athena... Damon looked past Elysia toward the altar and the statue of Athena behind it.

"Damon." Elysia shook him.

"There are no weapons," he managed. "None except..."

Elysia turned toward the statue of Athena in her warrior armor, a sleeve of arrows strapped to her back, a real sword at her side in one hand and a bow in the other.

"*Skata.*" Elysia pushed to her feet. "I'll get them."

Damon's brain cued in to what she was planning, and fear wrapped an icy hand around his throat and squeezed. He grasped her forearm before she could get more than a step away. "No. You can't."

"One of us has to."

She jerked free of his hold and sprinted across the temple. A harpy screeched and dove toward her, but Elysia ducked behind a column before the monster could reach her.

Damon jerked to his knees. And something in the center of his chest condensed, finally kicking his ass into gear. "No. Godsdammit. Elysia!"

She darted behind the statue as the three harpies shrieked and circled inside the temple. Grasping the back of the statue, Elysia began to climb.

Damon's gaze darted to the floor, searching for something he could use to buy her more time. He spotted a broken piece of marble as large as his fist.

He slid across the floor, grasped it in his palm, and jumped to his feet. "Hey!"

The harpy closest to Elysia jerked her head his way. Damon yanked his arm back and chucked the stone at the beast as hard as he could.

The rock hit the monster in the side. It yelped and flapped its wings as it tumbled through the air toward the floor of the temple. At the last second, it regained its strength, screeched again, and darted toward Elysia.

Elysia reached the middle of the statue and pulled the sword from the statue's hand. "Damon!"

He raced toward her. She dropped the sword and darted around the other side of the sculpture. Damon caught the hilt of the blade in his hand just as another harpy spotted him and charged. Swinging out with the sword as the second harpy reached him, he hoped like hell there was still some sharpness to the blade. The blade made contact with the beast's wing. The harpy screamed. Feathers flew up into the air. Something whirred over Damon's head. The harpy Damon had just hit sailed through the temple and out through the opening in the ceiling, one wing barely flapping.

Another whir echoed above, followed by a screech that brought Damon around. He watched an arrow strike a harpy dead in the chest. It flapped once and dropped to the floor of the temple with a thunk.

Shocked, Damon swiveled and looked up at the statue of Athena where Elysia stood on the platform, the bow poised perfectly in her arms, an arrow at the ready, her gaze locked on the third and final monster circling the temple.

Its blood-red eyes locked on Elysia. On a long screech, the beast tucked its wings and dove straight for her. Damon's pulse raced, pushing his legs into gear. He darted toward the pedestal of the statue to help her, but she was fifteen feet above him. The harpy would reach her long before he could. It would—

Elysia followed the flight of the harpy with the tip of the arrow. And just as the monster spread its wings and screamed for the kill, Elysia released the arrow.

The arrow struck the beast right between the eyes. The monster never even saw it coming. It dropped to the ground without another sound.

Damon stared wide-eyed at the female—no, the warrior—who'd just saved both their asses.

A beaming smile broke across Elysia's lips as she climbed down Athena's statue and dropped to her bare feet. "Did you see that? Did you see what I just did?"

"How did you do that?" He hadn't taught her that. None of the Siren trainers had taught her that. Three days ago when he'd worked with her after hours, she'd barely been able to ricochet an arrow off the trunk of a tree. There was no way the female he'd tutored in that meadow late at night could ever have been able to nail a moving target between the eyes.

"I don't know," she said in an excited voice. "I just felt this calm come over me. I knew what I had to do, and I did it. Wow. Did you see me? I was *good*. Wasn't I good?" She looked down at the bow still in her hand as if she'd found a new pet.

But all Damon knew was that she could have been killed. Because of him. Because he'd brought her here. He'd put her in danger. He'd risked her life when he was supposed to be the one protecting her.

He dropped the sword, wrapped his arms around her, and pulled her hard against his chest. "This won't happen again."

"Which part?" she squeaked.

Realizing he was crushing her, he eased his hold, but he still didn't let go.

"The sex or the fighting?" she asked. "Because I rocked *both*." Her lips curled into a smile against his shoulder. "I should definitely come here again."

Fear whipped through Damon. Gripping her shoulders, he pushed her back. "No."

Her brow lifted. "No?"

He wasn't making sense, even to himself. He knew he was acting like a complete loon. But the only thing he could think about was the moment that harpy had been ready to kill her and how helpless he'd been to stand there and watch.

Grasping her hand, he pulled her toward the front of the temple. "We're leaving."

She jerked back on his grip, but he didn't release her. Not even when they hit the steps outside and he dragged her onto the hard, cold ground.

"Drop the bow."

Defiance flashed in Elysia's dark eyes. A rebellious confidence he hadn't seen from her before. She tucked the bow over her shoulder. "No."

"We're leaving this place, and you can't take it with you."

She pushed the bow to her back. "Oh, I'm keeping it."

Down the hillside, another scream echoed up from the trees, telling Damon they were out of time. "Fine. Give me your hands."

Her eyes narrowed, but she slid her palms along his. "What's going on, Damon? What happened to you in there?"

Damon didn't know. And he couldn't think when she was close like this. Couldn't focus when sparks of heat and electricity were skipping across his skin from just the simple contact. Especially when he knew she was at the root of everything.

He closed his fingers around hers and pictured the field outside the Siren compound.

"Talk to me," she said softly.

He wanted to, but he couldn't. Couldn't because they were already flashing back to Olympus. And because he still didn't know what the hell he was going to say to her when they arrived.

CHAPTER FOURTEEN

"Things are not going as planned," the king of the gods grumbled.

From her office window, Athena glared down at the training field, barely listening to Zeus at her back. She zeroed in on Elysia swinging a wooden sword she'd barely been able to hold days ago with the skill of Athena's best Sirens. Hooking her leg around the Amazon recruit she was sparring, the Argolean princess dropped the larger female to the ground. Before the Amazon could respond, the tip of Elysia's training sword poised for the kill at the Amazon's throat.

The Amazon had been the most promising of all the recruits in the training class so far, and Elysia—the brunette embarrassment to the class—had just bested her. In fact, she'd bested everyone since she'd come back from her night on Pandora four days before.

"Did you hear me?" Zeus asked with an irritated clip in his voice. "We have a problem. We need to do something drastic. And fast."

Fury burned deep in Athena's gut as she watched Elysia hold her hand out to the Amazon and help the other recruit to her feet. She could think of something drastic. A poisoned arrow straight to Elysia's heart would take care of their so-called problem.

"Athena," Zeus said louder.

"She needs to be punished. Serpents in her hair would be a good start."

"You're not turning her into a gorgon."

Athena turned fiery eyes toward her father. "She fucked Aphrodite's man whore in *my* temple. She stole some of my powers." Holding her hand toward the window, she added, "She's no mighty warrior. She's a conniving little bitch of a thief who needs to be destroyed."

Zeus pushed away from Athena's desk where he'd been leaning and loomed over his daughter. Soulless, empty, black eyes locked on hers. "You will not touch her. She is the key to our plan. Without her, everything we've worked for the last twenty-five years is ruined."

Right now, Athena didn't care about their little plan. All she cared about was revenge. "But—"

"But nothing." Zeus's voice boomed through her office on the top floor of Siren Headquarters. "You're not to go after her now. She will suffer in the end. When we have our prize, then you can relish in the knowledge that she played a part in destroying her world."

Athena ground her teeth. That wouldn't be enough. She wanted the bitch to suffer now, to know not only heartache but unending agony and pain. Athena wasn't stupid enough to cross the king of the gods to make that happen today, but after he had what he wanted… Then she'd find a way to turn that bitch into a gorgon.

"So what's the big problem?" Athena folded her arms over her chest. "They fucked. *In my temple.* You should be happy about that."

Zeus pinned her with an irritated look. "I don't give a rat's ass about your temple. Sex was supposed to bring them closer together. Instead, it's pushed them apart. He's avoiding her. He's skipped their last three seduction sessions."

Athena's jaw locked again, but she didn't respond to her father's snarky comment. She knew Damon was avoiding Elysia. She'd gotten a sharp little thrill over the fact Aphrodite's boy toy had rejected the bitch. She wanted him to go on rejecting her. "I don't see the problem. He can't avoid her forever. And if he tries, I can threaten him with the pit. He doesn't like that place."

"We don't have time for your stupid pit. This process is already taking too long as it is. Assign a new seduction trainer to her. Tonight. That should light a fire under his ass."

Athena's eyes widened, and she dropped her arms to her sides. "But that is not what we agreed to." And it wouldn't prolong the bitch's suffering *now*.

Zeus moved for the door. "Our agreement was just revised. Everything hinges on what he does next. And I'm tired of waiting." He pulled the door open and sent Athena one last scathing look. "Do it tonight, or I'll send my Sirenum Scorpoli to destroy all your temples, everywhere in the human realm. Then you won't have to worry about anyone fucking on your sacred ground."

The door slammed shut behind him, and Athena bit down hard as she curled her hands into fists at her sides. The Sirenum Scorpoli were the best of the Sirens, Zeus's secret band of warriors who carried out his most devious plans. They were also completely out of her control. Athena had no doubt Zeus would follow through with his threat and have them destroy her temples if she didn't comply with his orders. And if that happened, she wouldn't just lose a little power, she'd lose all the power she gained from the humans who still worshipped her around the world.

She couldn't afford for that to happen. Which meant she had to spur Damon into action. And that meant giving that bitch exactly what she wanted—the male she'd clearly fallen for.

Her jaw clenched harder, and as she turned her narrowed gaze back to the training field, she told herself to be patient. Zeus didn't want her to go after the bitch now, but he hadn't said a word about later. Once he had what he wanted, Athena would find a way to make Elysia pay.

A smile slinked across her face. She'd find a writhing, snapping, slithering way to make the little bitch pay.

Damon paced up and back on the gravel path in the dark outside the Hall of Seduction.

Swiping a hand across his jaw, he told himself to stop dicking around and go in there, but he couldn't seem to make his feet listen to his brain.

He hadn't seen Elysia in four days. He'd skipped their sessions in the evening and avoided her in the training field during the day, arriving late and leaving early so she couldn't intercept him, choosing to work with recruits as far from her on the field as possible, even going so far as to avoid any kind of eye contact.

He knew he was being a dick. He knew she had to be pissed. Knew he owed her an explanation, but he still had no idea what to tell her. That pressure in his chest hadn't let up since they'd been back at the Siren compound. It had only gotten worse. And on top of that, the damn voice whispering, "She's yours," was only getting more demanding, pushing him to the point of wanting to scream.

The door to the hall opened, and a flood of light spilled into the darkness, illuminating the white rocks on the path in front of Damon. He stopped, hoping whoever it was would just pass him by. Feminine laughter met his ears, followed by a deep male voice.

Erebus. Damon turned the other direction, intent on rounding the corner of the building so they didn't spot him.

"Damon!"

Shit. Too late.

Damon turned and lifted his hand in a halfhearted wave. "Hey."

The door to the hall snapped closed, and gravel crunched as Erebus pulled the female with him to a stop. "What are you doing here?" Erebus asked.

Rays of moonlight illuminated the path, Erebus's dark skin, and the recruit's blonde hair.

"Just heading in," Damon lied. "I got hung up with some paperwork."

Sera and Erebus exchanged worried glances, and foreboding rushed down Damon's spine.

"Why?" Damon looked between the two. "Where are you headed?"

"For a walk." Erebus's eyes narrowed. "Who are you working with tonight?"

"Elysia. Hopefully she didn't fall asleep waiting for me." He forced a smile he didn't feel. Knew it fell flat when Erebus and Sera exchanged nervous looks once more.

Damon's stomach tightened. "Okay, you two. What's going on?"

Sera pulled her gaze from Erebus's and met Damon's. "Elysia was assigned to a different seduction trainer. I thought you knew that."

"She was *what?*" Panic ignited in the center of Damon's chest.

Worry wrinkled Sera's brow. "She told me earlier today that you hadn't shown up the last few nights. I guess Athena got tired of waiting for you and—"

Damon pushed past both of them and bolted for the door to the hall. At Damon's back, Erebus muttered, "What the hell was that about?" but Damon didn't stick around to hear Sera's response.

She's mine...

He sprinted down the hall to the room he and Elysia had been assigned and yanked the door open. Candlelight flickered over the walls, and the scent of some kind of musky flower filled the air. Fabric rustled, followed by Elysia's startled voice, gasping, "Damon."

Several things registered at once: the half-empty wineglasses on the nightstand, a fire crackling in the stone hearth, the dark-haired male leaning over Elysia where she sat on the edge of the bed, and her dress—not the sweet sundress style she'd been wearing the last few times he'd seen her, but something low cut, tight, and revealing. Revealing her body not to him but to another male, one Damon recognized as a trainer.

A roar grew in Damon's head. A roar that drowned out everything else. A roar that colored his vision red.

"Damon?" Silky brown tendrils fell over Elysia's shoulder as she pushed to her feet—her stiletto-clad, wobbly feet. But this time when she said his name, it didn't sound shocked. It sounded a little bit scared.

Petros, a mortal who answered to Apollo, the god of war, when he wasn't working with the Siren recruits, rose beside her. "Dude. This isn't your room anym—"

Damon lunged and shoved his fist into Petros's jaw. Petros sailed back and hit the wall. Elysia yelped.

Petros stumbled to his feet and rubbed his jaw. "What the hell, Damon?"

Damon barely heard him. Grasping the male by the shirtfront, he shoved him up against the wall and growled, "She's mine. If you touch her again, you're fucking dead. Do you hear me?"

"Damon!" Elysia screamed.

Petros's green eyes grew wide with their own fury. "What the fuck is wrong with you?"

"You're what's wrong with me, asshole," Damon growled.

"Damon!" Elysia grabbed at his arm and pulled hard, jerking him back a step. "Let go of him."

Damon released Petros's shirt. Breathing heavily, Petros swiped at his bloody lip with the back of his hand. "Holy hell, man.

She's just a recruit. You're losing your shit over a fucking recruit who means nothing."

The roar sounded again. And Damon lurched toward Petros, but Elysia darted in front of him and pushed her hands against Damon's chest, holding him back.

"Go," she yelled at Petros. "Get out of here."

Petros lifted his chest. "I can kick his ass."

The roar sounded louder, and Damon's muscles flexed.

"No." Elysia pushed harder, keeping Damon back from the knock-down, drag-out fight he craved.

Petros glanced once at her and then at Damon. "I don't need this shit." Sidestepping his way to the door, he shook his head. "You're going down for this, buddy."

"Go," Elysia yelled over her shoulder, her hands still pressed hard against Damon's chest. "Get out of here."

"Fucking lost it," Petros muttered, exiting the room.

The door snapped closed, but the red haze lingered, only dulling at the edges as Elysia dropped her hands and stared at him with both horror and shock in her pretty chocolate eyes.

"What in Hades was that?" she snapped. "You had no reason to go after him like that."

No reason? *No reason?*

The red haze sharpened, and this time when the familiar voice he'd been hearing in his head all week whispered, *"She's yours,"* Damon didn't ignore it.

Fuck no reason.

He flipped the table upside down. Glass shattered. Wine splashed across the floor. Elysia gasped, but that didn't stop him. Grasping her hand, he shoved the door open and jerked her out of the room.

"Damon." She fumbled in her heels, trying to keep up. "What are you doing? Where are we going?"

He hit the door at the end of the hall with his shoulder. Cool night air washed around him as he yanked her outside into the dark. She yelped and stumbled. Before she could hit the ground, he swept her up in his arms and tossed her over his shoulder.

"Put me down." Her fist landed hard against his spine as he crossed the grass and moved farther away from the buildings. "Godsdammit. Put me down right this second."

Damon increased his pace. She wiggled against him. Hit his back again—several times—but he only tightened his hold on her legs and kept walking.

"Damon, dammit. I said put me down!"

He yanked the ridiculous heels from her feet and threw them into the shrubs. She yelped and pushed up, trying to wriggle her way out of his arms. He didn't let go of her until he reached the middle of the meadow.

"What the hell is wrong with you?" she yelled in the moonlight as he dropped her on her bare feet. "You can't just waltz into a room and—"

The roar sounded again. But before it could drag him under, Damon grasped both of her hands in his and pictured the beach.

CHAPTER FIFTEEN

The ground disappeared. Elysia's shriek sounded in Damon's ears, but in the burst of light as the portal opened, he couldn't see her. Wind rustled his hair as they flashed, stilling only when sand formed beneath his feet.

"Oh my gods." Elysia immediately jerked her hands free of his. "You flashed us *back* to Pandora. Are you mad? It's the middle of the damn night!"

The cap on his temper finally blew sky high, but he remembered the monsters on the island and kept his voice to a harsh whisper. "You're fucking right I'm mad. I'm gone for a couple of days and you fall into bed with the first asshole who looks your way?"

"I didn't fall into bed with anyone," she hissed.

"You were on the fucking bed with Petros."

"I was *sitting* on the bed. Not fucking on the bed. And what do you care anyway? You clearly don't. You couldn't even be bothered to show up for our sessions. I've seen you in the training field during the day. I know you haven't been out on some mission for Athena. If something had come up, you could have gotten word to me. But no, instead you made me wait in that room alone for you, night after miserable night."

His eyes widened as he looked down at her slinky black dress. "So you decided to get dressed up like a whore and screw the first guy who came along?"

The flat of her hand connected hard with the side of his face, cracking his head to the side. "Fuck you, Damon."

She turned on her heel and made it five steps down the beach before he grasped her upper arm and yanked her back to face him. "Fuck me? I don't think so. You're the one who clearly wants to get fucked."

Her eyes narrowed to hard, sharp points. "Don't."

"Why not?" Something in the back of his head said not to push this, but he couldn't stop. He dropped her hand, but instead of moving back, he stepped forward, closing the distance between them. "You did your hair and makeup. You slipped into this slutty little dress. You're wearing those fuck-me heels. Obviously, you were hoping to get a little tonight."

She moved back a step. "I thought you sent this outfit."

He moved toward her again. "You obviously realized it wasn't me when you got to that room. I saw the wine. And the fire. Did that guy turn you on, *oraios*? Did he do it for you?"

"No." Her dark eyes glistened in the moonlight. "I wasn't interested in him."

"I think you're lying." He moved closer still. "I think that's all you want. Just a warm body to fuck."

She stopped moving and stared at him with hurt eyes. And the minute the words were out of his mouth, the pressure re-formed in his chest, telling him he'd gone too far.

Regret immediately swamped him, and he softened his voice. "*Emmoní...*"

Tears filled her eyes. He reached for her, cursing the fact he'd let his emotions get away from him—something he'd never ever done before. Her fingertips landed on his biceps, but instead of letting him pull her in, she hooked her leg around the back of his knee and jerked. Air whooshed over his spine before he realized what was happening. His back hit the sand with a crack.

She planted her hands on her slim hips and glared down at him. "The only person I wanted to fuck was *you*, you son of a bitch. But not anymore. I don't have any desire to be with someone who doesn't really want me."

She swiveled in the sand and made it one step before his brain kicked into gear.

She's mine...

He captured her ankle and pulled. She hit the sand with a grunt. Flipping her to her back, he climbed over her, braced both knees against her hips, and pinned her hands near her head. "I do want you, *emmoní*. You're all I want. You're all I can think about, and it's making me fucking crazy."

She struggled against his grip. "You've got a really twisted way of showing it."

He did. She was right. And he knew only one way to make her believe it was true.

He lowered his mouth to hers. She grunted and struggled harder against his hands. Forcing her lips apart with his tongue, he dove in and kissed her deeply.

Pain spiraled across his tongue, and he jerked back when he realized she'd bitten him.

"Don't kiss me," she growled.

Fire flared in her eyes. Fire and heat and passion. The same passion he'd seen the other night in Athena's temple. But now it was fueled by anger and what she perceived as rejection.

"You like it when I kiss you."

"No, I don't." She struggled again, tossing her head on the sand so her hair flew all around her. "Let me go."

He couldn't. At this point, he knew he could never let her go.

His hands continued to pin her wrists to the sand, but he scooted back with his knees and lowered his face to the curve of her neck, breathing hot all over her silky flesh. "You love it when I kiss you here."

He pressed his lips against the base of her throat. She swallowed hard and pulled at his grip once more, but the fight was already fading. "I hate it when you kiss me there."

He smiled against her skin and trailed a hot, wet line of kisses to the other side. "I bet you hate it here as well, then."

She bit back a moan, but he felt it rumble deep in her chest. His blood warmed. His cock came to life, thickening in his pants. He shifted lower, dragging his lips down the exposed V of her dress and across the top of her cleavage.

The tip of his tongue traced the line between her succulent breasts. "And here."

"Don't do that," she whispered, rocking her hips from side to side between his knees.

"Why not?" He licked at the spot again.

"Because you're an ass."

He lifted his head and met her gaze. Her gorgeous, mesmerizing gaze. "I am an ass. But I'm *your* ass. And you belong with me. Not with Petros. Not with anyone else. Just with me."

Her eyes narrowed. "And you thought attacking him would prove that to me?"

He shifted her hands together, pinned them with one of his, then reached down to grasp her dress at the V. "No, I think this will."

He yanked hard. Fabric ripped all the way to the hem, revealing her sexy black lace bra and matching low-rise panties.

Elysia gasped and lifted her head. "You prick."

He smiled, because there was no venom in her words. Only heat. A heat he recognized was about to flare out of control.

He lowered his mouth to hers, and this time when their lips touched, she opened and drew him in, licking and tasting with the same force and fury consuming every inch of him.

He shoved the tattered sides of her dress open, flicked the clasp on her bra, and freed her gorgeous breasts. Soft flesh filled his palm. He pulled away from her mouth and lowered to her nipple, taking the pink tip between his lips and sucking until she moaned. She wiggled against the grip he still held on her wrists, but he didn't let go. Moving to the other breast, he licked the tip, then took the whole areola into his mouth and suckled.

"Damon…" Her breaths grew shallow. Fast. "Let my hands go. Right now."

He released his grip on her wrists but didn't lift his head. Pressing kisses all along her toned belly, he shifted lower, trailing his tongue down to the edge of her lacy black panties.

She moaned. Dropped her head back in the sand. He grasped the lace between his teeth and pulled.

Elysia's fingers threaded into his hair. She lifted her hips as he tugged the lace down. When he reached the top of her thighs, he let go with his teeth and yanked her panties the rest of the way with his hand.

"Open your legs, *emmoní*."

She dropped her knees open, and he drew in the heady scent of her arousal. Moving between her legs, he groaned as he looked down at her swollen flesh. His gaze lifted, skimming her gorgeously naked body up to her beautiful face, illuminated in ribbons of moonlight.

She's mine. Only mine. Always...

Emotions closed his throat. Made his cock swell so hard. Parting her sex with his fingers, he lowered his head and licked. She moaned. Lifted her hips. The sound turned his blood to fire. He dragged the flat of his tongue down to her opening, pressed in, out, in again. Fucking her with his tongue the way he wanted to fuck her with his cock. She groaned again and let go of his hair, dropping her hands to the sand as she lifted her hips higher and rocked against his face. Trailing his tongue back up her silky center, Damon found her clit and flicked it back and forth before finally drawing it between his lips and suckling.

"Oh my gods." Elysia tossed her head from side to side on the sand and pressed against his mouth. "Oh gods, yes..."

Her orgasm was rising. But he didn't want her to go over without him. Pulling his mouth from her dripping sex, he pushed to his knees and grasped her hips to flip her over.

She grunted and caught herself on her hands and knees. Jerking the ruined dress free, he threw it into the darkness, then grabbed her hips again and pulled her back into his groin. She groaned and rocked her ass back into him. With one hand, he trailed his fingers through her dripping arousal. With the other, he yanked his pants open and freed his aching cock.

"Damon..."

He fisted his cock and pressed forward, sliding the tip through her silky wetness. "Is this where you want me to fuck you? Right here?" He drew back. Stroked himself and brushed the head over her clit until she shivered. "Say yes. Say yes, and I'll give you what you want."

She moaned and pushed back. The head passed over her opening, and a tremor racked her luscious body. He pressed inside, just until it stretched her, then pulled back again.

She dropped her forehead and groaned.

"Say it. Tell me to fuck you, and I'll give you what you want."

"Oh my gods..." She gasped and lifted her head, arching her back ever so slightly in the process, revealing more of herself to him. "What are you doing?"

He did it again, stroking himself there until she trembled. "Tormenting you. And me."

She dropped her head once more and groaned, her breaths shallow and fast as he slid a fraction of an inch in and back out again, then down to circle her sensitive spot. "Tell me to fuck you, and I will. Tell me you want me. Tell me, and I'll give you everything. All of me."

"Oh gods..." Her body quaked. "Yes. Yes. Give it to me. Fuck me, Damon. Fuck me so hard..."

Oh yessss... Shifting his hips forward, he slammed inside her in one deep thrust.

She cried out when he hit bottom, groaned as he slid back and almost free, then shoved deep once more. A shudder rushed down his spine, and he did it again, her slick channel gripping him so tightly, closing like a hot velvet fist around his slippery cock every time he thrust in, out, in, out...

"Damon..." She spread her legs wider. Dropped to her forearms on the sand, arching her back so he could drive in one more reaching inch. His hand slid down between her legs to find her clit, and he flicked in time to his thrusts, wanting to feel her climax around his cock, wanting her to send him over the edge into sheer, mindless oblivion with her.

Sweat beaded his forehead. Tingles rushed down his spine. He needed to get her off before he lost it. Needed to take her with him. Bracing one hand on the sand near her head, he leaned over her sexy spine. Plunging deep with long, hard, slow strokes, he struck her G-spot again and again. She squeezed tight around him, sending electrical charges all through his body. His balls drew up tight. His cock pulsed and twitched inside her. At her ear, he whispered, "Elysia. My Elysia. Only mine. Say you're only mine."

"Oh..." She pushed back against him. Curled her hands into fists in the sand.

"Say you're mine." He flicked faster with his finger. Her pussy grew wetter, tighter, slicker, hotter...

He drove deeper and pinched her clit hard, and when she rocked into him, when she dropped her head back against his shoulder and groaned at the mix of pleasure and pain, he knew she was his. "I'm yours. I'm yours, Damon. Oh gods... I'm yours. Don't stop... Don't ever stop..."

"Yes, *emmoni.* That's what I want. Come for me." Damon grunted as he thrust into her and let go. The orgasm raced down his spine, exploding through his balls. The moment his cock swelled and his seed erupted inside her, she shattered, contracting around him in a release that sent him spinning through a sea of erotic pleasure that sucked him under and seemed to have no end.

Long minutes later—or maybe it was hours, he had no sense of time—Damon blinked and realized he was lying against Elysia's back, pressing her into the sand. Groaning, he pulled free of her sensual body and flopped onto his back as the last dregs of the most incredible orgasm he'd ever felt flittered through his veins.

Elysia grunted beside him and rolled to her back. Waves lapped against the sand near their feet, and high above, some kind of bird cawed.

"You decimated my dress."

Damon dragged his eyes open and stared up at the twinkling stars, still trying to catch his breath. "I hated that dress."

She shifted her head on the sand and looked up at him. "I thought you sent that dress. I wouldn't have worn it if I'd thought it had come from anyone else."

He looked over her beautiful face. Shards of moonlight highlighted the gentle slope of her nose, her high cheekbones and plump lips. And as he stared at her, everything that had just happened—that he'd done—came back in a rush of memories.

"*Skata.*" He covered his face with his arm in abject mortification. "I'm a complete dick."

She laughed and rolled toward him, plastering her naked body to his side in the sand. "Maybe not a complete dick. But close. Good thing I like your dick. Oh my gods, that was good."

He lowered his arm and looked at her, amazed she could laugh and flirt and be so happy after the things he'd done. "I'm sorry. I'm sorry I assumed the worst. I'm sorry for what I did to you in the sand. I'm—"

"Look at me." She climbed over him and braced her hands on each side of his face. "I'm not sorry. I've spent the last four days thinking you didn't want me anymore. This, us, here like this… This just proved you do want me."

His heart squeezed tight. "I always want you. That's the problem. I can't stop wanting you."

Her sweet little brow wrinkled. "Then I fail to see the problem."

He sighed. "It's a problem because I don't understand it. Because it's never been like this for me. Because…" He searched for words but came up empty. "Because I can't control it."

"Neither can I," she whispered. "But I don't consider that a bad thing, Damon. Right now, after what you just did to me, I consider that good. Very, very good."

Emotions closed his throat, and he wrapped his arms around her slim waist, pulling her down to his mouth for a kiss that started with their lips and traveled through every cell in his body.

His cock thickened against her thigh. He wanted her again, but he didn't want her to think this was just about sex. Because it wasn't. What she did to him, the way she overwhelmed him, the things she made him feel, it was way more than sex. It was deeper. Stronger. A connection that was only intensifying with every passing hour.

Breathless, she rested her forehead against his and just held him. "Don't pull away from me, Damon."

"I won't." He trailed his fingers up the pearls of her spine. "I won't again, I promise. Unless you wear that dress. I lost it when I saw you in that thing."

She chuckled. "I think you're safe there. You shredded it. My only choice now is to walk around naked."

No way anyone else was seeing what belonged to him. "You can wear my shirt."

She smiled. "Staking your claim?"

He closed his eyes and drew in a deep whiff of her honeysuckle scent. "Absolutely."

They held each other long moments in the sand. Finally, she said, "You know...we might want to think about getting up. You flashed us to Pandora. It's night. Anything could come along and spot us."

Any kinds of monsters, she meant.

Reluctantly, Damon let go so she could climb off him. Pulling off his T-shirt, he handed it to her, then tugged up his pants and buttoned them.

She pushed to her feet and fluffed her hair out of the collar of his T-shirt. The black cotton fell to her thighs, looking more like a dress on her than a shirt. "It's getting late. We really should start getting back."

Damon dusted sand off his legs as he rose. "We're not going back to Olympus."

"What?"

He reached for her hand. "They're trying to take you away from me. I can't let that happen. You're mine. No other trainer is touching you."

She frowned up at him in the moonlight. "And you didn't think to discuss this with me first?"

"There's nothing to discuss."

She tipped her head and lifted her brow.

Something in his chest pinched, almost a stab of pain telling him he'd fucked up…again. Which he *totally* didn't understand. "Fine. Yes, I should have discussed it with you. But we can't go back now. Petros has probably already told Athena what I did. She's looking for an excuse to separate us. You heard him say I was going down. I'd rather live one day on the run with you than a lifetime without you. You're *mine*."

He was being a total barbarian and completely possessive, but he didn't care. She was his, and he'd do anything to keep her with him. *Anything.*

Her eyes softened. "You are entirely sweet and adorable when you're in domineering warrior mode, but there are limits. Next time, talk to me before you go all nutty on me."

He breathed easier. "Yes, *emmoní*."

Sighing, she crossed her arms over her chest and glanced around the dark beach. "So what's your plan? To stay here? We're less safe here than we were on Olympus. There are a thousand different predators on this island."

He pulled her toward him and slid his hand down her slim back. "I've seen you with a bow and arrow. I think we're pretty safe. Plus, I'm not bad with a sword."

She snorted and rested her hands on his biceps. "Did you happen to bring any of those weapons? Because I didn't."

"We'll come up with something. There are a lot of ruins on this island. More than just Athena's temple."

She leaned into him, resting her head against his chest in a way that didn't just warm his heart, it filled his soul with light. "It's too bad you can't open a portal anywhere else besides Olympus."

Yeah, no shit. That would make their lives way too easy.

"Oh my gods, I can." She pushed out of his arms and looked up with wide eyes.

"You can what?"

"I can open a portal."

"You can? To where?"

"To Ar—I mean, the human realm."

His gaze narrowed. "How?"

"On sacred ground. Everyone from my race can open a portal from sacred ground. And lucky us, we have that right here on this island."

At Athena's temple. "If it's that easy, why didn't you open a portal so we could escape those harpies the other night?"

"Because I just remembered it now. Blame the Sirens for wiping my memories." She gripped his forearms. "Damon, we can really be free."

Escape… From Olympus, from the gods, from Zeus and Athena and Aphrodite and everyone who used him for their own gain.

Hope pulsed inside Damon. A hope he'd never let himself dream of before. A hope he felt thanks to the female beside him.

Warmth filled his chest as he looked down at her in the moonlight. So much warmth and heat and life, whatever pressure he'd felt before disappeared and was replaced with nothing but joy.

Twigs snapped in the forest to his right, and his adrenaline shot up as he looked in that direction. He squeezed Elysia's hand. "Only if we make it to Athena's temple unseen."

"We'll make it," she whispered, stepping back on the sand and pulling him with her. "You'll see. We'll make it together."

Freedom sounded pretty damn good to him. He just prayed they stayed free wherever they went from here.

Demetrius couldn't sleep.

Standing at the balcony railing of the suite he shared with Isadora in the Argolean castle, he gazed out at the moonlight sparkling over the surface of the Olympic Ocean like sunlight on newly fallen snow. He rubbed the heel of his hand over his heart, but it did no good. The ever-present ache he'd lived with since he'd heard the news his daughter had been taken by Sirens didn't ease. In fact, as he stood there wondering where she was this very night, it intensified, spreading through his chest to rouse the darkness he'd worked so hard to bury over the years.

The darkness rolled and gathered strength, urging him to forget the bonds of brotherhood he'd forged with the Argonauts, to ignore the fate of the land his mate ruled, to release the shadows inside him and go after that which rightly belonged to him. His fingers curled around the balustrade. His pulse pumped hard and fast. But he fought the darkness back for one simple reason.

Elysia had made the choice he couldn't. Demetrius had been livid when he'd heard what Max had done, but knowing Elysia was unharmed—and that she'd chosen to stay with the Sirens to keep their realm safe—had gotten through to him when nothing else could.

He drew in a shaky breath. Released his fingers from the cold stone. Reminded himself he needed to stay strong for his mate. That he had to keep it together at least until Elysia was allowed to cross into the human realm. It might take three years, but then he could rescue her. Then he could hide her away and protect her. Then he would make sure no one could ever touch her again.

"Demetrius?"

He turned at the sound of Isadora's voice. Her cotton nightgown swayed around her feet in the open doorway to their bedroom, and her blonde hair fell in messy waves past her shoulders. But it was her eyes he focused on. Her glazed coffee-colored eyes that told him something was wrong.

"*Kardia?*" He stepped toward her and reached for her hand. Her skin was cold and clammy, and her fingers shook as they slid over his. "What is it? What's happened?"

"She's in danger."

Demetrius's heart rate spiked. "Max said she was safe. That she was okay. He said—"

"It's not the Sirens that threaten her." Isadora looked up at her mate, and horror reflected in her eyes. "It's not the gods either. It's someone else. Someone she trusts."

"What did you see?"

Isadora had the gift of foresight, but her visions were muddied when they involved those she loved. Since Elysia's abduction, the most Isadora had seen were hazy images…a training field, a bow and arrow, a candle burning in the night.

She squeezed his hand. "I saw a great sword, blazing with the fire of a thousand suns in the darkness, and I saw our daughter unable to move as the flaming blade pierced her chest."

Every muscle in Demetrius's body contracted, and his blood turned to ice.

"I saw our daughter fall to her knees as the sword was pulled free, and a mighty hand reach deep into the cavern of her chest to pull out her still-beating heart. And I saw agony and heartbreak brimming in her eyes as she looked up and watched the hand curl around her heart, crushing it to ashes in its palm."

Demetrius's own heart pumped hard and fast against his ribs, and a new sense of terror consumed him.

Tears filled Isadora's eyes. "We have to bring her home before it's too late."

That darkness sizzled and rolled inside Demetrius, and as he pulled his mate into his arms, he knew he wouldn't be able to hold it back much longer.

Because some things were more important than duty and honor and brotherhood. And knowing Elysia was in mortal danger changed everything.

Making it to Athena's temple in the dark without disturbing any kind of monsters had been tricky. Damon could flash from Olympus to Pandora but not from location to location on the island. Twice Elysia had stopped and pushed Damon back into the shadows because she'd spotted a manticore and a chimera. Luckily, neither had noticed them, and they'd been able to pick their way through the forest untouched and finally climb the hillside to the ruins.

Elysia's soles hurt from walking barefoot, and her skin was sweaty beneath Damon's baggy T-shirt, but there was no one else she'd rather be with. And she was already envisioning where she'd open the portal in the human realm.

Common sense told her the smartest move was to take him to Argolea, but she didn't want to do that. Not only because it wouldn't be any safer there for them—the Sirens could cross into both Argolea and the human realm and possibly come after them—but also because she wasn't ready to face her family. They'd tried to arrange a political binding for her. To a male she didn't love. Damon had spent his life as nothing but a slave. Regardless of who he was before his time with the Sirens, his social class now was far below hers. They'd never accept him. For all her parents talk about helping the common person in need, she knew that was all well and good unless it involved their daughter's future.

She closed her hand tighter around Damon's in the dark as he pulled her up the hillside, remembering the way he'd looked at her on the beach. As if he couldn't breathe without her. As if the thought of losing her had destroyed him. As if she were his everything.

She'd never been anyone's everything, had never wanted to belong to someone else or be in a relationship. But the connection she felt to him was getting stronger, and every moment they spent together only made her want to be his.

They finally reached the temple. The moon had set during their hike, and the sun would soon be rising. A monster screamed far down the hillside, but Elysia ignored it and followed Damon inside.

Heat rushed to her cheeks when she remembered what they'd done on the altar, and more than anything, she wanted a repeat of that moment right here, but she knew there would be plenty of time to explore his body somewhere safer.

"I thought you said the monsters on this island couldn't enter sacred ground," Elysia said as he drew her to the base of the broken steps, trying to take her mind off the images replaying in her brain—the moaning and rocking and mindless pleasure.

"They're not supposed to be able to."

"Then how were the harpies able to enter?"

"I have a theory on that. I think Athena sent them. I think she sensed what we did here and the power you took from her. I'm pretty sure she sent the harpies because she was pissed."

Skata. Then Elysia had gone back to the Siren compound and shown off her newfound skills. Perhaps leaving Olympus for good wasn't a bad idea after all.

Damon turned to face her and clasped her hands. Above, stars sparkled through the open roof. "So how does this work?"

"I just have to focus." She drew a deep breath, closed her eyes, and pictured a damp forest.

Nothing happened.

"I thought you said you could do this on holy ground."

"Shh." Elysia pictured the trees, the moss, the rocks and lake.

Still nothing happened.

"Need a little help? I could focus too. Where are we going again?"

She frowned and tried to concentrate. "You'd probably accidentally flash us back to Olympus."

"True." He squeezed her hands. "How 'bout I just focus on you while you focus on wherever it is we're going. I could spend all day focusing on your gorgeous face."

She opened her eyes to find him grinning at her. A childish, happy grin she hadn't seen on his face before. One filled with...hope.

A roar sounded outside the temple, and Elysia's gaze darted toward the door.

Damon's smile faded. "Uh, *emmoní*. If you're gonna flash us out of here, now would be a good time."

"I can't do it." Panic and fear filled her chest as understanding dawned. She looked up at Damon. "That's why the harpies were able to enter. Because Athena stripped this temple of its sacredness."

The roar grew louder. Followed by a thunder of footsteps.

"*Skata*," Damon's hands tightened around hers. "We'll never be able to outfight that. *Focus*. One more time. Do it for me."

"It won't work."

"Try!"

Elysia had no hope this would work, but she closed her eyes and pictured the forest again.

And felt the temple spin around them and the world fall apart at her feet.

Solid ground formed beneath her legs, and the smell of pine and moss and damp earth filled her senses before she even opened her eyes.

"Whoa." Damon let go of her with one hand and glanced around the old-growth timber and dewy forest. "Where the heck are we?"

Elysia could barely believe what she was seeing. "Near the half-breed colony. Or what's left of it. In Montana. In the human realm. I was born here."

He grinned down at her. "Told ya you could do it."

"That's just it, though. I didn't do it." Her brow wrinkled. "I think you did."

"Me? All I did was imagine you focusing on opening a portal."

Which didn't make any kind of sense, because she couldn't open a portal on anything but holy ground, and she was absolutely sure now that Athena's temple on Pandora was no longer holy. "Damon, do you have any gifts?"

"Gifts?"

"Abilities?"

He looked at her like she'd grown a second head.

She sighed. "Powers?"

"Like the gods?" He huffed. "No. I'd know by now if I did."

"I think you must. I couldn't have opened that portal alone."

"Trust me, *emmoní*. If I could open a portal like that on my own, I'd have done it years ago to get the hell out of Olympus."

Her gaze skipped over the dark stubble on his jaw, down his thick shoulders and strong pecs as she tried to figure out just how he could have opened that portal, then dropped to his carved stomach and his hand still holding hers in the moonli—

"Oh my gods."

"What?" Damon looked down and froze. In the dark of the forest, the whites of his eyes appeared all around his chocolate irises. "What the hell is that?"

Elysia's stomach pitched as she stared at the ancient Greek text appearing on Damon's forearms and running down to entwine his fingers. "Those are the markings of the ancient Greek heroes. The strongest demigods who ever lived."

Wide-eyed, she looked back up at Damon's shocked features, and in a rush realized why he'd always felt so familiar. Because she'd seen his face in a photo on the wall in the castle where she'd grown up. In a photo that had been taken long before Zeus's Sirens had struck him with an arrow dipped in Medusa's poison that had turned him to stone.

"What does that mean?" he asked in a low voice.

Holy *skata*, this couldn't be real.

But it was. She was seeing it with her own eyes.

"It means you were an Argonaut." Her heart beat like wildfire against her ribs. "It means you *are* an Argonaut. And it means your name isn't Damon. It's Cerek." She held his gaze. "Your name is Cerek, and oh my gods, you're alive."

CHAPTER SIXTEEN

A whisper of foreboding rushed down Damon's spine. "Of course I'm alive. I'm standing right here."

"No, you don't understand," Elysia said. "You were dead. Zeus's Sirens killed you. All the Argonauts watched it happen twenty-five years ago."

Twenty-five years ago... Damon's gaze dropped to the markings on his arms, growing darker by the second, and his stomach rolled because he knew who the Argonauts were, but he had no memory of them. No memory of anything but Olympus. He let go of Elysia's hands and took a shaky step back. "I don't understand."

"I should have realized it sooner." Elysia brushed the hair back from her face, but her dark gaze stayed locked on Damon's, so intense and unwavering, his pulse sped up. "I was a baby when you were killed, so I had no memory of you myself. But the moment we met, I knew there was something familiar about you. I just didn't put the pieces together until right now. Your picture hangs on the wall in the castle, next to pictures of all the Argonauts who have ever served. I've walked by it hundreds of times."

He swallowed hard. "That can't be."

"It is." She stepped close once more. "Your name is Cerek. Your forefather is Theseus. You were one-hundred twenty-five years old when you died, one of the younger Argonauts in the Order at the time. Your father is Aristokles. You took his place with the Argonauts when he went missing. He was gone for fifty years and reappeared the day you died. He's been serving in your stead ever since. I remember my father talking about it. About how heartbreaking it was for Ari to finally reconnect with you only to lose you. He was there that day. My father watched you die along with the other Argonauts."

Damon's heart beat hard and fast as he stared at Elysia. She was talking about people and things he didn't remember. Could it be true? Could he really be an Argonaut? He glanced down at the markings once more. They still held no familiarity, no recognition. "I don't—"

"Look at me." She placed her fingers at his temples and stared into his eyes, and, in a rush, pictures flashed inside his mind.

A group of males, all massive and muscular and each sporting the Argonaut markings on their arms and dressed in the same heavy dark clothes as they stood in some kind of grand office with soaring ceilings and massive arched windows. A great Alpha seal was embedded in the middle of the marble floor, and a female who looked a lot like Elysia but with blonde hair leaned against a decorative desk, frustration lines evident on her forehead while a dark-haired toddler—a girl—played with blocks on the floor at her feet. But one male stood off to the side, staring out the window toward the ocean, barely paying attention to whatever discussion was happening. And when he turned, sad, lost, heartbroken mismatched eyes came into view...one green, one blue.

The image shifted, and this time it was of a young girl, no more than seven, wearing a pink dress, her dark brown hair flying behind her as she laughed and ran down a long hall flanked by columns. Framed photos covered the walls. All of males dressed in the same dark clothing Damon had seen in the previous image. But one stood out from the others as the girl ran by. One who looked exactly like Damon.

Damon gasped and stumbled back, away from Elysia's touch. "W-what was that?"

"My gift. I'm sorry. I didn't know how else to make you believe me."

His eyes widened, and he stared down at her hands. "Gift?"

"All Argoleans have some kind of gift. Mine deals with memories. I can transfer memories. The girl was me. The first memory was the Argonauts, how distraught they were after you were killed. The second was the great hall where photos of the Argonauts all hang. Your pictu—"

"How do you know all this? You said your memories were still scattered."

"They are. But when I saw the markings on your arms and realized who you were, that all came back to me."

It still sounded crazy, but Damon couldn't deny what he'd seen in those memories Elysia had shared with him. Urgency pushed Damon toward her. "Tell me everything. About who I used to be and what happened."

Elysia glanced warily around the forest. "We should leave this place first. Hades's daemons still roam these forests. I can tell you when we get to—"

"No." Damon grasped her hand, holding her in place. "Tell me now."

She held his gaze and sighed. "Okay, but the short version. Zeus sent a Siren to kill your father, Aristokles. He was living in the human realm. I don't know the whole story, just that Aristokles lost his soul mate years ago, and the grief drove him out of Argolea and away from the Argonauts. He'd been hiding in the human realm for fifty years, but he was still protecting the humans and half-breeds in the area, fighting Hades's daemons who prey on the innocent and messing with Zeus's Sirenum Scorpoli. Zeus grew tired of Ari's meddling and sent Daphne, a recruit in the last stages of Siren training, to kill him. But she didn't. They fell in love. And she brought him back to the Argonauts. But Zeus found out and sent his Sirens to kill them both. The Argonauts arrived just after the attack happened. You were there. You helped the Argonauts defeat Zeus's Sirens, and in the process you reunited with your father. Zeus became enraged. And just before it was all over, one of his Sirens hit you in the chest with an arrow and killed you."

Damon glanced down at his bare chest. There was just enough moonlight filtering through the trees to highlight his skin. He saw no marks. Had no scars. "How is that possible? I'm clearly not dead."

"The arrow was dipped in Medusa's poison. It turned you to stone. Zeus then took your body. I don't know how he did it, but somehow he brought you back. You said you have no memory before waking up on Olympus twenty-five years ago. What if Zeus wiped your memories? They do it to the Siren recruits. What if he used magic or witchcraft or something to bring you back? It makes sense. He imprisoned you on Olympus. He's been using you all this time, and because you couldn't remember your old life, you had no idea what he was doing."

Using you... His mind skipped back over the years. To his first memories, blinking up at a gorgeous female with emerald-green eyes and fire-red hair. To hearing her chanting words he didn't understand and feeling something warm swirl in his veins. To his time with Aphrodite, to all the things the goddess of lust made him do in her sickening pleasure palace, the females she'd ordered him to fuck for her entertainment, the orgies she'd made him participate in, the hours she'd kept him isolated in her bed. The times she'd loaned him out like property to the Sirens to use for warfare training and seduction. To the hundreds of females he'd pleasured because he had no other choice, and finally the nights he'd lain awake staring at the ceiling thinking there had to be more to life.

His vision turned red, and a roar grew in his ears. "Zeus did this to me? He stole my life. Why?"

"Because he hates the Argonauts. Because they've bested him too many times and interfered with his plans. Because he doesn't care how they suffer, just that they do. Taking you like that... It cut them all deeply. They're your brothers."

Damon wasn't sure of that. He felt no brotherly connection to anyone. All he knew was a boiling rage and the need for retribution.

Every muscle in his body contracted. "Open the portal again. I'm going back to Olympus."

"No." Elysia grasped his hands tightly. "Look at me. You can't go back. Not now. Not when you know what you are. He'll kill you for good this time."

"Not before I do some serious damage. I'll slaughter all his Sirens if I have to. Open the damn portal."

"I can't. I don't know how I did it before."

She was lying. He saw it in her fear-filled eyes. His jaw clenched. "Fine." He pulled his hands from hers and stepped past her. "I'll find someone who can."

She rushed into his path and pressed her hands against his chest. "You can't."

"Watch me."

"No." Her voice shook as she pushed harder, stopping him. "You can't leave me here. I need you. I need you more now than I ever did. Can't you see what's right in front of you? Can't you tell that I love you?"

Something in his chest cinched down hard, a sharp bite of pain that squeezed so tight it stole his breath. "You...what?"

"I love you." Her eyes grew damp. "I think I fell in love with you on Pandora, only I was so confused and hurt when you disappeared for that month that I didn't know what to do. But this feeling I have for you has only grown since. Every moment we're together, I feel like I'm exactly where I'm supposed to be, and I don't want to lose that. I *won't* lose you. Not to Zeus or anyone. Not when we've finally found each other. You can't leave me now. I love you too much to let you go."

His heart raced again as he stared down at her, but this time it wasn't fury fueling his blood, it was fear. So much fear, he was afraid to move. "How?"

"How what?"

"How can you love me knowing the things I've done with Aphrodite, with those other recruits, with—"

"How can I not love you when you've protected me, when you've supported me?" She stepped closer, brushing her body against his in the cool night air until heat was all he felt. "I couldn't have gotten through any of what I did with the Sirens if you hadn't been there. And I don't care about what you did in the past because we both know it wasn't your choice. This, though—you and me—this is a choice. And the way you just swept me out of Olympus told me loud and clear that I'm your choice."

All the rage slid right out of him, and as his heart swelled, a love he'd always been too afraid to hope for filled the space left behind.

"*Emmoní...*" He lifted his hand and gently cupped her cheek as he looked over her beautiful face. She was his obsession. Had been from the beginning. And now he knew why. "All these years, I thought I was alone. I thought no one cared. I thought..." His throat grew thick, and the hot sting of tears burned his eyes. He lifted his other hand to her face. "You awakened me. You brought me back to life. You are the reason my heart beats. I won't leave you. I can't. I'm yours. Always yours."

"Oh..." Tears spilled over her lashes and slid down her cheeks as he lowered his lips to hers and kissed her. She wrapped her arms around his neck, pulling him into the heat and life of her body. That fire only she could ignite flared hot inside again, sparking through every nerve ending, every cell, even into the depths of his soul, telling him he was finally home.

Releasing her mouth, he wrapped his arms around her and held her close, lowering his face to her neck and drawing in her sweet honeysuckle scent. She clung to him just as tightly, showing no signs of letting go, and he was glad for that. Glad because the reality of everything she'd shared hit him hard in the silence. Made him realize nothing would ever be the same. Changed every one of his thoughts and plans and ideas for the future.

"Damon," she whispered against him. "Damianos. Who gave you that name?"

"I don't know," he said into her hair. "It's always been my name."

She drew back. "It's an old name. Ancient Greek. Translated, it means to tame, to subdue." Her eyes held his. "Indirectly, it means to kill."

Zeus had done all those things. The king of the gods had tamed him, subdued him, and in the process, he'd killed the person Damon used to be. "I can't use that name anymore."

"You're not that person anymore. Your name is Cerek."

"Cerek." The name still held no familiarity. Sounded foreign on his tongue.

"My Cerek," she whispered. Rising to her toes, she brushed her lips against his and, added, "All mine."

He opened to her kiss, dazed, confused, but steady because she was with him. She was right, he couldn't leave her. He never wanted to leave her. They were free now. And all he wanted to do was lose himself in her love and never look back.

She shivered against him, and as he broke the kiss, he finally cued in to the fact it was night and they were standing in a damp forest, him wearing only pants and boots, her dressed in nothing but his thin T-shirt.

He ran his hands up and down her arms, hoping to warm her. "We need to find some kind of shelter."

"The half-breed colony isn't far. It's in ruins now and abandoned, but we can safely stay there as long as we'd like. I brought us here because there are therillium stores in the tunnels beneath the colony."

"The invisibility ore?"

She nodded. "Once we light the ore, no one will be able to find us. Not even Zeus."

Being totally alone with her with no outside distractions sounded absolutely heavenly. "Lead the way."

She stepped back, gripped his hand, and smiled. A shiver racked her body once more as she drew him into the trees. "That's weird. It feels like it's getting colder."

It was getting colder. He felt the temperature drop, and a tingle rushed down his spine.

Daemons... Hades's daemons were somewhere close.

The realization hit like a wave, consuming every thought. He didn't know how he knew, he just did. He pulled Elysia to a stop. "We have to leave."

"But we haven't even—"

A roar sounded through the trees. His head jerked in that direction and spotted the vile, seven-foot beast with the body of a man, the head of a lion, and the horns of a goat rushing straight toward them.

Protect her. Take her home. Keep her safe...

Instinct brought his hands together.

"Damon—Cerek"—panic filled her voice—"what are you doing?"

His pinky fingers connected, and a portal opened with a pop and sizzle of light that illuminated the forest. He jerked back in surprise, his eyes growing wide, but he didn't care where it took them. With one look, he realized two more daemons had joined the first.

He grasped Elysia's hand.

"No." She jerked back against him. "No, we can't go through!"

He darted into the portal. She yelled again and jerked against his hand, but he only held on tighter.

Somehow he knew they weren't heading back to Olympus like she thought. It was instinct—again. An instinct he didn't understand, but wasn't about to fight.

Panic stole Elysia's breath. No, they couldn't go back. They couldn't go—

Her feet connected with stone, and she stumbled forward. The portal popped and sizzled at her back as it closed. Beside her, Cerek gripped her hand tightly so she didn't fall.

"What the...?" a voice muttered somewhere close.

Elysia's gaze swept over the room. Tall stone columns. Guards dressed in armor, holding spears. She whipped around and stared at the arched portal, silent now after they'd come through, the familiar words she'd read hundreds of times as a child etched into the stones:

> *Herein lies the boundary of worlds. Protected on this side, bound only by sacred land on the other. Those who cross do so at their own risk. But be forewarned: passage herein invites the bringer of nightmares, the watcher of madness, the light and dark in constant flux. And always, waiting...the thief at the gate taking stock for the deathless gods.*

Panic turned to an icy fear that gripped her chest and squeezed so tight, she could barely breathe. Footsteps sounded close as she shoved her hands against Cerek and pushed hard. "Go back. Go back through. Quick. Before—"

"Holy Hades."

Elysia froze because she knew that voice. Had listened to it sing to her at night when she'd been young. Had heard it scold her when she'd gotten into trouble and read her stories late into the night when her mother thought she was sleeping.

What in the name of all things holy is he doing in the Gatehouse right now?

Cerek looked past her. The male at Elysia's back gasped. "Call the others," he said in a dazed voice to the Executive Guard. "Call them at once and tell them to get over here."

Elysia dropped her head against Cerek's chest and bit back a groan. There was no way they could escape now. Not when her father had just spotted Cerek.

Footsteps sounded again as Demetrius moved up the stone steps. Against her, Cerek tensed and whispered, *"Emmoni."*

Elysia drew in a breath for courage, lifted her head and finally turned. "*Patéras.*"

Demetrius's feet drew to a sharp stop halfway up the steps, and his eyes grew so wide, the whites could be seen all around his black irises. "Elysia? Oh my gods..."

She nodded, and even though she wasn't ready to come home, even though she just wanted more time alone with Cerek, tears filled her eyes. "It's me." She ran to him. "I'm home."

Her father's arms closed around her, and he swept her off her feet and hugged her close. Tears spilled over her lashes, and as his familiar scents of pine and leather and citrus filled her senses, love and home and safety surrounded her.

"My *ageklos*," he whispered, turning her in a slow circle. "Oh, how I've missed you."

She held on tighter. "I missed you too, *pampas*. So much."

He lowered her to her feet, drew back, and looked down at her, his own eyes wet with tears. "Are you hurt? Are you okay? Are you—"

"I'm fine. I'm not hurt. I promise, *pampas*. I'm good."

His gaze swept over her again, as if to make sure, and then he pulled her tight against him again so her cheek pressed against his beating heart. "My *angeklos*," he whispered again.

She smiled and sank into him, knowing Cerek was behind her, watching the whole scene. Maybe she'd been foolish not to want to come home. Her father loved her. Cerek was a part of his brotherhood. Once she told him she and Cerek were—

"*Ageklos*," her father said in a low voice, "why are you wearing a male's shirt? And why is *he* missing his?"

He. Cerek. There was no warmth of brotherhood in her father's voice.

Skata. This could go downhill fast if she wasn't careful. She drew back and gripped her father's arms. "*Pampas*, it's not what it looks like."

"Not what it looks like?" Elysia's father pushed her to the side. "I think it's exactly what it looks like."

He stalked up the rest of the stone steps to the portal's platform, muscles clenched, eyes black as night and focused right on Cerek as if Cerek were a bug he wanted to squash beneath his shoe.

Cerek tensed and stepped back, wondering how the heck he'd opened the portal to this realm in the first place and whether or not he could open it to somewhere else right this second.

"*Pampas*, stop!" Elysia rushed up the stairs and stepped in front of Cerek, pushing her hands against her father's chest to force him back. "We ran into a pack of daemons when we reached the human realm. My clothes were ripped in the fight. Cerek gave me his shirt so I wouldn't have to walk around naked."

The Argonaut's feet stilled, but his calculating black as night eyes never once wavered from Cerek's face. "Is that true?"

Think quickly, dumbass. "Yes."

"He saved my life, *patéras*. You should be thanking him, not trying to hurt him."

The Argonaut ignored his daughter's pleas and narrowed his gaze on Cerek. Darkness pumped off him in waves, and Cerek's stomach tightened when he realized—again by some weird instinct he'd never felt before—that the male was part witch.

"*Pampas*," Elysia said again. "Cerek didn't hurt me. He helped me. He's not a threat."

"I'll find out what he did or didn't do to you later. But you're wrong about him not being a threat. Dark magic surrounds him. I can feel it. He's not what you think, Elysia."

Cerek's pulse sped up, and a strange energy urged him to move forward, to leave, to run.

Though to run where, he didn't know.

Elysia turned confused eyes his way, and the pull lessened. But when he saw the questions swirling in their chocolate depths, he keyed back in to what her father had just said. Sweat broke out along his spine.

Dark magic... What did that mean? Was that the energy he was feeling in his limbs? And if so, why was he feeling it now when he'd never felt it before?

His stomach tightened. Before he could find a way to voice the questions, footsteps sounded near the arched doorway. He looked in that direction just as two large males, both sporting the same ancient Greek text on their arms, stepped into the room with wide eyes.

"Holy Hera," the one with shoulder-length dark hair said. "I can't believe it."

The other male moved up the steps without stopping, bypassing Elysia and her father and slowing only when he was directly in front of Cerek.

Short, dark hair fell across the male's brow as his mismatched eyes—one green, one blue—searched Cerek's face. He was roughly the same height and build as Cerek, but otherwise they shared no other similarities besides the markings on their arms. But Cerek's pulse turned to a roar in his ears as he stared back, because he'd seen those eyes before. In the memory Elysia had showed him just after they'd arrived in the human realm.

"*Yios?*" the male whispered. "Is that you?"

Unease tingled down Cerek's spine, and he moved a half step back. "No, I—"

"Holy gods." The male closed the distance between them and threw his arms around Cerek's shoulders. "It is you."

The air whooshed out of Cerek's lungs, and his body went stiff as a board. He recognized the word *yios*, knew it meant "my son," and figured from everything Elysia had explained that the male must be his biological father. But there was no familiarity. No warmth or vibration that told Cerek he was family. He felt nothing except that growing energy, urging him to leave, to rush, to search...

"I can't"—his breaths grew shallow and fast. He lifted his arms, braced them against the other male's and pushed—"breathe."

The male dropped his arms and stumbled back, but his brow wrinkled and confusion filled his mismatched eyes when he said, "Cerek?"

Perspiration broke out all over Cerek's body. Even the name was unfamiliar. His stomach tossed as he tried to find words. He believed everything Elysia had told him, but nothing about this male or this place was familiar, and that strange energy—

Pressure formed along his forearm, distracting him from his thoughts.

"He doesn't remember you, Ari."

Elysia's voice drifted up to his ears, and Cerek looked down to see her standing beside him, her soft fingers hovering over the strange markings on his arm. He drew in her honeysuckle scent, let it filter into his soul, and relaxed little by little, knowing she was close.

"What do you mean he doesn't remember me?"

Footsteps sounded on the platform, and Cerek sensed the third Argonaut, the one with the long dark hair, move up beside Elysia's father, but all he could focus on was her. On her calming presence, on the fact she hadn't left him, on her silky fingers against his skin and the way he wanted her entire body pressed against his as it had been only hours ago in the sand.

"Zeus wiped his memories. He doesn't remember anything before his time on Olympus. The markings didn't appear on his arms until we arrived in the human realm. He didn't even know he was an Argonaut until very recently."

"I don't understand." Questions swirled in Ari's mismatched eyes as he looked from Elysia to Cerek and back again. "Then how did the two of you—"

"I recognized him," Elysia said quickly. "He was one of the Siren trainers"—she glanced over at her father—"in the field. Archery and combat. That kind of thing. As soon as I saw him, I knew who he was."

Her fingers dug into Cerek's arm, and his own confusion grew as he looked down at her. She was lying. She hadn't recognized him. She'd only just figured out who he was when she'd seen the markings appear on his arms. And he'd trained her in a helluva lot more than just archery and combat.

"We both knew we weren't supposed to be there," she went on, "so we helped each other escape." Her gaze remained fixed on her father. "So there's nothing for you to worry about."

Ari glanced over his shoulder toward the long-haired Argonaut, the one Cerek instinctively guessed was some kind of leader, and the two exchanged puzzled looks. But Elysia's father's gaze was still hard and appraising as it hovered on Cerek, and Cerek sensed the male had already guessed what other skills Cerek had trained Elysia in. Or, if he was being accurate, what skills she'd trained him in.

The long-haired Argonaut turned his gaze toward Elysia's father. "Demetrius?"

Demetrius's jaw clenched. "Elysia, come with me."

"*Patéras.*" Panic filled her voice. "You have to believe me."

Demetrius held out his hand. "Come." But still he didn't look toward his daughter. He only continued to watch Cerek the way a predator watches its prey just before it strikes. "Your mother will want to see you."

"Go with him," Ari said quietly. "We'll take care of Cerek."

Elysia cast a worried look Cerek's way. Indecision brimmed in her dark eyes. "I'll find you," she whispered.

Her fingertips released his arm, and she stepped away. Cerek's stomach twisted hard, because she was the only thing familiar in this place, the only thing that made sense, and he couldn't let her go. "*Emmoni...*"

He reached for her, but Ari and the long-haired Argonaut both moved in his way, blocking his view of her.

"It's okay," Ari said, lifting his arms in a nonthreatening way. "She's just going to the castle to see her mother. This is Theron. He's the leader of the Argonauts. You've got nothing to be afraid of."

Footsteps sounded on the stairs, followed by soft words Cerek couldn't quite make out fading in the distance. His muscles tensed. He tried to look past the two Argonauts to see where Elysia was going, but her father had already whisked her out of the room.

"We need Callia to take a look at him," Theron was saying. "If Zeus really did block his memories, maybe she can find a way to bring them back."

"That's a good idea," Ari replied. "Is she at home?"

"No, she's at the castle. The sisters were having dinner together tonight."

"Let's take him there, then."

Cerek's attention snapped back to the males. They were taking him to the castle—wherever that was. To the same place Elysia's father had taken her?

"I know this is all confusing, *yios*," Ari said. "But hopefully we can get it sorted out quickly. I'm just glad you're home. You have no idea how happy I am that you're home."

Cerek stared at the male Elysia had said was his father. Still nothing familiar passed through him. And Demetrius's words...dark magic...floated in his head.

Energy tingled all through his limbs again, some unseen force urging him forward. A tiny voice in the back of his head warned whatever it was couldn't be good, but he ignored it and this time didn't fight the pull.

It was tugging him in the same direction Elysia had disappeared. And right now, he was determined to follow it. And her.

CHAPTER SEVENTEEN

"Oh, my darling." Elysia's mother held her in a tight embrace, one that left Elysia feeling safe and protected, just as she'd felt when she was young. "We've been so worried. I can't believe you're here."

Isadora drew back, framed Elysia's face with her hands, and smiled as tears filled her warm brown eyes. She was roughly the same height as Elysia, and their features were eerily similar save their hair color, which Elysia got from her father, "I just can't believe you're here."

She pulled Elysia in for another hug, and Elysia blinked back her own tears. She hadn't realized just how much she missed home until she'd been standing in the middle of her parents' suite, surrounded by pictures of their family, looking out at the familiar view of the Olympic Ocean.

"I still don't understand how it's possible," Isadora said, easing back once more. "When Max returned from Olympus, he said you wouldn't leave. And now here you are."

Unease rolled through Elysia's belly. "Well, I wanted to come home, but I was worried about putting the rest of you in danger."

Her mother's challenging gaze scanned her face. "What changed your mind?"

Perspiration dotted Elysia's forehead. She glanced across the room toward her father, standing with his arms crossed over his chest, his eyes locked on his daughter, listening to—no, analyzing—every word she said. "Cerek changed my mind."

Demetrius's jaw hardened.

Be careful... Elysia's pulse ticked up. "I couldn't go with Max because I'd just realized Cerek was there." Gods, she was so going to Tartarus for lying. "I couldn't leave without him. Not when I knew so many here would want him back."

"Why didn't you tell Max about Cerek?" Isadora asked. "He could have helped get both of you out of Olympus."

Skata. That was a logical question. "Because Cerek didn't trust me then."

Isadora turned to look toward her mate near the window, still watching Elysia like a hawk. And in his dark eyes, Elysia knew what her father was thinking...specifically just how his daughter had convinced a virile male to trust her.

She swallowed hard and looked back at her mother. "I also didn't want Max to get caught. The Sirens would have killed him if they'd found him."

Isadora brushed the hair back from her daughter's face. "We didn't know Max had used Orpheus's invisibility cloak to gain access to Olympus. Had we known, we wouldn't have allowed him to risk himself that way. But I have to admit, I was heartbroken when he returned without you." She clasped Elysia's hands in her own. "We tried to come up with a plan to come after you, but every one put you and us and our people in danger, and we just couldn't risk that."

Elysia's throat grew thick. "I know that."

Remorse filled Isadora's eyes. "Do you? Skyla assured us you were safe. If we'd thought you were in any kind of immediate danger, we'd have been there to get you. As it is, your father was on his way to find you tonight. That's why he was at the Gatehouse when you came through the portal."

Elysia's gaze darted to her father. "You were?" She looked back at her mother. "But...why would you think I was in any kind of danger?"

"Because you are." Demetrius pushed away from the wall and stopped at his mate's side. "You're not to see that male again."

That male.

His Argonaut kin.

Cerek.

Shock rippled through Elysia. She'd expected him to say she was in danger of the Sirens finding her again, not this. "What do you mean I can't see him? He's an Argonaut. The Argonauts are always in the castle. Are you planning to lock me up so I can't 'see' him within these walls?"

A don't-get-smart-with-me look flashed in her father's eyes. "You know what I mean."

Yes, Elysia knew exactly what he meant. He was so old-fashioned, he couldn't get over the fact she was still wearing Cerek's shirt.

Anger simmered beneath her skin. Regardless of what he thought he knew, he didn't understand her or Cerek or what had happened between them, and he never would. It wasn't enough that her parents had tried to bind her without her consent. Now they were telling her who she could and couldn't be friends with.

"No, I don't think I do." She crossed her arms over her chest and glared at her father. "Explain it to me, *patéras*. Just so we're clear."

Demetrius's jaw tightened. "Elysia, I don't like your to—"

"It's been a long night." Isadora placed a hand on her mate's chest and sent him a pointed look. "We're all tired, and I think this conversation would best be put on hold until we've each had a chance to rest."

Demetrius's dark eyes held on Elysia, and in his gaze, she saw mistrust. Who was he to mistrust her? He didn't have a clue what she'd been through these last two months. Or what she'd done to survive.

"Demetrius?" Isadora said softly.

Elysia's father frowned down at his mate and nodded. But not before Elysia caught the look between her parents, the one that said they'd convince Elysia their way was best tomorrow.

He sighed, and his features shifted from the unbending Argonaut the world knew to the warm and loving father she remembered. "Yes, you're probably right. We're all tired." Crossing toward Elysia, he leaned down and kissed her cheek. "Get some sleep, *angeklos*. We'll talk more tomorrow. And just know that, contrary to what you think right now, I am glad you're home. I missed you very much."

He stepped past Elysia and moved into her parents' bedroom, closing the door softly at his back.

"The last few months have not been easy on your father," Isadora said softly. "He wanted to go after you right away."

Elysia knew that, and even though she was still good and ticked, a bit of her animosity trickled away. She recognized that his overprotectiveness came from a place of love even if she didn't agree with it. Sighing, she dropped her arms. "I get that. But I'm not a child. I just spent two months with the Sirens. Not only that, but I held my own with them."

Isadora stepped close and squeezed Elysia's arms. "I know you're not a child. You've grown into a beautiful and strong *gynaíka*. And that worries your father even more because now that he has you back, he doesn't want to lose you again."

Elysia frowned. "He's not going to lose me. The Sirens can't get into the castle. It's too heavily guarded. Even if they try to come after me again, I know I'm safe here."

"Elysia, your father is worried because I had a vision."

"What kind of vision?"

"About you. In great pain. Betrayed by someone you trust. By someone you love."

Elysia's heart sped up. Her mother couldn't possibly know she'd fallen in love with Cerek. She'd only just realized that herself. "But…your visions aren't accurate when it comes to those in your immediate family."

"No, they're not. But this one was very clear. Your father senses there's something off about Cerek. I haven't spoken with Cerek yet, but I've learned over the years that your father's intuition is strong. He's rarely wrong."

Elysia's pulse turned to a roar in her ears. Her father was wrong this time. There was nothing "off" about Cerek. He was not any kind of threat. And she wasn't about to let her parents convince her otherwise.

"It's late," Isadora said, squeezing Elysia's shoulders once more. "You should get some rest. Don't worry. Cerek is with Ari and Callia downstairs. Whatever's going on with him, they'll figure it out. In the meantime, just try to get some sleep. Everything will seem brighter in the morning."

Elysia wasn't convinced of that, but she nodded for her mother's benefit. "Okay."

Isadora hugged her again and kissed her forehead. "I love you, *angeklos*. And I'm so very happy to have you home." She drew back. "Tonight why don't you stay with us in your old room?"

Elysia absolutely did not want to stay in her old room tonight. Though she hadn't gone far when she'd officially "moved out" at the age of twenty—only to her own suite of rooms across the main corridor—tonight she needed the space. "I think I'd be more comfortable in my own bed, *materas*. I'm looking forward to sleeping in."

"I understand." Linking her arm with Elysia's, Isadora walked her toward the suite's main door. "I'm sure you're also ready for your own clothing as well."

Elysia's step faltered, and heat rose in her cheeks. "I'm not at all sure what you mean."

Isadora stopped at the door and faced her daughter with a knowing, motherly look. "And I'm entirely sure that you do. Be careful, daughter. Some things are not always as they seem. Having been on Olympus, you, of all people, should know that by now."

Isadora kissed Elysia's cheek, then turned into her suite. And, alone, Elysia stared after her mother as her heart beat hard against her breast.

Some things were exactly as they seemed.

Her gaze drifted to her door on the far side of the corridor, but she wasn't tired, and she didn't want to go into her room. She wanted Cerek. She wanted him and nothing else. And she wasn't about to let anyone convince her otherwise.

"Go ahead and put your shirt on, Cerek." The auburn-haired female Cerek was pretty sure was somehow related to Elysia stepped back from the bed where he sat on the edge and slung the stethoscope around her neck.

He was never going to get used to people calling him Cerek. The name sounded foreign, strange, so *not* his name. But he didn't want to use Damon, and, short of choosing something new, he was stuck. Sitting up so his legs fell over the side of the bed, he told himself he'd get used to it. Eventually.

"Well?" Across the suite where he'd stood with his arms crossed over his chest while he'd observed the medical exam, Ari stared at the healer with his eerily mismatched eyes. "Did you figure anything out, Callia?"

Cerek shrugged into the black button-down his father—now there was a title he'd never get used to—had given him when they'd arrived at the castle. He didn't like being a specimen, and he liked even less that the Argonaut—father or not—wouldn't let Cerek out of his sight. Especially when all Cerek wanted to do was find Elysia.

"I don't think it's a block," the healer answered. "It's as if his memory has been completely wiped. I can't find anything to access, even if we wanted to."

"So he'll never get his memory back?" Ari asked.

"No, I'm sorry," Callia said.

Across the room, Ari's jaw tightened. "What else?"

"Well, I definitely sensed some kind of energy. But I can't say if it's dark or light or what it's related to. If Zeus used witchcraft to wipe his memory, it's possible I'm picking up lingering elements from that."

An image flashed in Cerek's mind, and his fingers stilled against the button at his chest. A female with fire-red hair, emerald-green eyes, and the body of a seductress, looking down at him as she called him back from the darkness with one word: *Damianos*.

"So it's not dark energy," Ari said.

He gave his head a swift shake and resumed buttoning. He was not Damianos. He'd never go by that name again. And he *really* wanted to find Elysia.

Callia reached for her healer's bag from the table to her left. "I honestly can't say."

"Demetrius thinks there's something wrong with him," Ari went on. "That he's a threat."

Callia tugged the stethoscope from her neck and placed it in her bag. "Physically, I can tell you he's in perfect shape. His vitals are good, his heart is strong, he shows no signs of abuse, mentally or physically. As for Demetrius, I don't know what to tell you. He's a descendent of Medea. He can sense and use spells. If magic was used to wipe Cerek's memory, Demetrius could be sensing that himself." She glanced Cerek's way. "What do you think? Are you a threat we should be worried about?"

Cerek's pulse raced as he stared up at the healer, and that energy pulled at his limbs again, telling him to get up, to go, to search—

"Cerek?"

He blinked twice. "Yeah?"

"I asked how you feel," the healer said. Her eyes were a different color but shaped so much like Elysia's, they made him blink twice. "Is there any reason to be worried?"

Sweat broke out across his spine, and that energy intensified. Yes. there was a reason to be worried, he just couldn't explain why, even to himself, and he knew these people would never understand if he tried. As for how he felt? Restless. Unsettled. Boxed in. Desperate for Elysia.

He pushed to his feet. "No reason to worry. I'd like to take a shower if there's somewhere—"

"Oh, sure." Callia crossed the room and opened a door. "Through here."

Cerek cast one quick glance at Ari, unsure what to say. This was worse than awkward. When the Argonaut only continued to stare at him, he figured there was nothing he could say. "Thanks," he said to the healer.

"I'll make sure fresh clothes and pajamas are left on the bed," Callia said as he stepped toward her. "I'm sure you're exhausted."

He was. But he wanted Elysia more than he wanted sleep.

Callia stepped back so he could move into the bathroom. Just before he closed the door, Ari said, "Don't worry about this, *yios*. We'll figure everything out."

Cerek's hand hovered on the door handle, and that energy grew stronger, urging him to rush out of the room. Unable to form a coherent response, he nodded and closed the door.

Skata. He dropped his forehead against the hard wood when he was alone and breathed deep. What the hell was happening to him? What was this energy pulling at him? And why was it happening now when he'd never felt anything similar in twenty-five years?

He crossed the room, leaned into the open stone shower, and flipped on the water. After wiping his wet hand on his pant legs, he paced the length of the marble and stone bathroom, trying like hell to settle his roaring pulse.

Steam filled the room. His thoughts pinged back and forth between what Elysia's father had said and the questions the healer in the other room had asked him.

Was he a threat? Was it possible the red-haired female with green eyes he kept remembering was a witch? And if so, had she somehow cursed him?

But if that were the case, then why? What would she get from it? What would Zeus get? And wh—

Across the room, the window above the soaking tub creaked, bringing Cerek's feet to a stop. He looked up as the window pushed open and a sultry bare leg he'd recognize anywhere slipped through the space.

"Elysia?" He crossed the floor in two strides, pushed the window wider, and helped her climb all the way through. "What are you doing?"

"I needed to see you," she whispered, stepping on the edge of the tub with bare feet. "I would have come through the front door, but Callia and Ari are still in your room."

She was still wearing his T-shirt. Grasping her at the waist, he helped her down, then pulled her into his arms. Warmth filled his chest, distracting him from the strange energy.

"*Emmoní.*" He lifted his hands to her face. "Gods, I missed you."

He took her mouth, driving his tongue between her lips so he could touch and taste and feel her. She opened to his kiss, stroked her tongue along his, and gripped his arms tightly at the biceps.

"I missed you too," she murmured against him as he changed the angle of the kiss, as she pressed her sensual body against his from knee to chest.

Need erupted inside him. The need to lose himself in her and forget everything else. He kissed her deeper, pushed her back until her spine hit the wall, groaned when she rose up on her toes and rubbed against his swelling erection.

"I need you." He kissed the corner of her mouth, her jaw, nibbled at her neck. His hands streaked down her shoulders and sides. Grasping the T-shirt that hit at her thighs, he pulled it up and palmed the soft skin of her ass.

"Ah gods." She swallowed hard. Trailed her hands down his chest and grasped the button at his waistband. "I need you too. Right now."

Need turned to a roaring demand he couldn't ignore. He claimed her mouth as she worked the button free and tugged the zipper down. Grasping her around the waist, he lifted her off the floor and pushed his way between her legs. She groaned against him, wiggled her hands inside his pants, and pushed the fabric down his hips. Cool air washed over his cock as she pulled it free, but heat was all he felt when she wrapped her hand around the steely length and stroked.

Her tongue tangled with his. Pulling him close so her soft, slick center brushed the tip of his aching erection, she whispered, "Now, now, now." She lined him up and let go to wrap both arms around his neck. "Take me now."

He was powerless to do anything but. He drove into her body as he licked into her mouth, tasting her deeply while he thrust hard and bottomed out, as he drew back and plunged in again. Breaking their kiss, she dropped her head back against the wall and moaned. He gripped her ass tightly, lifted and lowered her against his cock. Shoved in and out again and again until they were both sweating.

"Oh yes," she moaned. "Don't stop."

Her slick channel constricted around him, and he knew he couldn't stop even if he wanted to. The need to take her, to fuck her, to own her drove him faster, harder, deeper than ever before. She gasped and lifted her head from the wall. Tightened her arms around his shoulders and held on. Sweat slid down his brow as his cock hammered inside her, as he dropped his forehead to her throat and pleasure raced down his spine, teasing his control.

"Come for me, *emmoní.*"

"Yes, yes…" Her body tensed; her fingernails dug into his shoulders. "I'm so close, don't stop."

He wasn't going to last. The need was too strong. But he wanted her to spiral over the edge with him. Drawing the soft skin at her throat between his lips, he shifted one hand around to her front, between their bodies. And the moment he pinched her clit, he suckled.

"Oh my GO—"

He lifted his head and captured her scream with his mouth. Her slick sex spasmed around him in ecstasy, causing his orgasm to ricochet down his spine, explode in his balls, and pull a grunt from his throat as hot jets of pleasure pulsed deep inside her.

He swallowed her groans as he thrust deep once, twice, three more times, and finally stilled. She broke their kiss and sucked back air. Dropping his forehead against hers, he simply tried to breathe.

"Oh my gods," she whispered, dragging her fingers through the damp hair at his nape, her chest rising and falling against his. "That was—"

"Loud." A smile curled his lips when he thought of the way she'd cried out and how knowing she was climaxing had pushed him right into oblivion. He shifted his hand around her back to squeeze one delectable cheek. "I'm pretty sure my father and that healer are still in the other room."

Her fingers paused in his hair. "Callia? *Skata.* Do you think they heard us?"

He turned his head and listened. He couldn't hear any voices over the hum of the shower, but that didn't mean they were alone. "Hopefully not. She's related to you, isn't she?"

Elysia nodded. "She's my aunt. My mother's half sister."

Of course she was. And if she'd heard any of what they'd just done, she was probably already on her way to tell Elysia's parents.

Reluctantly, he disengaged from Elysia's sultry body, lowered her to the floor, and tugged up his pants. "You have to leave."

"What?" Worry rippled over her features as his T-shirt fell back to her thighs, covering that secret, succulent place that belonged only to him. "No. I just got here. I want to stay—"

"*Emmoní.*" He gripped her shoulders and kissed her, cutting off her words. "I don't want you to leave either, but I don't want you to get into any more trouble than you're already in."

"I don't care about my father."

"I do."

Her brows drew together. "You do?"

He exhaled, trying to find a way to say what he felt. The energy was still there, but close to her, it was muted, not as insistent, and he knew that was because she did something to him. She calmed him in a way nothing else could. She believed in him in a way no one else ever had. As much as he wanted her with him, he couldn't be the cause of any more trouble or pain in her life.

"Your parents are worried about you."

"I'm fine."

"Yes, but they don't know that. All they know is that you showed up here with me, someone who's supposed to be dead."

Her eyes darkened. "My father's wrong about you. Don't you go believing what he said. Because I don't."

There she went, loving him again like no one ever had. His heart filled, and for the first time since he'd stepped through that portal, he felt as if he could think clearly. Gripping her hands in his, he lifted them to his mouth and kissed each one. "I don't. But I don't want to give your father any more reason to hate me."

"But—"

"But nothing." He pulled her into his arms. "I'm not going anywhere. It'll kill me not being with you every minute like I'd planned when we left Olympus, but I think for now it's best if we keep what's between us secret."

She sank into him and wrapped her arms around his waist. "I'm not sure I like the sound of that. But I might be able to go along with it if you answer one question."

"Anything."

"What *is* between us?"

He drew back and looked down at her, stunned she didn't already know. "Love."

"You love me?"

"Madly." His heart squeezed tight. "Which is why I want to make sure we do this right with your parents. Because I plan on being part of your life for a very long time."

Her eyes grew glassy, and she rose up on her toes and kissed him, throwing her arms around his neck and holding on as if she never wanted to let go.

A knock sounded at the door. "Cerek?" a male voice called. "Are you okay in there?"

"*Skata.*" Elysia drew back from his mouth long before he was ready to let her go. "That's Ari."

Right. His father. He still couldn't get used to the fact he had a father.

"I should go," she whispered.

Reluctantly, he nodded and walked her back to the window. When she was perched on the sill, one foot out and one foot in, he whispered, "Wait. Maybe you should hide until he leaves and go out another way."

She flicked him a bemused look. "Seriously? I'm perfectly safe. I made it here okay, didn't I?"

"Yeah, but"—he glanced down at her toes—"your feet are still bare. You might slip."

"Won't happen," she said confidently.

"Won't happen?" He lifted his brow.

"I trained with the Sirens, remember?" She smiled, a mesmerizing warm smile that filled his heart with joy. "Not to mention all that warrior power I stole from Athena, thanks to you."

The memory of her riding him on the altar in that temple filled his mind, and his cock thickened with the need to have her do it again.

She leaned back into the room and kissed his cheek. "I'll find you tomorrow when you least expect it. Forbidden secret rendezvous might be fun."

He chuckled as she climbed out the window and disappeared into the dark, imagining just what she could be planning for him tomorrow.

"Cerek?" Ari called from the other room again.

"Yeah," he managed over the sound of the running water behind him. "I'm okay. I'll be out in a few minutes."

His smile faded as he closed the pane. The energy was already growing stronger now that he was alone. The one urging him to do something or go somewhere he didn't understand. As much as he wanted to believe it was a pull toward Elysia, something in the back of his head warned whatever this was, it had absolutely nothing to do with her.

And he had no idea if that was good or bad.

CHAPTER EIGHTEEN

Kneeling in front of the ottoman near the crackling fire, Zagreus cringed as Atropos lifted her gnarled, wrinkled feet onto the silver satin pillow he'd just plumped.

"What are you waiting for, Ziggy?" The Fate wiggled her twisted toes as she reclined in her overstuffed chair. "These nails aren't gonna trim themselves."

Bile rose in Zagreus's throat as he reached for the clippers and went to work cutting Atropos's thick yellow nails. For an immortal deity, one would think she'd take better care of herself. Then again, why would she bother? She had "Ziggy" around to do everything for her.

Fucking Hades…

"I think now is definitely the best time," Clotho said, reaching for her goblet of wine from the coffee table. "If you wait much longer, you're going to miss your window of opportunity."

Beside Clotho on the couch, Lachesis sighed. "Perhaps. The queen is planning a welcome-home festivity for Cerek and Elysia tonight. I'll need to intercede before that. Aristokles can't accept the healer's assessment of Cerek. He's taking Cerek to see his home in the mountains today, hoping the familiarity will trigger his memories. I could wait for a moment to catch him alone there, when his father is preoccupied."

"That's the dumbest idea you've had yet," Zagreus muttered as he snipped a nail.

"What's that, Ziggy?" Atropos lifted her white brows. "You say something'?"

Zagreus knew he should bite his tongue, but he just couldn't anymore. These old hags took meddling to the nth degree, and more often than not, their efforts produced zero results.

"You're damn right I said something." He lowered his hands to the ottoman. "The dude clearly doesn't understand what it means to be an Argonaut. He's already wigged out enough. You show up in your diaphanous robes, floating off the ground, pulling that glowing-eye thing, and rambling incoherently, and you're gonna push him right over the edge into looney-land."

Lachesis and Clotho exchanged wide-eyed looks.

"Gryphon was more unstable than Cerek," Clotho said, "and he turned out fine."

Zagreus snorted. "That's still up for debate. That dude will forever be fucked in the head from Atalanta's shit. But regardless, you all didn't let Lachesis mess with Gryphon until he'd already figured things out for himself. Not to mention," Zagreus went on even though he knew he shouldn't, "if your goal is to make sure Zeus doesn't win now, interceding with Cerek here is only going to guarantee the sonofabitch god *does* win."

"How do you figure?" Atropos asked with narrowed eyes.

Gods, he was surrounded by morons. And *these* were the wisest and most powerful beings in the cosmos? "Because Cerek's already over the moon for that princess. He's not going to leave Argolea no matter what you say."

He went back to trimming Atropos's nails with a scowl.

"What would you have us do in this situation?" Lachesis asked.

"I'd stay the fuck out of it. Let things play out. Maybe he'll wise up on his own."

"And if he doesn't?"

Zagreus shrugged and moved to Atropos's other foot. "Then I'd just deal with it. Your meddling hasn't changed anything in, like, thirty years, has it? Yeah, that bitch Atalanta might be dead, but not because of your influence. The gods are all still scrambling for power. The threat of war is still imminent. And have you influenced one soul to shift from the side of darkness to light?" Glowering, he shook his head. "Not a single one. All you've done is stick your noses where they don't belong."

The room grew quiet but for the crackle of the fire at Zagreus's back and the snip of the clippers in his hand.

His fingers paused their work, and he looked up. All three Fates were staring at him with perplexed expressions. "What?"

Lachesis looked toward Atropos, and then Clotho, and some kind of secret communication passed between the three Fates. One that sent a warning trickle straight down Zagreus's spine.

Fuck. *Fuuuuuck.* They were planning something. Something that had to do with him. He should have kept his big mouth shut. If there was one thing he'd learned over the past twenty-five years serving the Fates, it was that anything the old crones could come up with had nightmare written all over it for him.

Which meant he was about to get royally fucked. And not in any of the depraved ways his wicked mind could imagine.

Soft music from the three-piece orchestra on the far side of the ballroom floated around Elysia as she smiled and shook hands. Outwardly, she was the image of the perfect princess returned home after a terrifying abduction—pale pink ball gown, slippers on her feet, a golden crown of grape leaves in her hair...smaller, of course, than her mother's. But inside, she wanted to scream. If she had to fake one more smile or pretend she was having a good time, she was seriously going to lose it.

Her gaze drifted toward the stately columns on the edge of the ballroom and locked on Cerek, standing in the shadows next to Phineus. She'd never seen him dressed up, and every time she caught sight of him, her heart did a little flip. He wore the traditional Argonaut dress attire—dark trousers, white tunic cinched at the waist, leather breastplate decorated with the seal of his forefather, and a cloak made of differing colors based on a guardian's lineage, which fell over his left arm and was anchored at his shoulder with a bronze leaf. Phineus's was a bright orange. Cerek's was a pale yellow that only made his hair and eyes look even darker.

Phineus was clearly talking, but Cerek barely seemed to be listening. His gaze was locked on Elysia, and as her eyes met his, heat pulsed through her veins. She hadn't been able to meet up with him since last night, since he'd frantically taken her to the brink of passion with his mouth and hands and body. Her parents had kept her busy all day, first making her meet with Callia to ensure she hadn't actually been harmed on Olympus—or by

Cerek—then fitting her for this stuffy gown and insisting she help with the pre-festivity preparations. She was desperate for a few stolen moments alone with him. Desperate to feel his touch and sink into his kiss. And she was starting to think if she didn't find a way to escape this claustrophobic party and do just that, she wasn't going to be able to keep their relationship secret much longer.

"Elysia?"

She blinked at the sound of her mother's voice and looked to her left. "Yes?"

The queen's gaze skipped past Elysia, and a frown pulled at her lips. Elysia's stomach tightened as she turned to see what her mother was looking at, and when she realized it was Cerek, her pulse jerked.

"Yes." The queen's voice drifted back to Elysia, and without even looking, Elysia knew her mother was smiling that fake smile she used when dealing with Council members. "We're all very relieved to have Elysia back, Lord Eugenios."

"As am I," the lord answered in a deep voice. "And before any permanent damage was done."

Elysia's brow lowered as she turned to face the portly politician with receding gray hair. "Before what damage was done?"

Her mother sent her a scolding look.

Lord Eugenios didn't seem to notice Elysia had even spoken. He looked past her as he lifted his arm and waved. "Ah, there's my son now. Nereus, we're over here."

Great. Nereus. Elysia had almost forgotten he existed.

She steeled her nerves as the future Council member joined them. He was thinner and taller than his father, but his hair was already beginning to thin at the temples. And though Elysia guessed he was handsome enough for most—green eyes, brown hair, and a good complexion—when he reached for her hand and brought it to his lips, his palms were too soft from hours behind a desk. He wore the traditional *chison*, a crisp white shirt buttoned up to his throat with a long collar that looped from one side around his neck to drape over the opposite shoulder, and crisp black slacks, but he didn't fill the clothes out the way Cerek would. He wasn't muscular or commanding or heart-stopping in any way, and not for the first time, Elysia wondered what the hell her parents had been thinking when they'd considered a match for her with him.

"I'm so happy you are home," Nereus said, lowering Elysia's hand but refusing to let it go. "I'm sure your days on Olympus must have been absolutely frightful."

Frightful? Was this guy for real? He was looking at her as if she were a piece of meat rather than a living person. Elysia's fingers grew damp as an unseen pressure condensed in her chest. She had to get out of here before she screamed.

"They weren't all that bad," she managed. Tugging her hand from Nereus's, she turned toward her mother. "If you'll excuse me."

"Elysia." Her mother reached for the sleeve of her dress, but Elysia sidestepped her hand.

"I'll be right back."

She made it three steps before her father moved in her way and narrowed hard, black eyes down at her. "Where do you think you're going?"

Skata. Think fast. "The restroom. That's still allowed, isn't it?"

Demetrius's jaw clenched, and she knew she should have bitten her tongue, but she couldn't anymore. They were treating her as if she was five instead of twenty-five. As if she knew nothing about taking care of herself when she'd kicked ass on Pandora.

"Don't be long," her father said after several seconds. "Everyone in this room is here for you."

She wanted to tell him she'd take as long as she liked, but bit back the words and nodded. Her temper skyrocketed as she stepped around him, though. Everyone *should* be here for Cerek, not her. He'd been missing for twenty-five years, not two simple months. But the only people who even seemed to care were the Argonauts…and her.

Weaving through the crowd, she glanced toward the column where she'd last seen Cerek. He was still watching her, his chocolate eyes as focused and intense as ever. Her heart picked up speed as she glanced toward the doors, hoping he could read her silent plea.

"Hold on, Princess."

Elysia startled just as she reached the open door and drew up short. She pressed a hand to her chest. "Oh, Titus. You scared me."

The Argonaut was dressed in the same formal outfit Cerek wore, though his cape was blue. A few wisps of wavy dark hair framed his face, but the rest was tied with a leather strap at his nape, and he stared down at her with knowing hazel eyes. Eyes that put her on immediate alert. "What's going on between you and Cerek?"

Elysia's heart stuttered. "I-I don't know what you mean."

"Bullshit." He took a half step closer but was careful, she noticed, not to touch her with his gloved hands. "You're both projecting so loudly, my eardrums are about to burst."

Skata. Titus had the ability to read minds. She'd forgotten that until just this moment. Her face grew hot, and her pulse turned to a roar in her ears. "You don't think anyone else knows, do you?" she whispered.

"No. Most of the guys think Cerek's gay."

Elysia nearly choked on her tongue. "*What?*"

"We never saw him with a female. In all the years he served with the Argonauts, he never once even talked about a female."

Cerek…gay? She glanced across the ballroom, and heat rushed through her when she saw the way he was watching her—as if he couldn't wait to get to her, as if she were all that mattered. Memories of the way he'd all but devoured her last night rushed through her mind, making that heat trickle lower. There was no way he was gay. He was the most heterosexual male she'd ever met.

"Your father suspects something happened between the two of you," Titus said.

Elysia looked back at Titus. His gaze was fixed beyond her, in the direction of her parents. Panic whipped through her chest before she reminded herself that suspecting and knowing were two very different things.

Titus looked down at her once more. "Callia knows for sure."

"How? Did you—"

"She did your exam this morning, remember? She knows you're no longer untouched."

Elysia's face absolutely burned, and her eyes fell closed. The healer had asked her this morning if she'd been forced to do anything against her will, and Elysia had answered—truthfully—no. But she hadn't expected anyone could know whether or not she was a virgin based on a quick magical scan.

"She asked me earlier if there's something going on between you two," Titus went on.

Elysia looked up at him. "And what did you say?"

"I said no, of course. She's your mother's sister. They share secrets like candy. Besides which, if your father finds out, Cerek's dead. Demetrius is projecting loudly as well. He thinks Cerek's a traitor. That Zeus brainwashed him and sent him to bring you back only to kill you in front of your parents."

Elysia's eyes widened. "What? That's ridiculous. Why on earth would he do that?"

"To inflict as much pain as possible. To make us all suffer. Zeus is all about revenge. We've bested him one too many times. Cerek could be nothing more than a means to an end."

A protective urge bubbled through Elysia. "And what do you think?"

"I think..." Titus glanced across the room toward Cerek. "I'm not sure what to think. His thoughts are all over the place. I can't get a read on him." Titus looked back down at her. "But I do know this much, you need to be careful."

"I'm not afraid of Cerek."

"I don't mean him. Your parents are moving up your arranged binding with Nereus. They're worried about Zeus coming after you again. Zeus can't claim a bound female for his Sirens. But Nereus is not a good match. He cares only about how the union will benefit his political status. Nothing more."

The pressure in Elysia's chest intensified, and her throat grew thick. "W-when?"

"Tomorrow night."

No. Her heart squeezed so tight, the air felt as if it were wrenched from her lungs. She wanted to whip around and stare at her parents in horrified disbelief, but she forced herself not to move, not to turn, not to show any emotion that would give their awful secret away.

She couldn't bind herself to Nereus. She wouldn't. "I-I need some air."

She sidestepped Titus, but he moved in her path before she could get away. "I didn't tell you so you'd run. I told you so you could prepare an argument to use against them. Running will only get you in trouble, as it did last time."

Oh yeah, he'd read her mind. He knew exactly why she'd run and how the Sirens had caught her. But more than that, he was right. She couldn't run this time. Not if she had any intention of staying in Argolea. And she had to stay in Argolea so she could be near Cerek. He wasn't safe outside this realm either, and she wasn't about to let Aphrodite or any of those Siren recruits sink their claws into him again.

"I understand," she said calmly. More calmly than she expected. "And I'm not running. I just need to use the restroom."

He stared at her several long seconds as if he didn't believe her, then finally stepped back and let her pass.

Elysia moved out the tall double doors, away from the lights and people and music and into the foyer. But that pressure in her chest didn't ease. It only intensified. Felt as if it were burning a hole right through the middle of her heart.

Shaking, she darted past the bathroom, up the curved stairs to the second floor, and into the closest suite. Shoving the French doors opened, she staggered out onto the veranda, where she gripped the stone balustrade as she gulped in air.

Only it didn't help. Because she still had no idea what she was supposed to do next.

She wasn't on the first floor.

Cerek's heart rate picked up speed as he skipped steps to get to the second floor. He'd checked every room—even the restroom, where he'd scared the shit out of a couple of females who were probably going to report him as a pervert—and there was no sign of her.

He passed an office, a library, tried a door only to find it locked. His heart beat faster. If she'd gone outside, if she'd moved to an upper floor in this monstrosity of a castle, he might never find her. And he *needed* to find her. Something was wrong. He'd seen the flash of panic in her eyes when she'd been talking to the long-haired Argonaut with the gloves. Something he instinctively knew had to do with him.

He passed an open bedroom door, then jerked back when he noticed the French doors on the far side open.

The dark room consisting of a sitting area, a fireplace, a bed, and two end tables. "*Emmoni?*"

Sniffling sounded from the veranda. Closing the main door quietly, he crossed the floor and stepped out into the darkness. The balcony overlooked the gardens below, and, beyond the castle walls, the twinkling lights of the city of Tiyrns. But his attention immediately shot to the female leaning against the railing, swiping at her eyes.

"*Emmoni?*"

"Oh, Cerek." She moved into him and buried her head against his chest.

"What's wrong?" He closed his arms around her, trying to keep the panic at bay. "What's happened?"

She sniffled again. "My parents are what's happened. They're arranging my binding."

His fingers stilled near her spine, and thoughts of whips and chains and some kind of sadistic ceremony only Hades would like filled his head. "Tell me that's not as bad as it sounds."

"It's worse." She pushed out of his arms and swiped at her damp eyes. "It's a marriage. They're forcing me into marriage. They're going to say it's to keep Zeus from coming after me, but I know the truth. It's a political arrangement to smooth things over with the Council. They've been planning this for months. That's how the Sirens found me. I overheard my parents arranging it months ago, so I ran. Before I could get to the human realm and freedom, the Sirens intercepted me."

Cerek had no idea what the Council was or what she meant about smoothing things over with them, but he understood the words marriage and force. He gripped her shoulders. "The weasely-looking male? The one who couldn't stop staring at your breasts?"

Elysia's shoulders slumped. "Yes. He's the Council leader's son. He'll one day rule the Council that advises the monarchy, but really they just want to overthrow the monarchy. The political situation in this country is a mess. My mother's been trying to fix it but—"

"You're not doing anything with that male."

Elysia's expression softened. "I don't want to. But I don't have much of a choice here. I can't run off again. Zeus will find me if I leave this realm, and if that happens, I'll be sent back to Olympus." She gripped his forearms. "And I don't want to leave you."

"So bind yourself to me."

She stilled beneath his hands. "What?"

His blood pumped hot and fast. "If their reason is Zeus, bind with me. Then he can't take you. He can't take a bound female from any race."

"You…would want to do that? With me? It's forever. It's not just a simple—"

He lifted his hands to her face and stepped closer. "I want you with me forever. It is simple."

Her gaze searched his face. "But…my father—"

"He doesn't like me. I know. Which is why we need to do this right away. He can't say no after it's done. And he can't force you to marry someone else when you're already bound to me."

She stared at him and swallowed hard, and he knew she was wavering. That he had to convince her.

He lowered his head and pressed his lips against hers. Then he looked down at her with every bit of emotion he hoped she could feel. "I need you, Elysia. Say yes." He kissed her again. "Say yes to me. To us."

Her hands landed on his hips, and a soft moan echoed from her chest as she opened to his kiss, drawing him into the heat and life of her mouth. "Yes," she whispered against his lips. "Yes, yes, yes."

Relief filled his chest like air, but it was fleeting. He drew back. "Is there someone you know who can do the ceremony?"

She bit her lip. "Yes. One person. I can send word."

"Do it."

"We'll have to go tonight," she said. "My parents are moving up the binding with Nereus. Titus told me they're going to announce it tomorrow."

He nodded. "To—"

Voices echoed from the corridor. Cerek looked toward the closed door and pushed Elysia deeper onto the veranda, out of sight of the door in case anyone came in the bedroom. "Someone's coming." He kissed her again and let go. "I'll find you at midnight."

Reaching for the balustrade, he climbed onto the railing and moved toward the castle wall.

"Wait." She turned after him. "Meet me in the downstairs library."

He stopped and looked back. "You're sure you'll be able to get away?"

"I'll make it happen."

He smiled. "It's a date, *emmoní*. Now go back to the party before anyone notices we're both gone."

"Can't you just use the door?"

"People are in the hall. I don't want them to see us together. Besides, I can't let you have all the fun climbing sides of buildings."

A smile spread across her beautiful face as she turned for the bedroom door. "Just don't fall to your death between now and midnight, *ómorfos.*"

"Not a chance," he said after her. "You're mine."

And in a few hours, she'd be his forever.

CHAPTER NINETEEN

The party had run later than she'd expected. After Elysia had excused herself close to midnight, she'd had to hide out in her room until the last of the guests had left. Now, at just before one a.m., she rushed down the dark stairs, hoping Cerek hadn't given up on her.

He'd left the party with his father sometime around eleven. She'd watched him go, wondering where they were heading. Elysia knew Aristokles was still worried about Cerek, but she hoped that worry wasn't translating into constant supervision.

She reached the lowest level, crossed the massive Alpha seal in the foyer's marble floor, and soundlessly moved toward the library. Stepping into the dark room surrounded on all sides by two-story bookshelves filled with leather tomes, she let her eyes adjust and searched for Cerek.

"Cerek," she whispered. It still felt strange to call him that, and she knew it was strange to him as well. Knowing he was having trouble responding to it, she whispered, "Damon."

Silence met her ears, and inside the library, nothing moved.

Panic rose in her chest. "Cerek!" she hissed again.

"You called?" a voice said over her shoulder.

She whipped around and pressed a hand against her heart. Cerek stood behind her, dressed in a dark shirt and pants, moonlight through the tall arching windows in the library highlighting his tousled hair, dark gaze, and mischievous smile. "You scared me."

"I'd rather dazzle you." He pressed a kiss to her lips. "Are you ready?"

"Yes." She closed her hand around his as nerves jumped in her belly. "We have to go down to the tunnels. It's the easiest way out of the castle unnoticed."

She stepped past him and pulled him with her, leading him to a set of stairs hidden near the kitchen.

"Did anyone see you leave?" he asked as the door closed behind them and she lit the torch hanging on the wall.

"No. You?"

"No." He took the torch from her hand as they started down. "Ari and his mate…what's her name?"

"Daphne."

"Yeah. Daphne. They left about thirty minutes ago and went back to their house. Or my house, I guess. They've been staying there since I left. Or died. Or…whatever."

Elysia drew to a stop as she stepped off the last stair and turned to look up at him. The air was colder down here, the torch illuminating only a circle of light as he joined her.

"What?" he asked.

"You went there this morning, to your old home. Did it trigger any memories?"

"Not one."

Torchlight cast shadows over his handsome face. Shadows lurked in his eyes. She squeezed his hand. "We'll make new memories."

"We will." He let go of her hand, wrapped his arm around her waist, and drew her into his heat as he leaned down to kiss her again.

The nerves she'd been feeling skittered away, and as she rose to her toes, wrapped her arms around his neck, and kissed him back, she knew this was the right choice. The only choice. Everything she'd never known she wanted.

Breathless, he drew back and rested his forehead against hers. "As much as I want to stay here and go on kissing you, I think we've already kept the priest waiting."

Reluctantly, she let go and dropped to her heels. "We have. And it's not a priest, it's a priestess. Only here, the ancient word for priestess is *hiereia*, so use that when you address her."

He chuckled as she pulled him with her down a long dark corridor. "See? I learn something new every day because of you."

"Oh, and she's not just a *hiereia*. She's also a witch."

"Even better. Will this be legal if it's overseen by a witch?"

"Yes." She grinned back at him. "Especially because my bloodline is part witch."

"It is?"

"Don't worry. I'm not going to turn you into a toad or anything. My father hails from Jason and Medea. He can make spells work, but I've never had much luck. Probably because I didn't ever like to practice."

"Your father's an Argonaut *and* a witch," he muttered. "I knew there was something different about him. Man, I am totally dead when he finds out about this."

She laughed as they reached a door on the far end of the corridor. "No, you're not. Once we're bound, he can't change it. He'll have to accept you."

Relief pulsed through her as she pushed the heavy door open and stepped out into the moonlit forest beyond the castle walls. She drew in a deep breath of freedom and smiled. But Cerek's hand tugged her back before she could take another step.

"*Emmoní*," he said, looking down at her, his brows drawn together. "Are you sure this is what you want?"

The full moon cast enough light that they no longer needed the torch. Taking it from his hand, she dropped it on the ground and stomped the flame out with her boot. "Want what?"

He grasped both of her hands, drawing her attention back to him. "Me. Once your father finds out what I did for the gods on Olympus, bound or not, he's going to try to take you away from me."

"That won't happen."

"Yes, it wi—"

She laced her fingers with his. "Listen to me. That won't happen, because I choose you, Cerek, Damon...whatever you want me to call you. Your name doesn't matter to me. Your past doesn't matter to me. The only thing that matters is that I love you. And I will always choose you."

"*Emmoní*." His eyes filled with emotion. And when his mouth met hers and his tongue slipped between her lips, the wicked taste didn't just set off a burst of desire in her body. It ignited a craving deep in her soul only he could fill.

She closed her eyes as she kissed him back, imagining the small clearing beneath the stars where she'd watched Delia, the high priestess of the coven, perform more than one binding ceremony over the years.

The ground disappeared beneath their feet, and she felt the world tip and sway, but she didn't stop kissing Cerek.

"Whoa." He pulled back when stones formed beneath their shoes. Wide-eyed, he looked at the trees and mountains rising around the small circle, illuminated and shining like silver in the moonlight. "I didn't know you could do that."

"Only here. Argolean trick. Just don't try to do it through walls."

He cast a sexy, half grin down at her, for the first time since they'd arrived in her realm, seeming to relax. The lines were gone from his forehead, his eyes sparkled in the moonlight, and his smile was one of pure delight that absolutely made her heart melt.

"*Paidí*," Delia, the leader of the coven, said to Elysia's left. "We were beginning to think you'd changed your mind."

Elysia let go of Cerek and turned toward the high priestess, dressed in a flowing red robe, her snow-white hair hanging to the middle of her back. "*Hiereia.*" Elysia closed both of her hands around the one Delia offered. "I'm sorry we kept you waiting. Thank you for arranging this."

Delia nodded. "I've heard rumblings of the queen's plans. As saddened as I was to hear of your father's agreement in those plans, I understand his rationale. I'm just happy you've made your own choice. You must be bound, or Zeus will return. The coven will do anything we can to keep the Sirens at bay." Delia turned her brilliant blue eyes Cerek's direction. "Welcome home, Guardian. You don't remember me, do you?"

"No, I'm sorry."

Delia's gaze hovered on Cerek, and as Elysia watched, she had the strange sense the witch knew something about Cerek she wasn't saying.

"'Tis of little importance." Delia smiled and looked back at Elysia. "All is prepared here for the *Hieros Gamos*. Juniper will take you to be cleansed so we may begin. Guardian." She looked back at Cerek. "Follow me."

Juniper stepped forward from the shadows, a willowy witch with dark hair, dressed in a purple robe similar to Delia's, and began walking away from the circle. Elysia turned to follow, but Cerek captured her by the wrist.

"Hold on," he whispered. "Where is the priestess taking me?"

Elysia squeezed his hand for reassurance. "Just to the pools. For a ceremonial bath called a *loutra*. It's part of the ritual. Trust me. You're not going to get turned into something unnatural."

"I'd better not be," he muttered as he let go of her. "Or you're gonna be in big trouble."

"Like the trouble I was in on that Pandoran beach?"

Heat filled his sexy eyes. A heat that ignited a fire deep in Elysia's core. "Exactly like that." He kissed her quickly, then moved away with a wicked smile. "On second thought, maybe you'll be in that kind of trouble again either way."

She laughed as he disappeared into the darkness. At her back, Juniper said, "This way, Princess."

She followed Juniper into the trees. Moonlight lit their way. In a matter of minutes, they came to a small pool flanked by rocks and filled with steaming water.

"Everything off. This is for your hair." The witch handed her a ribbon. "Climb in."

Elysia wrapped her hair in a knot, then tugged her shirt up and off and let it drop to the ground. As she reached for the snap of her pants, a memory flashed—of her and Cerek in the hot springs on Olympus, of the way he'd kissed her, how hard he'd been beneath the water, and just what she'd wanted him to do to her right there under the stars.

She smiled as she climbed into the pool. Heat surrounded her. Sinking back into the water, she sighed as the scent of heliotrope filled her senses.

Juniper sat on a rock near Elysia's back, poured some kind of oil into her hands, and began to knead the muscles in Elysia's shoulders. "I was shocked when Delia told me of your impending binding."

Yeah, Elysia knew several people were going to be shocked when they heard the news. "Why? Because we haven't known each other long? When you know who you're meant to be with, there's no sense in waiting."

"Not because of that. Because you're binding yourself to the Argonaut Cerek. I never expected him to be bound."

Elysia's conversation with Titus rolled through her mind. "And why is that?"

"Because of his celibacy. He was the talk of the coven for many years before his disappearance. More than one witch tried to tempt him."

Elysia's back tingled. "He's not gay."

Juniper chuckled. "I never implied he was. I take it he didn't tell you about his prophecy?"

Elysia sat up straighter and glanced over her shoulder toward the witch. "What prophecy?"

Juniper lifted Elysia's left arm out of the water and massaged the heliotrope-scented oil into her skin. "Many moons ago, before Cerek was inducted into the Argonauts, he began seeing one from our coven. Astrid advised the young witch to stay away from him. Astrid, you see, was an oracle. She had the gift of sight, and she prophesied that the sins of Cerek's forefather would follow him. Do you know the story of Theseus, Cerek's forefather?"

"No."

Juniper lowered Elysia's arm into the water and reached for the other. "Theseus was a great hero, as great, some say, as Heracles himself. Born from the union between Aethra, a human mother, and the sea god, Poseidon, he was strong and accomplished many great feats. He even killed the mighty minotaur."

Elysia knew her history. As future heir to the throne, she'd been raised on it. "Go on."

"Theseus's greatest weakness, however, was lust, and some called him the 'great abductor of women,' as he saw females not as gifts to be revered but as objects to be conquered. It was because of this lust that he agreed to join his cousin, Pirithous, on a quest to abduct and bind themselves to two daughters of Zeus. Theseus chose Helen. Pirithous set his eyes on Persephone. After they abducted Helen, they left her with Theseus's mother and descended into the Underworld to steal Persephone from Hades. But all did not go as planned, for the Underworld is a cruel and demoralizing place. Rise, Princess."

Elysia pushed to her feet, letting the water hit at her waist. "What does this all have to do with Cerek?"

Juniper rubbed the scented oil down her spine. "Theseus abandoned honor for lust and lost his courage in the Underworld. When, in despair, he sat down on a rock, he was immovably fixed in stone and surrounded by furies. He was trapped in the Underworld for many years, until Heracles eventually rescued him.

Astrid, the oracle, foresaw that Cerek would follow in his forefather's footsteps. She foresaw that lust would cause him to lose his courage. She told Cerek and the young witch what she'd seen. Cerek, as you can imagine, was skeptical. But shortly thereafter, his father, Aristokles, lost his courage when his soul mate was killed. Aristokles left the Argonauts. He disappeared for nearly fifty years. Cerek realized that the cycle was destined to repeat and stepped back from all females. For a warrior, for an Argonaut, courage is the most sacred of virtues."

The witch lifted her hands from Elysia's back. "Turn."

Elysia's mind was a whirl of thoughts as she turned in the water and the witch began rubbing the oil across her collarbone. Was she cursing Cerek by going through with this binding? Would he lose his honor? His courage? He'd abandoned the gods for her, gone back on his vow to serve them. But that didn't make him a coward. No, to her it made him extremely honorable. And whether or not he chose to return to the Argonauts, he was still honorable and courageous and the mightiest warrior she'd ever known. Besides which, this—what was happening between them—wasn't lust. It was stronger, more real. It was meant to be.

"Climb out of the water, Princess, and I'll oil your legs."

Dazed, Elysia looked down only to realize the witch had already oiled her breasts and belly. She'd been so distracted by thoughts of Cerek, she hadn't even noticed.

Climbing out of the pool, Elysia took the wrap Juniper handed her and closed it around her body. As she sat on the rocks and extended one leg, the witch knelt in front of her and rubbed oil across her thigh and down to her toes.

"He doesn't know about the prophesy," Elysia said. "He doesn't remember it. And I don't want you to tell him, because it's irrelevant."

Juniper glanced up as she moved to Elysia's other leg. "You don't think he has the right to know about his destiny?"

"Destiny is a term people use to imply we have no control over our futures. There is no such thing as destiny. All paths can be changed."

"So you don't believe in the Fates?" The witch rose, stepped past Elysia, and reached for a purple gown with gold trim.

Elysia stood and looked after her. "I believe the Fates are real, meddling in future events, but even they can't see all ends. The future changes based on the decisions we make today."

Juniper lifted the gown over Elysia's head. "And you believe the oracle was making the prophecy up?"

"Not necessarily." Elysia tugged the wrap free and let it fall to her feet. Shrugging into the gown, she said, "I just don't believe all visions are accurate. My mother has the gift of foresight, and her visions are often muddled."

The witch moved around behind her and worked the buttons along Elysia's spine. "Your mother's gift is impeded when it relates to those she loves. Astrid's gift is not."

Frustration bubbled through Elysia as the witch began to mess with her hair. "So you're saying I'm dooming Cerek by going through with this ceremony."

"No." Juniper stepped around in front of her. "I'm saying be careful, Princess. There are forces at work here you and Cerek do not understand."

Elysia's pulse picked up speed as she stared into the witch's amber eyes. "I love him and he loves me. That's all that matters."

"For both your sakes, I hope that is true. And I hope love is enough to weather the coming storm."

The witch stepped away only to return with glittering jewels, which she began draping over Elysia. But Elysia barely noticed. Because her heart was suddenly pounding a staccato rhythm against her ribs, and her mind was spinning over everything the witch had just said, trying to fit together pieces that didn't seem to want to merge.

There was no coming storm. She and Cerek could get through anything so long as they were together. And he wasn't in danger of losing his honor or his courage because of her either. She wouldn't let either happen.

But as the witch finished her preparations and motioned Elysia to follow her back to the stone circle, Elysia heard her mother's voice saying, *"Be careful, daughter. Some things are not always as they seem."* And she also heard words from long ago that she didn't want to remember.

She heard her mother whisper, *"Twenty-five years is nothing but a blink of an eye to the gods. And peace is as fleeting as the wind. It will end. It will end soon."*

* * *

Okay, the whole bath thing was just plain weird.

Cerek had told the white-haired witch who spoke as if she were five hundred but looked only thirty that he was perfectly capable of bathing alone. The witch had chuckled and handed over the soap, but she hadn't left. Instead she'd moved off to the side and watched him as if he were the main event at a three-ring circus.

He'd had enough years of people watching him in Aphrodite's pleasure palace not to be self-conscious of his body, but it was just plain creepy to be watched like this when he was about to marry— no, bind with—Elysia.

"This is a good match," Delia said as he dressed in the loose-fitting tan cotton pants she'd left out for him and the white tunic with its purple sash. "A very good match."

Cerek thought so too. And he was anxious to get on with the ceremony so he could get back to Elysia and get away from the witch.

The witch lifted a crown of ivy and motioned for Cerek to lower his head. "Especially since she is your soul mate. A very good match."

"Soul mate?" Cerek adjusted the crown and looked down at the witch. "What do you mean?"

"It means exactly as it sounds. Hera cursed all the Argonauts with a soul mate. The other half of their soul. She is yours. That is why you are so drawn to her. You are lucky, Guardian. Many Argonauts spend their lives searching for their soul mate, only to come up empty. You are very lucky indeed."

A chill spread down Cerek's spine as the witch turned away and motioned for him to follow. Was that the energy he'd been feeling? A draw toward Elysia? No, he knew whatever that strange feeling had been, it had nothing to do with Elysia. Plus, ever since they'd left the castle and come to this place, he hadn't felt it.

But he did feel a closeness to Elysia he'd never felt to anyone else. A bond that had formed the moment they'd met, one that had only intensified when they'd made love in Athena's temple. Was she the other half of his soul? Was that why he'd fallen for her so quickly and completely? Why he'd become obsessed with her and couldn't imagine life without her?

Hera cursed all the Argonauts... A curse didn't sound good. A curse meant there were repercussions to the whole deal. For him?

Or for the female involved in the equation? Heat burned in his veins and tightened his chest. He couldn't let anything happen to Elysia. It wasn't enough that the gods had fucked with his life. Now they were fucking with his future? With Elysia's?

Moonlight shone down over Elysia on the far side of the circle as Cerek approached. She was dressed in a purple gown that matched his sash. A wide ballet collar showed off her delicate shoulders and dipped low at her cleavage. Long bell sleeves draped past her hands, and a fitted waistline gave way to an A-line skirt. Amethyst jewels dripped from her ears, a large gemstone was clasped at her throat, and a crown of ivy, like his, sat in her updrawn hair sprinkled with even more purple-toned jewels. But all Cerek could focus on was the fact someone had planned this, that the gods were pushing them together, that even though he'd asked her if this was truly her choice, she might not be able to fully comprehend the question.

"Welcome," Delia said, stepping into the middle of the circle. "Tonight we gather for the *Heiros Gamos* of Cerek and Elysia."

Several witches emerged from the trees, dressed in hooded purple cloaks, each holding a lantern. They lined up on the outside of the circle, closing the space after Elysia joined Cerek in the middle.

Delia turned toward Juniper at her side. "We begin with—"

"Wait." Cerek reached for Elysia's hand. "I need to talk to you for a minute."

Elysia's smile faltered. "Okay."

"Not here." To Delia, he said, "We'll be right back."

The witches exchanged perplexed looks, but two moved aside, opening the circle so Cerek could pull Elysia through and into the trees.

"What's wrong?" Elysia asked when they were out of earshot. "Did you change your mind?"

"No. Gods, no." He stopped and looked down at her. "I just want to make sure you don't."

"I already told you that I want to do this. I—"

"You might not have a choice in this. You're my soul mate."

She blinked like he was a total fool. "I know I am."

"You do?"

"I suspected it when you went all ape-shit alpha on Petros. That was a classic Argonaut response to his soul mate with another male."

"Why didn't you say anything?"

"Because I didn't fully understand until we got to the human realm and I saw your markings. That's when I knew for sure I was your soul mate."

"And that doesn't bother you?"

She laughed. "Why would that bother me? Aside from the fact you went a little overboard—which we already discussed—it means you'll always protect me. That's not exactly a bad thing."

"But..." His gaze searched her flawless face. "You don't care that this has all been preordained by Hera? That you don't have a choice in what you feel for me?"

"Cerek." She laid her soft palm against his cheek. "Yes, Hera cursed you to feel an attraction toward me, but it's one-sided. The female in Hera's soul mate curse doesn't feel the same pull. I'm here because I want to be here. Because I love you with every fiber of my being. No one is making me bind my soul to yours. I choose to do so freely."

His heart swelled. "You do?"

"Of course I do." Her voice softened. "You have a choice as well. You don't have to go through with this ceremony if you don't want to. I will still love you if you're not ready or if you're unsure or—"

He dragged her close and kissed her. "I am ready. I'm more than sure. I just needed to know that you weren't being forced into it. I've been forced by the gods to do things I didn't want to do. I'd never put you through that."

Her fingers curled into his tunic, holding on tight. "No one's forcing me, I promise. I love you. I need you. I want us."

He closed his mouth over hers again, and as her tongue tangled with his and her hands slid around his neck to draw her succulent body against his, all the doubt and worry drifted away. Yes, some silly soul mate curse might have made him take notice of her, but he loved her because of her spirit and her warmth and her unfailing belief in him. Not because any stupid god was making him love her.

He drew back and clasped her hand, pulling her with him. "Come on. Let's finish this so I have plenty of time before the sun rises to show you just how much I love you back."

She laughed as he tugged her toward the witches.

Pushing his way back into the circle, Cerek clasped Elysia's soft hands in his and looked toward Delia. "Okay, Priestess, we're set. Let's do this."

Elysia giggled.

"As I was about to say," Delia began, holding her hands out wide. "We are here to celebrate the blessed union of these two souls, separated at birth, brought together this night by the will of the Creator."

"Blessed be, *Dimiourgos*," the witches around the circle chanted, lowering their heads.

Leaning toward Elysia, Cerek whispered, "They're not going to start worshiping the gods, are they? Because that won't go over well with me."

"No," she whispered back. "We don't worship the gods here. Only give thanks to the Creator of all life."

That he could deal with. After all, the gods were nothing more than fallen angels, hell-bent on their own power and pleasure. He wasn't sure how much of the great Creator he believed in, but he wasn't about to say so now. Now all he wanted to do was finish this ceremony so he could go about worshiping the female who held his heart.

"The elements, please." Delia held out her hand. Juniper shook a small velvet sack over Delia's palm. Five silver coins dropped free. Delia handed two to Elysia and two to Cerek.

Cerek turned the coins in his hand. The backs of each were stamped with the Omega symbol. The opposite sides were different. One was a flame, the other a cloud in the shape of a face, blowing air as if to create wind.

"The classic elements make up all life in the cosmos," Delia said, "gifted to us by the Creator. Fire and air are inherently male, whereas earth and water are female. She knelt where she stood and placed the fifth coin—blank, it appeared to Cerek—into a slot he hadn't noticed in the center of the circle. "As the female is the beginning, the male is the end. That which is joined together shall not be undone. Elysia." The witch looked Elysia's way. "Place your elements opposite each other and say the great words."

Elysia let go of Cerek's hand and knelt. "May water be here, pure and unmixed. May I live in its presence, and may this union be guided by its spirit." She placed the coin with the water droplet stamped into one side to the right of the witch's blank coin. Reaching across the blank coin, she placed the other, this one stamped with a picture of mountains, on the opposite side to form a line. "May earth be here, pure and unmixed. May I live in its presence, and may this union be guided by its spirit."

As she pushed to her feet, Delia turned to Cerek. "Argonaut, place your coins above and below, forming a perfect circle, and repeat the words."

Cerek really had no clue what he was doing, but Elysia's nod of assurance urged him on. Kneeling, he placed the fire coin above the witch's and said, "May fire be here, pure and unmixed. May I live in its presence, and may this union be blessed by its spirit." Placing the air coin in the last space, he said, "May air be here, pure and unmixed. May I live in its presence and may this union be blessed by its spirit."

Elysia grinned and reached for his hands as he pushed to his feet.

He mouthed the word *whew* and gripped her warm fingers. That wasn't nearly as bad as he'd expected.

Delia held out her hands. "Blessed be water and earth and fire and air. As to all the gifts the Creator has given us, may these elements bind male to female, beginning to end."

The ground shook, and Cerek looked down to see two symbols forming on the witch's blank coin. The first was the Alpha symbol, and over the top of that, entwining with the symbol's lines, the Omega.

"Whoa," he whispered, looking back up at Elysia.

She grinned wider.

"Cross hands," Delia instructed.

Elysia's left hand reached for Cerek's left, and her right for his right, forming an X between them. "This is the binding part," she whispered.

Juniper stepped forward from the edge of the circle with several lengths of rope, all in different colors.

Cerek lifted his brow. "Looks kinky."

Elysia laughed and quickly pursed her lips.

Delia took the purple rope from Juniper. "Will you share each other's pain and seek to ease it?"

"Yes," they responded together.

Delia wrapped the purple cord around their hands. "Will you share in each other's laughter?"

"Yes," they said again.

She draped the orange cord over their hands. "Will you share the burdens of life so that your spirits may grow in this union?"

"Yes."

The blue cord wove around their hands. "Will you dream together to create new realities and hopes?"

"Yes."

After tying the red cord around their hands, she said, "Will you use the fire of passion and the heat of anger to strengthen this union?"

Elysia blushed as they both said, "Yes."

Lastly, Delia added the yellow cord. "And will you honor each other from now until the end of time, never giving cause to break that honor?"

Cerek stared into Elysia's mesmerizing eyes and said, "Yes," along with her.

Delia held out her hands. "The knots of this binding are formed not by these cords but by the vows you make today. May the union of your souls be blessed by the elements and the Creator, and may the warmth of hearth and home, the heat of the heart's passion, and the light you find in each other guide you on the path of life together." She lowered her hands. "You are bound."

Cerek looked toward the witch. "That's it?"

Delia smiled as Juniper rushed over and began untying the cords from their hands. "That's it."

Breathing easier, he grinned down at Elysia. "After the ground shook earlier, I expected something more cataclysmic."

"That part comes later." Delia winked and held out her hand toward the cloaked witches walking away from the circle in two lines. "After you."

Elysia pulled Cerek with her and followed the witches.

"Where are we going?" he asked in a low voice as they stepped out of the circle.

"To finish the rest of the ceremony."

"There's more? The priestess said that was it."

"That was it for *her.*"

Cerek had no idea what Elysia meant, but he hoped it meant they were headed someplace where they could be alone. Ever since he'd stopped the ceremony to talk to her about the whole soul mate thing and she'd kissed him in the trees, he'd been itching to kiss her like that again.

The witches stopped in the middle of a clearing. Turning to face each other, they formed two lines and held their lanterns high, creating an archway of light. Down the path they created, Cerek spotted a tent illuminated by a warm glow from inside.

"Here we part ways," Delia announced behind them. He and Elysia turned to look her way. Delia held out her hands, her white hair catching the rays of moonlight until it appeared almost silver. "Go forth and complete the binding ritual with the blessing of the classic elements and of the Creator, whose gifts make this union possible."

Elysia bowed. Cerek did the same. Turning quickly, Elysia pulled him with her beneath the witches' lanterns.

"She didn't mean what I think she meant, did she?" Cerek asked in a whisper as they passed under the light.

"She meant *exactly* that." Elysia grinned back at him with so much heat he grew hot and hard and achy.

"In that case…" He swept her up into his arms. "What are we waiting for?"

Her laughter rang through the meadow as two witches at the far end pulled back the tent flaps. Applause echoed behind him, but the second he stepped into the tent illuminated with dozens of candles of all shapes and sizes, the central space filled with a fur rug and more pillows than he could count, he blocked out the witches, the ceremony, even what was happening back on Olympus and in Argolea. Because all that mattered was this. All he needed until the end of eternity was *her.*

Lowering Elysia to her feet, he drew her against him. "Come to me, *emmoni.*"

Her whispered, "Yes," as she lifted to his kiss was the sweetest word he'd ever heard.

CHAPTER TWENTY

Warmth flowed through Elysia's entire body as she wrapped her arms around Cerek and kissed him.

His hands slid down her back as his tongue stroked against hers, molded to her curves, and pulled her tight against him. He kissed the corner of her mouth, her jaw, nuzzled against her neck until she trembled. "Gods, I love you."

Her heart swelled. Lifting her hands to his face, she drew his mouth back to hers and kissed him again, walking backward and pulling him with her toward the mountain of pillows in the middle of the tent. "Show me," she said, angling her head the other way. "Show me now."

His groan was one of hunger, of need, of desperation...the same desperation bubbling inside her. His tongue swept over hers as he trailed his hands back up her spine and worked the buttons of her gown one by one.

When the last button slipped free, he drew back from her mouth, shifted his hands to the shoulders of her dress, and pushed the fabric down her arms. The gown fell to her feet in a puddle of silk, and the heat in his eyes as they traveled down her naked flesh made her nipples pebble, made her stomach cave in, made her limbs tremble with need.

"Mine," he whispered, raking her body with his lusty gaze. "This is mine."

He cupped her right breast with his warm, rough palm, lowered his head, and laved his tongue over the tip. Elysia gasped, gripped his shoulders, and groaned as pleasure arced from her nipple to her sex.

She'd never wanted to be any male's. Had always thought the soul mate curse was just that—a curse to the female because she didn't feel the same draw of the soul mate bond. But this wasn't a curse. This was a connection. A connection that told her this was exactly where she was supposed to be.

She grasped his face again, pulled his mouth back up to hers, kissed him crazy while she fumbled with the sash at his waist. Pulling it free, she tugged his shirt up at the hem, drew back from his mouth long enough to jerk it over his head, and tossed it on the ground.

His arms closed around her waist. Hers circled his shoulders to pull him in tight so her breasts pressed up against his strong bare chest. The swell of his erection pushed against her belly, and she squirmed against it, desperate to give him pleasure, to draw him to release, to join him as he crested the wave.

He pulled back, breathless, his lips swollen from her kisses. "I need you, *emmoni.*"

"Yes." Heat burned in her veins. She rubbed against him again, looking deep into his fathomless eyes. "Yes."

He groaned and claimed her mouth, lifting her feet off the floor so he could kick her dress away, then dragging her to the pillows. His hot, slick tongue traced hers as he pushed between her legs and palmed her breast. Pressure gathered in her nipples, shot straight to her core. She moaned as he kissed her jaw, her throat, as he worked his way down to lick and suck and nip at one swollen breast and then the other.

Her sex grew wet, hot, achy. She threaded her fingers through his hair and lifted her hips, desperate for friction, for him, for more.

He trailed his mouth lower, down her abs and across her belly button. She groaned as his hot breath tickled her skin. He kissed the top of her mound and the sensitive line between her torso and leg. She jerked back, moaning in frustration as she tossed her head against the pillows. Just when she was sure he was only interested in teasing, he pushed one leg wide and drew the flat of his tongue up her core.

"Oh...." She arched up against his mouth. Groaned when his tongue flicked her clit, then slid back down and circled her opening. "...yes."

"That's it." He licked the length of her slit again. "Say my name, *emmoní*. Know who you belong to."

Him. She belonged to him. Her sex tightened as he drew his tongue over her clit again and again. As he slid one finger down to her opening and pressed inside, stretching her. Groaning, she rocked against his mouth, against his thick digit pumping slowly inside her.

"Oh, Cerek..." Her hands fell out to the sides to grip the pillows around her. She lifted and lowered her hips, reveling in the erotic sparks growing in her core. "Yes. Oh yes, that feels so good. Don't stop."

He flicked faster with his tongue, drew his finger out, then pressed back in with two. Pleasure gathered deep inside.

"Tell me," he said, breathing hot over her mound. "Tell me who you belong to. "

"Ah..." The orgasm spiraled in like a tornado. She clenched around his fingers. Lifted toward his mouth.

Just before it hit, he pulled free of her body. Fabric rustled as cool air washed over her. Panting, Elysia opened her eyes to see where he'd gone, then gasped as he knelt between her spread legs, grasped her around the waist, and tugged her upper body from the floor to pull her against him.

She grappled for his shoulders so she wouldn't fall. His arms closed tight around her. Then he was there, pressing between her legs, the blunt head of his cock sliding through her wetness to rest at the apex of her body until she groaned.

"Tell me," he breathed against her lips. "Tell me who you belong to."

Her heart filled with love, with devotion, with purity and an overwhelming sense of completion. "You," she whispered. "I belong to you, and you belong to me. Always."

His mouth captured hers, his tongue thrusting inside just as his cock speared deep inside her body.

Pleasure streaked through her core. She gripped his shoulders and cried out. Held on as he drew back and drove inside again. Her sex grew tighter, wetter, hotter around his thick length. His strokes came faster with every thrust, harder with every retreat, deeper with every plunge. Sweat slicked her skin. Fire raced along her nerve endings. She braced her knees on each side of his hips, lifted and lowered to his strokes. And just before the orgasm hit, an image flashed in her brain. An image of a cave, stone walls, candles burning, and a female with fire-red hair chanting the words of a spell.

She gasped because the image came out of nowhere. But before she could process what she'd seen, he drove deep once more and groaned. And when his climax hit, it triggered hers, sending her into a dark orgasmic bliss that consumed every nerve and cell and thought. Blue and silver light filled the tent, spiraling together above them in a conjoined helix until the orgasm faded and the illumination slowly dissipated to nothing more than candlelight.

Panting, Elysia blinked several times and looked up at the peaked ceiling of the tent. Shadows danced over the walls. Somehow she'd ended up on her back in the pillows with a sweaty Cerek draped over her.

"I'll move in a second," he mumbled against her.

"You don't need to move. I like you right where you are."

"Good. Because my brain's having trouble coming back online."

Smiling, she ran her hands down his damp spine. But the smile faded as she thought back to the image she'd drawn from him. An image she knew instinctively was a memory.

Groaning, he rolled to his back in the pillows, but he dragged her with him, pulling her against his side. "Holy *skata*. What was that weird light?"

"The end of the binding ceremony."

He glanced down at her with the cutest confused look, his brown hair mussed and damp, his brow wrinkled and lips swollen from her kiss, she couldn't help but laugh. "Twisting binding souls, Cerek."

"Through sex?"

Perching her elbow on the pillows, she rested her head on her hand. "You're the one who told me there's power in sex. It's amplified in the binding ceremony, which is no different from the Great Rite covens have been practicing for millennia."

"Does it happen this way for all who are bound, or just when a witch performs the ceremony?"

"For all. The ceremony's the same whether it's done by a high priestess in nature or high priest in a temple in Tiyrns. So long as the participants involved are in love and committed."

He smiled and pulled her closer to his side. "I guess we qualify."

They definitely did. She snuggled into him and drew in a deep whiff of his musky scent.

"Oh!" Pushing away, she sat up and lifted her foot from the floor. "I almost forgot."

"What?" He eased up onto his elbows.

"Proof we're bound." She held up her foot so he could see the marking on the inside of her right ankle. The Alpha marking all Argoleans were born with signifying the origin of their race, only now her marking was intertwined with the Omega symbol.

"It's the same as the coin Delia put into the ground," he said, studying the mark.

"Yep." She lowered her foot. "The Alpha marking changes after a person is bound. And you have one too. Somewhere."

"No, I don't."

"You have to. You're Argolean. I bet the gods hid it on Olympus, like they did with your Argonaut markings." She glanced over his strong, sexy, naked body. Stilled when she spotted it. "Look at your arm."

He glanced at his left arm, then to his right. And when he spotted the same intertwined Alpha and Omega on his right biceps, where Aphrodite's rose brand had once been, his eyes grew wide. "Whoa."

"You're not hers anymore." Elysia leaned down and kissed him, pushing him into the pillows once more. "You're mine."

They kissed until they were breathless. Sighing, she snuggled into him and laid her head on his chest.

"I like being yours," he said softly, running his hand up and down her arm in a languid way that sent tiny shivers all across her skin.

She liked it too. And she planned to keep him hers, no matter what Zeus or Aphrodite or Athena had planned.

"Cerek," she said after several minutes. "What's the first thing you remember from Olympus?"

"I'm not sure. A lot of the past is a blur. I don't really remember meeting Aphrodite or being assigned to her. I just remember being in her temple."

"Nothing before that?"

"There is one thing. I remember a female with fire-red hair and bright green eyes. I know she spoke to me. But I'm not sure what she said."

Elysia pushed up on her elbow again. "I think she was a witch."

He looked up at her with an amused expression. "Why?"

"I told you my gift is accessing memories. A few minutes ago, I picked up one from you. You were in a cave somewhere, and a very tall female with red hair and green eyes was chanting over you. My father comes from a long line of witches. I recognized the spell she was chanting. It was an eradication spell."

His brow dropped. "An er-what spell?"

Elysia sat up and brushed a lock of hair out of her eyes. The ivy crowns they'd both worn during the binding ceremony had ended up on the floor, and she pulled at one of the jewel's Juniper had used to decorate her updo. "Eradication spells are used to get rid of things. I think she used it to wipe your memory. An eradication spell could do that."

"Why would a witch be on Olympus?"

"I don't know. Unless Zeus needed her for something."

He stared at her so long, a tingle ran down her spine. "What are you thinking?" she asked.

He sat up next to her. "I think we should leave."

"This tent? But we just got here."

"No, leave Argolea."

"Why? We're safe here. The Olympians can't cross into this realm, and now that we're bound, the Sirens can't come after me again."

"I'm not afraid of the gods or the Sirens. I'm worried about something else."

That tingle intensified. "What are you talking about?"

He glanced around the tent with a wary expression. "Ever since we crossed into this realm, I've had a strange feeling. Like something's waiting to happen. Like I shouldn't be here." He looked into her eyes. "Your father feels it too."

Her pulse sped up, but she told herself what he was feeling was just stress. "Cerek." She reached for his hand. "My father's judgment is clouded because he's worried about me and because he's overprotective. Don't let him dictate what happens between us."

"Maybe he has a reason to be worried."

Panic spread all through her chest. "What do you mean?"

"I don't know. I just know how I felt at that castle. Something there isn't right."

At the castle... Her panic ebbed. "I'm sure you're just picking up my father's anxious vibes." When he frowned, she squeezed his hand. "Look, I know you don't remember this place. I know everything feels new and that you've been inundated by people expecting you to remember them. I get that it might make you want to leave. But this is home for both of us. You have to give it a chance to feel like home."

"Home isn't a realm or a castle or a city, *emmoni*. Home is wherever you are. As long as we're together, we can make our home anywhere."

Her heart swelled. She felt that way too. But there was too much at stake now to just leave. "Cerek, I've dreamt of running away my whole life. I never wanted to rule. I grew up hating that my every move was observed and recorded. But these last few months with the Sirens taught me one very valuable lesson. You can't run away from your destiny. After I was taken from here, I thought I was destined to serve with the Sirens, but now I know that wasn't my path. My path was to come back here"—she squeezed his hand—"with you. I didn't have choice in whom I was born to and neither did you. But our paths intertwined for a reason. I have to believe that wasn't a coincidence. We're destined to do something important, together."

His worried gaze searched hers. "And what if our destinies aren't the same?"

"We're bound now. We won't let them be different."

His jaw clenched as he stared at her. Panic trickled in again, but she tried to force it back.

"You're right," he said after several long moments, pulling her against the warmth of his chest. He kissed her temple. "We won't let them be different. We're together now no matter what."

She wrapped her arms around him and held on tight. "No matter what," she repeated.

But worry niggled at the back of her mind, because he didn't sound convinced. And as she thought back over the memory she'd pulled from him, she couldn't help but wonder if the strange feeling he'd spoken of really was just her father's disapproval or if there was something more sinister at work beneath the surface.

"Cerek's missing too." Orpheus moved into Theron's office where Demetrius stood next to his mate, discussing Elysia's disappearance.

A darkness Demetrius only just barely held back swirled inside him. "Are you certain?"

"Pretty damn. He didn't go back to his room last night after the party, and Max called from Ari's place. No sign of him there either."

"*Skata.*" Demetrius's jaw clenched down hard, and he stepped toward the door.

"Demetrius," Isadora called at his back, but he didn't turn. She didn't want to believe the worst, but he was done pretending this wasn't happening.

"Hold up." Theron moved in front of Demetrius before he could reach the door and pressed a hand against his chest. "We don't know that they're together. We all need to stay calm until we have more information."

"I know they're together. And don't tell me to stay calm. If it were Talisa he'd targeted, you wouldn't be so fucking calm."

"He's one of us, D," Zander said from across the room, his thick arms crossed over his chest.

"I don't fucking care who he is," Demetrius answered, glaring at the blond Argonaut. "He bears the mark of the rose. You know what that means."

"He does have a point," Orpheus said. "I spent plenty of time slinking around Olympus in the old days. The rose is Aphrodite's symbol. All her pleasure slaves have them. Lotta sick shit goes on in her palace, let me tell ya."

Isadora glared Orpheus's way. "You're not helping."

"What?" Orpheus shrugged and crossed to sit on the arm of the leather couch. "I'm just sayin'. D has a right to be stressed." Leaning toward Titus on the couch, he muttered, "This is why I never wanted to have young."

"Yeah, you really put your foot down on that one," Titus muttered back. "Got two for the price of one."

Orpheus frowned and folded his arms over his chest. "Melita's getting locked up until she's two hundred."

"Might want to think about locking your Siren up instead," Titus answered. "She's projecting loudly these days. Female's got a serious case of baby fever. Again."

"She does not." Panic filled Orpheus's gray eyes. "Does she?"

"Oh yeah." Phineus chuckled from his seat beside Titus. "And you thought the Underworld was a wild ride. Orpheus with a whole litter. This is going to be fun to watch."

"Fuck me," Orpheus mumbled.

"Can we please focus?" Demetrius glared at Phin, Titus, and O. "We need to find my daughter before the Sirens show up to take her to Olympus or before Cerek takes her back for them."

"He wouldn't do that," Theron said.

"And how do you know?" Demetrius turned his glare on Theron. "There's something off about him. I know you've sensed it too." He glanced around the room. "I know you all have, only none of you want to admit it. Even Callia picked up some kind of dark energy radiating from him when she did his exam."

Theron looked past Demetrius toward Zander, Callia's mate.

Zander frowned. "Callia's not sure what she sensed."

"But she suspects the energy was likely related to whoever wiped his memories," Isadora added.

"It's more than that," Demetrius said, turning his attention to his mate. "And you know it too." To the rest of the room, he added, "It's time we all stop pretending he's fine, because he's not. I don't care what story he and Elysia are telling. They didn't escape Olympus. No one escapes the Sirens that easily. Zeus let them go. He let them go for a purpose."

"And what purpose would that be?" Gryphon asked from the opposite side of the room.

"To attack the heart of who we are," Demetrius answered. "Zeus hates the Argonauts not just because of what we've done, but because of what we stand for. Family, faith, the future of Argolea. I wouldn't put it past him to go after the people who mean the most to us in his sick need for revenge. If we collapse, then Argolea is ripe for the Sirens to conquer. Forget about any political threat from the Council. Right now, our biggest threat is Zeus and what he has planned."

The guardians all exchanged glances, and a heavy silence spread over the room. None of them were safe if that was Zeus's plan. They all had mates, children, attachments in this realm that kept them whole. And a broken Argonaut—as Ari had proved when he'd lost his soul mate—was a danger not just to himself but to anyone around him.

"Any word?" Ari's voice echoed from the hall.

All eyes turned to look his way where he stood with Max in the doorway.

"What?" Ari asked, glancing from face to face.

Theron moved to Ari's side. "We might have a problem."

Worry darkened Ari's mismatched eyes. "Shit. Not Sirens again."

"No." Theron's jaw clenched. "Some concerns have been presented. About Cerek."

"What kind of concerns?" Max asked.

"The kind that don't matter," a female voice said behind Ari.

Demetrius's pulse skipped as he glanced past Ari toward Elysia, standing in the doorway. "*Angeklos?*"

"Yes, I'm here, *patéras*. And you can stop talking about Cerek as if he's Zeus's evil minion, because he's not." Cerek stepped into the doorway beside her, and as she reached for his hand, the darkness inside Demetrius screamed to be released. "He's my mate now. We were bound last night."

CHAPTER TWENTY-ONE

Silence settled over the room. A silence that should have made the hair on Cerek's nape stand straight but didn't because all he could focus on was the weird energy again. The one he'd felt tingling in his limbs as soon as they'd stepped foot in the castle. The one urging him to walk out of this room right now and find...

Holy hell, he didn't know what he was supposed to find. All he knew was that it was tugging at him to find something.

Fighting the pull, he glanced around at the eight Argonauts staring toward the doorway where he and Elysia stood. Though the office was big, with two-story ceilings and arched windows that looked out over the city shimmering in the morning light, the males seemed to suck up all the space, dwarfing Elysia and her mother.

"What did you say?" Demetrius asked slowly, a vein in his temple bulging as if it were about to explode.

"You heard what I said." To the Argonauts, Elysia said, "I'd like to speak with my parents in private if you don't mind."

The Argonauts exchanged worried looks, but when the queen nodded, they slowly filed out of the room. Several—Cerek wasn't sure who—muttered comments as they left. He picked up "Way to go," and "Good luck, buddy," and the long-haired guardian who always wore the gloves mumbled, "Well, that was one way to go." But Theron's warning gaze caught Cerek's attention as he passed, and when the leader of the Argonauts said, "I'll be right outside in case he tries to kill either of you," Cerek realized the shit storm he'd started when he'd stayed on Pandora with Elysia wasn't simply going to hit the fan, it was about to rain holy hell down all over him.

His spine stiffened, and he stood a little taller. Maybe he deserved whatever was coming his way, but her parents deserved it too for trying to bind her to someone she didn't want.

Only Ari stayed. Elysia's father shot him an intimidating look, but it had no effect on the guardian. Ari perched his hands on his hips and shook his head. "If they're bound, that makes us family. Sorry, D, but you're stuck with me now."

At least Cerek had one person on his side. Correction, two. He had Elysia. He squeezed her hand.

"I don't believe you're bound," Demetrius said when the Argonauts had all left.

"Believe it." Elysia let go of Cerek's hand and tugged the edge of her pant leg up so her parents could see the Alpha and Omega marking on her ankle.

"Holy *skata*." Demetrius stiffened, and that vein in his temple pulsed faster. "Who did this?"

"Delia," Elysia answered.

"Fucking witch," Demetrius muttered.

Elysia crossed her arms over her chest. "Well, seeing as how you're part witch, I guess that's a diss on you, and me, *patéras*."

"Elysia." The queen squeezed her mate's arm and stepped forward. She sent Cerek a worried look before focusing on her daughter. "Your father has every right to be upset. We had no idea where you'd gone last night. We've been sick with worry for hours. And then we find out you ran off and were bound? How could you do that without—"

"How could *I*?" Elysia's voice lifted, and her arms dropped to her sides. "How could both of you? You were going to bind me to Nereus like I was nothing but property. And don't try to deny it," she added when her father opened his mouth, "because I know it's the truth. You're not upset I'm bound. You're upset you didn't get to benefit politically from the arrangement."

Tension curled like a thick fog all through the room. A tension Cerek knew he was responsible for.

"That's not true," the queen said softly. "Your father and I talked last night and we both agreed there would be no binding, to Nereus or anyone, unless you were in favor of the union. And any discussions we had on the matter were done in an attempt to keep you safe—then and now. That's our duty as your parents, Elysia, to keep you safe. If Zeus—"

"If Zeus comes after me, I know how to take care of myself. I killed harpies on Pandora. I trained with the Sirens on Olympus. Not only that, but I escaped from both the gods and that hellhole of an island. How many Siren recruits do you know who've done either of those things? How many Argoleans? I'm not the weakling you both think I am. And I wasn't about to be bound to someone you picked out just because you think I can't take care of myself. I'm not a child anymore—"

"We know you aren't," the queen said.

"—and I'm done letting you treat me like one."

"Then start acting like a grown-up," Demetrius cut in.

Elysia's mouth snapped closed, but her hard, narrowed eyes pinned on her father told Cerek she wasn't about to back down. And the way Demetrius glared back at her was a big red warning flag that this argument was nowhere near over.

Cerek didn't want to be the cause of a rift between her and her parents. Family was something he'd never known. He wouldn't be able to live with himself if he was the reason she walked away from hers.

"The binding was my idea," he said. "Not because I think she needs me to keep her safe, but because I love her."

Elysia turned his way, and when their gazes met, he felt that connection deep inside. The one he'd felt from the very first. Her eyes softened, and she reached for his hand once more. As her warm fingers slid around his, he knew this was right. That they were meant for each other. That it no longer mattered what anyone thought.

He looked back at her parents. "*She* saved *me*, more than once. On Olympus, on Pandora, here. And I wasn't about to lose her, to you or Zeus or anyone. So if you want to be pissed at someone, be pissed at me."

Demetrius crossed his arms over his chest and leaned back against the desk, but his jaw was a little less clenched, his expression a bit more relaxed. The queen's mouth softened, and her chocolate eyes grew damp. From the corner of his vision, Cerek saw Ari smile like an idiot.

The tension in the center of his chest uncoiled.

"*Materas*," Elysia said, her voice gentling. "*Pampas*... I know this is not what you envisioned for me, but this is what I want. This is my choice. I love Cerek, and I would have chosen him even if I'd never known about the arranged binding with Nereus." She looked toward her father. "You, of all people, should understand. Once we found each other and realized who he was and that I was his soul mate, this was inevitable. I know you have—"

"Whoa." Demetrius dropped his arms and pushed away from the desk. "Soul mate?" He looked between Elysia and Cerek. "She's your *soul mate*?"

Icy fingers squeezed the air from Cerek's chest. He tried to remember back to what Elysia had told him about the whole soul mate connection.

"Holy *skata*." Demetrius's jaw tightened once more, and he glanced toward the queen, whose own worried expression sent Cerek's pulse up all over again.

Elysia had made the soul mate bond sound like a good thing, but Delia had called it a curse. Was it a curse? Had he missed something in his rush to make Elysia his?

Scowling, Demetrius pinned Cerek with a hard look. "I guarantee Zeus knew about this. That's why he took Elysia."

Cerek's spine stiffened.

"You don't know that," Ari said.

"Why else would he take her?" Demetrius glared at the Argonaut. "Immortal law states Zeus can choose any female from the age of twenty to join the Sirens. She's twenty-five. Why did he wait five years? I'll tell you why. Because he didn't know she was Cerek's fucking soul mate until recently."

Ari held up his hands. "D, you need to dial it down a notch, because you're jumping to all kinds of conclusions that make no sense. How would Zeus even know that? The soul mate bond is Hera's curse, not his."

"Which Zeus clearly discovered when he fucked with your son's head."

A warning tingle raced down Cerek's spine, one that grew in intensity even when Elysia squeezed his hand in reassurance.

"So you're saying Zeus set this up?" the queen asked. "Forced them together so they'd be drawn to each other? Why would he do that?"

"Hell if I know," Demetrius answered, leveling a look on Cerek again. "Maybe so she'd do exactly what she did and bring him here to Argolea. The soul mate bond is, after all, a curse. And we still don't know what Zeus has planned for him."

"This is bullshit." Ari stepped forward. "You're letting your personal feelings about this binding interfere with rational thought. There's nothing wrong with Cerek."

"Maybe not," Demetrius answered. "Then again, the soul mate curse fucked you up for a good fifty years. Maybe that's all Zeus is banking on here. That, like father, like son, the curse will tear him down the way it did you. And in the process destroy the rest of us." He glared at Cerek once more. "I'm not about to let that happen."

That weird energy tingled stronger, urging Cerek to leave, to flee, to search. The one he didn't understand but knew instinctively was somehow related to all this.

"I don't care what you *think* might happen," Elysia said to her father in a hard voice once more. "And I'm done listening to your theories about Zeus and what he may or may not have planned for Cerek. This male is an Argonaut. He's your kin. And he survived twenty-five years of hell to come back to this realm and the people who are supposed to care for him. If you can't accept him for who he is now, then you can't accept me. We're bound, whether you like it or not. And that means where he goes, I go, even if that's out of this castle forever."

Cerek glanced Elysia's way. At her strong jaw, determined chin, and the fire in her dark eyes as she met her father's gaze. No one believed in him the way she did. No one had ever stood up for him the way she just had. Warmth and love pushed aside the weird energy. A love he planned to show her tenfold as soon as they were alone.

"Come on, Cerek." Stepping back, she pulled him with her toward the door. "This conversation is over."

Relief trickled through Cerek.

"Elysia." Demetrius's voice rang out. Stopping in the doorway, they both turned and looked back. "Stay within the castle walls."

"Is that an order?" she asked.

"No." Demetrius's shoulders relaxed. "It's a request. At least until we can send word to Olympus that you're...bound."

Elysia nodded. Looking up at Cerek, she said, "Are you okay with that?"

Cerek wanted nothing more than to leave this castle for good, but he didn't say so. He nodded. Because more than fleeing, he wanted Elysia to be happy, and he knew she never would be until she mended her tattered relationship with her parents.

He just hoped she did so before whatever this odd energy was grew too strong to resist.

"You know, if you can't sleep," Elysia said, rolling to her side and propping her head on her hand, "I can think of something way more exciting for you to do right here in this bed than staring out the window."

Cerek turned from the moonlit view of the city with a half grin that warmed Elysia's insides. "Sorry if I woke you. I thought you were asleep."

"I can't sleep when you're stressing."

"I'm not stressing."

She huffed. "You've been pacing. I know the sounds of an anxious male. Have you met my father?"

Frowning, he leaned back against the windowsill and crossed his arms over his chest, the movement pulling at the thin white T-shirt he wore over all those strong, sexy muscles she wanted to trace with her tongue. "I'm not like your father."

She smiled, because deep down, he was exactly like her father—gentle, loving, protective—which was part of the reason she was so attracted to him.

"Your parents are right across the hall, and your father thinks I'm Zeus's yes-boy. I'm pretty sure I have every reason to stress."

He did, but that wasn't why he was so anxious. She couldn't put her finger on what exactly was bothering him, but she knew it wasn't just her father's little rant. The only time he'd seemed like the relaxed Cerek she'd known on Olympus was when they'd left the castle for the binding ceremony. Logic said *that* should have stressed him out more than anything else, but it hadn't. Here in the castle, though—anytime he'd been in Tiryns, really—he seemed agitated, unsettled…restless. And she couldn't stop thinking back to his words in that tent after they'd been bound, when he'd begged her to run away with him.

Tossing back the covers, she threw her legs over the side of the bed and crossed to where he leaned against the sill. "There are at least four doors between us and my parents, who, by the way, are clear across the corridor. They can't hear us."

He unfolded his arms as she straddled his legs, and his hands landed at her waist to tickle the silky fabric of her nightgown against her skin. "You know there's no way your father's sleeping tonight with me here in this room alone with you."

"I know." Elysia brushed her hands over his warm chest and smiled. "But I really don't care. You're mine, Guardian."

She leaned in to kiss him, but he eased back and frowned. "What's wrong?" she asked.

"I'm not a guardian. I might have the markings, but that doesn't make me an Argonaut."

"Maybe not yet. But in time, you'll start to feel like one of them. They're all thrilled to have you back."

"All except your father."

She rolled her eyes. "My father's just being overprotective."

"Aren't you worried he could be right?"

"No."

"Why not? You heard what he said. It makes sense in a sick sort of way. Zeus killed me, brought me back to life with some kind of magic, and then he took you... five years *after* he could have taken you. He wouldn't have done that unless he knew we were soul mates."

In some way, yes, it made sense. But it was the rantings of a worried father, not of a logical warrior. "Cerek. How would Zeus know that? The Argonauts don't even know who their soul mates are until they meet them."

"If he used a witch to wipe my memories, he might know. I don't know how magic works, just that it does. Your aunt, the healer, said she sensed dark magic in me as well."

"She said she sensed the residual effects of dark magic. Nothing more."

"Isn't that enough to worry you?"

"No." She shifted her hands to his shoulders and squeezed because she sensed he was growing more agitated by the second. "What you're talking about is some elaborate plan. To what end? To bring you back here so you can destroy the Argonauts as my father predicts? That won't happen. Memory or not, we both know you wouldn't hurt them. And as far as Zeus taking me for the Sirens, I think it's pretty clear he did that to get back at my parents for messing with his plans all these years. It's no secret he hates my mother and the Argonauts. My father has no proof, Cerek. He's just trying to put doubt in your mind so you'll stay away from me.

Well, I'm not falling for it. There's nothing wrong with you. Absolutely nothing. You're mine and you're perfect."

His dark eyes, filled with so much uncertainty, searched hers. "How can you be so sure?"

She lifted her hands to his face and brushed her palms over the soft stubble along his jaw. "The same way I knew to trust you on Pandora. The same way I knew to believe in you on Olympus. The exact same way I knew binding my soul to yours was the right thing to do. Because I know your heart, and it is good and true and, above all else, honest."

His eyes slid closed, and as he dropped his forehead against her shoulder, her heart squeezed tight over the stress and worry he was struggling to make sense of. She trailed one hand up and through his silky hair, hoping to reassure him. "No one dictates this life but us. Not my parents. Not Zeus. Just you and me."

He lifted his head, and his gorgeous brown eyes opened and held on hers. But they were pained eyes. Tormented eyes. Eyes that still didn't look a bit convinced. "I love you, Elysia. I love you so much it hurts. And I would never, ever do anything to cause you pain or distress."

"I know that," she whispered.

"I hope you remember it."

She had no idea what he was talking about, but her pulse sped up and her heart beat so hard against her ribs as he stared at her, she was afraid it might leave bruises in its wake. Sighing, he wrapped his arms around her waist and drew her close, but he didn't kiss her as she wanted. Just buried his face in her hair and breathed long, shaky breaths against her neck that sent her own anxiety straight up.

He couldn't be right. She closed her arms around his shoulders and held him. Her father was just causing problems. There was nothing wrong with Cerek, and she'd do whatever it took to convince him of that fact.

A knock sounded at the outer door of her suite, causing Cerek to draw back. The muscles in his shoulders and legs immediately tensed as he looked toward the living area.

The last thing she wanted was for him to be subjected to another of her father's rants. Pushing away, she grabbed her robe from the foot of the bed. "I'll get that. You just get back in that bed so we can finish celebrating our binding the right way."

He tipped his head and shot her a sexy look. "Not happening. You're way too loud."

She slid her arms into the robe and smiled. "Maybe you should gag me, *ómorfos*."

His brow lifted, and his suddenly interested expression made Elysia laugh. "Hold that thought, Guardian."

She tugged the bedroom door closed at her back and tied the sash of her robe as she crossed the living area of her suite. But her mood darkened as she approached the door. She didn't really want to deal with her father right now either, but the sooner she found out what he wanted, the sooner she could get back to Cerek. Drawing a deep breath, she squared her shoulders, pulled the door open, and faltered when Ari and Daphne smiled her way.

"Hi," Ari said. "Sorry about the hour. Can we come in for a few minutes?"

"Um. Sure." Elysia pulled the door open wider so they could both enter. "Cerek?" she called as she shut the door. "It's your father."

The bedroom door opened, and Cerek stepped out, his brow drawn low. "What is it? What's wrong?"

"Nothing." Ari crossed to hug him, an action, Elysia noticed, that caused Cerek to tense all over again.

"Nothing's wrong." Ari must have felt it too, because he let go just as quickly and glanced toward his mate. "We both just wanted to come over and offer our congratulations."

"Yes." Daphne tucked her mahogany hair behind one ear. "We wanted you to know how happy we are for the both of you."

Elysia's stomach settled. She looked toward Cerek and smiled. He only continued to frown.

"We also wanted to tell you not to worry about anything Demetrius said." Ari glanced toward his son. "D's an ass." He cringed. "Sorry, Elysia. I meant—"

"I know what you meant." Elysia's smile widened. "My father is not always the easiest person to deal with."

"He's a lot better since he and your mother were bound. Before that"—Ari rested his hands on his hips and shrugged. "You don't remember what he was like before, Cerek, but trust me when I say none of the guardians wanted to be around Demetrius any more than they had to be. All this—everything he's been saying lately, though—it's only because he's been so worried about his daughter." He looked toward Elysia. "Someday, when you two have young of your own, you'll understand. It nearly killed your father when you were taken. And then when none of us could go after you because of the ramifications that would have on our so-called treaty with Olympus... Well, it was rough."

"He was continually trying to find ways to rescue you," Daphne said. "And when Max disobeyed the queen and went to Olympus only to return empty-handed, he was devastated."

All the animosity Elysia had been feeling toward her father slipped away, and her heart softened. Yes, her father was overbearing and protective and, yes, he was even an ass at times, but he was all of those things because he loved her. As much as she wanted to fault him for that, she couldn't, because she loved him just as much.

"He'll come around." Ari glanced back at Cerek. "He's just in shock right now. He got his daughter back only to lose her to you. Give the *ándras* some time."

Cerek's gaze met Elysia's from across the room, and though she still saw worry and doubt in his beautiful brown eyes, she also saw the first stirrings of belief. A belief that gave her hope.

"We also came by," Ari said, his tone lightening, "because we wanted to give you something."

Daphne handed Ari a small black box.

"This was your mother's." Ari laid the box in Cerek's hand.

Cerek lifted the hinged lid and stared down at whatever was inside.

"What is it?" Elysia asked, stepping closer.

"Rings," Ari said. "Gia was fascinated with human culture. Years ago, when the borders between our world and the human realm were more fluid, she used to travel there a lot. She picked these up on one of her trips. When two humans are bound—or married, as they call it—they exchange rings, which they each wear on the fourth fingers of their left hands. Gia thought that was terribly romantic, and she bought these for her and her future mate." His voice hitched. "Only she never found him."

Daphne moved closer to Ari and wrapped her arm around his waist. He slid his around her shoulder, tugging her tight to his side. "After, when I was moving your things to my house, *yios*. I found these in your mother's things."

Elysia stepped up next to Cerek and looked down at the twin platinum bands nestled in the velvet box. One was thicker, more masculine, the other thinner and feminine. Both were engraved with ancient Greek words. Words, Elysia realized when Cerek lifted the thicker ring and turned it, that read *η ελπίδα είναι η ζωή της αγάπης.*

Hope is the life of love.

"They meant a great deal to her," Ari went on. "I know she'd want you to have them."

Elysia looked up at Cerek, and when his eyes met hers, she saw the softest shimmer. One that told her even though he might not remember his mother, he felt her love. As strongly as he felt Elysia's love.

Elysia laid her hand over the markings on Cerek's forearm and squeezed. He blinked several times and lowered the band back into the box.

"Well." Ari let go of his mate, and they both moved toward the door. "We should probably go."

"Yeah." Cerek closed the lid on the box and followed them toward the door. "Thanks for coming by." He held up the box. "And for this."

Daphne stepped out into the hall, but Ari stopped in the doorway and laid his hand on Cerek's shoulder. "You're not alone. The Argonauts are all behind you. Even Demetrius. No matter what, we've got your back."

Cerek nodded, but Elysia couldn't see his expression.

In the awkward silence that followed, Ari cleared his throat, dropped his hand, and finally left. Cerek stood where he was long seconds as he watched his father and Daphne walk away. Closing the door quietly, he finally turned with the box in his hand.

Nerves gathered in Elysia's stomach. Unsure how to read him, she clasped her hands at the small of her back and rocked on her heels. "Feel any better?""

"A little."

A little was better than nothing. "That was very nice of them."

"Yeah, it was." He stopped in front of her and opened the box, turning it so she could see inside. "What do you think of these?"

"I think your mother had very good taste."

"Yeah," he said softly, looking down. "So do I."

"And I think she was a very brave female."

"Why do you say that?"

She reached up to brush the hair back from his temple. "Because she picked your father. Whether or not it was love doesn't matter. They made you, and she chose to have you in a time when it couldn't have been easy for a *gynaíka* in this realm to raise a child alone. She loved you. I heard it in Ari's voice. I saw it in your eyes. Whether you remember her or not is irrelevant. I know you feel her. Love is the one thing that endures. Through good and bad, life and death, it's always there."

He looked down again, running his fingers over the cool metal bands in the box. Blinking several times, he tugged the rings free of the velvet and tossed the box on the couch. "Would you wear this, *emmoní?* For me?"

The way he looked down at her, his handsome face filled with so much love, her insides absolutely melted. "Only if you believe the words."

His eyes went all soft and dreamy. The way they had on Pandora. The way they had in Athena's temple. The way they had last night when they'd been bound. "I do." He reached for her left hand. "But not because they're engraved on these rings. Because of you."

Love and hope pushed away all the worry and fear lingering inside. He slid the ring down her finger, and the band encircled her skin like an unbreakable promise.

"I do too." She took the second ring and reached for his left hand, sliding it past his thick knuckle to the base of his finger. "I believe in us. Nothing can break this bond, Cerek. Absolutely nothing."

His lips met hers, and his arms wound around her back to pull her tight against him. And as she lost herself in the taste and feel and heat of him, she repeated the words in her head.

Everything will be okay.

She'd make sure of it.

CHAPTER TWENTY-TWO

Cerek opened his eyes in the dead of night and stared at the dark ceiling high above.

Against his chest, Elysia groaned and snuggled closer, her bare leg sliding over his beneath the covers while her warm breath heated the skin near his heart.

"Shh, *emmoní.*" Pressing a kiss to the top of her head, he trailed his fingers down the length of her hair to soothe her. "Go back to sleep."

She relaxed against him, and her breaths slowly lengthened as sleep overtook her once more. But he couldn't join her. He hadn't been able to sleep, not after his father had left and he'd carried her to this bed, laid her out, and made love to her until they were both sweaty and shaking. Not after she'd tugged his head against her breast and massaged his scalp. Not even after she'd sensed he was still not sleepy, slid beneath the covers, and taken him deep in her mouth until he'd exploded.

He should be wrecked from two powerful orgasms and a day—who was he kidding, *days*—filled with drama. But he wasn't. Because every time his focus turned away from Elysia, all he felt was that weird energy in his limbs. All he knew was some strange desire to climb out of this bed and go...he didn't know where.

Elysia groaned again and shifted against him. Knowing his anxiety was ruining her rest, he gently tugged his arm out from beneath her and watched her roll to her side away from him.

His heart pinched as his gaze drifted to the ring on her finger. Gods, he really did love her. Not because she was his soul mate but because she understood him in a way no one ever had before. She was right. Nothing could break this bond between them. He needed to stop worrying, because that worry was only causing her stress.

She sighed and relaxed into her pillow. Not wanting to disturb her any more, he pressed a soft kiss against her temple. "Sleep, *emmoní*."

Carefully, so as not to wake her, he climbed out of bed, tugged on his sweats and T-shirt, and moved soundlessly out of the room. Closing the door at his back, he stood in the dark living room and drew a deep breath that did nothing to relax the tingling in his limbs.

Food might help. He hadn't eaten much the last few days. Maybe this weird energy was hunger.

He headed for the hall, hoping like hell the whole way that it was hunger.

At the main corridor, he turned left. The marble beneath his bare feet was cool. Low light from sconces along the walls lit his way. He passed massive oil paintings, pillars that rose to the arced ceiling, wide doorways that opened to libraries and offices and suites. At the grand staircase, he didn't stop. Just moved up the steps to his right as soundlessly as he'd moved across the floor.

Something was pulling him. Something that had nothing to do with nourishment or hunger. It was like a magnet, pushing his legs into motion, drawing him closer. Dragging him toward a purpose he couldn't see.

He followed the curved staircase to the highest level. The stairs came to an end at a set of double doors. Pulling the right side open, he stepped beneath the archway and moved into the octagonal-shaped room with walls of glass.

His feet slowed. The floor here wasn't marble but wood. Not a single piece of furniture, art, or adornment decorated the empty room. The eight walls rose fifteen feet and angled in to form a peak. Moonlight shone through the glass to cast shadows along the hardwood, and the twinkling lights of Tiyrns far below and the stars high above illuminated what was left.

The energy vibrating in his legs and chest intensified, pushing him farther into the room. He stopped beneath the peaked ceiling and looked down. The hardwood gave way to intarsia, an elaborate mosaic of inlaid wood that created a 3-D image of a winged Omega symbol.

He ran his bare foot over the pattern. It was flat, the illusion of depth created by the different colors in the woods of the image. His heart beat hard as he lifted his gaze four feet above the intarsia. Energy gathered in his arms and shot to his hands, making him draw the three middle fingers of both hands together to form a peak.

Nothing happened. He wasn't sure why he was here. Didn't know what he was doing. But the heavy vibrations in his limbs wouldn't let him leave. Staring at the empty space above the winged Omega, he heard words echo in his mind. Words that were foreign and made no sense. Before he knew what he was doing, he spoke the words aloud:

"*Hekàs, ô hekàs, éste bébêloi.*"

A flash of light illuminated the room, followed by a pop and a sizzle. Cerek's spine tingled as the words he'd just spoken translated in his head: *Begone whatever is unholy.*

Confusion rushed in. What could be unholy in this room? There was nothing here but air.

No sooner did the thought hit than a small portal the size of a porthole window opened above the winged Omega, sizzling with energy all around the edges. A warning blare echoed in his ears when he spotted a small metal disk in the window, one with four chambers, three of which were filled. One chamber held a diamond. The second housed a teardrop-shaped glass container swirling with a white cloud of gas. In the third sat a vial of red liquid that looked like blood.

His eyes grew wide, and his heart raced when he realized what he was seeing. The Orb of Krónos. The magical medallion that was home to the four classic elements—earth, air, water, and fire—and had the strength to grant the owner powers never seen before, not by any god.

Some unseen force lifted his hand away from his body, reached through the open portal, and closed his fingers around the Orb. Power raced into his fingers, up his arm, and straight into the center of his chest, obliterating every other thought and desire and want.

In a moment of absolute clarity, he realized this was his purpose. This was what he'd been reborn to find. This disk did not belong to the Argoleans but to the king of the gods, and it was his destiny to return it to its rightful owner.

* * *

Elysia sat upright in bed and gasped.

"Cerek?" She looked across the bed to find his side empty. "Cerek?" Her gaze darted around the dark room.

Her heart beat strong and fast, and perspiration dotted her spine as she threw back the covers, pulled on her nightgown from the floor, and found her robe. Something was wrong. Something didn't feel right. Her hands shook as she belted the robe and rushed for the living area. Again the dark room was empty.

She darted out into the hall, looked up and down the dark corridor. Turning to her left, she pushed her feet into a run, her bare soles connecting with the cold marble. Her pulse turned to a roar in her ears. When she reached the staircase, she stopped, looked up and down. Wasn't sure which way to go.

"Son of a bitch."

She whipped around to see her father rushing toward her in the dark, dressed in sweats and a T-shirt, his dark hair mussed, his black eyes focused and intense.

"You felt it too?" he asked.

She swallowed hard, unsure what to say.

"Where is your mate?"

"I-I don't know."

"Holy *skata*." He swept past her for the stairs. "The Orb."

No. Her eyes widened. That wasn't what she'd felt. Panic swirled in her chest. "*Patéras…*"

When he didn't stop, she rushed up the stairs after him.

He climbed to the highest level in the castle and yanked open the double doors. Elysia raced after him and drew to a sharp stop inside the glass room with a gasp.

Cerek stood facing away from them. Energy snapped and sizzled at his front as the portal closed. As the flash of light slowly faded, Cerek turned toward them with the Orb of Krónos cradled in his hand.

"Oh my gods, Cerek." Elysia stepped farther into the room. "What are doing?"

His gaze lifted from the Orb to her. And she drew in a sharp breath when she saw his eyes. No, not *his* eyes. These weren't the same warm chocolate brown she'd gazed into only hours ago as they'd made love. These were black as night and empty as death.

"Not Cerek," he said in a voice that wasn't his. This voice was deeper, darker, possessed. "Cerek's usefulness has now been spent."

"Zeus," her father muttered at her side.

Cerek's crazed eyes shifted Demetrius's way. "Circe predicted you would try to protect the Orb. Your miniscule spells are nothing compared to her power, *Guardian*."

He sneered the last word and glanced back at Elysia. "Thank you for being so predictable, female. It's because of you he was able to answer his calling." Cerek's hand closed around the Orb. "This now belongs to me."

"No." Elysia reached out and stepped forward. But before she could touch him, another flash of light filled the room, followed by a swirling cloud of black smoke.

Demetrius jerked her back.

Elysia coughed as the smoke filled her lungs. Her father drew her to his chest, but Elysia struggled against his hold. When she was finally able to break free and turn, Cerek was gone.

"*Skata*," Demetrius muttered. "I'll fucking kill him."

Her father swept out of the room and rushed back down the stairs, but Elysia couldn't move. Couldn't think. Could barely breathe.

The whole time…

The whole time?

Cerek had been working for Zeus the whole time? Oh gods… He'd tricked her on Pandora, on Olympus. He'd made her fall for him so she'd bring him to Argolea, where he could then find the Orb and steal it for Zeus. Her father had been right. The black magic Demetrius had sensed around Cerek was real.

Circe… The witch Circe had been involved. She must have been the one who'd wiped his memories. Who'd set this whole plan in motion. Who'd forced him to—

The memory Elysia had picked up from Cerek when they'd made love after their binding ceremony flashed in her mind. The red-haired female standing over him, chanting an elimination spell. Except that wasn't just an elimination spell she'd heard. She replayed the memory, focusing on the words. It had also been a reprogramming spell. One that was specifically targeted to begin at a set time and in an explicit place.

Elysia covered her mouth with her hand in horror. The warm metal around her ring finger pressed against her lip, drawing her attention. Lowering her hand, she stared at the platinum band and had another memory flash. Of being in that tent with Cerek. Of the worry in his eyes when he'd tried to convince her to run away with him. Of his words as they'd lain together in the candlelight.

"Home isn't a realm or a castle or a city, emmoní. *Home is wherever you are."*

No, he hadn't betrayed her. Not on purpose, at least. No male who'd been planning something as treacherous as this could have said those words with such conviction, she'd felt them deep in her soul. She didn't believe he'd known what Zeus had planned. Wouldn't. Because she knew in her heart he was as much a victim in all of this as she was.

Panic pushed aside the shock. Panic that gave way to bone-melting fear.

Zeus had said Cerek's usefulness had now been spent. What did that mean? Was Zeus going to kill him once and for all? She couldn't let that happen. She wouldn't.

Shaking, she turned for the stairs, intent on finding her father, but stopped when she remembered her father's words.

"I'll fucking kill him."

He thought Cerek was a traitor. He'd never help her rescue Cerek from Zeus. And the Argonauts would be no help either. As soon as her father told them what Cerek had done, they'd take his side.

Her mind spun. Her hands grew sweaty. She couldn't do this alone. She needed help. She didn't even know how to get to Olympus.

Max...

Max had snuck into Olympus to find her. Max could help her get there. And Ari. Ari wouldn't side with the Argonauts over his son. He'd do whatever was needed to rescue Cerek.

Hope trickled in to swirl with the panic threatening to pull her under. A hope she prayed would carry her to Cerek before it was too late.

CHAPTER TWENTY-THREE

Cerek gasped and fell forward, landing against the cold stones beneath him on his hands and knees as a wave of consciousness returned.

"Thank you, Guardian," Zeus said somewhere above him. "You have been most useful."

Dazed, Cerek looked up and watched as Zeus smiled a malicious grin and turned the Orb of Krónos in his hands. Holy *skata*. Zeus had the Orb. Zeus had the Orb... *because I gave it to him.*

Nausea rolled through his belly, shot up his throat, and made him gag. Dropping his head again, Cerek coughed several times, trying to dispel the horror and disgust. But he couldn't get rid of it, because the reality of what he'd done hit him with the force of a tidal wave.

The energy he'd felt in the Argolean castle had been the draw of the Orb. Zeus had sent him to find it. And he'd used Cerek's connection to Elysia to ensure his victory.

Oh gods... Elysia...

His heart squeezed so tight, he groaned at the sharp slash of pain. She must hate him right now. He needed to get to her. Needed to tell her he hadn't known what he was doing. On shaky hands, he slowly pushed to his feet. He needed her to know he hadn't planned it or that he—

"So you're done with him?"

Cerek froze when he heard the familiar voice. The familiar *goddess* voice.

"Yes," Zeus answered. "He's yours, Aphrodite. After my Siren makes one slight adjustment."

Cerek glanced to his left where Zeus stood with a smug-looking Aphrodite. The Siren at his side lifted her bow, the arrow aimed directly at his heart.

"We can't have him causing any more trouble now, can we?" Zeus said. "And since we don't know when he might be of use in the future…"

A whir sounded as the arrow torpedoed away from the bow. Before Cerek could react, the tip struck him in the chest. He stumbled back but didn't fall. The arrow turned to stone inside his flesh, hardening the cells outward from the spot in a chain reaction that left him nothing more than a statue standing in the middle of Athena's temple.

A statue that could hear and feel and sense everything around him but couldn't move.

"Are you sure this is going to work?" Elysia asked, glancing through the trees outside the gates of Olympus where they stood in the shadows, hidden from view.

"It'll work." Max shrugged into the invisibility cloak. "There's enough magic in this thing for one more use. Once I'm through the gate, I'll create a diversion. The guards will investigate. They're totally predictable."

Nerves rolled through Elysia's belly as she looked up at Ari, remembering how frightened his mate Daphne had been when they'd left. "And you? You don't have to go with me, you know."

Ari sheathed the dagger at his thigh. "I'm going with you."

Elysia breathed a little easier, but not much. Shifting the bow across her back, she reminded herself that a thousand different things could go wrong between here and Circe's cave. She didn't even know if Circe would help them, but she had to try. Cerek could be anywhere on Olympus. She was banking on the witch telling them what Zeus had planned for him now that he'd brought the god the Orb.

"You're sure she's on Mount Olympus?" Max asked, drawing Elysia's attention.

She nodded. "The details of Cerek's memory were clear. It was a cave in the highest mountain. That has to be Olympus."

"I'll meet you both there," Max said. "Don't leave until I reach you."

Ari nodded. "Be safe, Guardian."

"You too, old man."

He stepped away, but Elysia grabbed Max by the sleeve before he could pull up his hood. "Wait."

He turned to face her. "What, Lys?"

He hadn't hesitated to help her in this, even though she knew he wasn't completely convinced of Cerek's innocence. He was helping her because he cared. Because they were family. And since she'd returned to Argolea, things had happened so fast, she hadn't had the chance to tell him what his support meant to her. She needed to make sure he knew now...before it was too late.

"Don't do anything stupid."

A crooked smile pulled at the corner of his mouth. "I wouldn't do something like that."

"Yes, you would. You think because you have the power of transferability, you're safe, but you're not. Not here. Your ability to access and use others' gifts is something Zeus covets. The king of the gods considers you a much bigger prize than the Orb."

"I'll be fine. Don't worry about me."

"I do, though," she said softly. "I wouldn't be able to live with myself if anything happened to you. Especially because of me."

He closed his arms around her and hugged her tight. And in his familiar embrace, tears burned her eyes. "Nothing's going to happen to me, Lys. I promise. I may be reckless from time to time, but not when it comes to you." He leaned back and looked down at her. "I want you to be happy. If he makes you happy, then I guess I have to accept that."

"He does make me happy." When Max frowned, she added, "Someday when you find your soul mate and you fall in love, you'll understand."

His grim expression said he didn't agree, but as he let go of her and stepped back, he didn't argue. "Just stick to the plan. And don't leave Olympus before I get there."

Elysia swallowed hard and nodded. As she watched him pull up the hood of the invisibility cloak and disappear, she said a silent prayer that their plan worked. Because she couldn't live without Cerek or Max in her life.

The massive wrought iron gate of Olympus rattled. Even though she couldn't see him, Elysia knew he was climbing up and over the structure. Seconds later, the gate creaked open.

"He unlocked it," Ari said at Elysia's side. "Now we wait."

Elysia's pulse raced. Now they waited for the guards stationed inside the gate near the small stone structure to follow Max and his diversion.

Long minutes passed in silence. The only sound was the roaring pulse in Elysia's ears. One guard stepped out of the gatehouse and looked up the paved road that angled toward the gods' temples. Something had caught his attention. Some*one* Elysia hoped stayed true to his word and didn't do anything reckless.

The first guard motioned to the other. Seconds later, the two grabbed spears leaning against the gatehouse wall and jogged up the path toward whatever had piqued their interest.

"That's our cue," Ari whispered. "Quietly."

Elysia's stomach tightened as she followed Ari out of the shadows. They pulled the gate open wider and slipped through the space, then tugged it shut behind them so it looked latched but wasn't. Ari ducked behind the gatehouse and moved into the forest on the far side, motioning for Elysia to follow.

The trek to Mount Olympus took longer than she'd expected. Without the power to flash in this realm, they had to move on foot. By the time they made it through the thick forest to the path at the base of the mountain, Elysia was hot and sweaty and wishing she'd worn a tank rather than the tight pants and long-sleeved fitted black shirt that made her blend into the shadows.

They paused for water. Elysia took the canteen Ari handed her, drew a deep drink, and gave it back.

"How do you know she'll help us?" he asked, capping the canteen and reattaching it to his belt.

"I don't." Elysia started up the steep path that wound around the mountain. "But something in that memory Cerek showed me made me think Circe is as much a prisoner as he was. I don't think she's on this mountain by choice."

"You think Zeus tricked her?"

"That or she made a deal with him that didn't go the way she planned."

"She's still a witch, you know."

"I'm part witch."

"Yeah, but she's the strongest witch in all the realms, whether she's trapped on Olympus or not."

Elysia was fully aware of that and hoped they could use it to their advantage.

Thirty minutes later, Elysia swiped her windblown hair back from her face as she stood on the stony path and eyed the opening of the cave high in the mountain. "Don't draw your weapon. We don't want to spook her."

Something moved inside the shadows of the cave. At Elysia's back, Ari muttered, "Something tells me she already knows we're here."

"Enter, warriors," a female voice called from beyond the darkness. "If you dare."

They could be walking right into a trap, but Elysia had to try. She just hoped that if they failed, Max would find Cerek and free him before it was too late.

Drawing a deep breath, she stepped into the darkness and paused to let her eyes adjust.

Rock walls, a stone floor. The tunnel led deep into the cave. At the far end, a red hue beckoned her forward.

Elysia followed the path, winding through the mountain until the tunnel opened to a massive room. Three steps led up to a raised platform where a woman dressed in a long flowing green robe stood in front of a golden pedestal topped with a bowl. Flames shot high from the bowl, twisting and turning in the darkness just as the fire-red curls spilled down the female's bare spine.

"I saw you coming," Circe said. "I see all in the flames." She glanced over her shoulder with piercing green eyes. "Even your destiny. The Argonauts will fail."

Urgency pushed Elysia forward. "I'm not an Argonaut."

"No, you are not." Circe turned fully to face them. "But you have the power of Athena within you, and that makes you as much a warrior as him." She nodded toward Ari but kept her gaze locked on Elysia. "I cannot help you in your quest."

"We don't need your help," Elysia said. "We just need to know where he is."

"You already know where he is," the witch responded. "Search your intuition. Zeus's use for him is done. There's only one place where he is wanted. Flesh or stone."

Panic swelled inside Elysia. Stone… Zeus couldn't have turned him to stone again…could he? She opened her mouth to ask the question when another thought hit.

Where he's wanted…

Elysia turned toward Ari. "He's with Aphrodite."

Ari's mismatched eyes widened. "He's *where?*"

Elysia whipped back to Circe. "How do we bring him back? You brought him back once before."

"That I cannot tell you."

"You have to tell me."

Circe only blinked.

Frustration bubbled inside Elysia. She moved up the three steps and grasped the witch's arm. Circe didn't step back or flinch. But when Elysia's hand made contact, a memory hit Elysia. This one from Circe's point of view. Standing over Cerek, chanting the spell that had brought him back to life twenty-five years ago.

Elysia gasped and stumbled back, breaking the connection.

"Now you know." Circe eyed Elysia three steps down. "And I did not break the rules. Your powers are not strong, little witch, but you know the words. Cerek's gift is that of augmentation. If you give him the words, he can amplify your powers and free himself from his confinement. But be forewarned, as soon as he is free, the gods will know. You will have to choose—him or the Orb. You cannot save both."

It wasn't a choice for Elysia. She'd choose Cerek a thousand times over any Orb.

"Thank you," she whispered and turned to leave.

Ari captured her arm and looked up at the witch. "Wait."

Elysia looked back.

"Why are you helping us?" he asked.

"Because no one deserves to suffer at the hands of the gods," she replied. "Not even those who deserve it."

Elysia wasn't sure what the witch meant, but she had a feeling Circe was talking about herself, not Cerek.

"Go," Circe said. "Go now before it's too late."

"Mm, *erastis.*" Aphrodite trailed her hand along Cerek's buttocks as she circled his stone body. "How I've missed my favorite toy." She slid her fingers down his chest, pausing at his waist. "I do have to say, though"—her hand dropped lower to cup his groin—"I rather like you hard as stone. It's just a pity that the Siren's poisoned arrow didn't strike you when you were erect."

Cerek couldn't move, couldn't respond to her teasing, but he felt every caress and squeeze. Tingles echoed all through his body as she tormented him with her hands. And the bitch knew that. Grinning, Aphrodite pushed to her toes and pressed her mouth hard against his stone lips.

"Luckily, there's still enough here to work with," she said, lowering to her heels as she palmed his cock once more. "More than enough. We'll find a way to make do, I'm sure."

Laughter echoed from a nearby room, and Aphrodite turned. With a licentious smile, she let go of Cerek and stepped toward the sound. "I'll be back soon, *erastis*. And when I return, I'll bring a friend or two to keep you entertained. Don't you worry. We're going to have all sorts of fun together. You're my prize now. From now until the end of time."

She swept out of the room like a breeze, her sheer white robe flowing in her wake, her curly auburn hair bouncing as she moved. The relief he thought he'd feel at her departure didn't come. Only her words echoed in his head...*from now until the end of time.*

He was trapped. This truly was all that life held for him. And he deserved every minute of it for what he'd done to his father, to the Argonauts, to Elysia—

Elysia...

"Look at me..."

He could almost hear her saying those words. When she'd climbed over him on that beach after he'd flashed them away from Olympus and she'd told him she wanted him. When she'd grasped his face after they'd flashed to the human realm and she'd transferred her memories to him. Gods, how he desperately wanted to hear her say those words now. To know she hadn't given up on him. That she didn't believe the worst about him. That she still loved him even after all the horrible things he'd do—

"Cerek, look at me. Just me. Focus on me."

That was her voice. He could hear her. Concentrating his attention, he realized he could see her. She was standing in the middle of Aphrodite's courtyard, her dark hair pulled back into a messy tail, her sexy body covered by a long-sleeved black T-shirt and fitted black pants that showed off her curves. And she was looking at him. Touching his face. Talking *to him*.

"Cerek, look at me. Hear me."

"This isn't working," Ari said from somewhere close. Voices echoed from a nearby room. "We're running out of time. Max can't hold them off much longer."

Max... Elysia's cousin.

"Cerek. Listen to me. Hear my words. Your gift is the power of augmentation. You used it to help me open the portal from Pandora to the human realm, do you remember? Circe gave me the spell to break you out of this stone, but my witch powers aren't strong enough to do it alone. You have to help me. Hear the words. Repeat them with me. *Hekàs, ô hekàs, éste bébêloi.*"

He'd heard those words before. He'd said them. When he'd broken the spell protecting the Orb.

A wave of guilt washed through him.

"It's not working," Ari said again, his voice more frantic.

"Cerek." Elysia's fingers moved to his temples. "I can't do this alone, and we're running out of time."

Footsteps echoed close, followed by a breathless voice. "We have to go. Those nymphs are crazed. And Aphrodite saw me. I think she went to tell Zeus."

Max again. Cerek's attention drifted toward the guardian. His clothes were ripped, his hair mussed, his face stained with bright red lipstick.

Elysia pressed her fingers against Cerek's temples. "Focus on me. *Hekàs, ô hekàs, éste bébêloi.* Dammit, Cerek. I love you. *Hekàs, ô hekàs, éste bébêloi.* I love you."

She loved him. Everything else came to a stuttering stop. She loved him even knowing what he'd done. A flood of memories filled his mind—him training her to fight in the moonlight on Olympus, the night they'd made love in Athena's temple, the way she'd kissed him on the beach of Pandora, binding their souls together beneath the full moon of Argolea.

He focused on the words she said over and over again. Heard them in his head. Repeated them with his mind. And when he did, the stone around him started to crumble. The block in his mind broke free, flooding him with memories...of his mother, of his years with Ari, of training with the Argonauts and serving with his kin, the day he'd lost his father in a fire, only to discover he was alive fifty years later, followed by their reunion on that snowy mountain and Zeus's Siren hitting him with that poisoned arrow.

He stumbled forward, but Elysia was right there to catch him. Her arms closed around his waist, and she leaned her weight into his to hold him upright. "I've got you," she whispered. "I'm here."

His muscles were stiff, his body tight, but he lifted his arms and scrambled to find her face with his hands. Pulling her close, he drew her mouth to his and kissed her with all the love and sorrow and guilt still swirling inside him.

"Guys." Ari tugged at Cerek's sleeve. "I hate to break up this happy moment, but we have to go. *Now.*"

Cerek drew back and looked down at Elysia. "I didn't know what he had planned. I didn't realize what was happening until it was too late. I wouldn't—"

"I know." She squeezed his hands. "It's okay. I already know."

She did. Hope filled his chest. Hope and love and the promise of a future only she could give him.

Footsteps sounded close. Ari pulled on Cerek's sleeve again. "I wasn't kidding when I said *now*. Let's go already."

Cerek's warrior instincts clicked into gear. He pulled Elysia with him and looked at his father. "What's the plan?"

"To get to the gates as fast as possible." Max handed Cerek a blade. "You steady enough to use this?"

Cerek closed his hand around the weapon, the grip heavy and familiar in his palm. As familiar as Elysia's hand in his. "Yeah. I'm fine." When he realized Ari was leading them toward the west wing of Aphrodite's palace, his pulse ticked up. "No. That'll take you to the grotto. This way."

He led them under an archway, down a long corridor and into a rose garden filled with thousands of blooms. Footsteps sounded behind them. Echoes of voices. He pulled them into a row between two hedges and picked up his pace. "Hurry."

"What is this?" Ari asked.

The hedges rose ten feet. The path turned to the right. They came to a T-intersection, and Cerek immediately shifted to the left, running through the twists and turns they needed to take in his head. "A maze."

"Holy *skata.*" Max turned to look behind them. Voices had entered the maze. Were on the other sides of the hedges. "I hope like hell you know where you're going."

Cerek gripped Elysia's hand tightly in his as he turned right, left, right again. After a series of switchbacks and angles, they finally emerged on the far side of the maze. A dark forest lay ahead, followed by a hill. At the bottom of the hill, the gates of Olympus opened to a vast open plain where they could flash back to Argolea.

"We're almost free," Elysia breathed.

"Almost," Cerek said. "Through the trees. Come on."

Freedom was the sweetest word, but it fizzled in Cerek's head as branches and twigs crunched beneath his feet like snapping bones.

That freedom came with a price. The enormity of what he'd done hit him hard. Zeus had the Orb. Once the king of the gods found the last element, he'd have the power to release the Titans from Tartarus. He could start the war to end all wars. No one would be safe. Not those in the human realm, not those in the oceans or the heavens, not even his kin in Argolea. Because of him, the people he loved would never be free.

He stopped, drawing Elysia up short. She turned to face him. "What?" Her brow wrinkled; worry darkened her eyes. "What's wrong?"

"I can't go."

"What?" Panic filled her voice. "You have to."

"I can't leave the Orb. Zeus has it. I gave it to him. Do you know what that means?"

"I know exactly what that means. It means we have to get out of here."

Ari jogged back toward them, urgency filling his mismatched eyes. "Kids, now is not the time to have a marital spat. We've gotta keep moving."

Cerek looked at his father. "I have to get the Orb. I can't leave without it."

Ari's jaw clenched. He glanced down at Elysia. Behind them, Max appeared, his brow drawn low. "What the hell's the holdup? Gotta go, gotta go. By now Zeus knows we sprung this boy. Time's a-tickin', folks."

Cerek squeezed Elysia's hand. "I have to go back. I won't be able to live with myself if I don't. This was my fuckup. I have to make it right."

Fear filled her eyes. "Circe said we couldn't get both. That we had to choose. I don't care about some stupid Orb. Zeus doesn't have all the elements. He can't even use the Orb yet. I won't lose you for that. I choose you. I always choose you."

His heart filled with so much love, he pulled her close and kissed her, sliding his fingers into her silky hair and breathing hot against her luscious lips. "All my life I've been an outsider looking in. I never thought I mattered. I never felt as if I belonged. Not with my family. Not with the Argonauts. Never on Olympus. But you... You changed all that. You gave me a purpose and a reason to live. That's why I have to go back. So you can live. So Zeus can't take anything else from us."

"But—"

"I love you." He kissed her again. "Just you. Always you." Letting go, he looked toward Max and Ari. "Take her to the gate. Get her out of here while you can."

"No," Elysia protested, "I won't—"

"Take her and go." Cerek stepped back and gripped the sword tighter. "Now, dammit."

Max grasped Elysia's arm and pulled her with him. "Come on, Lys."

"No." Elysia stumbled backward. "I can fight."

"I know you can," Cerek said. "But I need you to live. Do this. For me."

She stopped her struggling. Tears filled her eyes. Tears that gave Cerek courage. A courage he knew he would never lose.

"Come on," Max said again, pulling on her arm.

She let Max tug her with him down the hillside, but she didn't look away, not until they disappeared from sight. And as tears burned his own eyes, Cerek knew hope wasn't the life of love as his mother had thought. Sacrifice was.

"You got your memory back."

Ari's deep voice drew Cerek's attention, and he looked to his left where his father stood with knowing mismatched eyes.

"I did. When Elysia broke the spell, it all came flooding back. How did you know?"

"I heard what you said to her." Ari stepped closer and laid one hand on Cerek's shoulder. "You do matter. You always did. To me, to the Argonauts, to everyone. I'm sorry I was such a shitty father and didn't tell you that before. I should have. If I could go back, I'd do a lot of things differently."

Cerek had waited a hundred and fifty years to hear these words. And now they were here when he didn't have time to embrace them. He swallowed hard. "You have to go."

Ari shook his head. "I'm not leaving you again. I made that mistake once before. I won't do it again."

His chest pinched. "But Daphne—"

"—will understand. She knew when I left that this might be a one-way trip. We talked about it. And she knows if I don't make it back, I'll be waiting for her on the other side." He squeezed Cerek's shoulder and grinned, his eyes sparkling in the dim light. "Now what's your plan?"

What was his plan? *Skata*, Cerek didn't have one. His mind spun. "The Orb will most likely be in Siren Headquarters. There's a vault in the lowest level. I'm guessing Zeus stashed it there where his Sirens can guard it."

"Makes sense. What's the easiest way in?"

"Through the orchard on the back side. We'll have to go out and around Olympus to get there."

"Let's go, then." Ari took three steps deeper into the trees before Cerek reached for his arm, stopping him. "What's wrong?"

"Nothing. I just…" Emotions tightened Cerek's throat. Emotions he wasn't prepared for. "I'm glad you're here, *patéras*. With me now. At the end."

"It's not the end, *yios*. Not even close." Ari closed his hand over the ancient Greek text on Cerek's forearm. The same text that ran over his forearms. "No matter what happens tonight or tomorrow or next year, our spirits will live on. You'll see your mate again. And your kin. And when you do, they'll know what you did for them here. That I promise."

The words steeled Cerek's resolve. He nodded. Let go of his father's arm. Knew what he was doing now was as right as binding his life to Elysia's.

He stepped forward. The crackle of twigs around them brought his head up. Every muscle in Cerek's body went rigid as eight Sirens emerged from the trees, bows drawn, arrows pointed right at them.

"Well, well, well," Zeus said in a deep voice at Cerek's back. "The Orb and two Argonauts for the price of one. This day is turning out better than I planned."

CHAPTER TWENTY-FOUR

They were fucked. Completely fucked. Before they'd even gotten out of the damn trees.

Cerek's pulse raced. He gripped the blade tightly and turned.

Ari moved up at his side and glared at Zeus. "Your little stone spells won't work anymore. Cerek knows how to break free of them."

"No thanks to a witch, I'm sure." Zeus's dark gaze narrowed. "I'll deal with her later. Right now, I'm going to enjoy killing both of you once and for all."

"I want the girl," Athena hissed, moving up next to Zeus, her eyes filled with fury.

"Patience, daughter," Zeus said. "As soon as we're done here, you can have her. She hasn't passed the gate yet."

True fear swept through Cerek as he shifted so his back was to Ari's. His gaze darted right and left at the Sirens around them. His gift of augmentation wasn't going to help them here. He lifted the blade. The weapon was useless against flying arrows, but he had to hold them off long enough for Elysia to get free.

Run, emmoní...

"The only good Argonaut is a dead Argonaut as far as I'm concerned." Zeus grinned. "Ladies? Fire away."

"Remember this isn't the end," Ari muttered at Cerek's back.

Not the end... The words had a calming effect as Cerek drew a breath. He pictured Elysia rushing past the gates of Olympus where the gods couldn't touch her, flashing back to Argolea where she would be safe, the wedding band that matched the one he wore snug around her finger.

No, this wasn't the end. He would see her again. He'd wait for her on the other side as long as it took because she was worth the sacrifice. She was worth everything. And he knew the next time he saw her, he could hold his head up high and not feel ashamed for all the things he'd done here because of Zeus.

The Sirens drew their bows back. Twigs crackled. Cerek tightened his hand around the hilt of the blade.

Silence met his ears, followed by Zeus's muttered, "Fucking Argonauts."

Cerek squinted to see past the Sirens to where an Argonaut stood behind each one, a blade at their throats.

"Draw off your bitches," Theron yelled. "Or each one of them will die."

"I'd do what they say," Skyla called toward Zeus, her blade also at a Siren's throat. "These heroes are unpredictable."

"This is my realm," Zeus growled.

"And these are our boys," Theron said. "Tell your warriors to drop their weapons, or we'll make mincemeat of them."

Zeus lifted his hands. Before he could draw on his powers, Nick, Demetrius's half brother and a god himself, stepped out of the shadows and shot a beam of energy forward that knocked the god off his feet and slammed him up against a tree.

"Your power is broken until we leave this realm," Nick announced.

"You can't do that," Zeus growled, scrambling to his feet.

"I just did, *adelfos.*" Nick held out his hands, ready to use them again. "I'm as strong as you. Now tell your dogs to lower their weapons."

Zeus's black-as-night eyes narrowed, brimming with retribution and rage. But he motioned for his warriors to drop their weapons.

The Sirens tossed their bows on the ground and muttered derogatory comments. Orpheus shoved the Siren at his front forward and moved from tree to tree, picking up the bows.

"You can't let them do this," Athena hissed.

"Shush," Zeus said to her.

Cerek ignored the gods and looked from face to face, stunned the Argonauts were all there—Theron, Zander, Orpheus, Gryphon, Phineus, Titus…even Demetrius. They'd all come after him, even knowing he'd given up the Orb.

The Argonauts released the Sirens. The females glared back at their captors before moving to stand behind Zeus and Athena.

"You think this means you win?" Zeus shook his head. "Whether you rescue these two traitors or not, you still lose. The Orb is mine."

"We didn't come for the Orb." Demetrius moved up on Cerek's right. "Some things are more important than trinkets and jewels. You wouldn't understand that, but then you don't understand anything about brotherhood and sacrifice."

"Brotherhood doesn't win wars." Zeus sneered. "You're all going to die when I use the Orb."

"That will never happen." Theron stepped up next to Ari. "You don't have the water element, and you'll never find it before we do. We have two gods on our side now. One of whom knows exactly where the water element is hiding."

Zeus growled at the mention of Prometheus, the Titan currently lurking in the mountains of Argolea, a realm the Olympians could not cross into. With one last glare, Zeus nodded toward the gate. "Leave Olympus now. And take your pathetic traitors with you."

Athena startled at Zeus's side. "But—"

Zeus grasped the goddess's hand and poofed them away in a cloud of dark smoke. The Sirens glared at the group before turning up the hill and heading for their compound.

Voices echoed around Cerek. One by one the Argonauts each slapped him on the shoulder, muttered encouraging words he couldn't quite grasp, before moving through the trees toward the gate. Orpheus and Skyla followed.

When Ari and Cerek were the only ones left, Ari grinned down at his son. "What do you say we get back to our women?"

Still too dazed to answer, Cerek nodded and followed his father into the trees. But nothing made sense. He should be dead. They hadn't retrieved the Orb. The Argonauts should be gunning for him as much as Zeus, but they weren't.

He stepped out of the trees onto the stone path that led down the hill and spotted Demetrius, standing only a few yards ahead. A scowl pulled at the guardian's mouth, making the hairs on Cerek's nape stand straight all over again. Swallowing hard, he stopped in front of the Argonaut he'd served with for fifty years before Zeus had taken him, understanding—now that he had his memory back—just what he'd done. Not to the Argonauts as a whole, but to someone he'd once considered a friend.

Demetrius didn't speak. In the silence Cerek shook his head, more confused than ever. "Why are you here? You were right about me. You were right about everything. If I were you, I'd be handing me over to Zeus, not defending me."

Demetrius angled his head to look down at Cerek in the moonlight. At six-eight, Demetrius was the biggest and most intimidating of the Argonauts. But in his dark eyes, Cerek no longer saw threats. He saw camaraderie.

"You have a long way to go to earn my respect," Demetrius said. "I'm still pissed about the way you and Elysia kept your relationship a secret, and I'm not sure I'll ever be okay with you and her, well..." He cleared his throat and shifted his weight. "But we're kin. The bonds of brotherhood run deep. Regardless of what you think, you're not a traitor. Not even close. I—we—all knew what you did was not done intentionally. But more than that, I know my daughter. I know she would not risk everything for someone who wasn't worthy. The second I learned she'd gone after you, I knew you were innocent."

Elysia... "Is she—"

"Already on the other side of the gate. Probably freaking the hell out because we're not back yet."

Cerek glanced down the hill past Demetrius.

"Know this, though." Demetrius stepped in front of him, blocking Cerek's view. "If you ever hurt her, I'll find out."

"I won't. I promise I won't."

Demetrius stared at him. Frowned. Finally shook his head and turned away. "I know you won't, dumbass."

He moved down the path. Alone, Cerek drew in a shaky breath. Ari chuckled and slapped Cerek on the shoulder as he followed Demetrius. "You're screwed with that one as a father-in-law. Totally fucking screwed."

He was. Cerek knew there was no way around it. He vowed to find a way to earn back Demetrius's respect.

"Hey," Ari said. "Slow down."

Footsteps sounded on the path, and Cerek spotted Elysia rushing past his father seconds before she threw herself into his arms.

His heart leapt, and he captured her around the waist and pulled her close. "You're supposed to be back in Argolea. What the hell are you doing on this side of the gate?"

"Rescuing you, *ilithios*."

All the worry and stress and disappointment and fear leaked out of him. Smiling, he lowered his face to the curve between her shoulder and jaw and drew in a deep whiff of her sweet honeysuckle scent. "You did. More times than I can count. Did you send the Argonauts?"

"No." She drew back and looked into his eyes. "They were already at the gate when Max and I went through. They believe in you as much as I do."

He brushed a silky lock of hair back from her face. "Not quite as much as you do. I don't think anybody could."

"That's true." Her beautiful eyes narrowed. "Which is why sending me away was a really bad idea."

"I was trying to protect you."

"I know. That's the only reason I'm not spitting mad right now."

She would always challenge him, always push him, and he loved that about her. Loved everything about her, especially the way she loved him back. He'd never believed anyone before her could. He'd been so afraid of that witch's prophecy that he'd lose his courage because of lust, he'd never let anyone try. Something for which, now, he was so very grateful.

"We didn't get the Orb," he said softly.

"I know. But it'll all work out."

Amusement toyed with the edge of his lips. "How can you be so sure?"

"Because, *ómorfos*, I'm never wrong."

He thought back to the choices she'd made on Pandora. To the decisions she'd made when they'd been attacked by those harpies. To her unwavering belief that binding her soul to his was the only path. His gaze narrowed. "You are never wrong. Why haven't I noticed that before?"

Grinning, she wrapped her arms around his neck. "Because I'm so completely talented in the ways of seduction, I distract you from my unwavering perfection."

"Talented in the ways of seduction… You must have had a really good trainer."

Her grin widened. "The very best."

Her lips found his, and as he kissed her, he knew that regardless of the ups and downs and twists and turns of his life, everything was finally the way it was supposed to be.

"If you get my daughter killed because you couldn't get your ass outside these gates before Zeus's Sirens showed up again," Demetrius called, "I'll take back everything I said and deliver you to the fucking god myself."

Elysia dropped to her heels and giggled.

"That's not funny." Releasing her, Cerek steered her in front of him and pushed her down the path. "I'm pretty sure your father still wants to kill me."

"I know." Swiveling back toward him, she grasped his hand in both of hers and pulled him with her toward the gate. "Isn't it awesome?"

Cerek couldn't stop himself. He laughed. She was right. It *was* awesome. Awesome and normal and messy and right. And it was his life.

A life he couldn't wait to get back to living.

EPILOGUE

"Where are you taking me?" Elysia reached out with her hand to try to feel her way in the darkness. The blindfold Cerek had tied around her head blocked out all light, and she stumbled up the step.

"Gods, you're so impatient." Cerek's warm hands against her upper arms sent tingles rushing all across her skin as he guided her forward. "Just a little farther."

"You like when I'm impatient."

"In bed. I like when you're impatient in bed, not when I'm trying to surprise you."

She smiled at the memory of her impatience last night. He'd recently rejoined the Argonauts, and last week was the first time they'd been separated since their binding. His four-day mission in the human realm as the guardians intensified their search for the water element had felt like twenty, and she'd been more than impatient when he'd finally come home. So impatient they hadn't even made it to the bed. She'd torn off his clothes in the living area of their suite and rocked both their worlds right out from under them before he got even three steps into the room.

"Okay," he said, drawing her to a stop. "That's far enough."

His hands lifted from her shoulders to untie the sash from the back of her head, and as the fabric fell from her face, she blinked several times at her surroundings.

"Oh my gods."

Cerek turned to look over the suite. Pale yellow walls framed a living room with plush furnishings and a rock fireplace that rose to the ceiling. The great room opened to a kitchen with granite counters and gleaming appliances. A hallway led back to what she guessed were the bedrooms, and a wall of windows overlooked the white-capped, blue-green Aegis Mountains in the distance.

Wide-eyed, Elysia moved toward the windows to gaze out at the view. "This is the north wing of the castle."

"Yep."

She glanced over her shoulder. "It's been empty for years."

He tucked his hands into the front pockets of his jeans and smiled, a warm, sexy smile that did crazy things to her insides. "I talked your parents into letting us have it. If it were up to me, we'd have our own place outside the city, in the trees, far from anyone who might interrupt us. But we can't."

She gazed back at the view. She wanted that too, but being heir to the throne came with a number of sacrifices, and on this point she'd had to agree with her parents. It wasn't safe for her to live outside the castle walls. There were still political factions within Argolea that wanted to see the demise of the monarchy. Until that changed—or until her parents produced a son who would overtake her in succession to the throne—she had responsibilities, and those responsibilities outweighed her personal wishes and desires.

He moved up behind her and wrapped his arms around her waist. "What do you think?"

She lifted her hands to his and ran her fingers over his rough and sexy skin. "I think it's incredible. Did you do all this?"

"Your mom helped. And Daphne. It was their binding gift to us. They did the decorating. All I did was some of the renovations."

"When?" She angled her head to look up at him.

"At night. When you were sleeping. I wanted it to be a surprise."

"I love it."

"Yeah?"

She nodded.

"So do I." He turned her in his arms and brushed the hair back from her face. "Especially because this far from your parents' suite, they can't hear your throaty, sexy screams when you fuck my brains out right here on the floor."

She laughed, then sighed as his mouth found hers. And as she sank into his kiss and wrapped her arms around his neck, she thought back to the day she'd run from this castle. Back then, she'd believed binding herself to another and accepting her role as heir to the throne would signal the end of her life. She'd had no idea then that it would be the start of something wonderful.

He drew back and gazed down at her with warm, gorgeous brown eyes she sometimes couldn't believe she was lucky enough to stare into for the rest of her life. "Happy?"

"Yes. Sublimely." She trailed her fingers through the silky hair at his nape and grinned. "Or I will be. If this carpet you picked out is half as soft as it looks."

His eyes lit with an erotic light, and he chuckled. "Oh, it is, *emmoní.* Extremely soft." He wrapped his arms around her waist and pulled her to the floor. "Let me show you, right now."

She fell on top of him and giggled. But her laughter turned to sighs of pleasure when he rolled her over and kissed her. And as their hands explored and their mouths fused, she couldn't help but be thankful that Zeus's Sirens had kidnapped her all those months ago. Because if they hadn't, she never would have found Cerek, and she wouldn't have the one thing that now mattered more than anything else.

She wouldn't have love.

"Ah." Lachesis sighed and leaned back from the bowl of water in the courtyard behind the home she shared with her sisters and waved her hand so the image of Cerek and Elysia faded in a swirl of water. "They both fulfilled their destinies. And we didn't have to intervene after all."

Frowning, Zagreus went back to deadheading roses in the courtyard. Leave it to the fucking Fates to cut the feed just when things were about to get interesting between the Argonaut and his hot little mate.

Atropos harrumphed as she tucked her hands behind her head and reclined on the chaise in the sunlight. "I still think we could have cut that boy loose and the girl would have ultimately fulfilled her destiny."

"Maybe," Clotho pointed out from her seat on the edge of the fountain. "But she would have accepted her fate as heir begrudgingly. And she wouldn't have been happy."

Atropos rolled her eyes. "Happy schmappy. Happiness is overrated. Look at Ziggy over there. He's not happy, and he's fulfilling his destiny just fine."

Zagreus clenched his jaw. He'd like to use these shears to snip the bratty Fate's head off, but he didn't dare. Fuming, he glanced down at the blades in his hand. Oh, how he wanted to, though. Just one good snap to shut the bitch up.

"Well," Lachesis said, sitting in the chair beside her sister, "regardless of what you think, everything worked out. That was a good idea by us, I must say."

Zagreus huffed.

"What was that, Ziggy?" Lachesis called. "Did you say something?"

"What the hell worked out?" he snapped before he could stop himself. "Zeus has the fucking Orb. He's one element away from being able to release Krónos from Tartarus. And if that happens, hold on to your boobs, bitches, because that sick fuck will find a way to mess up every one of your so-called 'good ideas.'"

The Fates exchanged glances.

In the silence, Zagreus looked from face to face. "Oh, you don't like hearing the truth? Too fucking bad." He went back to snipping roses. "Someone needs to say it. Might as well be me. You can't fuck up my life any more than you already have."

The sound of water spraying in the fountain echoed through the courtyard. Frowning, he tossed a rose hip in the bucket at his feet and went back to pruning. Holy hell, he was ready to use the damn shears to snip off his own head. And he would. If it would work. But of course it wouldn't, because he was a minor god and therefore im-fucking-mortal.

"Atropos is right," Lachesis said, "you don't seem happy here, Ziggy."

"Ya think?" Zagreus tossed another rose hip in the bucket, this one with more force than necessary. The rose hip hit the bottom and bounced out to land in the flower bed.

"When Hades sent you to us," the Fate continued, "it wasn't supposed to be forever. Just until you had time to reflect on the error of your ways."

Zagreus's shears stilled against the rosebush, and a tingle raced down his spine. Was the Fate saying—

"As much as we enjoy your company," Clotho added, "we think that time has come and gone."

Heat spread through Zagreus's limbs as he turned to stare at the Fates. Holy shit… They were letting him go.

"Not quite," Atropos said, clearly reading his mind. "We have one stipulation to granting your freedom."

Zagreus dropped his shears into the bucket. "I'm listening."

"We agree with you in that Zeus cannot have the Orb." Lachesis tipped her head and pinned him with her hard gaze. "The repercussions, should he find the last element before the Argonauts, are unacceptable to the balance of the universe."

"Well, no shit."

"In order to earn your freedom," the Fate went on, ignoring his comment, "you must complete one task for us. You'll steal the Orb from Zeus."

Excitement burned hot and wild inside Zagreus's belly. Zeus had stored the Orb with his lusty Sirens. Zagreus had no problem fucking his way through that Order to steal the Orb. "Consider it done."

Atropos cleared her throat. "Ah no. That is *not* what you're going to do. You're going to keep your dick in your pants, find the Orb, and return it to the Argoleans."

Whoa. Wait. What the fuck? His eyes widened. "You want me to give it back to them? They want to destroy the damn thing."

"Exactly." Lachesis folded her hands in her lap. "That is the only way order will be restored to the universe."

"If you want your freedom, Ziggy," Clotho said, "you'll steal the Orb from Zeus, return it to the Argonauts, and you won't touch a single Siren in the process."

Where the hell was the fun in that?

"The point is not to have fun," Atropos said. "The point is to do something for the good of all mankind."

Zagreus huffed. "What the hell do I care about the good of mankind? I'm not human."

"No, you're not." Lachesis pushed to her feet. "You have the potential to be a whole lot more."

Clotho and Atropos rose and stood next to Lachesis, smiling knowing, secretive grins. And as Zagreus looked over each Fate, a tingle of apprehension rushed down his spine.

"That is the offer for your eventual freedom, Ziggy." Lachesis lifted her brow in anticipation. "The decision is up to you. Now what is your choice?"

ETERNAL GAURDIANS
LEXICON

adelfos. Brother

agkelos. Term of endearment; my angel

agapi. Term of endearment; my love.

ándras; pl. *ándres.* Male Argolean

archdaemon. Head of the daemon order; has enhanced powers from Atalanta

Argolea. Realm established by Zeus for the blessed heroes and their descendants

Argonauts. Eternal guardian warriors who protect Argolea. In every generation, one from the original seven bloodlines (Heracles, Achilles, Jason, Odysseus, Perseus, Theseus, and Bellerophon) is chosen to continue the guardian tradition.

Binding. Marriage

chará. Term of endearment; my joy

Chosen. One Argolean, one human; two individuals who, when united, completed the Argolean Prophecy and broke Atalanta's contract with Hades, thereby ejecting her from the Underworld and ending her immortality.

Council of Elders. Twelve lords of Argolea who advise the king

daemons. Beasts who were once human, recruited from the Fields of Asphodel (purgatory) by Atalanta to join her army.

*Dimiourgo*s. Creator

doulas. Slave

élencho. Mind-control technique Argonauts use on humans

emmoní. Term of endearment; my obsession

erastis. Lover

Fates. Three goddesses who control the thread of life for all mortals from birth until death

Fields of Asphodel. Purgatory

fotia. Term of endearment. My fire.

gigia. Grandmother

gynaíka; pl. *gynaíkes.* Female Argolean

hiereia. Priestess

Hieros Gamos – Ritualistic binding ceremony

Horae. Three goddesses of balance controlling life and order

Isles of the Blessed. Heaven

ilithios. Idiot

kardia. Term of endearment; my heart

Kore. Another name for the goddess Persephone. "The maiden"

ligos-Vesuvius. Term of endearment; little volcano

loutra. Ceremonial bath

matéras. Mother

meli. Term of endearment; beloved

Misos. Half-human/half-Argolean race that lives hidden among humans

Olympians. Current ruling gods of the Greek pantheon, led by Zeus; meddle in human life

ómorfos. Handsome

oraios. Beautiful

Orb of Krónos. Four-chambered disk that, when filled with the four classic elements—earth, wind, fire, and water—has the power to release the Titans from Tartarus

paidí. Child

pampas. Daddy

parazonium. Ancient Greek sword all Argonauts carry.

patéras. Father

sotiria. Term of endearment; my salvation

Siren Order. Zeus's elite band of personal warriors. Commanded by Athena

skata. Swearword

syzygos. Wife

Tartarus. Realm of the Underworld similar to hell

therillium. Invisibility ore, sought after by all the gods

thisavrós. Term of endearment; my treasure

Titans. The ruling gods before the Olympians

Titanomachy. The war between the Olympians and the Titans, which resulted in Krónos being cast into Tartarus and the Olympians becoming the ruling gods.

thea. Term of endearment; goddess

yios. Son

**Read on for a sneak peek at
UNCHAINED
The next book in Elisabeth Naughton's
Eternal Guardians Series**

PROMETHEUS – *One of the keenest Titans to ever walk the earth. Until, that is, his weakness for the human race resulted in his imprisonment.*

For thousands of years, Prometheus's only certainty was his daily torture at Zeus's hand. Now, unchained by the Eternal Guardians, he spends his days in solitude, trying to forget the past. He's vowed no allegiance in the war between mortal and immortal, but when a beautiful maiden seeks him out and begs for his help, he's once again powerless to say no. Soon, Prometheus is drawn into the very conflict he swore to avoid, and, to save the maiden's life, he must choose sides. But she has a secret of her own, and if Prometheus doesn't discover what she's hiding in time, the world won't simply find itself embroiled in a battle between good and evil, it will fall in total domination to Prometheus's greatest enemy.

UNCHAINED

CHAPTER ONE

"*Find me. I'm waiting. I'm waiting only for you...*"

The words echoed in Prometheus's head as he wandered the empty halls of the ancient castle high in the Aegis Mountains. He heard them in his waking hours now, not just when he was asleep. Heard them tickle the hairs on his nape, heard them whisper like a lover in his ear, heard them call like fire to his blood until he twitched with the need to find her and claim her as his own.

Her. The female with the flame-red hair and eyes like glittering emeralds he'd conjured with his mind. The female who was now more real to him than, well, him.

Damn, but he'd fantasized about her so often over the last few months he wanted her more than he wanted his precious isolation. But the voice wasn't real because *she* wasn't real. Not even a Titan, a god with the power to match that of any ruling Olympian's powers, could make her real. The only person in the cosmos who could summon life was the Creator, and the Creator had screwed Prometheus over so long ago, Prometheus knew there was no chance in this world or the next that he'd ever be blessed with a living version of his endless fantasy.

Life didn't work that way. Correction, *his* life didn't work that way. His life was a series of bad choices and never-ending repercussions. Which was exactly the reason he was determined to stay right here in this dank castle and *not* follow the sultry voice that made him so hard he could barely walk.

He waved a hand, using his telekinetic powers to light a torch along the wall in the cold, dark hallway as he moved. Maybe he was going mad. Maybe all these years of isolation were finally catching up with him. After the Argonauts—warrior descendants of the strongest heroes in all of Ancient Greece—had freed him from Zeus's chains, Prometheus had craved nothing but solitude. To do what he wanted, when he wanted—or to do absolutely nothing at all. But now, more than twenty-five years later, he was starting to wonder if his self-imposed seclusion in this ancient castle was at the root of all his problems. He was hallucinating, for shit's sake. Not just visions, but voices now, too. A sane person didn't do that. A sane person—mortal or immortal—recognized when he was standing on quicksand and got the fuck out.

"Find me. I'm waiting, Titos. I'm waiting for you..."

She always called him Titos in his hallucinations. A nickname that translated to fire. One that now brought him around to stare down the dark and empty hallway even though he knew she wasn't real.

Nothing moved. No sound met his ears. The castle was as silent as it had been since the day he'd arrived. But his spine tingled with apprehension, and his god-sense, something he rarely relied on because no one knew where he was, shot a warning blare straight through his ears.

The witches in the valley at the base of Mt. Parnithia had told him this castle in the Argolean realm had once belonged to an evil sorcerer who'd chosen darkness over light. That sorcerer's quest for power had cost him his life, and he now resided in the lowest levels of Tartarus, tortured endlessly by Hades much as Prometheus had been tortured by Zeus. His energy still lingered, though. A vile and murky energy Prometheus felt vibrating in his bones. As a divine being, Prometheus wasn't worried that energy would claim him—he was too strong for that—but he couldn't help but wonder if the sorcerer's dark energy was somehow affecting him. Could it be the source of the voice?

"Titos... I'm waiting..."

"Who's there?" he called.

Silence met his ears. His pulse ticked up as he scanned the darkened corridor, the only light coming from the torch behind him. Still nothing moved. Even the wind outside the castle walls had died down as if it too were afraid to utter a sound.

His imagination. It had to be. A hallucination or whatever the fuck he wanted to call it. Frowning, he turned away only to catch a flash of white out of the corner of his eye.

He whipped back. Some kind of gauzy fabric disappeared into the library, followed by the sound of laughter.

Sexy, feminine laughter.

Prometheus's stomach tightened as he rushed to the threshold of the room, grasped the doorframe, and peered inside. Shelves lined with books covered all four walls. A cold, dark fireplace sat across the distance. An empty couch, two side chairs, and a small coffee table lingered in the middle of the library.

Nothing moved inside the room. No fabric rustled. No laughter sounded in the cool air.

His stomach dropped when he realized he was hallucinating again, and he lowered his head into his hand and rubbed his aching temple. What had he said to himself earlier? A sane person recognized when he was standing on quicksand and got the fuck out? Maybe it was time he did that. Maybe it was time he moved on from Argolea and refocused on what he should have been doing these last twenty-five years. Namely, finding a way to screw Zeus over for everything the asshat god had done to him.

"I can help you."

Prometheus's head jerked up at the sound of the sultry feminine voice he'd heard so many times in his dreams. Only this time when he looked the room wasn't empty. This time a gorgeous female with hair as wild as fire and eyes like chipped emeralds peered back at him from the couch.

"I can help you exact revenge on Zeus," she whispered, sitting forward so her breasts heaved in the low-cut white gown. "All you have to do is help me first."

"Help you how?" The Titan took one step into the library and stopped. "Who are you? And how did you get here?"

This was where she needed to be careful. Circe slowly pushed to her feet and brushed the thick curls over her shoulder. If he suspected too much, all her efforts would be for naught. She had to play this cool, had to stick to the plan, had to wait for just the right moment to strike.

"My name is Keia." Not entirely a lie, she figured. For thousands of years, humans had called her a goddess pharmakeia, which was just a fancy nickname for witch or sorceress. She was simply borrowing from that label. "But I am not here. I am only an apparition."

"I don't believe you." Prometheus stalked forward. He reached out to grab her but his wide palm and long fingers passed through nothing but air.

His hazel eyes widened as he looked from his hand back to her. "What the hell?"

He was only a few inches taller than her nearly seven feet, but he was bigger everywhere. A wall of solid steel that stood between her and eternity. Power radiated from his broad shoulders and chiseled muscles. A power that made her heart beat faster and her blood warm in a way it hadn't done in ages.

His dark hair was cut short, his jaw strong and square and covered by three days worth of stubble that made him look both dangerous and sexy. He was thousands of years old—like her—but he didn't look a day over thirty. And when his eyes narrowed and his luscious lips thinned, she had an overwhelming urge to dive into his mouth to find out if he tasted as good as he looked.

"How did you find me?" he said. "What do you want with me?"

Circe blinked, his voice pulling her back to the moment. She'd not been sexually attracted to anyone in so long, she'd forgotten what that rush of excitement felt like. Then again, she'd not had the chance to be attracted to anyone. Zeus kept her locked up tight and had for way too long.

Focus. Sexy as hell you can use to your advantage.

She lifted a foot-long length of heavy chain. "Look familiar?"

His face paled as he looked at the chain Zeus had used to bind him to that rock. The rock where he'd been tortured daily by a giant eagle that had torn into his side and consumed his liver day after day. "Where did you get that?"

"Find me and I'll tell you."

His confused gaze lifted to her face. "Find you?"

"You're a Titan. You have powers others don't. Find me and I can help you make Zeus pay for everything he's done."

He glanced over her from head to toe, a careful sweep of his green-brown eyes that was filled with both skepticism and interest. "Who are you?"

She could tell him she was a witch, but instinct made her hold her tongue. Prometheus was wary of all otherworldly beings. Many had known about his torture over the years, but none had dared rescue him from Zeus's clutches. None but the Argonauts.

"I'm no one of importance. Just a maiden who helped another and is now trapped because of it. Much as you were trapped for helping mankind."

Prometheus had given fire to humans. That was the big sin Zeus had punished him for. On a grand scale, she could see how his punishment made sense. Fire had led to the industrialization of man and the advancement of society. Zeus would have preferred man continue to worship and rely on the gods. Circe, on the other hand, had only helped free another of Zeus's prisoners, one who'd already fulfilled his required destiny for the king of the gods. But Zeus was determined to torment her forever for that crime.

She'd learned one very valuable lesson then. If you crossed Zeus you were fucked whether your offense was a major or minor violation.

She had to get out of here. She'd go mad if she had to spend eternity in this prison. Urgency pushed her forward. "Please help me."

"I can't. I don't know how." He looked over her again. "You're nothing but air."

"I—" Footsteps echoed close. Her pulse shot up. Zeus was back. Waving her hand, she broke the feed as she swiveled toward the sound. Prometheus's frantic "Wait," faded in the air as she faced the king of the gods.

Zeus strolled into her cave high on Mount Olympus and stared up the three stone steps where she stood next to the copper cauldron she used to conjure her magic. The flames in the bowl slowly shrank and eventually died out.

His black as night eyes narrowed. He was taller than most gods, over seven feet, and nothing but muscle. And though she supposed some probably found his dark looks attractive, Circe realized he paled in comparison to Prometheus.

"Well?" Zeus asked, hands on his hips and a perturbed expression across his angular face.

"These things take time, my king." She lowered her head in a reverent bow but gritted her teeth because just doing so made her want to scream.

"I grow tired of your lack of progress. I want the water element, and I want it now."

Of course he did. Ever since he'd stolen the Orb of Kronós—the magical disk that housed the four basic elements and had the power to unleash the Titans from Tartarus—from the Argonauts, he'd been pressuring her to figure out where Prometheus had hidden the last element. The god who possessed the Orb with all four elements intact could lord ultimate power over every living being. Forget controlling simply the heavens. With the water element, Zeus would finally control every realm and each being in them.

Circe was determined not to let that happen. Though Zeus was allowing her to contact Prometheus with her powers so she could find the element for him, she was really planning to convince Prometheus to break her free from this hell. Because it was hell. Being trapped in this mountain, even though she was allowed to use her magic, was as much a prison as any other. She was tired of doing what Zeus wanted. Tired of being his yes-witch. Tired of living half a life tucked away from the world.

"My magic cannot be rushed," she said, careful not to give her plans away. "We've discussed this before. You must be patient."

Zeus's jaw clenched down hard. "Do whatever you have to do to get me that element. But you'd better get it quickly because I'm a god of only so much patience. If I don't see results soon, witch, things are going to change."

Circe lifted her chin as he turned to leave. He couldn't threaten her. Because of him, she was the strongest witch who'd ever lived, and he knew that. Oh, she'd get results, but they'd be for her, not him.

When his footsteps faded in the tunnel that led out of her cave, she turned back to her cauldron and bit her lip. She couldn't go on visiting Prometheus as an apparition. He was already fascinated by her. She needed to step up her game.

A wry smile pulled at her lips as an idea formulated. One that would take him from fascination to obsession and set the wheels of change in full motion.

Learn more about
UNCHAINED
at
ElisabethNaughton.com

Elisabeth Naughton

Don't miss the other books in the Eternal Guardians Series:

UNCHAINED

ABOUT THE AUTHOR

Photo by Almquist Studios

Before topping multiple bestseller lists—including those of the New York Times, USA Today, and the Wall Street Journal—Elisabeth Naughton taught middle school science. A voracious reader, she soon discovered she had a knack for creating stories with a chemistry of their own. The spark turned to a flame, and Naughton now writes full-time. Besides topping bestseller lists, her books have been nominated for some of the industry's most prestigious awards, such as the RITA® and Golden Heart Awards from Romance Writers of America, the Australian Romance Reader Awards, and the Golden Leaf Award. When not dreaming up new stories, Naughton can be found spending time with her husband and three children in their western Oregon home.

Visit her at www.ElisabethNaughton.com to learn more about her books.

CPSIA information can be obtained
at www.ICGtesting.com
Printed in the USA
FSOW01n0906050717
36004FS